THE JEWELLED DARKNESS

THE JEWELLED DARKNESS

by

Virginia Coffman

SEVERN HOUSE PUBLISHERS

This first world edition published 1989 simultaneously in
the U.S.A. by SEVERN HOUSE PUBLISHERS INC.,
New York and in Great Britain by SEVERN HOUSE
PUBLISHERS LTD. of 40–42 William IV Street,
London WC2N 4DF.

British Library Cataloguing in Publication Data
Coffman, Virginia, *1914–*
The jewelled darkness.
I. Title
823'.54
ISBN 0–7278–1737–X

Distributed in the U.S.A. by
Mercedes Distribution Center, Inc.,
62 Imlay Street, Brooklyn, New York 11231

Typeset in Great Britain by Selectmove Limited

Printed and bound in Great Britain

CHAPTER ONE

Very much aware of the six o'clock curtain, Elisa Carlisle, born Elsie Catlow, could scarcely hear her own thoughts above the bawdy chatter of the gentlemen in her dressing-room.

No matter. Every other thought vanished before the immediate necessity of getting these 'admirers' out of her sight.

She glanced anxiously at the little clock on her scarred old making-up table. Less than half an hour before the curtain.

Her shimmering first act costume hanging from the dressing screen was a reminder of difficulties ahead. Twenty pearl buttons down the back required attention, and her dressing maid was busy with the actress's manager, checking on the evening's probable profits.

According to a tradition hallowed by time, these aristocrats in the actress's dressing-room, all titled and/or decorated, expected to replace Tuttle, her maid, by helping to dress Miss Carlisle, London's newest idol.

They had no concept of her real feelings about this intimacy from comparative strangers. They seemed to think she enjoyed it. After all, she had been known to accept delicate pieces of jewelry from time to time. These items were not given from any charitable impulse.

On the other hand, few of her admirers would admit how often they were nudged out into the dark theatre passage and urged to take their seats before the first act curtain, because Miss Carlisle disliked noisy arrivals while she was on-stage. They generally obeyed. Despite her reputation, she was equally adept at dismissing admirers in her private life.

She resented her reputation as 'an enchantress who lures men to ruin'. Peg Tuttle, her maid and confidante, was aware of how much she disliked warm, sweating, or even gloved hands on her flesh when she dressed, but Tuttle, being a practical woman, had pointed out that 'This reputation has made you the most popular actress in London, two years running.'

Tonight, since Tuttle was busy elsewhere, and could not help her, Elisa hit upon the hoary idea of inventing a visit from the Prince Regent himself.

'Gentlemen, His Royal Highness prefers not to find the room so – busy.'

'Good old Prinny. Got in his bid early,' was the disrespectful response but she bestowed upon these slightly drunk admirers her smile, the famous smile that promised so much more than it gave. Her male 'claque' was in terror of her gently distant air sometimes followed by a frown, so they obeyed her, joking and reluctant, leaving her quite alone.

Curtain time was upon her. Elisa hurriedly stepped behind the painted Cathay screen again to strip off the violet redingote and crepe gown in which she had arrived at the old theatre on the South Bank of the Thames.

The screen itself had come from far away China and after her fingers completed the buttons on the underdress she touched the long panels of the screen with their ancient Oriental designs of exotic plant and human life.

She had decided some years ago that she too must be unique, special in some way. It was the only possible hope she had of rising above her birth, her terrible childhood and, finally, the disgrace of being 'an actress'. In many ways she had succeeded in becoming unique. Unlike the style of the present year, 1819, with its fuller skirts and ruffles, she had her own gowns made in the manner of 1810, a high-waisted, fragile style extremely flattering on her slender form.

She had not yet risen to that other dream of being a 'lady' accepted as an equal by the Prince Regent's circle, but

2

considering how far she had come, this ultimate goal did not seem unattainable. She was convinced that no other goal would thaw the cold disgust of the one man who remained in her thoughts, night and day.

Her arms were still bare; the long, white gloves so necessary to a lady, even on-stage, lay on her dressing-table. Suddenly, she felt the bare flesh of her shoulders caressed by sweating male hands. The touch ruined her mood of concentration. Its crudeness disgusted her.

She knew she invited this treatment by ordering that the door into the passage always be left ajar. No one but Tuttle knew the real reason she had a terror of being shut in and alone. This clumsy fellow must believe he was welcome.

'If you please,' she protested, trying in vain to shrug off his grip. She looked over her bare shoulder into the perspiring face of the Conde da Spada, a member of the Piedmont King's diplomatic entourage in London. As he kneaded her flesh with those crude hands he licked his flabby lips.

She winced, but the painful pressure did not repulse her as much as his innocent assumption that she was public property.

She tried to accept his disgusting familiarity as a humorous gesture.

'My dear count,' she teased, 'you will make me late. Would you have me hissed and bombarded off the stage? They do not always throw apple cores. I assure you, oranges can be brutal weapons.'

He tittered but retained his advantage, breathing heavily.

She shrugged and she thought for an instant that she had freed herself, but his thick fingers shifted from her upper arms to her elbows and then to her waist, which he squeezed uncomfortably just under her breasts. He leaned closer, whispering hoarsely in an incomprehensible patois that was partly Italian, partly French.

The passage door remained open. She knew Peg Tuttle would return at any minute. She stood very still for several seconds, lulling him into further liberties. Though she didn't understand his words, she knew exactly what he suggested as his fingers prowled over her bosom and into her bodice, lingering and caressing and pinching her breasts.

With a sudden, twisting motion that caught him by surprise she broke away, calling loudly, 'Tuttle! Where is the silver overdress? And hurry. I shall be late.'

Da Spada reached for her but she eluded him, taking up the mahogany-framed make-up mirror and holding it between them as she pretended to examine her face.

'I must ask you to leave, Sir.' She had enough bad publicity recently, and felt the necessity of preserving as much good will as possible in the circumstances.

'But my little enchantress . . . my little *Circe*, I thought . . .'

She forgot the necessity of remaining good-humored. 'Do not call me by that odious name! Please. Go.'

His hands groped for her around the edge of the mirror. She raised the mirror abruptly, nervous as always when about to make her first appearance on-stage immediately after the tiny orchestra had warmed the audience and, she hoped, silenced it.

Fortunately, before she could bring the heavy, sharp corner down on his fingers, Peg Tuttle came along the passage, escorting Elisa's most fervent admirer, Arthur March, not quite eighteen years old, but passionately devoted to the woman he called his 'Goddess'.

The Conde da Spada reacted with shock and hauteur, pulling himself together, drawing up his portly body to look nearly as tall as his youthful rival.

He managed to bow and assure Miss Carlisle in tolerable English, 'Your servant, Madame.' Then he strutted to the open doorway, avoiding any contact with Arthur March, inclined his head to the imperturbable, leathery Peg Tuttle, and was gone.

Relieved, Elisa accepted Tuttle's help with her gown while she gave young March her warm, charming smile. He moved closer in a gingerly way, trying not to seem interested in what went on behind the delicate, painted screen.

'Dearest Miss Carlisle,' he began. 'Might I see you alone for just a few minutes?'

Tuttle and Elisa exchanged glances. Elisa nodded. Tuttle fastened the last pearl button on the silver gauze overdress, gave March a look that expressed cynical amusement, and went out into the passage.

Elisa was fond of Arthur March and did not join in Tuttle's amusement. At twenty-six and with her background she had no illusions about the kind of love he offered her. She did not intend to ruin his life by accepting his boyish attentions as more than a fleeting juvenile adoration.

Then, too, she did not wish further to antagonize Jeremy March, his older brother and guardian. Lord Jeremiah March was a hero of the recent Napoleonic wars, the fascinating and wholly indifferent object of her romantic dreams. It would have surprised many cynics to know a woman like the celebrated Elisa Carlisle could still have romantic dreams, but he was the one man in the Regent's dazzling world who made her feel like a desperately gauche maiden, fresh out of an academy for genteel young females.

The idea was absurd under the circumstances, but she listened to every word about Jeremy March, knew how he was working to get laws passed that would ameliorate the terrible conditions of the indigent elderly and the poor. She was sure she could love him, but meanwhile her friendship with his naive young brother had hopelessly compromised her in the eyes of the one man upon whom her light flirtatious charm had no apparent effect. She did not feel she could hurt young Arthur by a deliberate break with him. It must come gently.

Meanwhile, to his intense and nervous joy, young Arthur found himself alone with his idol. Shaking with nerves and hope, he dropped a pair of his grandmother's small but flawless diamond ear-bobs onto the actress's make-up table. They almost slipped off. Elisa caught them in time and held them up to the lamplight, studying them in an interested and almost professional way. She had no intention of keeping them, but gems did fascinate her, primarily for the safe haven they gave one who had known extreme poverty.

Watching her, he murmured, 'Your fingers are like delicate porcelain.'

After a moment she offered the jewels to him with one of her gentle smiles, saying, 'I am persuaded these are family jewels. They should remain in the March family.'

'No, no. I want you to have them, my dearest . . . I mean, my dear Miss Carlisle. They were part of my inheritance from Grandmama March. She was the beauty of her day, and if I may say so, you are the loveliest ornament of the Regent's world.'

'But I am not a part of His Highness's world.' She offered the diamond drops to him. 'Nor am I likely to be.'

When he did not immediately take the diamonds she had a chance to enjoy their flash, the kaleidoscope of colors in their depths, before offering them again with the teasing reminder, 'Then they would ask, "What did your ladybird offer in exchange?"'

Young March was shocked beyond measure that his fragile goddess should be aware of such language currently being used against her. It was true that Jeremy, his brother and guardian, made remarks like that to his gaming friends behind the sacred portals of Brooks's Club, but Arthur doubled his fist at the thought of his own reaction if he had overheard such a calumny. He was in awe of his brother Jeremy but he would never permit an insult to this angel.

'As though I would ask any payment, Miss Carlisle! Only . . .' He almost choked on his high cravat at the mere idea. He was carried away by the emotion of the moment. 'I ask only a light in those beautiful tawny eyes of yours.'

He caught her gaze in the mahogany-framed mirror while she added a trifle of lip rouge and a very light touch of kohl to accentuate her eyes with their golden light. They were wide, soft eyes that gave promise of bliss. Most of Elisa Carlisle's admirers existed on the promise alone, which didn't prevent their boasting to rivals of their imagined conquests.

She offered Arthur the earrings again. A wiser man might have thought she hesitated too long over the jewels, studying all the facets that flashed around the dressing-room.

'You are too generous, dear young friend,' she said finally. 'And now, forgive me, but I must send you away. It is almost six o'clock. Curtain-time.'

She turned away from him again to finish dusting rice powder over her cheeks. Behind her, Arthur March, like a child greatly daring, touched the soft, warm flesh at the nape of her neck. His fingers would have gone further down, beneath the silk of her gown, but she shrugged him off. He blushed and apologized, backing away from her, not seeing her amused smile.

'They are yours,' he insisted as she held the jewels out to him again. 'They are very small. It isn't as though . . .' His voice trailed off lamely.

She seemed to have forgotten his recent impropriety.

'My dear, generous friend. Please. No.' She gave him her hand. He took advantage of the moment to clasp the delicate fingers between his and to press his lips passionately to the knuckles. With a gentle reluctance she began to draw her hand away, but he was so overcome by his luck that he tried to kiss her hand again, stopping only when he saw that his impetuosity displeased her. He looked up to see her pretty white teeth set in her lower lip and the faintest of frowns creasing her brow.

He would not have offended her for the world and quickly freed her fingers. 'Of course, Miss Carlisle. I only wish I might stay for your performance. Splendid, you know. Simply splendid. And all alone. How you can stand upon that stage reciting so beautifully. But no. Jeremy insists that I owe it to the family name to be present at the wretched soirée, as they call it. His Highness may attend. You do understand?'

'I understand, dear friend. Another time.' As she turned back to the mirror he watched her for a second, then silently placed the diamond drops on a table by the doorway, and hurried out into the passage with its dim, smoking oil lamp. He left the door open, well aware of her order.

She heard his footsteps fading along the aged wood planks of the floor. He made no response when Miss Carlisle's manager, Strawbridge, gave him an eager, obsequious, 'Fine evening, Sir. Just a trifling of fog, but nothing keeps away the Lovely Carlisle's admirers.'

Elisa Carlisle listened carefully, but there was now an old dis-illusionment in her smile that would have surprised her would-be lovers. From their indifferent treatment of her employees she knew how they would despise the real woman behind the mask of Elisa Carlisle. They were infatuated by a carefully created vision. They would pass Elsie Catlow, born in the workhouse, without a second glance.

A knock on the open door reminded her that it was nearly six o'clock. She stood up and smoothed out the white silk lengths of her gown, then the silver gauze surcoat. She glanced once more at the making-up table. The little diamond ear-bobs lay there. Arthur was nothing if not persistent.

Feeling a warm tenderness toward this boy who gave so much and received so little from her in return, she turned instinctively to call him back. Too late. By now, he would be off with his aristocratic friends where diamonds were a commonplace.

With a sudden movement she clawed her fingers and picked up the little ear-lobes. She fastened them so that they glistened among the lustrous clouds of her brown-gold hair.

She spoke to her reflection in an abrasive voice no theatregoer ever heard. 'Go away, Elsie Catlow. You died a long, long time ago.'

'Miss Carlisle? Elisa?' her manager called.

Elisa moved gracefully out into the passage. 'Yes, yes. Coming.'

CHAPTER TWO

As was the custom, crowds of the young actress's admirers gathered in the wings leading to the shallow stage, but toward the end of her performance another of Miss Carlisle's presumed lovers made his way backstage and stood in the front wing near the proscenium. Here she could not fail to see him as she stepped out to the apron of the stage and took each curtain call.

Captain Ronald Hawtree was a dazzling young officer in his regimentals but he had an unfortunate combination of traits, a hot temper and a talent for braggadocio. When he swaggered forward, others around him, at first resenting his proprietary manner, were soon warned in whispers that this was a firebrand whose luck in the legally banned duels was legendary. It was said that he would challenge any man, and last year had actually killed his opponent with a pistol-ball between the eyes. But that was the Bois de Boulogne outside Paris, and he had been whisked out of the country before retribution struck.

Tonight Hawtree soon found himself alone. A splendid-looking figure, especially in uniform, he was very much aware of his more popular attractions as he stood in the wings where he must be seen by those gossiping female playgoers who sat chattering in the lower box, just above the stage-right. He made it plain to all who saw him that he was mesmerized by the notorious Elisa Carlisle and brooked no rivals.

Elisa herself was fully aware that his passion fed on her evanescent fame. At the moment it was considered the popular pastime to hang about the actress. His boyhood friend, Arthur

March, found the lady elusive but fascinating; therefore, Ronald Hawtree must show him that she could be won.

It was whispered that her bedchamber was a bower of sexual pleasures. None of the captain's friends seemed able to furnish precise details. Therefore, Captain Ronald Hawtree would manage where they failed, and bribery was one of his tools.

Elisa had repeatedly refused to favor him, and even refused the more ostentatious jewels he offered, but the captain saw his friend Arthur in attendance on the Enchantress and suspected the worst, or the best, despite Arthur's denials and her own.

There seemed to be no stopping the hot-tempered captain.

The theatre was small and not in the fashionable quarter of London, though the audience, driven by gossip and curiosity, crossed the Thames nightly to see this 'Circe, who drove men to ruin'.

The cramped space backstage made it necessary for Elisa Carlisle to pass the young captain each time she took the final calls and made her graceful curtsy in the glow of the footlight lamps. However, old customs were ingrained in her. When she slipped past him she always gave the captain her gentle smile. It satisfied him for the time, especially since he was able to press his body hard against hers as she passed him.

Her critics had only one fault to find with the smile which parted her soft, moist, enchanting mouth in a promise of pleasure. Delighted admirers, dreaming of future ecstasy, did not realize that Elisa Carlisle's smile was democratic, exactly the same for everyone.

Captain Ronald Hawtree was obsessed as much by her reputation as by her tawny eyes and brown hair gleaming with reddish gold lights. He carried in his gloved hand what knowing gallants claimed was the talisman to win her: a small, emerald-studded locket.

Containing his own miniature, she had no doubt.

During her first curtsy a creaking noise in the wings made her glance that way before she remembered how old the timber in this building must be. Captain Hawtree had simply shifted one elegantly polished boot on the uneven backstage floor. Having attracted her attention, he opened his palm once more to display the jewelled locket nestled in his white glove. It gave off wondrous lights as it caught the candle-glow from the stage set.

Elisa Carlisle knew the value of jewels. Elsie Catlow had found out long ago what the lack of them could buy—a dirty wall in the yard of Debtors' Prison, or a pile of straw in the workhouse after eighteen hours' work.

As the shouts and applause swept up to her across the flickering footlights, she sank once more in a low curtsy. The difficulty of performing this act in the Early Regency style of costume she favored always fascinated her admirers.

Diamond gifts or not, until recently she had not cared for any man as she cared with a passion for the waves of excitement that poured across the footlights from the audience out there on long benches in the pit, two-tiered boxes, and the noisy galleries of the theatre.

How well she knew those Gallery Gods! When she first appeared on the stage in provincial towns like Leeds and York and even Bristol, in a troupe of itinerant strolling players, those citizens who paid their shilling and fought for the few benches in the gallery came armed with half-eaten fruit, hurling rotten apples and even harder fruit at the stage when something displeased them. The fruit usually struck the helpless theatregoers in the pit below, who were too tightly wedged in to escape this hail of critical opinion.

No rotten fruit tonight, she thought with satisfaction and, looking up at the galleries, gave them a special wave with her flawlessly gloved hand.

Occasional flashes of many-faceted lights from jewelled hands, jewelled necks, even the little ear-bobs below elaborate silk and velvet turbans, reminded her that these aristocrats of the *ton*, seated in the boxes or the pit, had come to pay tribute to Molly Catlow's daughter. Though they were far from knowing it.

Men and women who would not have paid the least attention to the desperate, penniless seamstress or her skinny little workhouse brat fifteen years ago, now happily paid whatever

11

Strawbridge, Elisa Carlisle's indefatigable manager, demanded for the privilege of watching Elisa perform in light romantic comedies, delicate romances and, occasionally, a seasoning of heavier fare. She was equally successful when she performed, as tonight, entirely alone, offsetting classic soliloquys with the gentle raillery in her modern scenes of Sheridan and Goldsmith.

Part of her popularity was based on her mysterious reputation as a kind of *Circe* with her male admirers. She knew that many in the audience came to see her out of curiosity, titillating themselves with the question: 'What poor fool is she luring to his downfall tonight?'

Thus far, the insulting and absurd idea had worked to her benefit. Since the Duke of Pentland's only son and heir had drunkenly thrown himself off a Channel packet into the North Sea, leaving a note that blamed 'that *Circe* Elisa Carlisle', theatre seats for Miss Carlisle's performances were hard to come by. Her own price had gone from sixteen pounds for each performance to six hundred for ten performances, out of which, of course, she paid the other actors and actresses who appeared with her when she performed in plays.

Half a dozen other males of the Prince's set found it romantic to use Miss Carlisle as their scapegoat when they wanted to excuse everything from drunken brawls staged in public to that most heinous of crimes, cheating at cards in Brooks's Club. At first, it had troubled the actress. Now, she shrugged and remembered all those jewelled creatures glittering in the darkness of the theatre pit and its boxes. They added to the profits that would keep her out of Debtors' Prison and even worse horrors.

In the end, money and jewels seemed to be all that really mattered in the mercenary London world which surrounded His Royal Highness, the Prince Regent.

Rising slowly, gracefully, she gave that jewelled audience one more smile and the curtain came down, leaving her momentarily alone. The old terrors gripped her for a minute and she spun around on the stage, calling with that uncontrollable hint of panic, 'Where have you gone? Where is everyone?'

They swarmed out onto the stage, a number of admirers, male and female, who were persuaded to wait for her out in the street by Strawbridge. Even he was pushed aside by leathery Peg Tuttle, and, of course, there was Captain Ronald Hawtree, looking magnificent in his scarlet regimentals.

He got to her first and brought her fingers to his lips. 'My adored, adorable one! You were never more exquisite.'

'Dear Captain, how very kind you are!'

To her intense relief, Elisa Carlisle was no longer alone. It didn't matter what was said to her, so long as that all-important fact remained. With tawny eyebrows raised in a question about tonight's performance, she looked at Peg Tuttle over the captain's bent head.

Peg Tuttle shrugged. 'Might've been worse. Your last reading wasn't too bad.'

Elisa smiled, satisfied. 'Thank you, Tuttle.'

After making another effort to interest her in the little locket tucked into the palm of his glove, Captain Hawtree insisted that his carriage would take her home to her house in Portman Square. He regretted that Tuttle must be included when he hoped for Miss Carlisle's company alone, but in spite of her profession the actress had all the manners of a lady, and her presence without her maid must sink her beyond redemption. As the captain had discovered, she was always more vulnerable when caught without her retinue of friends, admirers and servants. For some reason, the actress would do almost anything, yield to any pleas, rather than find herself alone.

Tonight Miss Carlisle was not quite so obliging, however. 'Perhaps later we shall have our little talk. But now, I must change. Come along, Tuttle.'

'I've something to show you. I'll wait,' the captain promised.

'As you like, my friend.' She patted his arm gently, while asking Strawbridge, 'Were you happy with the profits tonight?'

'Never better, Elisa, my angel.' Strawbridge bustled to her side, lowering his voice in a futile notion of confiding a secret. 'Everyone was here. You'll not credit it, but I'll go on oath I saw Lord March in the box stage-right. Fancies himself the savior of every Crabbed Ancient. Even wanted to refuse the peerage because it would destroy his chances to attend the Commons. Doesn't seem to have stopped him, though. By the by, he's also the guardian of that lad who's taken such a fancy to you.'

'Arthur March.' She said it casually, retaining the calm she had schooled herself to show when Lord Jeremy March's name was mentioned.

Captain Hawtree showed more interest in young Arthur March, whom he recognized not only as an old acquaintance but as a rival for the enchantress's favors.

'Shouldn't take young Arthur's attentions very seriously, Miss Carlisle. March practically keeps the lad on leading-strings. Great difference in ages, I fancy. His Lordship is in his late – well then, middle – thirties. And Arthur, much too young for – that is . . .

'For me?' She was more amused than offended.

'Lord, no! A goddess isn't born like we mere mortals.'

'But I am bosom-bows with your stepmother, and I am persuaded you would regard Lady Hawtree as much too mature for Arthur March.'

'My adorable creature, everyone knows you are only . . .'

'Very near on twenty-six. I do understand. The exact age of your stepmother.' She gave him her hand in a token of peace. 'I really must change now. Tuttle?'

'Then I shall wait, though it were an eon.' Carried away by his own eloquence, Captain Hawtree bowed low over her hand, watching its progress as it was gently withdrawn. While the actress crossed the hundred-year-old stage toward the little cubicle that was her dressing-room, Captain Hawtree strolled out to see if his closed carriage and team were being properly cared for.

This neighborhood south of the Thames, near breweries, Marshalsea Prison and a glue factory, was famed for its footpads and occasionally for matters even more unpleasant; the odors wafted on the foggy air from a tanning works.

Elisa returned to her dressing-room with Tuttle. Small, airless, tight rooms with bolted doors and blank walls were a part of the

14

old, childhood horror to the actress. Tuttle and her manager had vainly pointed out that these open doors only encouraged unwanted attentions from male visitors.

'Screens are quite adequate,' she retorted.

Peg Tuttle, who had first acted as a protective dragon for that pretty orphan, Elsie Catlow, over fifteen years ago, treated her employer with little ceremony. While shaking out the silver overskirt of the stage gown, she suggested in her hoarse, abrupt way, 'Best wear the green satin with the silk lace overskirt. It draws them and warms them at the same time. Did you see that locket your bird-witted captain was flaunting?'

'I could scarcely miss it. What did you think of the audience tonight? Was Strawbridge right?' Elisa busied herself with the buttons of the underdress she wore on-stage and slipped off the silken folds.

Tuttle said, 'About that odious Lord March?'

'Certainly not. I mean – was the house full?'

'Full enough. Some hurly-burly young females in the gallery was wearing their hair all Greek fashion like yours last month. Or so they hoped . . . Here. Stand still . . . To answer what you didn't ask, that Lord Jeremy March was sitting as near the stage as makes no matter. He never took those nasty eyes off you. Wicked devil that he is, he means you no good, Elsie, me girl.'

'He is polite to me when we meet. At first, he was genuinely charming. But that was before he learned that Arthur was my friend. God knows, I would never hurt that poor boy. I like his sincerity, and he keeps me from being lonely. He is gentle, unlike most of the others. He will tire of this pursuit. Then he will find some suitable young bride and wonder what he ever found in that tiresome old actress.'

Peg Tuttle shook her head at what she considered a misinterpretation of the facts. 'As if you could help it when these addled boys persist in laying trinkets at your feet.'

'At my head, in this instance. He insisted on leaving these ear-bobs. Then there is our valorous Captain Hawtree. I could wager what he has in mind.'

'I doubt he will be content with your sweet smiles.'

15

'It requires thought.'

'Not from me, Girl.'

Elisa laughed and wrinkled her nose. 'He amuses me. That is all.'

'You mean, he'll keep you from finding yourself alone.'

Elisa's smile faded.

While Tuttle fastened the willow-green, untrained gown behind her back, Elisa studied her own form and features in the pier-glass which was her prized possession. Talk of jewels, like talk of the night's profits, reassured her when she analyzed her face and slender form, watching for the first flaws that would eventually destroy her as a saleable commodity.

No lines yet. But sometimes she felt the lines were accumulating within.

'Will I ever escape the fear, Tuttle?'

Tuttle sniffed and began to hang tonight's costumes in the big wardrobe, while a stiff autumn wind moaned through the passage outside the windowless little room.

'All this is pure nonsense. You've the money invested in the funds. Then there's the five thousand you let them talk you into investing in the steam experiments. And there's –'

'The workhouse, Peg. And Debtors' Prison. And there are other things.' The actress looked into the mirror. Elsie Catlow looked out at her. She shuddered.

Peg Tuttle slammed the wardrobe door shut with a harsh, crunching sound. 'Well, then, you can sell them trinkets if you must.'

That brought laughter with an hysterical edge. 'Of course. My diamond trinkets. I'd forgotten.' She considered her reflection, decided her pale, bare arms above the elbow-length white gloves needed a shawl.

'The Belgian lace. Where did I leave it?'

Tuttle looked around the ugly room, clearing away various garments used in the actress's first three readings tonight.

'It must still be over the back of the settee on the stage. You tossed it there during the Sheridan scene. I'll find it.'

Peg Tuttle took up one of the two candleholders and went out into the passage where an oil lamp smoke unpleasantly, dangling from its wall brackets. She coughed at the fumes writhing through the drafty theatre. Elisa heard her footsteps retreating towards the stage. Then silence engulfed the old theatre which had once been a lively Guild Meeting Hall but now smelled of stale perfume, sweat, powder-stained garments and ageing wood.

She was alone.

Elisa hurried through the last of her chores, buttoning her left glove and frowning as she became aware of other sounds drifting through the building. Strawbridge? No. Strawbridge would be busy counting the profits at the front of the house.

She listened. No ghostly apparitions. Just the night wind, tipped with fog.

She started to the door, opened it wide, then remembered the remaining candle flickering on the scarred old table where she painted her face lightly before a performance. She retraced her steps, pinched out the little flame while the room was still illuminated by the passage light. Seconds later, a ghost of wind slammed the door shut with a force that made her jump.

In the darkness she reached for the door but found only space. Her fingers were ice-tipped already and she knew from long experience that this was how the haunting fear always began. An absurd and childish fear. Her groping fingers found the door. She lowered the latch and pulled. It did not yield. She tried again, putting some force into it, but her fingers felt numb.

Trying to eliminate all the panic from her voice, she called out, 'Peg, the door is jammed.' Her voice rose in spite of all her efforts to remain calm. It sounded desperate and terribly, terribly afraid.

'Tuttle?'

She turned around in the darkness, feeling for furniture, the candle, her reticule. Anything that would tell her she was not locked in that dark place with the blank walls, that living tomb where they had put Molly Catlow . . .

She raised a three-legged stool in her stiff fingers and swung it against the heavy oak door. It bounced back painfully. The door

17

did not give. She dropped the stool and kicked it away before pounding on the door with both fists.

'Are you out there? Anyone? Please . . .'

In her panic it took a minute or two before she realized that there was activity on the other side of the door. Then she heard an authoritative male voice order her.

'Stand aside!'

Trembling but hopeful, she stepped backward, coming to a stop against the table. The door burst open with the screech of timbers. The foul-smelling whale oil lamp in the passage cast a wide bar of light across the room.

Her rescuer stood with the light at his back, a tall, slim figure immaculately dressed for evening, the man she privately thought must be the most attractive male in London, though her acquaintance with him was a cool one.

She hardly troubled to conceal her relief. 'I can never thank you enough, My Lord. I was a prisoner in my own dressing-room. How absurd it must seem to you!'

She half-expected him to jeer at her childish fright, and was relieved when he said calmly, 'I have had my own experiences with fear. I seldom find them absurd. May I?'

It warmed and comforted her to read what appeared to be genuine sympathy in his dark eyes. No. Better than sympathy. Understanding. His manner was quite different from his puzzled, analytical gaze which she remembered from their most recent social encounters.

He stepped into the dressing-room as she moved backward before him. He was about to close the door behind him when she put out her arm quickly.

'No. Please.'

'Of course. Sorry.' The friendliness in his voice gave her a blessed calm. She began to feel more secure. He was one of the few who had never asked her for anything or tried to buy her.

He reached for her hand, which still trembled with shock. He bowed over it, touching her fingertips with his lips, a small, sensual gesture that he made more provocative when he raised his head and looked down into her eyes for a long moment.

18

'Miss Carlisle, Dr Brian Clifford has recently been employed by our housekeeper, Mrs Ponsonby. He will care for those who work in the household and the fields. He will also see to the poor and the elderly in the village. March Hall is among the hills, within a few hours' ride of the Hawtree place.'

'Yes, My Lord. I know. But I didn't know that Brian – Dr Clifford – was employed by you.' She would be anxious to hear what Brian had to say about the Marches when next she saw her childhood friend.

'At all events, he speaks of you in the highest terms.' His smile was exciting to her, indicating that his suspicions of her motives toward his young brother had been dismissed.

Surprised and pleased by his reliance on the word of her dear friend and trusted adviser, she said quickly, 'I am grateful to Dr Clifford. He has been a true friend. I have known him this age.'

He nodded. His manner seemed genuine, his interest in her sincere, and she left her hand in his fingers. The contact continued to give her a sensation of excitement she did not often know.

He said, 'As you may be aware, my brother Arthur was a boy of nine at the time of our father's death. He was left in my care. While I remained on the Continent during the War, he was reared, in a manner of speaking, by Mrs Ponsonby who adores him. But I believe you will have noted that he is not spoiled in any way.'

'I agree, Sir. And you must know I mean the young gentleman no harm.'

He hesitated, then said mater-of-factly, 'I hope you will believe, Ma'am, I am not one of Prinny's high-sticklers. We Marches have too bad a reputation historically to demand blue blood of others. But Arthur is an impressionable boy and it would ruin his life if he were to marry a woman who did not return his love, a woman who wanted only the material things he had to offer. Dr Clifford has given me to understand that you are not that sort of female.' She was mesmerized by his gaze. 'And perhaps I may guess that by my own brief knowledge of you.'

'I understand. And I agree.'

19

He seemed pleased. 'Excellent. Then we shall do very well. I will say no more.'

He studied her in a way that made her hope he had overcome his dislike of her. Then, as his gaze encompassed her face and hair, his fingers closed more firmly over hers until his grip became painful. Was it deliberate?

Suddenly, she noted a chilling loss of their new friendship. It was so unexpected she could not at first understand what had provoked it, or the contempt in his eyes.

'The tales about your greed for diamonds naturally make salty gossip.'

'I freely admit I am not in love with your brother. Therefore, I ask nothing but his friendship.'

'Do you?'

The change in his voice alarmed her. She raised her head and almost stammered, 'I don't – understand.'

Peg Tuttle was right in many ways. Lord March's smile struck her now as tigerish on that hard and rather cruel mouth, the lower lip sensuous, the upper lip thin, firm. His narrow eyes had a glitter in their depths that made Elisa think of Tuttle's description.

He was still smiling. A cat-and-mouse smile, she thought.

'Your earrings are exquisite,' he said. 'Have they been in the family long?'

She forced her hand out of his grip, but as she raised her fingers she remembered the March earrings that had belonged to Arthur March's grandmother, the grandmother of Lord Jeremy March, as well.

Why had she not returned them immediately? Worse, why had she worn them? That stupid fear of hers, the obsession to collect more and more jewels in some mad hope to fortify herself against poverty and Debtors' Prison!

It made her position with this man far more untenable, but she could not, in pride, take them off now and offer them to him.

'Well, *Circe*,' he prodded, using the name she had come to hate.

'I am not a thief. Nor do I turn men into . . .'

'Into swine?' This time the glint of malicious amusement in his eyes was unmistakeable. 'Come now. Miss Carlisle, this reputation as a sorceress waiting to turn men into their baser selves has been the making of what we may loosely call your career.' He looked her over from the crown of her head to her silver slippers, lingering all too deliberately at her bosom. The low, square neckline of her gown revealed the upthrust of her well-shaped breasts.

She stood there with her chin up and her cheeks reddening. He said at last, 'Your—er—career seems to have been highly profitable.'

She moistened her dry lips. He was determined to stab her with every word, and she felt that each of those words drew blood.

'Your Lordship would scarcely be in a position to know my private financial affairs. Or has Your Lordship's greed to know got the better of his honor?'

He reddened. She had struck a nerve. But he recovered. 'Whether my honor is at fault, I leave others to decide. But even in the company of ladies my manners are notoriously bad.'

Her fingers remained stiff with the remnant of the old fear. When the flat of her hand struck the flesh of his hard-boned cheek she was almost surprised by her own reaction.

A flicker of some other emotion crossed his face. Anger? Disappointment? He caught her wrist, giving it a painful pinch between his fingers before dropping it.

'You may now read your next line, Miss Carlisle. I am about to be treated to a burst of temper, fiery eyes and a crisp "Go, you Beast!" repeated at intervals until I slink away, duly chastised.'

A similar order had been on the tip of her tongue. Luckily, she was forewarned by his brutality and incredible bad manners. She managed to recover most of her poise.

'I trust Your Lordship's time is worth very little.'

Had she succeeded in surprising him at last? For the first time his eyes widened. 'May one ask why?'

'Because Your Lordship is wasting it here.' She gave him her professional smile. 'And what is infinitely more important, My

21

Lord, you are wasting my time. I trust we are about to say "good night". Or, even better, "a lasting farewell".'

His eyes lighted, though she saw no warmth in them.

'Bravo. Your talent is greater than I had suspected.'

A footstep in the passage made them both glance quickly at Peg Tuttle, who bobbed a very brief curtsy and squeezed by him to join Elisa and demonstrate her support. She asked, 'You feeling more the thing now, girl . . . Miss Carlisle?'

'Very much so . . . Does Your Lordship understand?'

He nodded. 'Exactly. We come now to the purpose of my visit. That you should better understand me. This affair with my seventeen-year-old brother will end. At once.' He turned, was stopped briefly by her question as Tuttle whispered at the same time, 'What affair?'

Elisa asked, 'Do you presume to threaten me, My Lord?'

There was steely politeness in his reminder, 'I never presume, Miss Carlisle.'

She snapped, 'You are overdue at the soirée to which you sent your charming young ward. Obviously, you wanted to keep him from guessing what you were about when you watched my performance.'

'Here? Or on the stage?' He bowed and left her.

Peg Tuttle stayed in the doorway to watch him vanish into the darkness beyond the passage, but Elisa said sharply, 'Come, Tuttle. That odious creature has delayed us long enough.'

'Can he do it? Can he destroy you?'

'Probably.'

'He might at least have offered to buy off your affections, like any decent older brother.'

Elisa laughed and was still laughing when Captain Hawtree came to escort her and Tuttle.

'All right, my angel?'

'How sweet of you, Captain! You don't think me a devil, a *Circe* who turns men into swine; do you, my dear – my very dear Captain?'

'Good God, no! Swine? You, Elisa? I beg pardon. Miss Carlisle. We fellows must look heavenward to find anyone like you, if I may say so.'

'You may, Sir. And I thank you with all my heart.'

When he took this as permission and dared to kiss her on the corner of her mouth, she made no objection. Nor did she feel anything, any sensuous excitement such as she had known during her brief armistice with Arthur March's detestable brother.

Her cruel rejection by the one man she thought she might have loved was soothed by this honey-talking young soldier, but the humiliation and pain remained, buried deep, with other injuries she never forgot.

CHAPTER THREE

For several nights afterward Elisa Carlisle's sleep was badly disturbed by dreams of black pits from which there was no escape. The sheer walls seemed to enclose her, but most disturbing was the face peering down at her from the mouth of the pit. Jeremy March watched her with his curious expression, at once hard and thoughtful. No doubt he was trying to balance everything he personally knew about her with the amiable portrait drawn by her lifelong friend, Dr Brian Clifford.

Tuttle guessed the true source of her dreams almost at once.

'If you'll take my advice, girl, you'll stop giving over so much thought to that fine gentleman. He means you no good and yet you spend all your waking hours thinking – aye, and running on about him.'

'Don't be ridiculous. It's at night I see his face. I can't control my dreams, can I?'

'That's as may be,' Tuttle sniffed, but at least she had put Elisa on her guard and the actress stopped confiding her dreams so freely.

She also sent the diamond earrings back to Arthur March on the excuse that she could not in honor receive heirlooms that should remain in the March Family. This produced an absurd situation in which Arthur returned them, stating categorically that they had once been March property but now belonged to him by the terms of 'Grandmama's Will.'

Elisa tried to give them to him in person, pointing out that the gift reflected upon her reputation. This aroused hurt on his part and she suspected a secret pride, because now society in

London would be sure Arthur March, of all young newcomers, had become her lover.

Tuttle shrugged at the contretemps. 'Let them think so. What's the odds? They think so, in any case.'

There was a deal of worldly advice in this. Eventually, Elisa added the earrings to her 'Security Collection', those jewels meant to protect her against her mother's fate.

Luckily, Gwenna Hawtree, young Captain Hawtree's step-mother, provided a friendly, gossiping, malicious confidante. She not only urged her 'Dear Elisa' to repeat all that had occurred between the actress and the insulting Lord March, she made her own analysis of Elisa's dreams. She promised that she would assure Lord Jeremy that Dr Clifford's assessment of the actress had been correct.

This was followed in less than a fortnight by a gift from March Hall, the family estate in the Cotswolds, not far from the Hawtree properties. Surely, it was a peace offering! Gwenna Hawtree herself was the messenger for the presentation of half a dozen bottles of champagne 'to be delivered to Miss Carlisle with the compliments of Lord March', as Gwenna put it.

According to Her Ladyship, this gift demonstrated Lord Jeremy's good will. Gesturing to a footman with the small trunk full of neatly segregated bottles, Her Ladyship hurried immediately to Elisa's narrow, elegant, three-storey house in the very correct Portman Square. She had barely taken time to instruct her coachman about the care of the landaulet and her own fractious team during the minutes she remained with the actress. It was always a sign of her extreme preoccupation when she failed to instruct anyone on anything.

Gwenna Hawtree was a tall, lean woman with an aquiline nose. She had never been pretty, was famed for her malicious mischiefmaking and, through some mysterious alchemy, was enormously popular.

The only child of the unsavory Duke of Severn who had died under a cloud, she was in the habit of getting her way. She liked nothing better than intrigue, unless it was flouting the rules accepted by the froth of Regency society. Her friendship

25

with Elisa Carlisle, an actress and therefore on the very fringe of respectability, was regarded as one more eccentricity by the Prince Regent's world. She had been told that not even she could make an actress welcome in her house, and immediately set out to disprove this out-of-fashion idea.

The friendship began when the new actress, Elisa Carlisle, gave her light, gentle caricature of the Princess of Wales, whose absurdities and uncouth behavior made her the butt of the Prince's set.

Of them all, only Elisa felt any regret afterward at the success of her performance. It occurred to her, too late, that the Princess of Wales, despite her highborn position, must feel herself on the ragged edge of decent society, thus suffering precisely as Elisa suffered.

While society debated the propriety of an actress doing for money what they themselves did for pleasure, Lady Hawtree laughed herself into a coughing fit at the theatre and ended by inviting Elisa Carlisle to attend a masque ball at Hawtree House.

In costume as Nell Gwyn, Elisa managed to charm a great many males and entertain the females with her theatre gossip. At the unmasking she was considered to have behaved 'very nearly like a lady'.

His Highness, the Prince Regent, detested the unconventional princess he had been forced to marry to produce an heir, and this went far to assuage the resentment at Elisa's performance.

Still, Lady Gwenna did not find the going perfectly clear. Regency society had rigid rules about the admission of commoners. Having set out on this laudable campaign to make an actress into a lady, she persisted, meanwhile amusing herself by reciting to Elisa every insult and 'set-down' she received from her friends before she succeeded. She did not hesitate to injure every feeling of her protégée, including repeating the universal name given to 'That Wicked *Circe*, the Carlisle Woman,' because a drunken aristocrat had killed himself after she rejected him.

Elisa may have been sensitive but she was also determined. By her own elegance and charm she managed to achieve Lady Hawtree's goal.

As Her Ladyship was being shown into the small gold and white salon with the gift of champagne, she announced, 'Surely, this gift from March Hall should cheer you. It was brought to Hawtree by one of the March footmen for delivery. Naturally, I agreed. We like to oblige the Marches.'

Elisa had been looking over the small chest. 'I find no card. Was the message a verbal one?'

Her Ladyship reached deep into her reticule and brought out a card which stated merely, 'March', a habit of Lord March who ignored his newly acquired peerage, the reward, not for his services to humanity, but for his mysterious work in France during the late war. Elisa examined the card. There could be no doubt. It must be a peace offering.

She said, 'It was kind of you to me. We must certainly discover whether the March tastes run with our own. Tabitha?' She signed to the red-cheeked, plump little maid who led the Hawtree footman with the wine chest off to the nether regions inhabited by Elisa's small staff.

'Poor Barnerd!' Lady Hawtree laughed. 'He will dream about that girl's hips for a month.' But she heartily endorsed the glass of champagne. 'Good. There is a certain decadence about it. My Hugo would think me quite beyond saving. Let us drink to his health.' She winked. 'And that of the Marches, of course.'

Chattering on, she stopped tilting her head to one side to give herself a better over-all view of her hostess. 'Are you feeling quite yourself? Forgive me, but you looked a trifle pale as I came in. Heavens! Has that fascinating man been threatening you again in spite of his gift?'

'Fascinating? The last man in the world I would –' Annoyed at having been trapped so easily, Elisa caught herself. 'What man?'

Lady Hawtree chuckled. 'Very well, then. Tell me, have you seduced my husband's clothheaded son yet? He implies as much, and heaven knows this rivalry over you has separated Ronald from both the March brothers. They have been friends from childhood, you naughty girl. Used to wager which of them, Arthur or our Ronald, would stand closest to the edge of that roof on March Hall.'

'I am not responsible for their childhood idiocy.'

'That may be. I do believe our Ronald had expectations.'

'I don't intend to fulfil them.'

'No more than that? Poor Ronald. His appalling imagination.' Lady Hawtree leaned forward as though to confide a state secret. 'Dear Elisa, the boy has a lamentable habit of bestowing the family jewels upon his friends.'

'His *chères amies*?' Elisa asked easily, trying not to be offended.

There was a slight, very slight hesitation. 'No. No. My dear, you are hardly of that class.'

'Thank you.' But the sting remained and Elisa decided her dear friend deserved one in exchange. 'At all events, what he had insisted on forcing upon me are only a few trinkets. You've no interest in a large and doubtless flawed pearl in a nest of diamonds, I daresay.'

Lady Hawtree gasped and half-rose from the white and gold damask settee. 'Not the Hawtree Pearl! Elisa! Elisa, you have never accepted it!'

'But if I were to become Mrs Colonel Hawtree, wife to the Hawtree heir, such family jewels would inevitably come to me, in time.'

While Gwenna Hawtree stared in horror, Elisa found it impossible to retain her gentle, innocent expression and began to laugh. Watching this display which was rather more genuine than the laugh so many admirers mistook for the real thing, Her Ladyship settled back, her tension visibly relaxing. She accepted the glass of champagne and the macaroon from Tabitha's crystal tray and sipped the wine.

'What a rogue you are, making me believe such a thing! You are much too intelligent to marry my absurd stepson.'

Elisa raised her own glass to her lips but did not drink. She found champagne more satisfying at a later hour.

'If I were only a painter, to catch your face when I told you of your precious pearl!' she went on, with a great deal of pleasure.

Her Ladyship took it in good humor. 'You know quite well I have set my heart upon having that ring. Hugo has promised it to me, times out of mind. For a minute, I could have murdered you.'

'I know.'

'But I forgive you, because it has made you laugh and taken away that sad look I surprised in your eyes a few moments since.'

'Nonsense. It is only that I wish I might be performing tonight. I feel lost on the days when there is no theatre, no stage, to occupy me.'

'Only your lovers, my dear?'

Elisa agreed lightly. 'Only my many lovers.'

Lady Hawtree sighed. 'I wish I knew how you manage it, I do swear.' Another slight pause followed, which Elisa read very well. She had not been in the theatre twelve years without learning the purpose of such nuances. Her Ladyship went on: 'Now, Elisa, about our villainous Mad March. I confess, I never believed it of you.'

'Me?' Indications were growing clearer.

'I mean to say, you were never a coward. Confess it. You are afraid of that man. Such an attractive rogue, I always thought. And he has sent you these bottles of wine. He means to be your friend. He is often received at Hawtree Place, you know. His manorhouse is within a day's ride of ours, in those hills and valleys of the Cotswolds. His is more lonely than ours, of course.'

'I leave him to Your Ladyship.' Elisa guessed where this was leading. Gwenna Hawtree wanted to keep her away from Captain Hawtree, for reasons that had a great deal to do with the Hawtree jewels and fortune. Elisa was amused. Nothing could be more absurd than a permanent relationship between Captain Ronald Hawtree, aged twenty-three, and Elisa Carlisle with her Elsie Catlow antecedents.

Lady Hawtree studied the crystal glass whose contents were half gone. She shook her head.

'Perhaps I am too hasty in pronouncing him your friend. I do t like his taste in wines. Evidently, March sent you what his rs reserve for the servants. Some such notion.'

ery likely.' Elisa tasted the bubbling wine. She found nothing al in the taste except that it seemed to be a trifle bitter. The color was not the best, either. 'Clouded,' she agreed, holding the glass up to the window light from the square.

Lady Hawtree set the glass down and rose. She appeared to sparkle like the lines of her shot-silk gown and the matching pelisse whose color brought out the brassiness of her red wig; her own hair was sparse.

'I am disappointed in your lack of courage, Elisa. Bad wine or no. I had thought you would face down our friend Lord March. In point of fact, I would not have been the least surprised to discover that you had won him over and he was quite taken with you.' Her eyes saw a good deal, and Elisa was uncomfortable under that survey. 'But of course, if you had rather be enemies – well then, you are not the incomparable *Circe* they all claim you to be.'

'I detest that name, Your Ladyship.'

But no one knew that better than Gwenna Hawtree. She smiled sweetly and took Elisa's unwilling arm, walking with her to the small but beautifully proportioned entrance hall.

As they parted Lady Hawtree said, still watching her friend with those prominent eyes that saw too much, 'I know Jeremy March. He can be won, and by a woman like you. He is not to be taken by anyone less resourceful, and he won't settle for one of those wretched niminy-piminy creatures the Regent is always thrusting at him.' She tapped Elisa's wrist with her fan. 'Mark me. He is yours, if you play your cards well.'

It took all Elisa's histrionic efforts to prevent a show of excitement over her friend's hint. She managed to laugh off the suggestion and even to pretend that it did not matter.

'Should this remarkable event occur, My Lady, yours will be the first invitation to the ceremony at St Margaret's.'

Even Gwenna Hawtree was forced to laugh at the likelihood of a marriage between Lord Jeremy March and Miss Elisa Carlisle, actress.

'To be sure, I wish you well.' She lowered her voice so t she would not be heard by McFee, the butler-coachman h by Peg Tuttle to protect Elisa. He was small but very tough Elisa's over-enthusiastic admirers had learned, to their sor

'But I beg of you, my dear Elisa, not the Hawtree Pearl. You must promise me.'

Elisa said nothing but gave her a mischievous, tantalizing look. Gwenna Hawtree, determined on revenge for this new challenge, leaned still closer. 'By the by, if you still believe Mad March dislikes you, I would suggest you refrain from drinking any more of that odious wine.' She yawned, covering her lips daintily. 'Whatever he sent you, it has a curious effect upon me. I shall be asleep before I am home in Grosvenor Square.'

Elisa was amused and stood there on the steps waving good-bye as Her Ladyship was assisted into the old-fashioned Hawtree landaulet and driven off around the busy square.

Elisa was left to her brief dreams. She felt sure Gwenna Hawtree's remark about the champagne was merely an attempt to trouble her, as revenge for Elisa's remarks about the Hawtree jewels. No. The important thing about the gift of champagne was that it came from Lord March.

She had first met Jeremy March six months earlier at Vauxhall Gardens one evening when, for a brief few minutes, His Lordship was perfectly charming. Until, in fact, he discovered she was the 'harpy' who held his seventeen-year-old brother in thrall. Arthur escorted her to the popular rendezvous, and abandoned her briefly in order to search for a small cameo she had lost on the path near the orchestra pavilion. She hated being left alone, but at least she was out of doors among trees, fairy-tale lights, and distant sounds of drinking, laughing, romantic trysts.

It was not as though she had been locked into a windowless room.

The two brothers bore no resemblance in either appearance or disposition. Arthur was incurably naive, never having known any suffering greater than the death of his favorite hound on his first fox hunt. His complexion was light, his hair the color of wheat, his mouth soft and sensitive. It was the face of a sheltered boy.

This man who strolled along, fresh from one of the leafy arbors, was much taller, very lean, with a fencer's grace. His dark hair was dishevelled and windblown. Unlike most male visitors to the pleasure gardens, he wore no hat. She saw at once

31

that the two brothers were violently opposite types, not least in their effect on her. There was an exciting attraction about Jeremy March, even though he had at first mistaken her for one of the well-dressed prostitutes who strolled what was called 'The Dark Walk'.

Her gentle reserve soon persuaded him of his error.

'You aren't really safe here,' he reminded her, having apologized for calling her 'a lovely doxy'.

She was amused but said gravely, 'I know. I am often accosted by strange peers who call me a doxy.'

He laughed at that. 'I take it that you have been abandoned by your escort. Come along. I'll at least provide you with a plate or two and a glass of Ratafia.'

She refused politely and he did not insist, but he remained with her, discussing the unseasonal warmth of the evening, the doings of Princess Lieven (was she a spy or wasn't she?) and the health of the unfortunate King George, while avoiding speculation on his 'madness'. She would always remember how March had talked to her as an equal, perhaps in the way he would have talked with a male, assuming she was intelligent enough to exchange gossip on political matters.

Her friend, Lady Gwenna Hawtree, had told her several times that Lord March was 'unusual'. Exceedingly popular with women, both ladies and 'bits of muslin', he had managed to reach the mature age of thirty-three without marrying – possibly because his time was occupied with political maneuverings to push his precious Indigent Elderly bill, and partly, no doubt, because he had never found whatever he looked for in a life companion.

She found herself mentally agreeing that Gwenna Hawtree was right in her admiration of Lord March. He was a man of many facets.

Elisa mentioned their common acquaintance, Her Ladyship, though she still wondered uneasily when he would remark upon his young brother's friendship with her. She had merely stated that her name was Carlisle and there were several Carlisles in the Prince Regent's circle.

He was amused when she mentioned Gwenna Hawtree but added, 'When next you are a guest at Hawtree Place, Sir Hugo must give me notice. I shall include you among my guests at March Hall. It is less than a day's ride over the hills.'

'You are most obliging, My Lord.'

She could not mistake the admiration in his eyes that glowed so flatteringly as they looked at her.

And then, in an instant, it all ended. Arthur March came loping along, waving her cameo brooch in boyish triumph.

'A fiddler kicked it with his boot-toe. But it seems quite safe. . . . Good Lord! Is that you, Jeremy? Have you made yourself known to Miss Carlisle?'

Elisa could not miss the change in Lord March. That delightful glow in his eyes hardened curiously into something that disappointed her. She did not often find herself the object of dislike and contempt, especially from men she found so attractive.

'You are that Carlisle?'

She made a brief curtsy. 'I am known professionally as Elisa Carlisle, Your Lordship.'

Arthur was a bit flustered. He almost babbled, 'Miss Carlisle is a perfect lady, Jeremy. I – I insist that you regard her as –'

'Mr March,' she cut in. 'I hope I need not leave the Gardens alone.'

Arthur offered his arm. 'No. Certainly not. Good God – I beg pardon, Miss Carlisle, but – Jeremy, what are you about, insulting a lady? It isn't like you.'

'It is very like me.' Jeremy March bowed to Elisa, an exaggerated gesture. 'Your servant, Madam. Arthur, I will see you at March House. Shall we say, some time before His Highness's reception at Carlton House tomorrow?'

Arthur waved him away nervously. 'To be sure. Come, Miss Carlisle.'

It had been the beginning of Lord March's animosity toward her. During the months since that first meeting she had met him on several occasions. Always, his manner was correct but distant.

He despised her no less when the stories of her sinister effect upon callow males were made public.

Arthur blamed their father, Sir Reginald March. 'His penchant for women of that sort prejudiced my brother. Not that you are remotely to be confused with such females, dear Miss Carlisle. But Jeremy was young at the time and perhaps he cared too much. The scandals, you know.'

Meanwhile, during the six months since Lord March's changeful behavior to her at Vauxhall Gardens, the tiresome gossip continued to surround Elisa Carlisle, further tarnishing her name. There seemed to be no way in which she could persuade Lord March that she was no '*Circe*,' except to enter a nunnery. His treatment of her had succeeded in arousing all her contradictory impulses.

At one moment he had saved her from sheer panic when the door of her dressing-room jammed shut; yet he had humiliated her only a minute or two later by assuming she had used her wiles to win the diamond ear-drops from his brother.

Why should she refuse gifts from admirers who could well afford them? Undoubtedly, nothing would satisfy Jeremy March but her starvation and death in the midst of degradation. She did not propose to satisfy that malicious desire of his. There was nothing noble about starvation. Nor was his good opinion worth a call in Bedlam where unfortunate women were sent who did not have the foresight to save the gifts given them by admirers.

All this animosity on Jeremy March's part did not explain today's gift of champagne.

Unless it was not a gift at all but a warning.

She called in pugnacious little McFee, whose ugly but likable grin spread when she mentioned her doubts about the champagne.

'If yezz'll give me leave, Mum, I'll be that pleased to try it on the tongue, as ye might say.'

Amused but nervous, she had to stop him before he poured an entire glass full of champagne and raised it.

'Please, McFee! If there is some dangerous substance!'

34

He waved aside such minor considerations, took a long drink and considered the results.

'Fair, Mum. Only fair. Color bad. Cloudy. And where'll be the bubbles?'

More uneasy than ever, she ordered the other bottles brought in. He examined them. Four bottles seemed normal but one other had been tampered with. McFee had his own ideas.

'Can't tell by the taste, but after making a night of it – excusing the thought, Mum – I've been known to drop a wee bit of laudanum in me mornin' mug of Blue Ruin.'

She shuddered at the idea of gin – Blue Ruin – in the morning, and at the notion that Lord March should hate her enough to send a dangerous drug like laudanum to her as a gift.

'You mean, it might kill whoever drank it?'

'That's as may be; on t'other hand, might be somebody's notion of a joke.'

She could scarcely write a letter to Lord March demanding an explanation. It was inconceivable that a lady should correspond with a gentleman who was not intimately related to her, and if she broke this inflexible social law, he would have reason to call her a 'doxy'.

But she was godmother to Dr Brian Clifford's young daughter, Susan, and a letter to her, franked by one of Elisa's friends, would be, in essence, a message to Brian. According to Gwenna Hawtree, Brian was frequently called in to care for the servants at March Hall.

She wrote the story of the champagne to Brian Clifford, who had been her friend long ago and done what he could to help the orphaned Elsie Catlow after Molly's death. He had been very young then, a handsome widower with an infant daughter, and young Elsie had loved them both.

He was as handsome and kindly as ever last year when he was in London to fetch home pretty, ambitious Susan from her Young Female Academy, but he didn't approve of Elisa Carlisle's style of life and quietly told her so.

A dozen years ago when Elisa Carlisle had created herself, more or less from the shreds of Elsie Catlow, she and Brian

Clifford drifted apart. She knew he had not approved of her ambition or her use of the male admirers she collected along the way. Nor had he been over-fond of Peg Tuttle, whom he blamed for the 'fall' of his friend Elsie. Though she pointed out that she gave very little of herself in exchange, he seemed to find this even more reprehensible. His morals were strict.

But he was a friend she could count upon, as he assured her last year.

The answer to her inquiry came to her in less than a fortnight. He was shocked at the champagne affair and assured her that no one at March Hall had sent the wine, either as a gift or as a joke.

'I am given to understand by the housekeeper, Mrs Ponsonby,' he wrote, *'that no March servant delivered the case to the Hawtrees. There is a strong suspicion here that Lady Hawtree has what Mrs Ponsonby calls "a very odd humor".*

'As you may know, Mrs Ponsonby was very like a mother to young Master Arthur; so I hear her ideas of you have been badly distorted by the ridiculous gossip that London sees fit to spread about Elisa Carlisle. I trust I have allayed her worst fears somewhat by the absolute assurance that the young lady I have known for fifteen years is incapable of behaving in such a fashion.

'But to return to the matter of the champagne. My dear Elisa, it troubles me that you should be subject to the odd humor of a female like Lady Hawtree. If she should not be the culprit, then the matter is far more serious and we must suspect such malicious humor actually came from March Hall, but, frankly, I find it difficult to believe. I have excellent relations with the household and am debating whether I should permit my Susan to be apprenticed, as one might say, to Mrs Ponsonby. The woman has taken a fancy to her and claims that at sixteen she is of an age to learn the rudiments of running a great household.

'Naturally, if there should be any danger, we must abandon such notions. Susan, of course, pleads with me night and day to give my permission. She adores March Hall.

36

'*Do take care, Elisa. Perhaps a surgeon of your acquaintance might discover what had been added to the mysterious champagne gift.*

'*Susan sends her dearest godmother all her affection, in which she is joined by,*

Brian Clifford'

The letter settled nothing and, in any case, Elisa had already submitted the wine to a surgeon in London. McFee was right. Laudanum had been added to two bottles. Possibly enough to kill, in some circumstances. If it had been a joke, it had an exceedingly unpleasant touch.

She began to wonder about Gwenna Hawtree. Brian and the March housekeeper were right in thinking this might be the sort of joke that lady would find amusing. But not to the extent of drinking it herself.

It was Gwenna Hawtree who called Elisa's attention to the odd effect of the champagne. It seemed absurd that she should have mentioned the matter when she was the only person who had drunk the wine. There seemed little humor in that, even for eccentric Lady Hawtree.

'No matter what Brian and the others think, I'll wager it was Jeremy March,' Elisa told herself and was chilled by the thought.

Having made the decision to continue her present life without being influenced by this nasty and unknown enemy, Elisa hesitated over Gwenna Hawtree's invitation to an evening of 'Poesie', performed by a somewhat bloodless young aristocrat who was her latest protégé.

Although in former days Elisa was flattered by such invitations, she still wondered occasionally about the champagne. Perhaps a closer acquaintance with her friend might discover the truth about that affair.

'Forgive me, but when your poet read at the Gala Ball for the Russian Tsar there was an appalling –'

'Exodus? Quite true, my dear, but you see, my husband is not in the least suspicious of poor Eustace.'

'Has he reason to be?'

'Elisa, child! You know me better.' Lady Hawtree grinned. 'Poor Eustace is a diversionary tactic. My adorable George Leith, the Viscount, you know, is more easily inserted among all those dull guests. You must come. That tiresome Eustace admires you so.'

Elisa's amusement was faintly edged.

'That is fortunate. Otherwise, my invitation would have no purpose. I trust your champagne will be better than mine was on your last visit.'

Lady Hawtree waved away such small details. 'How absurd! Do you know, I fell asleep on the way home to Grosvenor Square. Did you ever hear anything so nonsensical?'

Elisa was stunned by the implications. She was certain the woman said it quite innocently. She said, 'I will come, then, but I don't wish to encounter Arthur March's brother.'

'My dear, never. Jeremy March hasn't attended one of our London Evenings since his mother died. That would be eons ago. Of course, he was on the Continent for two years before Waterloo. Spying inside the French Empire, you know.'

How like the man! A wretched spy with a murderous sense of humor, and yet he put on these fine airs, as though a respectable actress was lower than a spy!

She agreed to attend, upon being assured that she would not run across Lord March unexpectedly.

It did not occur to her until the night of the Hawtree evening entertainment that Jeremy March had a talent for the unexpected.

CHAPTER FOUR

Tuttle set herself against Elisa's attendance at the Hawtree entertainment and pursued her own reasoning until the last moment.

'You are going to find enemies in every corner, Girl. You'll be crushed like an oyster.'

Elisa laughed at the comparison, although there was much truth in Tuttle's warning. Very possibly Lady Hawtree was guilty of that nasty little trick with the champagne. In any case, it was too late to change her plans. Arthur March had gallantly announced that he would escort Miss Carlisle, who then ordered a new gown to be made for the occasion. Arthur could not but consider this a tribute to himself.

The night had come and Elisa was willing to chance the rudeness of the Prince Regent's coterie. She was motivated by the dreams of her childhood in which she had watched the elegant, sparkling creatures of the aristocracy, and even royalty itself, leave splendid carriages, mount the few steps and enter the great houses in Grosvenor Square, Berkeley Square and Portman Place.

Occasionally, during moments of courage, she had peeked in behind the guests, watched them relieved of their weather garments in the reception hall and seen them mount the elegant staircase to be received by their host and hostess. Closing her eyes, she could still see the dazzling jewels, the shimmering materials of the women's gowns.

'Now it is your turn,' she reminded her mirror image as Tuttle carefully arranged the dainty little pearl tiara in her high-piled hair. But it was not entirely a triumph. There would always be the memory of one who could not live to enjoy this triumph. Pretty, generous, kind-hearted Molly Catlow had never known the pleasure of those jewels, the applause, the admiration. Above all, the money which would have been a blessing and a salvation, came to her daughter at twenty-six, fifteen years too late for Molly.

Elisa reached for a silk fan with its exquisite painted view of a far-off, perhaps non-existent Oriental land. The delicacy of the ladies and gentlemen pictured on the fan, with their curious long robes, the high curved bridge and the stylized trees so deep a green that they looked black, fascinated her. Female friends like Gwenna Hawtree, perhaps envious, claimed the portrait of an unknown land and civilization was sinister, but it was the first truly distinctive and rich present given to her, coming from an admirer fourteen years ago, and she could never tire of its fascination.

Tuttle followed her down the staircase which, like Elisa's house itself, was narrow, delicate and generally painted or decorated in white and gold. There was a daintiness about the furnishings whose style showed the influence of pre-revolutionary France. A first sight of the twin salons up on the first floor, above the stately formal dining room on the ground floor, invariably brought out the comment from her male admirers, 'How like you it is!' And sometimes, more elaborately: 'Anyone may see, Miss Carlisle, that you were born to such refinements of taste.'

This made her smile. She was never quite sure whether she should mentally thank the flatterer for his lack of insight, or congratulate herself for a performance far exceeding those on the stage of the Phoenix or the Adelphi theatres.

Arthur March looked proud and a bit puffed out at his coup in capturing the actress for the evening. It was said at the clubs that three peers who outranked his newly decorated brother had asked to escort Miss Carlisle and had been refused.

Elisa looked at him affectionately as he assisted her into the family carriage, while several street urchins hung about the heads of the team, discussing with the March footmen the fine points of these splendid blacks. Elisa saw nothing in Arthur that reminded her of his elder brother, for which she assured herself she was heartily glad. His pale gold hair glowed in the last of the bright autumn daylight and his honest blue eyes looked as though they had been washed clean of all that was sordid or cruel.

Or mysterious, sensuous and tantalizing.

She closed her mind to the forbidden figure this conjured up. 'You are looking most handsome, Sir,' she told Arthur when they were enclosed in the pleasant velvet confines of the March carriage.

He flushed with pleasure and felt for her gloved hand. She placed it in his fingers, murmuring, 'My dear friend, how good you are to me!' Before he could contradict her with more than a 'No – no – please –' she added, 'You have no sense of a difference between our stations. You do not share the prejudice of your family.'

'My brother, you mean. You may as well say it. He is incredible. I told him so, this very hour. I believe I took him aback. At all events,' Arthur went on proudly, 'he said no more but let James Larch, our first coachman, take out his precious black team. I suppose I should be grateful for that. Why Jeremy behaves so, I've no notion. He has certainly had his own share of such – I mean to say – not that you . . . Dear Miss Carlisle, I can't imagine how I came to blurt out such insulting nonsense.'

It was there. Always there, with these aristocrats. Even Arthur March. No matter. It was not expedient for her to notice it. Her fingers had curled in upon themselves at the clear implication and his stammered apology only made it more offensive. But one must be practical. Proud reactions could wait until she was as rich and mighty as the Marches. Richer. More powerful.

When she said nothing, Arthur ventured, 'Can you ever forgive my stupidity? Miss Carlisle, I have never known a female more admirable, more like a true lady of quality.'

'How generous of you, dear friend!' She smiled upon him benevolently.

It was just as well that she had learned long ago to let insults pass. Such youthful adoration, even from a foolish, babbling boy, often proved useful at odd moments. And besides, she liked him a great deal.

The Hawtree mansion in Grosvenor Square might have been mistaken for a royal town house. Its broad stone front reminded Elisa of a prison as well. Despite her own ambitions, it seemed inconceivable to Elisa that Gwenna Hawtree had married into this family for such uncomfortable displays of wealth. When she and Arthur entered the huge, cavernous interior of the reception hall she did not envy Lady Hawtree. All Elisa's dreams of splendor in her childhood were bound to beauty and grace, not this heavy, over-ornate style.

However, the sight of Lady Gwenna herself went far to overcome the gloom of the mansion. She stood just beyond the top of the staircase, on the gallery landing between the two double doors of the ballroom. Beside her the short, stout Sir Hugo Hawtree was flirting with a foreign lady in an astonishing turban of scarlet, purple and gold satin.

Lady Hawtree wore a gaudy red, black and white gown of some stiff, gold-threaded material that made her look taller, more imposing than ever and somehow called even more attention to the inquisitive nose that seemed to march before her.

The pompous voice of the Hawtree second butler called out: 'Miss Elisa Carlisle. Mr Arthur March.'

Several guests milling about the gallery turned to stare and whisper behind their fans. As Elisa Carlisle came up the stairs toward her host and hostess, with an inch of satin skirts gracefully raised on either side in her gloved fingers, Sir Hugo murmured to his wife, 'M'dear, one might be forgiven for supposing our actress was a lady.' He looked over Gwenna Hawtree who, like himself, had been flirting with a guest and added, 'and you the actress.'

Lady Hawtree laughed goodnaturedly and patted his arm with her ivory fan. 'Of course, Hugo. But I have a protector. She has not. And I have the blood of earls in my veins. I wonder what my dear Elisa has in hers.'

'Breathtaking thought, you will allow, my love.'

'I certainly will allow that . . . Dear Elisa, how good to see you! I trust it will not be pistols at dawn when our brave captain catches a glimpse of the young gentleman beside you. If it isn't the delightful Mr March! Welcome to Hawtree, as always.'

Captain Ronald Hawtree had been listening to the artless rambles of a pretty young female making her first appearance in London society. With renewed enthusiasm he made his excuses and approached the actress, who was dazzling in oyster-white set off by pearl jewelry. Pearls were also woven into the pattern that outlined the deep neckline and high bosom of the gown, as well as the panels down the front of the skirt.

Elisa had overheard snatches of the conversation between her host and hostess and was neither flattered nor offended. By this time she knew the Prince Regent's world fairly well. All was surface glitter. One must adapt or be swept under. In her seemingly gentle way she had no intention of being swept under.

Her response to her friend was easy, yet respectful. Although Gwenna Hawtree remained 'Your Ladyship' to Elisa, she herself had long been 'dearest Elisa' to Lady Hawtree, thus marking the proper distinction between them.

Elisa greeted Sir Hugo's compliments with the special warmth she used toward her audiences, her lashes modestly lowered, her voice soft, grateful, and sensuous. Sir Hugo was enraptured. He held her fingers too long and frankly stared at her, but she found his attentions far less repulsive than those of the Conde da Spada who trotted along the gallery to greet her.

She took care to accept Sir Hugo's broad compliments with due humility and a lovely smile. Then she turned to his son, allowing Captain Hawtree to come between her and da Spada.

In any case, she knew just how much all these attentions were worth. It had been made perfectly clear several years ago that whatever these males wanted of her, it had nothing to do with respect or any real affection. Even Arthur March placed her in the category of his brother's 'bits of muslin'.

This, however, did not keep Arthur from resenting the attentions of Ronald Hawtree, who was less than three years his senior. Arthur reached for her hand, asking in as stern a tone as he could muster, 'Shall we take our chairs, dearest—Miss Carlisle?'

Captain Hawtree refused to take him seriously.

'What? Where are your manners, my good fellow? Miss Carlisle, allow me to suggest a glass of champagne. Something to make this evening a trifle more palatable? Poets, imagine! What next for my stepmother, I wonder. Lord Byron himself?' Skilfully, he separated her from Arthur and strolled with her toward the small, overheated crimson salon at the end of the gallery.

They passed the crowded ballroom, where Elisa saw that most of the guests had gathered with champagne glasses precariously tilted in their hands as they searched for chairs. She thought of the reason for all this social hurly-burly, the effort to hide Gwenna Hawtree's latest *affaire* behind the reading of poetry that no one wanted to hear. She wondered if Sir Hugo suspected. She pitied the poor young poet 'entertainer', who probably thought this gathering of potential financial sponsors was all for his benefit.

The captain took two glasses from the footman's tray. Elisa stared at the golden bubbling flow of wine, remembering the last time she drank champagne with Gwenna Hawtree.

'We are certainly going to need this,' the captain warned Elisa as she took the glass from him. He had put his glass to his lips when Arthur March made his way through the little group around the footman and tried to take Elisa's arm. In doing so, Arthur jolted the captain's elbow and the wine spilled out in a spray which barely missed Elisa's gown.

While Ronald Hawtree swore and scrubbed his uniform sleeve with a napkin, Arthur begged pardon, adding in a lower voice, 'But Elisa, you came with me. I mean to say, Hawtree is an insinuating beggar. You know that.'

Several witnesses exchanged smiles and it was clear to Elisa that they would make poor young Arthur a figure of fun. She tried to be kind to him, at the same time reminding him lightly, 'I have two sides, my friend. Do come along with us.'

'Now, see here. . .' Hawtree began angrily, flourishing the damp, gold-fringed napkin. Whatever else he said was lost to

Elisa. She had looked up at that instant to see the latest guest appear in the doorway from the gallery.

Lord Jeremy March.

He had apparently seen the unfortunate accident between Arthur and the captain, in which Elisa Carlisle, that insolent, troublemaking actress, might be said to have encouraged both participants. It was maddening. So far as she could see, she had been completely innocent in the affair.

With this as consolation she tried to make peace between Hawtree and Arthur March, bestowing on them equal amounts of her attention. It did not relieve her when she noticed that the Conde da Spada had joined Lord March and was pointing her out, doubtless whispering some new scandal about her. She could not quite analyse Lord March's smile when he stared at her. It had seemed at first that he was pleased to see her. Perhaps he considered her a challenge. But the arrival of da Spada and his confidential whisper slowly altered whatever good will she read in that intriguing stare. The smile remained. Only Elisa's own nature, which was highly sensitive to insult, told her that Jeremy March's opinion of her had not changed for the better.

She raised her head haughtily and said in a tone she seldom used, 'If one of you gentlemen will oblige, I would like to take my chair for the entertainment.'

She moved toward the doorway, with Arthur and Captain Hawtree following in her train, arguing like children over whose rights had been violated. She paid little attention to them. Her thoughts were entirely wrapped around the arrogant peer who seemed to have tried to poison her as some sort of malignant joke.

She stopped before Jeremy March, drawing his attention away from the Conde da Spada who bowed low to her but whom she ignored.

'Your Lordship.'

Jeremy March had already taken her hand and brought it to his lips. She was aware of the all too familiar thrill of physical pleasure before she withdrew her hand. He looked a trifle surprised but, to her annoyance, he also seemed amused. 'The

Fair *Circe*.' He made a pretence of apology. 'But I had forgotten. You do not enjoy that title, Miss Carlisle.'

She made an effort to compete with his unpleasant banter. 'I received your card with the thoughtful gift, Lord March.' His dark lashes flickered in what appeared to be surprise.

'I beg your pardon?'

'But please, Sir, it was quite unwise to register your opinion of me with laudanum. How did you know your own young brother might not share the champagne with me?'

He said flatly, 'I'm afraid your humor escapes me.'

He must take her for a great ninny. 'Do you deny you sent me a present of champagne? How ungallant of you!'

'I certainly deny it. And what may this have to do with laudanum?'

She hesitated, uncertain now. She managed a sarcastic, 'If you do not know. I'm sure I cannot guess.'

As a woman in the eye of the public, a woman who had unconsciously made enemies by her conduct and the actions of her admirers, she had many who might wish her ill. Even some unknown, hearing of her supposed iniquities, might very possibly have sent her the laudanum-laced champagne.

With her heart beating rapidly she left Lord March there, frowning after her. She moved gracefully across the floor and into the ballroom, closely followed by her two wrangling suitors. She heard Jeremy March call to his brother and had the satisfaction of likewise noting that Arthur either ignored or didn't hear him.

But it was all in vain. Captain Ronald Hawtree had already found two heavy, dark Jacobean chairs in the double demi-circle around the poet. The chair next to Elisa was occupied by a stout, panting duchess whose stays were obviously too tight. She was not pleased to find the notorious Elisa Carlisle beside her and hissed a sibilant command to her jovial husband. They changed seats. But this proved to be a strategic mistake, since the duke was delighted to find himself beside the actress. His wife spent most of the next half-hour scowling around her husband's form at Elisa, who tried to remain unaware of her.

The frail young poet, Eustace Faraday, was introduced by Gwenna Hawtree with great fanfare, considerable fan-waving, and an occasional rap on the shy poet's knuckles by way of emphasis. Eustace Faraday imitated the fantastically popular George Gordon, Lord Byron, in every possible way, lacking only the two club feet and the arrogant beauty of the more celebrated poet.

He wore his nondescript hair in the Byronic fashion, rather like Lord March's unruly black locks. The poet was careful to leave his white silk shirt open, the cravat far too loose, revealing his prominent Adam's apple. He even affected a romantic limp, but from the comments around her Elisa was led to believe that all these affectations were useless. Lord Byron, though rude, shocking and cruel, was quite out of the ordinary way. Eustace Faraday was a pale substitute.

He began to read in a weak, passionless voice some equally passionless verses that had for their subject 'The Far Beauty of Samarkand'. Near or far, few of those present had more than the remotest notion where Samarkand was, and the audience soon began to yawn. Chairs shuffled back along the heavy Persian carpet, occasionally toppling over, as males made their way to the next room where champagne and an early midnight supper were laid out. These interruptions were made noisier by the demands to 'Hush!' and audible cries for silence from others in the audience with less foresight, as the poet fought his way valiantly from 'the caravan routes to Samarkand', onward to 'a single rose blooming fragrant in the dust of ages'.

As a performer herself, Elisa tried to keep her attention on the poet, frowning when Captain Hawtree beside her or Arthur March behind her made audible demands to take her riding in fashionable Hyde Park tomorrow. Her sympathies were all with the poet. He appeared to sense this and looked at her often when making an artistic point. Her smile encouraged him, but she was frankly relieved when the first interval occurred and the audience flocked out of the ballroom, in such a hurry there was considerable jostling and bustling.

47

The young poet's gaze shifted from an eager, plain young lady to Elisa Carlisle who was just leaving. He made stammered apologies, then rushed to ask Elisa, 'Oh, Miss Carlisle! Do you think they understood my medieval allusions?'

She replied with a slight evasion. 'Your scholarship is astonishing, Sir. I congratulate you.'

He blushed, thanked her and permitted himself to be captured by several very young females. Captain Hawtree, who had already drunk more than he could politely handle, was wrangling with a fellow officer in the gallery, and Arthur was gone; so Elisa went into the little salon, only to come upon Lord Jeremy March alone, drinking champagne and staring into the the coals that smouldered in the fireplace.

She was startled enough to turn away quickly. For a minute she failed to realize he was speaking to her when he called, 'Don't go. You are as free here as I am.' He added, catching her puzzled look, 'Unless you are afraid, of course.'

She knew that teasing tone very well but rose to it anyway. 'Afraid of you? Certainly not . . . I shall simply take care not to accept presents from dubious sources.'

Unexpectedly, he laughed. It was clear that he thought her remarks about the present of champagne were meant to be amusing. He might even think they were an attempt to win a genuine present of champagne from him by her hints that others (secret admirers?) favored her.

He took a glass of champagne off the tray on the sideboard and offered it to her. She had already taken it when he said in his teasing way, like a pin-prick, 'Your reasoning is that diamonds never come from dubious sources?' He was looking at her now in an odd way, almost as though he had turned serious, which was unlike him. 'You might do better as my pensioner than as my brother's evil genius. Give him up, *Circe*. Perhaps I will have a better offer.'

What a fool he must take her for! If she sent that nice young Arthur March packing, she would give Lord March the satisfaction of knowing she did so for a bribe, a hope of greater profit. He would never believe that when she freed Arthur from

48

his infatuation, it would be because she felt him much too fine a youth to be involved in the half-world of the theatre. There was no doubt that it tarnished him in some way to be considered one of *Circe's* admirers. But he was so clean, so decent, with that pure adoration of her that she found strangely compelling, perhaps for its unique appearance in her life!

How would Jeremy March guess that it was for this reason she had delayed sending Arthur on his way? He would never believe it anyway.

Meanwhile, other guests had found their way into the room, but she ignored them.

'Certainly, my diamonds come from cleaner sources than your champagne, My Lord. I wonder what you yourself bargained to obtain with it.'

'Please. Not that stale joke again, Madam. At all events, this is the Hawtree champagne I offer you. I never bargain for anything I can purchase outright.'

She felt as if he had slapped her. 'I assure you, I am not for sale to you at any price.'

Engrossed in their quarrel, during which each of them wanted to hurt the other, they were startled by Captain Hawtree's furious, drunken interruption: 'How dare you, Sir! No gentleman would speak so to a lady.'

If something wasn't done there would be more scandal attached to her name. With a nervous little laugh she fluttered her Oriental fan.

'No, Captain. I am persuaded you misunderstood the gentleman.'

Spurred on by a titter running through the audience which grew larger every minute, the captain persisted.

'I demand that you apologize to Miss Carlisle.'

Lord March examined his glass calmly, then drank down the contents. He made matters worse by handing the empty glass to the now thoroughly maddened captain.

'Nonsense, old fellow. Go up to bed and sleep it off. By morning you will see what a waste of time it is to defend every stray actress you may encounter in your nightly rounds.'

49

Several witnesses gasped. More shocking to Elisa, however, no one else came to her rescue.

Poor Captain Hawtree bellowed after His Lordship who was strolling out of the salon, 'I demand satisfaction, Sir. I will not be trifled with, nor see my friends insulted. I demand satisfaction on the field of honor, by God!'

In the doorway Jeremy March turned. 'Sleep on it first, my boy. Always the wisest policy.' Then he was gone.

Elisa could not mistake it. The guests were edging away from contact with her. They blamed her for the entire affair.

CHAPTER FIVE

'For what would you be going off to bed at this hour?' Tuttle wanted to know. 'You should've stayed and faced them down. You'll only lie there staring at the ceiling, scared you'll wind up back in the – well –'

'Gutter?' Elisa completed the remark, her soft, warm eyes bright with hatred of the world she had escaped from and the world she could not enter. 'By God, I'll not end in a gutter! Or in Bedlam!' She was stripping off the lovely gown so passionately Tuttle made vain grabs at the pristine white silk with its hundred of seed pearls.

'Now, don't you go and ruin this thing. It cost you a fortune.'

'Who cares? I could look like a saint and they would still treat me like a "bit of muslin", as Arthur March calls it.' She stepped out of the gown, picked it up in a wrinkled bundle and thrust it at Tuttle. 'Do you know what hurts the most?'

'I know who hurts you the most.'

Elisa ignored that. 'When we were alone in that little salon tonight and he spoke to me, I was idiot enough at first to think he might have softened toward me, even begun to like me.'

Rescuing the dress, Tuttle was philosophical. 'Well, maybe His Lordship will get stabbed through the heart in their duel. That'll teach him.'

'It would be just my luck if poor Captain Hawtree takes a pistol ball through the head.'

'Your luck! Won't be too great for the Captain neither, comes to that.'

51

Elisa's bad mood had been compounded by the nagging suspicion that the guests at Hawtree were right. It must be her fault that two respectable gentlemen of the Regent's circle were liable to blow each other's head off.

'Was it my fault, after all?' she asked plaintively half an hour later as Tuttle poured hot water over her pale, naked shoulders in the old hip-bath. 'I have separated men who were boyhood friends.'

Tuttle was nothing if not opinionated. 'Don't be so conceited, Girl. If they wasn't fighting over you, it'd be some other filly, like as not. Captain's been spoilin' for a fight, poor soul. This peacetime plays the devil with a young sprig like that.'

'Tuttle, you are as good as a glass of spirits, any day.'

'You aint drunk all yours, Girl. You just set back easy-like and finish that rum fustian. I stirred it with a hot poker, like Pa used to with the sailor-boys down to Portsmouth. Put you in fine fettle. Keep you from all them nasty dreams.'

Elisa followed her directions, relaxing in the steamy, perfume-scented water while she drank from the mug of rum. She went to bed just a bit befuddled, wrapped in a glow of warmth and unaccustomed optimism.

For several hours Tuttle's remedy worked its charm.

She awoke deep in the night. That first, warm comfort, aided by hot rum, had worn off. The little fire in the grate was dead now and she was aware of a chill in the air.

People were always telling her that her lovely, white bed-chamber was 'cold', that there should be bright colors around her. But Elisa remembered the dingy, dun-colored lodgings of her childhood, the dirt everywhere, and her longing for cleanliness. Purity. White.

How cold it was, too cold for early September.

She found it difficult to open her eyes. There was a weight on her eyelids, the remnants of the hot rum enticing her back to sleep. No sounds broke the night silence. All of London seemed – though it certainly wasn't – asleep.

Curious, because she sensed that Tuttle was in the room, wandering around, probably shutting away in the armoire the white gown Elisa had worn at the Hawtree Musicale.

But at two o'clock in the morning?

'Tuttle?' she murmured sleepily. 'Can't you do that in the morning?'

From the hall Peg Tuttle bellowed, 'You call me, girl?'

Confused, Elisa sat straight up in bed. Her flesh felt icy. Hugging herself, she rubbed her upper arms and looked around.

The room was empty. Starlight faintly illuminated the room at the point where the portieres met. Whatever presence she had sensed in the room, it was certainly not the one person who would have a legitimate reason for being there.

At the same time Tuttle pushed the white-panelled door open from the hall and a bar of lamplight cut across the rich, pale carpet.

'You calling me?'

Feeling foolish, Elisa wanted to satisfy herself that what she had felt or sensed in the room was no more than her imagination.

'Would you mind checking the windows? Nobody could get in that way; could they?'

Tuttle stalked around, holding the lamp high while she tested the locks of the two long windows.

'Not this high up. Unless they took to flying.'

Elisa knew then. She had dreamed again, one of those haunting memories that would not die. Whatever shared the room with her during those few seconds had been a figment of her own mind. She had created it. She wanted to scream. She laughed instead.

'If I keep to these stupid nightmares, I'll be dragged off to Bedlam for certain.'

'Over my body!' Tuttle informed her tersely.

So frightened was Elisa that she found herself thinking, surely, she means it. I can trust Tuttle can't I? But there were moments when she trusted no living being.

'Never mind. I'm sorry I disturbed you. It was nothing.'

'Go back to sleep.'

53

Trying to be playful, Elisa agreed obediently. 'Ay, Mum. Like 'ee say, Mum.'

Tuttle remarked, 'You got a real gift for that, what they call mimicking. You sounded just like your Ma when she used to play act, before them sailor-boys. She wasn't a bad actress herself. Kept you from starving, as you might say. I never knew a girl to try harder. Poor little thing. You look frail but you're a mite stronger. Taller, too. It helps, being taller.'

'It helps, being stronger.'

'You never spoke truer, girl.'

Tuttle went out, nodding.

To her own surprise Elisa eventually returned to a dreamless sleep. She was no more reassured, no less terrified than she had been at two in the morning, but her evening's performance lay ahead of her. There would be her work, a wardrobe change and a final rehearsal with other players on *Our Lady Of Victory*, a new confection by one of her admirers.

She had a pleasant relief from these pressures while she was in the midst of tedious wardrobe repairs, standing on a stool, turning slowly in the center of the stage, with all the footlight lamps glowing, to the brusque orders of Madame de Marsac, her dressmaker. Madame was concerned for the beauty of the lilac gown and its spidery lace overdress. Elisa's interest was entirely theatrical, hence the footlight lamps.

'How do the lamps strike the satin? When the lamps flicker there may be shadows. I don't want anything grotesque. Audiences always laugh. We are making the romantic tragedy of Josephine Bonaparte, not the comedy-melodrama of her early life.'

Madame sniffed. 'It is a lady's duty to appear at her best. One should not consider the audience, crude louts that they are.'

A welcome interruption came then. Elisa heard voices in the wings and a wave of relief washed over her, as always when she heard Brian Clifford in the wings.

'We won't interfere, I promise you. We are old friends. We haven't interrupted the rehearsal, I hope.'

Elisa ignored the muttered complaints of the seamstress and called out, 'Brian! Come on-stage. I haven't seen you this age. How is my pretty god-daughter?'

As the handsome doctor moved into the aura of the footlights, blinking his eyes at the brightness, the pretty self-confident sixteen-year-old girl with him answered for herself.

'I'm splendid, thank you, Elisa.' Her eyes opened wide. 'Oh, what a delicious gown! Some day I'm going to dress like that. It's good enough to eat. Turn around. Let me see it all over.'

Her father reproved her gently. 'That will do, Susan. Miss Elisa hasn't time to parade about just to oblige a harum-scarum girl.'

'Of course she has.' Slipping through Brian Clifford's arms, Elisa stepped down from the stool. She embraced the pretty child with the tangled mass of yellow hair dangling in a childish way below her bonnet. It was this very quality, the self-centered thoughtlessness of youth, that endeared her to Elisa. The actress often pictured a simple, protected childhood like Susan's as the ideal.

Elisa embraced the fluttering, excited girl, asking about Susan's life since she left Miss Fitch's Female Academy at Bath.

'And what are your future plans?'

Susan's school was one of those things Elisa had urged on Brian and offered to sponsor, but his pride made him refuse. It had been difficult financially and now, as Susan made clear, 'It is time for me to help Papa after he sacrificed so much for me. I shall see my dreams come true. *I know it.* And in doing so, I shall be Papa's savior.'

With an arm around her Elisa urged Clifford who was watching them with warm approval, 'Come along to my dressing-room.'

She ignored the mumbling of Madame de Marsac, still on her knees. 'We musn't let our heroine's advantages go for nothing. You and I are going to put our heads together and create a splendid life for Susan.'

'Not at all,' Susan announced grandly, with the tension of the young. 'I shall do it all myself. Indeed,' she smiled to herself, 'I am determined on that.'

'What do you say, Brian?' Elisa asked. 'Shall we marry our pretty Susan to one of the princes? The Prince Regent and the Princess have no legitimate heir, what with poor Princess Charlotte dying like that, and the Prince is trying for a divorce. Who knows? Susan, you might one day be Queen of England.'

Susan laughed. 'Who knows what I shall be?'

They were all laughing with her as they crowded into Elisa's little dressing-room where Brian, knowing Elisa's strong fears, left the passage door ajar.

Susan was thrilled by the utensils of Elisa's trade and immediately tried to darken her pale lashes with the sooty powder Elisa applied sparingly to her own lashes. As the girl worked, she assured them, 'I don't wish to be Queen of England. I want to be the mistress of March Hall . . . in a manner of speaking.' Her father looked at her and she added quickly, 'As housekeeper, Papa, of course.' She turned to Elisa, 'Oh, Ma'am, it's so wonderful, just cut off from the world like it was a fairy tale castle. Everyone is so kind. And I'll wager, some day I might have more power than the Queen of England.'

'I shouldn't be surprised.' Elisa looked hard at Brian, not liking all that talk of isolation and fairy tale castles when a girl like Susan might have so much more if properly launched. 'Do you have this enthusiasm for the home of the Marches?'

In a manner unlike the kind, straightforward Brian, he avoided her eyes and glanced at his daughter for help.

Susan shrugged. 'Papa thinks I like the household at March Hall too much and I persuaded him Lord March never sent you that wine. He's terribly attractive, and he's been ever so nice to me. So has young Master Arthur. Not so grown-up, of course.'

Elisa was disturbed. 'That is hardly a criterion – Lord March's attraction or Arthur's age. However, you are probably right. The wine may have come from someone who has heard of the wicked *Circe*, some total stranger. Am I to understand that you and your father disagree now about who sent the wine?'

'Not at all,' he insisted hurriedly. 'March may be quite innocent. Indeed, I expect he is. I lay the blame directly at Lady Hawtree's door, what with her peculiar form of humor.'

'Maybe Master Arthur did it,' Susan put in, giggling. 'He's a jokester, is Master Arthur. Such a child!' This from Susan struck her father and Elisa as very funny.

Elisa asked, 'Is that why you seem to disapprove of the Marches now, Brian?'

'Not precisely. But I've had time to think over your letter. Well, I daresay it's much ado about nothing. I confess I don't like Susan's aspirations. I hoped for something better than a housekeeper's post for her once, even after a suitable apprenticeship. I don't like to see her as a servant. But then, a housekeeper –'

'I like it, I tell you, Papa. As for being a servant, I shall have quite as much power as any March wife. Perhaps more. I haven't seen that country wives fare so well. But Mrs Ponsonby, who is the March housekeeper, orders everyone about in capital style.'

'What you like, my child, is flirting with those pretty footmen who come and go.'

Susan looked surprised, as if she hadn't suspected her father of such sharp eyes. But clearly she enjoyed the teasing.

'Well, he is most awfully elegant. But he has to be when you think how impressive the estate is. It's the only house of any consequence in those hills. The Hawtrees live in the next valley, but it takes half a day or more to reach them.'

'Sounds frightful to me,' Elisa murmured and began to plan for the entertainment of the Cliffords as well as their lodging. Her suggestion that they stay at her house in Portman Square was received with delight by Susan and protests by Brian Clifford.

'I'm sure you speak from your heart, Elisa, and it does you credit. But I am a widower and you are unmarried. It will not do.'

'Oh, fusty work, Papa. She is my godmother. Besides, people gossip about her anyway. What more can they say?'

Taken aback, Elisa thought 'the frankness of youth' was vastly overrated, but she wanted their company, Brian's in particular. Surely, their presence in the house would prevent those horrid nightmares about a creeping presence in her bedchamber.

Brian was scolding his daughter, but Elisa interceded for the girl. In the end it was agreed that the Cliffords should bring their boxes and portmanteaux to Portman Square, and dine there early in order to be at the theatre for the premiere performance of *Our Lady Of Victory* tonight.

With her spirits very much bolstered Elisa prepared for the evening curtain at six o'clock.

Since Strawbridge had orders from Elisa to be sparing of salaries, the company supporting her in *Our Lady Of Victory* was not of the first calibre. The plump little soubrette cast as Napoleon's second wife, Marie-Louise, spent most of her time edging toward the actor or toward Strawbridge, doubling as prompter, mutely asking for his assistance. She seemed to have become exceedingly well acquainted with the play's leading man.

The 'Napoleon Bonaparte' was Peter Tregaran, a small, ambitious Cornishman with a physical resemblance to the great Corsican and an iron determination to achieve overnight success in London. He had behaved well at rehearsal and, according to Strawbridge, showed talent if properly reined. Elisa did not doubt his talent but she was well aware that his blatant ambition might cause her trouble.

She had learned very early to protect herself.

She ate nothing before the first curtain. She sat at the old table, staring at her reflection but not seeing it, while Tuttle arranged her coiffure to match England's idea of the ex-Empress. The false diamonds in the chaplet glittered satisfactorily and reminded Elisa of the heirloom earrings that had been Arthur March's gift to her. She was wearing them tonight.

'I should return them. Again.'

Deep in her work, Tuttle rearranged a vagrant wisp of hair over Elisa's forehead.

'And what would that do? I wouldn't give tuppence for them diamonds in your crown.'

Elisa ran her fingers over the left earring, lingering on the little pear-shaped diamond. In the mirror she saw Tuttle shake her head.

58

'You earned it, girl, being nice to that addle-pated boy. Don't you forget it.'

Elisa touched the older woman's rough hand.

'Don't worry. You know me too well. I'll keep it.' She smiled without humor. 'Perhaps it will keep me warm on the cold winter nights of my old age.'

'It'll buy you the coal and kindling that will keep you warm.'

Then they both looked up as the call-boy stuck his head in. 'Curtain, Miss Elisa . . . By the by, Miss Elisa, that Captain Hawtree's in the wings yonder. Pot-valiant with drink, or I miss my guess. Best avoid him.'

She sighed. He had been likable and amusing when he was at least half-sober, but drunken, he was impossible.

'Well then, so it is, Billy. Thank you.'

It was curtain-time.

The ghastly doubts, the lack of confidence in her reputation, were thrust aside. Here was a field in which she had supreme confidence. She stood up. Tuttle ran a hand briskly down the silken length of her gown, looking for possible wrinkles, and set her out.

With all her movements as carefully studied as an opera-dancer's, Elisa walked to the wings. Captain Hawtree lolled against a side-wall. He caught her hand as she passed. She was almost suffocated by his breath.

'You've been avoiding me, damn you!'

She looked at him with her remote, puzzled expression that frustrated most unwanted lovers, who normally flushed and mumbled apologies.

The Captain reddened. 'Why d'you think I hang about here like an accursed urchin? I'll have you, and I'll have you tonight.'

'Not while you are in that state, Captain.'

He was still muttering when she heard her cue and moved out onto the stage and into the scene. She was annoyed by the disgusting quarrel with him but never let such extraneous matters interfere with the figure she presented on-stage.

She was only half-conscious of the thunderous disturbance by her romantic followers, particularly the young in the galleries.

She acknowledged the applause by her smile and then flashed the radiant look upon 'Napoleon', the young Cornishman, Peter Tregaran, and played out her scene.

She soon discovered that the young actor was upstaging her in every conceivable way.

She had learned her craft in a tough theatre world. When the young man moved upstage, maneuvring so that she must turn her back to the audience as she replied to his dialogue, she moved slowly, thoughtfully, downstage toward the footlight lamps, waving a delicate ivory fan, creating a stage business that attracted the eye of the audience. She resumed her dialogue, as if she could not face her persecutor, Napoleon. Once, she committed the unmentionable acting crime. She gazed down at the faces in the pit. The audience appeared to flicker out there in the jewelled darkness beyond the footlights and she gave them her mischievous look, as though she and they shared a secret from the rest of the cast on-stage.

These movements allowed her to get a good look at the aristocrats, obviously of the Regent's circle, seated in the box stage-right. A pretty little brunette with a ruby diadem glistening in her hair was busy chattering into the ear of Lord Jeremy March.

Elisa could scarcely believe that Lord Jeremy had come to see her perform after his insult at the Hawtree Musicale. His eyes stared at her with unnerving intensity, as if he wanted to read her soul. An absorbing thought. At least, it would prove that he thought she possessed a soul!

When he caught Elisa looking at him and realized that the audience began to follow her lead, he settled back in a bored way and made a remark to the plump little brunette who giggled behind her fan.

On-stage, Elisa turned to face her 'Napoleon' with his recriminations and ignored the titters of those who felt the dialogue was getting perilously close to Elisa Carlisle's scandalous private life. What followed was a totally unrehearsed scene.

At this point Tregaran as Napoleon was required to embrace her, on an irresistible impulse. With their faces close they would seem to be kissing passionately. The act itself, as performed regularly, was less romantic, a mere brushing of the lips, the position held several seconds, accompanied by sighs and sometimes the nervous titters of the audience.

Obviously, Tregaran hoped to win a clique of young admirers on his first London appearance. He seized her in his arms, swung her around with her back to the audience, and pressed his mouth rather amateurishly upon hers. There was force but no feeling.

Still, she earned all the attention he hoped to arouse.

It was not, however, a kiss to stir the recipient, being insensitive and very nearly childish. Also, it would further drag down her reputation. She wondered how he would react if he knew her real opinion of his supposed sexual attraction.

She would like to have thrust him off with all her strength, but a knowledge of the theatre warned her against such tactics.

She permitted the kiss, then, when he finally released her, she patted him gently on the cheek, making his apparently passionate kiss seem what it was, the work of a boy.

She saw too late that she had made an enemy. His face paled under its make-up. He looked stricken. But she thought he would not try that ploy again to get the better of her.

When she moved away and he picked up his dialogue, she saw Lord Jeremy March in the front box watching her with flattering attention, though there was little liking in his face. Did he suppose she behaved like this with his impressionable young brother? She longed to assure him that she would never consciously hurt Arthur.

Minutes later the scene was over and she hurried off to her dressing-room, thankful that Captain Hawtree was no longer around. She felt relieved. He was sure to grow more offensive after the last scene between Tregaran and herself.

'What happened to him?' she asked Peg Tuttle.

'If you mean that drunken Captain with his vile tongue not fit for a female's ears, he was gently urged out to his carriage, or his horse, or summut, and good riddance, say I. I'm sure I hope he's on his way straight home to Hawtree House. He's in no condition to escort you home.'

'Nor shall he. Peg, the other was out in the box tonight. Without Arthur.'

'Ah!'

'You know at once; don't you?'

'Who else would it be but His High and Mighty Lordship?'

'Not that I care.' Elisa waved away the idea, a gesture that interfered with Tuttle's busy work. Tuttle slapped away her hand.

'Likely.' Tuttle went on fastening Elisa into the glowing white satin Coronation gown with its yards of heavy train. 'Still following you about. He's got the sickness worse'n that young brother of his, I'll be bound.'

Elisa raised her head. 'Rubbish. If you mean he wants me. He hates me, I tell you.'

'He may despise you. There's a difference. These lordlings like to think they despise what others want, and maybe gets.'

'Peg! I have been excessively careful in my lovers. There isn't a female in the Regent's circle who can boast of as few lovers as I've taken in – or out – of my career.'

'But others don't hang about theatre boxes and musicales just for the love of the show. I'll wager he's got a fire in his loins this minute that he'd like to put out in your bed.'

'Good God, Tuttle! Where did you learn language like that?' All the same, she felt a burning in her own private parts at the thought.

'You know right well where I learned. First, at the Seaman's Rest in Portsmouth.'

Elisa stood obediently until Tuttle finished her work and upon being told 'That's about as good as I can do, Missus Empress,' she hurried out to make her next act entrance, still grateful that Captain Hawtree hadn't remained in the wings to cause her further trouble and perhaps give Lord Jeremy more reason to despise her.

Still, it wasn't like young Hawtree to give up so easily.

CHAPTER SIX

The new play was a success. Strawbridge's jowls stopped trembling and he also reassured Elisa excitedly by hugging himself as he stood in the wings. The audience was enthusiastic over Tregaran's Napoleon despite his sudden petulance after the love scene. Everyone seemed to be enthralled by the unhappiness of the 'forsaken Josephine'.

When the playwright had outlined the last act to Elisa, he had the usual author's anxiety to show 'the truth'. As he explained, 'She could scarcely be abandoned or heartbroken, Miss Carlisle, with all the millions the Emperor gave her, and some say she was more than friendly with the Russian Tsar and other kings when they came to call.'

Nevertheless, Elisa knew her audience, and the final curtain left more than one impressionable female blinking away tears as 'the Empress' lay on her deathbed, uttering the name of 'the one man she had loved' and expiring with a handful of the Bonaparte Parma violets dropping, one by one, from her delicate fingers.

Partly due to the nature of the final scene, and partly to a sense that they had witnessed the beginnings of a great love affair between Elisa and Tregaran, the audience gave her a standing ovation at the play's end, calling her name almost as a litany. Even Lord March and his young companion were on their feet. This might be a tribute to Tregaran. She did not flatter herself that it was on her account.

Adoring girls and boys from the galleries sent down bouquets of violets to be strewn at her feet as she took her graceful final curtsy. She had warm feelings toward these Gallery Gods. She had been one of them long ago, and they, in their turn, had made her the most popular actress in London.

She did not forget to lead out the young Cornishman, presenting him to the audience with the promise: 'I am persuaded you agree that Mister Tregaran will soon wear the mantle of Garrick and Kemble.'

He had the good taste to look modest at her praise but he managed to win the audience by picking up each of the violet nosegays, presenting them to Elisa with a flourishing bow.

'He will go far, that one,' Elisa remarked to Strawbridge on a note of amused irony.

She did not think again about Captain Hawtree until she left the theatre. While Tuttle went to summon her carriage in the coachhouse a block away, Elisa found herself surrounded by her young admirers from the gallery. As always, she tried to say a few words to each of them. Early in her career she had learned the importance of memory, not only on-stage but in dealing with her Gallery Gods.

She knew their names, and recalled anything they had told her about themselves. She was usually able to remark with affection on whatever they had told her in the past. This feat explained much of her popularity with them.

Suddenly, cries of indignation and shock ran through the crowd. They began to push and shove around her, propelled by something behind them. For a horrified moment Elisa thought a runaway team was causing the problem. In the narrow street carriages had rattled past for several minutes now, unnoticed by her little group.

The carriage horses were not involved. As she might have guessed, Captain Hawtree elbowed his way to her side where he swayed a little.

'Not good enough for a trollop like you? Yet you make indecent love to a dwarfish actor before the world.'

'Go home and sleep it away,' she said coolly. 'You are drunk.'

There were already murmurs and some smothered laughter, further infuriating him. Horses and carriages began to stall as the crowd grew in size. But he ignored the cursing of various coachmen and the uneasy fretting of the horses.

'I'll bed myself right enough, but you'll be with me, my cheap little *Circe*.'

Someone gasped at his insults, which made him retract loudly. 'No, by Gad! She's not cheap. She's the most expensive whore on the streets of London.'

This was too much even for Elisa's carefully controlled composure. She raised her gloved hand and slapped him across the cheek. The action probably made her hand sting a good deal more than his leathery face but it was a further provocation to the drunken man.

She saw his fist before her eyes and heard screams and vain scuffling as her friends tried to stop him. For a second or two she thought he would strike her in the face. But another hand, also gloved, seized his wrist, giving it such a wrench the Captain sank to his knees and fell back against the brick wall of the theatre, groaning as he was freed from that hard grip.

Jeremy March then held a hand out to him in a congenial effort to help him rise.

'What the devil were you about, Ronnie? Come along. You are positively bosky. Let us take you home.'

Captain Hawtree got to his feet, shrugging off all aid.

'I don't need help from you Marches. I've my own mount, thank you. You cried off from the duel like a coward and made me look the fool. And I've a score to settle with that precious brother of yours. He knew I loved the wench. He took her from me, damn him! I'll have his hide for it!'

He stumbled away, pushing through the crowd which yielded before him. Most of those present followed him with their eyes.

With an effort Elisa stopped shaking.

'Thank you, My Lord. This is not the first time you have saved me from –'

'Your doting admirers?' Jeremy March asked in the odious, sarcastic way that always chilled her.

'Saved me from fear.'

65

Again she saw that curious frown she had noticed before, as if she puzzled him. Then he said abruptly, 'I did it for Hawtree's sake. He was a boyhood friend of the family.'

She swallowed hard. 'Thank you, anyway, if nothing else, for coming to the theatre tonight.'

His carriage and restive horses were holding up traffic in the street. The brunette of the theatre box was watching these proceedings through the open door of the carriage. He smiled at her, a smile Elisa would have prayed for.

To Elisa's remark he answered, 'Oh, but our appearance here was my companion's doing. The Honorable Clarissa Hargreave was curious to see one of the *Circe*'s performances. It seems she got rather more than she bargained for. Good night, Madam.'

Seconds later he was in the carriage beside the Honorable Clarissa Hargreave and with his departure the traffic jam broke up.

'Thanks be to God!' Tuttle exclaimed when she reached Elisa. 'This is your biggest after-theatre crowd yet.'

'I take no credit for it. You may thank Captain Hawtree and Lord March.'

Tuttle looked around but both men were gone.

'So that's the way of it. I hope you didn't discourage Lord March. He always brings out that sparkle in your eyes. One day, he'll tumble into your arms.'

Elisa, who still smarted from the insults of the last ten minutes, suddenly came to a decision.

'Tuttle, I'm going back to my dressing-room to write an invitation. A late supper it shall be. Privately, in my home. I want it delivered within the hour. That will make him suffer.'

'What? You've invited Lord March only to make him suffer?' But she followed Elisa back into the theatre passage and on to her dressing-room. There Elisa removed her gloves, busied herself with quill and ink standish, writing in a flowing hand on her creamy note paper that carried the faint scent of violets.

'What are you about?' Tuttle demanded. 'Have you forgot you've got house guests, that Dr Clifford and his daughter? A shrewd little piece, that one.'

66

'Don't be ridiculous. I am inviting Arthur. Brian and Susan are sure to have retired before Arthur arrives – and, if not, they are discreet. My house is not so small as to hamper my having guests, I hope. It is time I repaid that dear child for those ear-bobs. And it will annoy His Lordship.'

'Will you take Master Arthur to your bed?'

'Certainly not. He is a mere boy. It would be most improper. I will let him amuse himself by kissing me with some fervor, if he likes.'

'He will like.'

'But I intend to send him home pristine and pure.'

'You haven't taken a lover in months. If you don't have a care, people will talk.'

'Let them. They will, in any case.'

She hadn't taken a lover since she met Lord Jeremy March. It was that simple.

Tuttle persisted. 'It'll be the ruin of your career. Do you want them to think you've lost your hold over men?'

'If I ever had it.' She thought of Jeremy March who hated her, and he was the only man she felt that she could have loved. But his sharp cruelty had driven her to a revenge she despised. Letting him think she was seducing a boy who hadn't quite reached his eighteenth birthday!

Am I trying for more than revenge, she wondered. Do I simply want to arouse Jeremy March's jealousy? To make him admit his real feelings toward me?

'Bah! His real feelings are a profound hatred of me.'

'What's that?' Tuttle wanted to know.

'Nothing. Talking to myself.'

'There lies madness, girl.'

Elisa shivered.

She completed the short invitation to Arthur March and watched Tuttle give it to the footman. Then she got into her own small, beautifully equipped carriage with Tuttle and sat back, still nervous, while they rode home.

For all her bravado, she had a revulsion toward letting Brian Clifford and his sixteen-year-old daughter suspect that the odious stories circulated about her might be true, and she was relieved when they showed signs of retiring before Arthur arrived.

For Elisa and the Cliffords, the cook had managed a satisfactory supper of a *céleri purée*, a very French eel pastry, a *ragout* of kidneys, some vegetables, several desserts and a syllabub to tempt Susan's appetite, which hardly needed tempting, plus wines to tempt Brian who drank sparingly. He had the extraordinary idea that doctors, and even surgeons, should drink with great moderation – not a common practice, even in these modern days of 1819.

Eventually, Susan went off to bed, to write in her journal as she announced on a note of pride, adding, 'I'm very good with words. Perhaps some day I shall write your lines, Miss Elisa. Or even create my own plays.'

'Perhaps you shall, indeed,' Elisa promised.

Susan looked at her for a long time with a mature and thoughtful expression. 'If you ever need help with – with anything, your lines, your plays, or anything where you wish a friend, I'd like very much to be the person you come to.'

Elisa was touched and took her hand. 'I promise you shall be my friend. My confidante.'

When he was sure his daughter could not hear them Brian set down the glass of Madeira he had been sipping and leaned toward Elisa.

'Now that we are alone, I want a word with you.'

'Of course.' She was puzzled and a little uneasy. Was he going to question her about her private life? Except for Arthur's expected visit tonight, it was undoubtedly less exciting than Brian thought. His own honesty made it difficult for him to understand anyone less direct and uncomplicated.

'My dear girl, I do not think you have been quite candid with me.'

'About what? If you mean these insulting items one hears in London about a person in my profession . . . You, of all people, must know that three-quarters of what is said or written is a pack of lies.'

He seemed angry at the suggestion. 'Certainly not. What do you take me for? Your private life is your own. I only wish I might have the power to protect your name.' His hand took hers briefly and let it go. 'But enough of that. You know I care for you, Elisa. I have never –'

'Dear Brian, I know. You are my closest—' she considered and added a sudden, rather saddening truth, 'my only true friend.'

His firm lips tightened, but his eyes were kind, despite his denial. 'I was not speaking of friendship. Now, no more on that head. I want to discuss something else. Your safety.'

'What on earth do you mean? If you are talking about my life in London, I do have Tuttle and the servants. And McFee is worth a dozen ruffians.' She laughed too brightly. 'Or is it my reputation that troubles you? Too late, my dear friend. Let them think what they choose. I am the only one who knows it is not true.'

'I know it is untrue. I know you, Elisa.' He rushed on. Evidently, he had given much thought to this. 'You troubled me very much when you asked me to make enquiries about the wine that was sent to you with His Lordship's card.'

'Oh, that. Very likely, he had nothing to do with it. He seemed puzzled when I challenged him. No doubt it was some enemy who believes all he hears about me.'

He shook his head, considering the matter seriously. 'I saw Lord March in the box tonight. His conduct was disturbing.'

'How so?' She hoped he was going to agree with Tuttle's theory that His Lordship might have a deeper interest in her than even he was aware of.

'That man still distrusts your motives.' She felt deflated and sat back. He went on. 'I saw it in his eyes, the way he watched your every move with such intensity. Only a man who feels violently could look so. And since we know his dislike of you – well . . .'

She tried to take this lightly. It was not like Brian to be so insulting. Couldn't he flatter her by suggesting that Lord March was passionately drawn to her and resented his own weakness? No. Not Brian Clifford. He did not flatter. His severe integrity

69

would not permit it, even in the intimacy of her small, exquisitely furnished boudoir-sitting room.

'All this may be very true, Brian, but I can do nothing about it.'

Brian looked down at his hands that were so skilful in their practice. He said evenly, 'You might marry me. There would then be no necessity for you to degrade yourself.'

'Degrade?' God in heaven! Did her old friend know her so little? 'Then you must share Lord March's opinion of me.'

He retracted hurriedly, in confusion, but it was clear that his apology was for the hurt he gave her, not for the basic truth of what he had said.

She borrowed a little of the glittering charm she used on-stage, to hide the pain.

'Dear friend, how fortunate I am to have one defender who loves me, despite my failings!'

'Elisa, I did not mean – I shall always be your defender. I think you know that.'

A shadow passed in front of the little bracket candles. Elisa and Brian both looked around. Tuttle was making gestures to Elisa. Embarrassed, Brian stood up.

'I beg your pardon. You have visitors. My daughter and I have been thoughtless, but I'll follow her good example. Good night, Elisa.'

'Good night, my dear friend.'

He took her hand, pressed it and left the room, passing Tuttle with a friendly nod. Tuttle looked out into the hall and then crossed the room full of suppressed excitement.

'That addled new footman who took your message to the Marches, he left it in the hands of a valet. Mister Arthur's valet.'

'Well?'

'Mister Arthur was expected home any minute. He'd been to Vauxhall Gardens with a duchess and her daughter.'

'He has my permission. Why the mystery, Peg? You are driving me to distraction.'

Tuttle hesitated. 'I've a notion that March valet was none too honorable.'

'What on earth do you mean?' As Tuttle didn't answer, she took a deep breath and dismissed this little game. 'Is he here?'

'Oh, he's *that*, right enough.'

'Then ask McFee to have a table set up with the lobster *patés*, the champagne, and the *gâteau glacé*.'

'McFee?' Tuttle repeated in a huff. 'This is delicate work. I'll attend to it myself.'

Elisa looked around the white and silver room which served to receive close friends or intimate callers. To entertain Brian and Susan she sat at the opposite end of the room on a settee near the low-burning fire in the grate of the fireplace. On the few more intimate occasions she occupied the chaise longue which was some yards from her bedchamber door.

Tonight she moved away from the chaise after Tuttle had gone to get the caller. She suspected that if Arthur found her reclining on the chaise he would expect a great deal more of her.

She turned away and started toward the far end of the room again when she realized that the door had closed. Tuttle knew better than that: No closed doors . . . *I will not be shut in. This isn't Bedlam . . .*

She swung around, ready to rush across the floor and throw the door open.

A tall man, like a slim black and white pillar, stood watching her with his back against the closed door. This was certainly not Arthur March. For an instant, in her panic at being closed in, she did not recognise him.

She lost all her carefully cultivated poise.

'The door! Please, please, open the door!'

Jeremy March frowned as he watched her.

'You did suggest that one of the Marches visit you. Well then, here is one of them.'

Gradually, she forced herself to a semblance of calm. Above all, she had to present some dignity before the man who so attracted her and yet remained her enemy. She was still alarmed but hoped he would not notice. The candles weren't that bright. She moved as gracefully as she could, putting all her courage into those simple movements. She sensed that she had puzzled him by her hysterical outburst.

She was always ashamed of her cowardice, and it seemed appalling that Jeremy March, of all people, should be a witness on two occasions. How he must despise her!

'That invitation was meant for another, as you know very well. What did you do, bribe your brother's valet? Or steal the invitation?'

He was still watching her with his hands behind him, pressed against the door. Her direct challenge brought a smile to those lips of his that had fascinated her in spite of herself.

'Arthur's valet is well paid. No need for bribery. Or theft. But I did think you might prefer someone with more experience of the world.'

It was maddening to be so insulted and have no defense. She managed a haughty order: 'Now that you do know, however, I trust you will leave.' She could not go on until something was done about the more pressing matter. 'And would you *please* open that door.'

He reached behind him, took hold of the brass latch and pulled the door ajar. He was still looking at her in his uncomfortably penetrating way. She decided it was the same look Brian Clifford wore when trying to analyze some illness of hers. She took a breath, and managed a wavering smile.

'Thank you. This is the second time you have seen me behave in this childish fashion. Undoubtedly, Your Lordship feels it is a jest of some sort. Let me admit you have managed to make me a figure of fun. I daresay this story will soon be circulated among the Prince's circle.'

For the first time she had disconcerted him. She was sure his high cheekbones colored a little as if he had been insulted. He moved away from the door and strode deliberately across the room toward her. There was a faint menace in his behaviour, or so she fancied, in spite of his elegance. Her heartbeat quickened.

'Whatever else I may be, I assure you, I am no talebearer, Miss Carlisle.'

He was much closer now, within an arm's length of her. She found his face unreadable. If she was going to call McFee to help her, the seconds were rapidly ticking away. She began again.

'You are welcome as a guest, Sir, but not if you are going to continue to insult me as you have at our previous meetings. Please stand aside. I'll ring for Tabitha and ask her to bring some wine. What do you prefer?'

'That won't be necessary.'

She watched, mesmerized, as his right hand reached out, his fingers closing firmly around her upper arm. She felt his warm grasp through the lace of her sleeve. Knowing her own weakness and her hunger for him, she turned to his left to escape this dangerous confinement, but his other arm was a barrier and she found herself backed against the chaise, imprisoned within his embrace.

Trembling against his body, she tried to speak but his mouth stifled her protest. He forced her lips apart with his and the fiery heat of his touch poured over her, leaving her drained of strength to resist. Almost of their own volition her lips responded, her hands raised to the nape of his neck and the skin beneath the brown tendrils of his hair.

Her body was joined to his so closely now she could feel the rising hardness of him. Her last fears of his trickery were gone. His own body betrayed his desire for her.

Breathless with her own passion for him, she returned his kiss. Seconds later, his lips moved with a feathery skill over her bared throat. He tore aside the neck of her gown. One finger traced the pale flesh with its delicate, milky fullness before he lowered his head again, his lips closing over one breast.

She heard herself moan and then betray herself with the whisper, 'I love you . . . I've always loved you . . . I only asked him to come because I wanted to make you jealous . . .'

But then, something strange and disappointing happened. He withdrew. Worse, she heard him chuckle.

She opened her eyes.

He wasn't even looking at her. He smoothed the immaculate folds of his cravat and turned away. She covered her bare

73

shoulder quickly with hands that shook, the remnants of that passion he had instilled in her.

Her throat was dry and she could not speak, even if she had thought of something cutting and cruel enough to say. She watched him cross the room. At the last second he stopped, dropped something on the tabaret by the door. Small and heavy, it rang on the delicately veined marble tabletop.

'For your kisses, Madam. I know you have a taste for diamonds. You need have no sentimental problems this time. I bought it myself.' He bowed, about to leave the room.

In her anguish she could only ask hoarsely, 'Why do you enjoy hurting me?'

At the door he hesitated. 'I beg your pardon?' For a few seconds he seemed about to return. They looked at each other. His gaze lowered to her hands. She saw that her arms had been held out toward him, beseeching him. Shameful. She drew them back quickly. She watched him take a deep breath. Then he bowed again and went out, carefully leaving the door ajar.

She was too stunned to move for a few minutes. She had a ridiculous desire to burst into tears, ridiculous because her reaction should have been deep anger and a desire for revenge. But there was that last curious and silent exchange between them just before he left. Could it mean that he had been ashamed of his action? Unlikely.

When Tuttle returned and peeked round the door Elisa sniffed hurriedly, trying to look as though nothing but a simple conversation had taken place. It was Tuttle who found Lord March's 'payment' on the tabaret. She took it up, weighing it in her palm.

'Lordy! He left his ring. Solid gold by the weight of it. And a pretty fair stone. Might be worth a thousand guineas in the shops. Wouldn't fetch you that much though. Not in our markets.' She glanced at Elisa to see what explanation she would give.

Elisa waved it away. 'His Lordship is a charitable man. He left it for those Quakers who help the poor and the Bedlam inmates.'

Tuttle opened her mouth in surprise. 'I'd never have thought he'd ask you to carry out his charities. How did you two get on?'

'Is that duel with Captain Hawtree still planned?'

'So they say, if the noble Captain has any weight in the business and the authorities don't get wind of it. There's talk that His Lordship just laughs it off.'

'If His Lordship does come up to scratch, as they say, let us hope Captain Hawtree shoots him through the heart.' Seeing Tuttle's suspicious gaze, Elisa added with a laugh, 'Although that might be difficult to find. Between the eyes would be easier, I think. And so very satisfying.'

'My God!' Tuttle rolled her eyes. 'He was scarcely here ten minutes. Was he that bad a lover? I'd never have thought it.'

CHAPTER SEVEN

She dreamed she was pursuing an unknown woman through the halls of an aged building. There were doors. She hadn't really looked at them as she passed. She was too concerned about catching the woman who ran from her.

A metallic noise echoed and clanged through the passage. One of the doors had opened and then slammed shut. Looking quickly over her shoulder, she saw that the doors had barred apertures and faces peered out at her, pallid, colorless, the eyes sunken, like bottomless holes.

A prison? She knew better, but she would not face it. She ran on.

Abruptly, the passage turned and she turned with it. She came upon the woman she pursued. Not a woman at all, but a girl who looked over her shoulder at Elisa in terror.

The girl she had been trying to catch was herself, Elsie Catlow. She knew that at once by the clothing, the made-over dress that had belonged to her mother, the dishevelled golden-brown hair with the touch of red in it, the questing, wondering eyes ...

While Elisa stared, trying to understand why she should see herself as she had been long ago, the girl cried out.

Elisa was awakened by the screams. Still half-asleep, she sprang out of bed. She was already crossing the carpet to the hall before she realized that her own throat had been strained by the screams. Badly shaken, she leaned against a wingchair, trying to recover herself.

The door had been left partially open as usual when she went to bed and now she heard voices. She realized she had awakened Brian and probably Susan. After a whispered discussion someone knocked on the door. It was a timid knock. She pulled herself together, wishing she had snatched up her velvet night robe before leaving the bed.

'Yes? Who is it?'

The door was pushed open a further few inches. Susan Clifford struck her head around the door, looking absurd but charming with her yellow hair tucked under a silk-ribboned night cap.

'I beg pardon. I heard somebody scream and I came out and here was Papa in the hall. He heard it too. Was it – I mean – did you hear?'

Elisa would much have preferred to deny the whole thing, but that seemed the depth of cowardice, and they would know better, in any case.

'I'm sorry I awakened you. It was a stupid nightmare.' She saw Brian's head in the doorway above his daughter's, and added with a deprecating smile, 'Awfully silly, I'm afraid. I dreamed I was chasing someone.'

'A common nightmare,' Brian put in. 'You mustn't let it concern you.' Brian was wearing a greatcoat, apparently over his night clothes. His thick brown hair looked rumpled, but, as usual, his manner and words calmed her. He added, 'I've had that dream myself.'

Not quite this dream, Elisa thought, but she thanked him.

Brian surprised her then by ordering his daughter off to bed, adding, 'I want to speak to Elisa.'

'Oh, Papa, can't I stay?' Susan grinned. 'As a chaperone?'

'Nonsense. I've known your godmother since she was a deal younger than you are; so run along.'

Susan went scuffing noisily down the hall while Brian suggested, 'You had best get a wrap. The fire seems to have gone out.'

'There are probably still coals in the grate of my sitting-room. If this is necessary.' She stood aside for him to cross the bedchamber and reach her boudoir. He had been about to walk down to the hall door.

He could not help looking at her in her thin silk nightgown as he followed her direction. She was amused to see the admiration

77

in his eyes. He had known her so long. Probably he had never really seen her before, despite his earlier, tender remarks about loving her. Then he excused himself, trying to turn the matter into a joke.

'You really are a disturbing sight to an old widower, even if I do remember that big-eyed little girl I used to comfort when she had nightmares.'

The memory aroused a tender warmth in Elisa. He was right. She trusted him, the only person in the world she felt she could trust. After Tuttle's outrageous trick tonight, in giving the invitation to the wrong man, one could scarcely trust her!

'Thank you, Brian. I'll be with you in a minute. Please leave the door open.'

'The same old superstition? Elisa. Elisa. At your age?'

'Not superstition. Fear.'

Still the same friend, but also the chiding, practical doctor as well.

No matter. She loved him and she loved her god-daughter. They were like blood relatives. She owed Brian more than she could ever repay.

She warmed her chilled flesh in the deep green velvet pile of her wrapper, stepped into the heeled slippers of quilted satin and went into the boudoir-sitting room with her hair tumbling down her back like a hoyden.

'A fairy princess,' Brian said, looking her up and down. 'Exactly like a princess in a fairy tale.' He had stirred up the fire in the grate and pulled an armchair over to the hearth for her. This warmth and care for her were doubly welcome after Jeremy March had left her feeling frozen and despised, like the 'bit of muslin' his brother mentioned so easily.

'Dear Brian, you were always too good to me.' She kissed him on the cheek.

'Don't.'

At this second repulsion in one night she backed away, not even troubling to hide the pain. He saw and understood.

'Sit here where it's warm.' He eased her into the chair and then explained. 'Elisa, I care for you. You know that.' She nodded. 'Then don't tempt me. You understand?'

She smiled at last. 'It's you who don't understand, Brian. There are all sorts of love. What I feel for you is a deep trust, a far stronger affection than for the usual men in my life.' She flushed in memory of that ghastly experience earlier.

'I had no idea that Lord March was one of them.'

'He wasn't,' she flashed. 'Nor is he. I was expecting his young brother. I sent His Lordship away.'

'I'm glad.' He seemed greatly relieved. She was surprised that he did not object to young Arthur as her lover. Then he went on. 'I will allow, Lord March is an excellent landowner, a man who cares about his tenantry, the fields, the crops. I deal with him whenever the villagers are ill, or when accidents occur. In all these matters, he is superior to most men of his station. But his reputation with women is quite another thing.'

'So I've discovered. I trust we are not going to spend the night discussing Jeremy March. A dull subject.'

'Far from it, now that I feel I have filled the role of a friend and warned you. It is about these nightmares of yours.'

This suggested that she had fresh ammunition against Tuttle. Surely, that tongue-wagging old gossip hadn't betrayed the many other nights when her sleep was broken! She began to bristle in her most imperious manner.

'Why do you talk of nightmares, as though I had them frequently? You are taking your guardianship of me a trifle too seriously.'

'Am I?' He pulled up a footstool and sat at her feet, reminding her of her own behavior when she was about ten years old and looked to him for advice and comfort on every occasion. 'You must remember, Elisa. I know what motivates you. I know the very core of your fears and those fears are groundless. If you were desperately poor—and you do not appear to be—I would never let you be taken to one of those wretched almshouses. And you are far too mature for the workhouse.'

'It isn't altogether poverty I fear. I mean,' she added honestly, 'I am afraid of it, but I am preparing myself to prevent it.'

He looked up into her eyes. 'I hope you aren't preparing by less than honorable means.'

'You must not believe all the gossip you hear.'

'Well then, what else troubles you in your sleep?'

She evaded, then admitted, 'The other. The place. Mother.'

That always made him nervous. He usually said things like: 'You musn't dwell upon it.' Or 'Your mother was unfortunate.' Or even, 'If that happened, you would never be placed there. I know other houses, quite pleasant, some of them.' This time he said: 'But this is absurd. I've seen no signs in you.' That answer was the worst.

She had 'seen no signs' in her mother. Only the weeping, the deep depression, the desperation. It was hardly surprising with not sixpence between her child, herself, and starvation. Even that friendly, goodhearted young doctor, Brian Clifford, could not feed four people.

She forgave him his clichés.

'Never mind, Brian. I am lucky. I've made my way. I shan't let something stupid like a dream destroy me. I've also had a deal of dreams that were *good*, and they never came true.' Certainly, her most romantic dream had exploded tonight.

She laughed. His eyes narrowed. He made her nervous, watching her. She explained her laughter with a quick lie.

'Here we are, you and I, with a very pleasant life, a reasonably pleasant future, our good health, and we sit discussing something that was over fifteen years ago.'

He was relieved. He slapped her hands. 'Good. Then we can dispense with the lectures for tonight.'

She watched him get up and leave her after kissing her temple chastely. She did not return his kiss.

Eventually, she went back to bed and dreamless sleep.

Contrary, to her fears during the next few days, the story of her abortive midnight rendezvous with Lord March had not spread. At least, she could admit Jeremy March was a gentleman in one sense.

It was Tuttle, behaving with unaccustomed civility, who brought the news that Lord March had refused to deal with Captain Hawtree's seconds.

'He dismissed the whole thing. Said it was all nothing but the hard drinking that was back of it all and he for one – mind you, this is what Lord March says – would drink a little less and stop fighting with his old friends.'

Well said,' Elisa agreed, having lost her bloodthirsty ideas in the interim. 'I hope Captain Hawtree took that good advice.'

'Took it! From all that's said, he near-on strangled his seconds for delivering the message. Thinks it reflects on his ability as a man. He's ready to kill both the Marches on sight. Can't stomach the gossip that says His Lordship don't want to do him any harm. Captain's bound and determined that someone's going to call him a coward. These males, fools, most of 'em.'

'I'm glad it may come off, for the Captain's sake.'

'Excuse me, Ma'am, but it's my thought that His Lordship thinks it's a great deal about nothing. Do you suppose that means what it sounds like?'

'Undoubtedly. He doesn't think I'm worth fighting for, when all's said. I couldn't agree more. And stop calling me Ma'am.'

'I hardly know what to call you, you're so prickly nowadays.'

At all events, Elisa thought with considerable relief, the absurd ending of the so-called duel would also end the gossip and the trouble in the theatre.

But in this her reasoning was false.

Several nights later the theatre disturbances began once more. Whether they were Tregaran's friends or genuine critics of the drama, Elisa could not tell. But out there in the jewelled dark were the creatures who had stared through the bars at her mother, faceless creatures laughing, sneering, even throwing things at her mother long ago. They were still there.

They were staring at Molly Catlow's daughter. It took all her resources to face them down, subdue them.

The trouble had started during a scene she shared with Bessie Maulders, who began to giggle so much she couldn't get her lines out clearly. Elisa covered her clumsiness but shortly after, in a

81

dialogue with Peter Tregaran, she was able to look up at the boxes near the stage.

In spite of all that happened between them, her heart gave a lurch of excitement when she saw that Lord Jeremy March was in his box with the Regent's coterie of chattering gossipers. He sat at the far end of the box and was staring at Elisa intently, as if he would read to her very soul.

A plump female, heavily jewelled, was in his box, accompanied by a haughty-looking pair, male and female. The plump woman leaned nearer Jeremy March to confide something behind her fan. His Lordship ignored it. The plump woman next whispered to the male and female. This time the reaction must have satisfied her. The pair glanced at Elisa in unison and attracted most of the audience with a sharp, cackling burst of laughter.

Still, Jeremy March paid no attention to the disturbance.

On-stage, Peter Tregaran pretended concern, but his expression of that concern gave fresh offense. He muttered, 'How rotten for you! Disgusting bad taste. Makes us youngsters shudder for our own future.'

She was deaf to this insidious sympathy and continued the scene, but she began to wonder how much Tregaran had to do with the kisses, occasional catcalls, and the all-too-audible remarks in certain areas of the audience. She knew that it took very little to set off the more clever members of the audience. They wanted to attract attention. What they regarded as Elisa Carlisle's scandalous effect on men gave them a perfect opportunity.

During the next act in which Elisa was alone on-stage for a minute or two, the insults from the pit became clearly audible to those in the boxes. Elisa's gallery admirers answered back, but Lord March's companions began to buzz among themselves and to laugh whenever a particularly nasty remark was hurled at her.

Suddenly, the other male in the March box leaned over to make a remark to Jeremy March; the peer got up, pushing his chair back noisily, and left the box. Elisa was astonished. She didn't dare to hope the insults angered him. But only minutes later he appeared in a box on the opposite side of the stage and settled into a gilt-painted front chair. Until his arrival the box had been dark and empty. Now, lamps were brought and the entire audience could see him as he leaned forward, his arms folded on the velvet-covered rail. He looked as if nothing in the world occupied him except the performance.

Elisa was terribly moved by the public gesture of support. She didn't understand but could only conclude that he might have revised his opinion of her since that emotional scene in her boudoir. She was so relieved she felt almost grateful to the bad manners of Tregaran's friends.

During the last scene in which she and Tregaran shared dialogue, two ruffians in the center of the pit began to call out: 'Jezebel!' 'Siren of the Stews!' and other insults. Her gallery friends took action. Between the acts they had equipped themselves with a pail of oranges of the variety often eaten during the performances. The young girls and their male companions began to pelt the disturbers in the pit below with the hard little Spanish fruit.

Screams went up as a few oranges missed their marks, striking ladies in elaborate feathered headgear, but, most startling of all, Lord Jeremy March stood up, waved to the galleries, called loudly, 'Bravo!' and began to applaud. The sight of this extremely attractive peer behaving in gallant support of a 'lady' on-stage appealed to the romantic instincts of the audience.

The applause spread until Elisa and Tregaran could hear cheers for their familiar favorite: 'The lovely Carlisle!' followed by the sorceress name even her admirers gave her: '*Circe!' Circe!'* '*Circe!'*

Tregaran bowed and waved to Elisa as if presenting her to her many admirers. But when the curtain was down he went stomping off in silence to his dressing-room.

Elisa glowed with relief. Thanks to Jeremy March she had regained control of her reputation, or what reputation an actress was allowed to possess. Certainly, it helped her career which could be destroyed if such outbreaks continued.

But even more important, he must think better of her. She prayed that he did.

A day later she received what she considered proof of his changed feelings in a message delivered by Gwenna Hawtree, of all people.

'My dear,' she burst out almost before she was seated in Elisa's Small salon. 'It is absurdly improper, but a certain party has entrusted an epistle to me. He knows I am your only friend among his clique. Do read it. I am in agony to know what it says.'

Elisa took the note, broke the March seal, and read the scrawled words: '*Forgive me for the past. Those were not the acts of a gentleman. But you must blame your attractions just a little.*' It was signed, '*March.*'

'It would appear to satisfy you,' Gwenna hinted.

'It does. He simply wishes me well. Was this your purpose in visiting me? It was exceedingly kind of Your Ladyship.'

Lady Hawtree squeezed her hand excitedly.

'Not entirely, my dear. You will never credit it. I am to play propriety for you at the March town house.'

Elisa stared at her, hardly daring to believe what she heard. 'But what would I be doing at the Marches' town house?'

'I asked myself that very question. Especially after that lamentable episode in the street outside your theatre. My wretched step-son! The boy is past praying for. But how flattering! Two grown men of the Regent's set almost coming to fisticuffs over an actress! Not that I object, mind. I rather hoped it might go further.' Lady Hawtree then admitted merrily, 'I did wonder if one of those delightful March lads would make me very rich by accepting my step-son's challenge. You know, Hugo's estate, for the most part, goes directly to Ronald. However, it was not to be.' She sighed over her bad luck, and in spite of her callous indifference to the captain's life she made Elisa laugh at this completely self-centered view of things.

'Forgive me, Your Ladyship, but you mentioned the March town house. How does it concern me?'

Gwenna Hawtree's mischievous grin made Elisa more nervous. The woman loved to tantalize her victims,

Her ladyship shrugged. 'Quite simple. Lord March believes we adults should make up the preposterous quarrel that has been

84

proceeding between his Arthur and our Ronald. There will be a reception and nuncheon on an early afternoon soon. Since the Marches were not provided with females of discreet years, he has asked Sir Hugo and me to fill the void. He happily obliged. Hugo says maybe His Lordship will now condescend to visit us more often at Hawtree Place in the country.'

'What will he say when he finds you have invited me?'

Lady Hawtree finished her announcement in triumph.

'But that is the delicious part. He told me I might especially invite you and two others. You will receive your invitations by delivery, of course.'

'Impossible.' It was too wonderful to be true.

'His precise words, let me see: "I understand you have taken up the cause of your actress-friend, the Fair Enchantress."'

'Oh, no. Not that again.'

Her Ladyship pretended confusion. 'Did I say that? No. I have it wrong. My deplorable memory. He said: "Your actress-friend, Miss Carlisle. Why not invite her? That should settle this absurd business once and for all."'

'I trust he doesn't want to make me a figure of fun, or try to show Captain Hawtree that I am unworthy of these noble lordlings.' All the same, she gloried in the chance to show them that she could behave like a lady, and that an actress was equal to their own ladies in the drawing room or otherwise.

Perhaps his first step in the matter of mending their relations had been his actions in the theatre, followed by that note she now held in her hand.

'But who are the two others you are to invite?'

Lady Hawtree was less interested. 'A man he proposes to make his estate agent, I believe. And a young daughter. Your house guests.'

'But how wonderful! Brian and Susan.'

'As you say. A matter for wonder. He seems to respect this Clifford very highly, though why he should find it necessary to include him and some addle-pated daughter is more than I can fathom. But Jeremy March always did take queer fancies. Very democratic.'

'Like yourself, dear Lady Hawtree. See what you have done for a wretched actress.'

'Nonsense. It was to spite the Regent's set. Why else?'

When the invitation arrived within two days Elisa, with the help of Tuttle and a wildly and anxious Susan Clifford, set about having appropriate gowns made for herself and for Susan. Brian insisted on paying for his daughter's pink muslin gown with its flounces and huge sash. It seemed to Elisa that the Cliffords were fully as excited as she was.

Brian reminded Elisa of his own position which was far from giving him entree to any social affair involving the Regent's circle. Even in the country his invitation always came as a pleasant surprise. Since Arthur March had occasionally accompanied Susan on country walks when no other chaperone was about, Brian supposed it must be Arthur who made himself responsible for the invitations.

This made it doubly important to Susan. The brother of a real-life peer had invited her to a glamorous affair and would be certain to pay her the attentions expected toward a lady.

With small, powerful McFee on the box the Cliffords and Elisa rode to Grosvenor Square on a lovely autumn day, with Tuttle along as maid to assist Elisa and Susan.

Elisa covered her own excitement by saying as little as possible while Brian teased his daughter who only expressed outwardly what Elisa was feeling within.

'I knew our Susan was much attached to March Hall and the countryside, but it seems the Marches themselves put that light in your eyes. Which of the gentlemen attracts my girl's fancy?' He appeared to consider. 'Probably Arthur. He is more nearly your age.'

Susan looked at him sharply, then laughed. 'Master Arthur is a gentleman. He is older than I but he is certainly a boy to Elisa.'

The actress admitted this. 'A sweet, goodnatured boy.'

'That may be,' Brian put in. 'But I don't want my girl reaching above her station. There is only pain in that.' He too looked at Elisa who snapped.

'I consider no man above my station.' She had a deep and secret belief that if she were ever given the chance she could make Jeremy March happy. Was it possible he would give her the opportunity? Most unlikely. But here she was, on her way to try and prove again that she was a lady and not some wicked enchantress who lured men to their doom.

The carriage drew up before the heavy stone building that looked uninviting from the outside and suggested a military edifice in a state of siege. The 'siege' was made up of two score elegantly gowned and suited members of the Prince Regent's court.

As she was descending from the carriage Susan whispered to Elisa, 'I'll wager we look quite as grand as any of these toffs. Master Arthur said once that I could grace any household.'

'And so you could.'

They went up the broad steps together. Elisa studied the girl. 'Wait until the Marches see you. You look enchanting.'

'And you. All in white, as usual. Quite like an angel.'

Elisa burst out laughing just as she and Susan entered the house between the cold, marble pillars of the reception hall. Here the hosts and hostess had decided to greet their guests on the ground floor just above the forbidding entry, thus giving more informality to the afternoon reception. By avoiding the dark, gloomy Jacobean staircase and a reception at the head of the stairs, the guests proceeded toward the airy, sunlit conservatory and the little terrace behind it.

While some guests milled around admiring the statuary, reputedly purloined from ancient Greek diggings, Elisa and her party were led forward. At once she saw Jeremy March standing beside Lady Hawtree, with Sir Hugo on her other side.

Elisa's laughter at Susan's remark had caught March's attention. He seemd mesmerized by her, or was he trying to mesmerize her? It was hard to know. She could only be sure that in some way she fascinated him.

Lady Hawtree and her husband ignored the Cliffords, paying great attention to Elisa. At the same time Elisa heard Lord March greet Susan and Brian with what sounded like genuine warmth. Susan was looking around anxiously and Elisa followed her gaze, wondering which of the footmen was the girl's Adonis.

Gwenna Hawtree confided impatiently, 'My tiresome step-son hasn't arrived, and we so hoped he would make peace with the March gentlemen.'

Then Lord March took Elisa's hand, welcoming her and pointing out his brother who was 'seeing to our guests on the terrace'. After a moment's hesitation, he added in a lower voice, 'May I hope that you have forgiven me?'

'Forgiven?' She could only pretend not to remember that midnight visit. Anything else would humiliate them both. He didn't seem to realize that and she fancied that he was disappointed. But that was incredible, considering his nature and his entire feeling toward her. He looked around at the crowded room, and said abruptly in the voice of an indifferent host, 'I thought I saw that wandering brother of mine. Where the devil has he got to?'

London's weather was not often conducive to parties on the terrace at the rear of the big, chilly house. The terrace overlooked a tiny pocket garden of herbs, as nearly as Elisa could make out, and several ladies and gentlemen were pretending to identify the weedy specimens.

The Cliffords had remained in the house, Brian recognizing the March butler, and exchanging a few words about the condition of the housekeeper's pleurisy, with Susan standing by, looking around hopefully.

Seeing Elisa, Arthur March made his way past several guests, unmindful of their greetings, and took her hand.

'How wonderful to see you, dear Elisa – I mean, Miss Carlisle! You are looking radiant.'

She was grateful for his kindness but wished his brother would stop watching her in that intent way. What was he thinking? She could only hope he was jealous. But why had he thrown them together?

She answered some question of Arthur's with a vague agreement before realizing that she had excited him unnecessarily.

He squeezed her fingers so painfully she frowned and withdrew her hand, trying to make a joke of the matter.

88

'Heavens! Even the mighty Gentleman Jackson would have fallen before your onslaught. You are surprisingly strong, Mr March.'

'If only I could ask you always to call me Arthur.'

'I am afraid that would shock these fine friends of yours.' She warmed to him then, seeing the devotion in his eyes. 'Dear Mr March – Arthur – can you tell me who is responsible for my invitation to these august portals? You or your brother?'

Arthur waved his hand. 'I, of course. That is to say, Old Jeremy saw me quite moped, and heard a few of my complaints, and you see what has come of it.' He added honestly, 'I confess, it was his idea. I had no notion he would come around so quickly.'

'He was exceedingly kind in the theatre the other night. Some tiresome groundlings caused us difficulty and Lord March defended us without saying a word except "bravo". But his manner!'

'Yes. Jeremy's manner can be deucedly cutting when he chooses.' He went on with passionate resolve, 'I wish I had been there. I'd have sent them packing.'

Other guests were watching them. She was sure they gossiped about the presence of a notorious actress in their aristocratic midst. Perhaps Arthur also felt these vibrations. He moved with her into the conservatory with its heavy jungle growth of plants and palm fronds and a long sideboard where peculiar, exotic fruits were set out in tantalizing array.

He saw Susan Clifford talking with great animation to a lanky, red-haired young footman looked confused but pleased. Susan smiled flirtatiously at Arthur and went on talking. He grinned, murmuring to Elisa, 'A delightful child. I trust those mischievous eyes won't end by breaking some poor devil's heart. I have come to know her little ways at the Hall.'

'She is young. It may be that she wants to test her skill as a female.'

'No.' His grin faded. 'That is cruel. To make a man care and then deny him.'

She saw the look in his eyes and resented its tug upon her pity. She suspected his remark about Susan had been a plea to her. So much for her attempts to return his boyish admiration with as much kindness as possible! She had tried to make the differences between them clear. Surely, he knew that everything made a deeper relationship impossible, not the least being her singleminded passion for his older brother.

She buried any flurries of conscience when Jeremy March strolled the length of the conservatory to join them. His actions piqued the curiosity of other guests who stood watching them while holding plates of strange gold, green, red and bronze-colored fruits which only the venturesome intended to eat.

Lord March stopped by the long, inlaid sideboard, gestured to a lackey and was given a plate of the exotic fruits. He presented the plate to Elisa, reminding his brother, 'This is something you should have done, my boy. Do you want your guest to think you are lacking in good manners?'

Arthur was flustered and cross at having been publicly scolded, especially before the one person he wanted to impress. Elisa thought his brother had been tactless. Their great difference in age had probably got Jeremy March into this bad habit.

She circumnavigated the matter by thanking Lord March as she took the plate while explaining, 'I was too interested in Mr March's conversation. I'm afraid it is my fault, not his.'

'Well spoken,' Lord March said and seemed to mean it. For once she was sure his smile was sincere.

Seeing that Arthur looked sulky, she began to eat the golden slice that Lord March called, 'A pineapple, from the Sandwich Islands. The yellow and green one is a paw-paw.' While he named them she herself offered a bit of deep pink fruit to Arthur with the light plea, 'Come now, do try it. If you survive, I shall eat it.'

Arthur took the fruit, grinning in reluctant good humor. It was at this moment that a commotion rang through the great, echoing reception hall. A loud male voice overpowered several agitated pleas for 'calm' from the March servants.

'What the devil?' March wanted to know. He started toward the doorway whose high arch was framed by twin marble columns. Arthur remained motionless with the fruit halfway to his lips. Everyone stared at the doorway.

Jeremy March had only taken a few steps when the latest guest, Captain Ronald Hawtree, appeared in the archway, closely followed by Sir Hugo and Gwenna Hawtree. He didn't look very steady on his feet.

'Bosky!' Arthur muttered. 'Fellow's been at the bottle.'

Sir Hugo made braying sounds, beseeching his son, who teetered slightly.

'No, Boy. I say, now. Not the way. Not the way at all. Don't want to make yourself a figure of fun.'

Captain Hawtree's scarlet jacket looked rumpled as though he had slept in it. His usually open countenance was so twisted Elisa scarcely recognized it. He lurched forward, heading toward Lord March, but shouted at Arthur over his brother's shoulder.

'Steal the woman I've set my heart to have. And then hide behind your noble brother. Ay. There's courage. As for you, Your Noble Lordship, you injured me in a way no real man can endure. Trying to shame me in the street, and gabbling to the world that you did not wish to kill me. Me, when I've already put one man under the sod, and by Gad, there'll be two in my reckoning before this is over.'

Everyone within hearing stood motionless. Jeremy March was surprisingly quiet. 'You have been misinformed, old friend. I said nothing of the sort.'

'Liar! How does it come about that the story's abroad? I'm met in the clubs with it. At Manton's. At Tattersalls when I'm bidding on a new mount. Everywhere.'

Still carrying the bit of fruit between his fingers, Arthur pushed past Elisa's restraining hand, protesting.

'I am at fault. You misunderstand, Hawtree. There was no intention to insult you. Good Gad! We were boys together. Old friends.'

Jeremy March said, 'Arthur, the matter is between the Captain and me. Don't interfere.'

Elisa saw that Jeremy's calm had begun to have an effect upon the Captain. He was impatient with Arthur but seemed willing to talk out his anger.

'Ay. Between us. Gad's life, you coward! You'll do anything to avoid my challenge. I might have guessed how it would be.'

'My boy, come,' his father urged, but at that instance one of the gaping witnesses chuckled and, as if infected, several others giggled.

Captain Hawtree reddened at what he conceived to be a personal sneer. His hand went to the breast of his rumpled jacket. Elisa saw the silver butt of a duelling pistol.

She caught her breath, afraid to utter a sound, for fear he would make the next move.

All sneers, whispers and giggles ceased.

Jeremy began quietly, 'Captain, I have no intention of meeting you on the field, with pistols or swords or fists, if it comes to that.'

'Do I have to shame you before our friends – before the world?' Hawtree blustered. He had the pistol out now, waving it around to punctuate his words.

To everyone's horror Arthur leaped between the two men, groping for the gun.

Jeremy March, now tense and pale, tried to separate the struggling men while Sir Hugo made vain pleas with his son. The struggle looked especially terrifying to the women, for most of whom it was the first sight of deadly male violence.

The two bodies, locked together grunting and panting, rocked back and forth as Arthur tried to wrench the pistol away from the captain. For a few seconds no one could see the weapon between their bodies.

Then the pistol went off, sounding like a cannon in the big room with its many glass windows. At the same time Captain Hawtree groaned. He fell against a now stupefied Arthur but it was Lord March who received his limp body, sinking slowly to the floor with him.

Arthur stammered, 'I – I didn't mean – I wouldn't have shot him . . . He meant to kill you.'

'Be quiet!' Lord March ordered. He and Sir Hugo hastily examined the wounded man who lay writhing in agony, dark gouts of blood slowly forming a pool beneath his right arm.

'My lad, my poor lad!' Sir Hugo whispered and looked fearfully at Lord March. 'His arm. Look.'

Lord March said, 'Someone find Dr Clifford. He is about somewhere.'

It was a trembling Arthur who ran toward the conservatory doors with young Susan. The girl found herself a part of male violence for the first time in her life, and was clearly excited by the drama of it.

Meanwhile, Elisa spoke to Susan's red-haired Adonis, the footman. 'Bring some clean clothes. Towels, sheets, anything.'

He went away hurriedly and returned with a great pile of kitchen cloths. When she knelt beside a confused and trembling Sir Hugo it was Jeremy March who took the clean pile, thanking her, but ignoring everything except the effort to staunch the blood that flowed inexorably from the shattered upper arm.

'Will he live?' Gwenna Hawtree asked.

No one answered her.

'My poor boy,' Sir Hugo muttered, taking up his son's good hand. The Captain was semi-conscious now. 'How bad is he?'

Lord March looked up. 'Ah, there you are, Clifford. The right arm. I'm afraid the ball shattered the bone. He is bleeding badly as well.'

Gwenna Hawtree nudged Elisa, urging her away from the tense figures around the wounded man.

'My dear, how ghastly! The unfortunate creature. So volatile. How does it feel to have men draw blood over you?'

Because she was badly shaken, Elisa snapped, 'Your sympathy for your step-son has been noted by all Your Ladyship's guests.'

Lady Hawtree did not seem to be offended. 'Of course. I think I must arrange for a bedchamber here in the March House. He should not be moved just yet to our place. Excuse me.' She added with her malicious smile, 'I shouldn't like to be remiss in my attentions to the poor boy.'

Elisa returned to the group around the wounded man.

93

'Is there anything I may do?'

Lord March raised his eyes from Captain Hawtree and studied her. To her intense relief he did not share Lady Hawtree's nasty ideas.

'Yes. Will you try and calm my brother? He needs you more than ever.'

She nodded and turned to find Arthur. He had propped himself against the wall beneath a forbidding portrait of the seventeenth- century General March. He was wringing his hands but didn't seem aware of the gesture.

She went to him and took his hands in hers.

'Don't. It was an accident. You were only trying to save your brother. We all know that.'

Choking back a sob, he whispered, 'Thank you, my dearest Elisa.' He leaned over their clasped hands and kissed her. At the last second she avoided his lips but she was deeply aware that she and Arthur were attracting unwanted attention from the witnesses to the Captain's tragedy.

CHAPTER EIGHT

Without knowing how she could have prevented Captain Hawtree's disastrous behavior, Elisa felt responsible and could not shake her depression when she learned that the tragedy had ended Captain Ronald Hawtree's army career.

The story being spread blamed the Captain's behavior on his drinking and his resentment over a 'fancied story' that Lord March had refused the challenge out of pity for his youth. Considering the character and reputation of each man, it was easy to believe.

All the same, Elisa's conscience did trouble her. She recalled Arthur March's remark about pretty little Susan Clifford with her teasing ways. It seemed wise for Elisa to profit by that warning. She certainly did not want to encourage him further in his delusion that he loved her.

She called upon Gwenna Hawtree to learn of Captain Hawtree's condition, only to be told by Sir Hugo that the wounded man remained at the March house for the moment.

'We are warned that he dare not be moved yet,' he told her, attempting to treat the matter with detachment. Also, Elisa sensed that whatever the Marches felt, Sir Hugo now blamed her in part for the disaster. He was stiffly polite. No more. No indication of wishing to prolong her ten-minute stay. She couldn't blame him.

She said hopefully, 'But he will recover?'

His heavy shoulders shrugged. 'Recover? My boy's entire life was the Army. His was among the British regiments that occupied Paris after Waterloo, you know. He was very proud of that. The great damage to the city and the parks was not committed by us, he said, but by the Russians. Or the Prussians. I always confuse the two.'

'Thank heaven his wound was no worse.'

Sir Hugo's answer came flatly, without emphasis, making it sound even more terrible.

'The Prince himself sent over his surgeon. But they could not save my boy's arm.'

She had no words to answer that. The bright scarlet uniform would be useless now. She got up. As she was leaving the room, she said, 'Please tell him he has my prayers and all my thoughts.'

'Do you think that is entirely wise, Miss Carlisle? I mean to say, in the circumstances?'

She felt as if he had thrown icy water in her face.

'Perhaps not. I beg your pardon. Good day, Sir.'

'Goodbye, Miss Carlisle.'

He did not escort her to the entry hall. A footman showed her out.

At home she protested angrily and a little desperately to Tuttle and Susan Clifford, 'I had no part in it. Why must I be ostracized?'

'At least, they don't pack you off to the country,' Susan grumbled, 'just when everything exciting happens and all the attractive men are remaining in London.'

Elisa didn't want her to go, and she would be even more sorry to lose Brian Clifford's company, but he had been adamant. His patients would need him. Besides, he made it clear he did not approve of life among the Prince's London and Brighton circles. He had added another and more disconcerting reason.

'I prefer not to find myself too much in your company these days.'

When she asked 'Why?' in surprise he said, 'I think you know why.'

She was too uneasy about the matter to say more. Now, he and Susan were both going and Elisa, with her dreadful fears, her nightmares and her passionate desire not to be left alone, would be once more thrown upon her own devices. It was an extremely uncomfortable thought.

'And mighty selfish, if it comes to that,' Tuttle reminded her when she complained.

Elisa threw a mirror at her, careful to aim wide of the mark, but both women were badly shaken when they looked down at the mirror, shattered on the floor between them.

Contrary to her deep-rooted superstitions, there was a very short time afterward during which Elisa thought the breaking of the mirror must have been lucky for her. The morning after her temper tantrum broke the silver-backed mirror, Elisa asked McFee to take her to Bond Street and the jewellers' shop she often patronized.

The two gentlemen who owned the shop were busy with a male patron and, as Elisa did not trust any of the clerks, she waited, staring at several jewelled mirrors on their gray velvet bed just out of her reach.

She was so startled she jumped when Lord Jeremy March spoke behind her.

'Well, this is fortunate. I have been hoping to meet you without your many admirers, Miss Carlisle.'

She borrowed courage from the warmth in his voice and turned to see him. He was looking very much his attractive self. He seemed especially breathtaking because he smiled as he took her hand.

She didn't know what to say without ruining her credit with him forever by seeming too eager. He misunderstood her silence.

'You are thinking of our last private encounter.' To her astonishment his expression was wry and apologetic. 'I behaved boorishly. I can scarcely blame you if you believe me past forgiving. May I say only that I regret the offense but not the deed?'

She colored. 'I believe I understand. That is to say, perhaps it would be best not to speak of that night. How is Captain Hawtree coming on?'

He almost seemed to regret the change of subject.

'You know, of course, that he lost his arm. Poor devil. He is home now. I trust there will be an end of his bitterness. My brother had to give evidence yesterday.'

'But Arthur is safe? Surely, they know it was an accident. He acted only to save you. He thought the Captain would shoot you.'

He was watching her again, studying her carefully. It made her uncomfortable.

'They know that. I was wrong about you. Arthur knew you so much better. Frankly, he won me over.'

'He?'

'He. And you yourself. Your conduct.' For some reason, just as she was beginning to hope he knew at last that she was sincere, he drew her further out of hearing of the two jewellers and said, 'I am persuaded you do not wish to hurt my brother.'

'Certainly not, Sir.'

'Then–' he had the grace to hesitate – 'it would hurt him if he knew the details of our — encounter in your boudoir.'

Pride gave her voice an unexpected sharpness.

'I assure Your Lordship, he will never learn it from me.'

His expression was almost one of regret. Again she wondered if there had been more in his kiss than even he had intended. He recovered. 'Thank you. We understand each other.' He lowered his head, brought her fingers to his lips and then, as he released her hand, he added without any show of sarcasm or lightness, 'I wish that encounter had ended differently.'

And I, she thought. How I wish it had!

But his attitude today gave promise for the future. She was far from crushed.

Returning home to Portman Square, she was particularly cheerful, until she found herself within the house, the servants gone about their business, room after room chill, empty, enclosed everywhere like lovely puzzle boxes that did not belong to plain Elsie Catlow.

'Tuttle? Where are you?' she called, rushing from the reception hall to the gold salon, the dining room and music room, and then back up the narrow, elegant white staircase to the chambers and salons above.

She came upon a startled chambermaid dusting Elisa's white bedchamber, and surprised the girl by her delighted greeting. It

98

was easier when Tuttle appeared, having returned from a friendly leavetaking of the Cliffords.

'They couldn't wait for you. Saw them off on the Oxford Mail. Hated to go, the lass especially. But he's a stern one, is our doctor. Duty calls, and all that.'

'I wish they might have stayed longer.' Then, to the further astonishment of the chambermaid, Elisa grinned and hugged Tuttle's lean, hard form. 'But you're here. Dear old Tuttle!'

'Never you mind. What's been giving you that glint in your eye? Some fool parted with his Mama's second-best diamonds?'

'Better than that.'

'Rubies. They never was your best color.'

'Much better.'

Tuttle's gray eyes narrowed. 'Zeffie, get on to Miss Susan's chamber. She left things in a bit of a muddle.'

The chambermaid sidled out, not without several backward glances.

'Now then,' Tuttle commanded Elisa, 'tell me what mischief you've been about.'

'No mischief. I'm going to make Jeremy March love me. I think we made a start today.'

Tuttle drew back and considered this surprising news. 'You surely have changed, lass. You mean to tell me this Lord March, him that insulted you so shamefully, is a better prize than diamonds, or rubies?'

'Or emeralds, or sapphires. I love him, I tell you.'

'I knew it. The man returns your love. I saw it in his eyes, the way they followed you at the March town house. It's my belief he envies his young brother.'

'It may be. Oh, Peg, if it should be true! But I daren't think about it until there is some proof. Mama believed things so easily.'

'That's a rubbishing thing to say,' Tuttle scolded impatiently. 'That dear little creature, your Mama, would be mightily disappointed if she saw you acting the fool.'

Elisa said something that shamed her when she heard herself. 'Mama was afraid of everything.' She winced and avoided Tuttle's eyes. 'I can still hear her pleading when I found her in that place. They'd partly drugged her. She told me so. She was no more lunatic than I, or you. Or anyone on the street, until after she'd been there a while in that – place.'

Tuttle busied herself putting away Elisa's hat, not looking at her. 'Don't talk about it.'

But Elisa could not stop herself. 'Mama did a deal of crying. She wasn't able to sew her embroidery toward the last, before they took her. She embroidered even when she was acting, in the early days. But she kept saying at the last that it wasn't any use. Nobody'd buy her pretty little collars. Then she tried to go on the street but she wasn't the sort.'

Tuttle shrugged. 'I tell you, Girl, it's a mighty dark hell if you're poor and you've a little one to feed, and no man.'

There had never been a father in Elisa's life. For a long time she had believed this was a normal condition. Her father was a young actor somewhere in the North, a feckless wanderer. Molly Catlow had never seen nor heard from him after their brief idyll while both played bit parts with strolling players.

Elisa banished memories and fears. In ripping off her mantle she tore away the diamond and pearl brooch at her neck. She knelt and picked up the glittering little jewels, her fingers closing around the brooch, holding it tight.

'Tuttle, should I sell more of the jewels and invest the money in the funds? Or in land? Or foundries? They say factories too are doing well in the North.'

'If you want to turn folk like Molly Catlow away from their jobs, aye, then it's mill and factory machinery for you.'

It was an old argument. Tuttle's ancestors had been weavers who sat spinning in the front window of their house in Yorkshire's West Riding. They were their own masters. But with each day since the turn of the century more hand weavers had lost their market to the great woollen mills with the machines manned by laborers, often consumptive, whose wages and hours were appalling, even to the government that sanctioned this new mechanical age.

Elisa envied the courage of Tuttle's parents who had packed

100

up, gone south to Portsmouth and finally opened a little tavern in London's Cheapside, and survived.

Elisa's reply was brusque, to hide those deep fears that made her feel 'weak' like her mother.

'Very well. Invest the proceeds in government funds. I have no intention of starving to death. Or finding myself bundled off to St Mary's of Bethlehem Asylum.' She spoke Bedlam's true name aloud, hearing herself and saying, 'There. I can pronounce it at last. That place of horror. I am not a coward, as you claim.'

'That's the girl. Stand up to the world. You've earned the right.'

That night at the theatre Elisa hoped against hope that she would see Jeremy March sitting in one of the boxes, perhaps with an idea of knowing the real Elisa Carlisle better. Not that he could ever know her, she confessed to herself. He would have to meet Elsie Catlow, the girl who sometimes looked out of Elisa's eyes in a furtive way. He would discover that the infamous Elisa Carlisle was only a costume, a mask of stage make-up, and he must never know about Elsie Catlow, or Molly, who had died in Bedlam.

Parts of the audience were unruly and insulting at times and Tregaran's timing was off until the final act at which time, perhaps from habit, he tried his old tricks of maneuvering Elisa's back to the audience. The moment he tried this, Elisa reached out and touched his cheek, caressing it lightly. Then she made a scolding motion with her finger. A number of the audience seemed to understand. Titters and open laughter followed.

Elisa waited a long minute until the noise subsided, after which time she repeated her previous speech. Tregaran reacted sulkily and the play ended shortly afterward, to everyone's relief except the galleries who were claiming their heroine.

Tregaran stalked off-stage while the curtain was still falling. On the way to his dressing-room he gave Strawbridge his notice.

'I won't act with that bitch. Everyone knows what she is. Shaming me before my audience. Bringing misery and shame to others. Will it be death next time? She's had everything else she can take from a man.'

101

His furious accusations were audible to everyone backstage, and not a few in the stage-boxes. Elisa had no doubt that all of London would hear of his outburst before twenty-four hours passed.

She went home shivering with delayed anger over the Tregaran episode, and wondering who else could be signed to take the place of the Cornishman. In the general way she got on very well with her hired companies. Despite her appearance and her manner of delicate loveliness, these players understood at once that the show and the company were her possessions, and the object of the plays was to show Elisa Carlisle to the best advantage.

She wanted to take laudanum to sleep that night but Tuttle called her 'coward' and, when that failed, said she couldn't find the dangerous liquid. Elisa finally slept after studying the latest 'One Woman' collection of speeches Strawbridge had arranged for her when the present season ended. After tonight it seemed that Elisa's single performances would come about sooner than she had planned.

She thought of every speech as a separate performance, and tried to give each of them a special mood and atmosphere. But she was not fool enough to indulge in heavy tragedy on-stage. She knew her limitations.

Once she got to sleep, she did not wake up until almost noon the next day. This was unfortunate because she knew there must be long conferences with Strawbridge over possible substitutes for Peter Tregaran, followed by interviews and try-outs. She couldn't put the try-outs off too long.

Early in the afternoon she crossed her cool, white sitting room to study the sketches and histories of several likely young provincial actors. She had just reached the inlaid drum table with its collection of portraits and articles laced together when her foot struck something beside a table leg. She looked down, discovered a little cylindrical flask and picked it up.

The laudanum that Tuttle had misplaced.

She weighed the charming little pewter and china flask in her palm. If she kept it within reach it would be much too easy for her to pour out a drop or two on impulse. Better to let Tuttle keep it safe. She put the flask on the table and settled down with a pile of letters, badly sketched portraits and a number of theatrical reviews.

When she heard footsteps along the gallery half an hour later she called out, 'Is that you, Tuttle? I've found the laudanum. It was here all the time.'

Tuttle stomped into the room.

'You've got a visitor. It's not proper, to say the least, at this hour of the day. But – well, he's here.'

Elisa caught her breath. Jeremy March must have come to her at home to tell her about Captain Hawtree's condition. Whatever his excuse, he wanted to see her.

Tuttle stepped away from the door, shuffling and looking as if she disapproved of the entire affair. She said more loudly than necessary, 'Mister Arthur March.'

The early afternoon sun glistened on Arthur March's hair and slanted on his light figure. He crossed the room to her, looking happier than she had ever seen him.

It took a high degree of acting for Elisa to welcome him in her usual warm, friendly way. She offered him her hand.

'Mr March, how dear of you to come! I trust you have better news about the Captain.'

He seemed nervous in spite of his apparent joy at seeing her.

'Dear Miss Carlisle—Elisa, how lovely you look, and by daylight, too!'

She laughed. 'May I accept that as a compliment?'

Arthur March raised her hand from his lips to his cheek. 'Of course, it is. What an angel you are! Always putting the welfare of others before your own. Yes, Hawtree is doing reasonably well. The shock, you know. Worse than the—the loss.' He restored her hand to her, recollecting his own responsibility for the Captain's injury. He added after an embarrassed moment, 'It was stupid. Clumsy. I should never have interfered. But I thought he would use it against Jeremy. Jeremy never takes any protection. He seems indifferent to danger.'

'But not to your danger. He cares very much for you.'

He agreed eagerly. 'Yes. You sense that, too. May I?' He pulled a chair up to the table, still gazing into her eyes so devotedly she lowered her eyelids and turned her head, pretending to examine the tiny cylindrical flask on the table.

'Tuttle forgot the laudanum,' she said.

His thoughts were elsewhere.

'How lovely you look!'

She laughed gently. 'I doubt that. I am feeling anything but lovely. So much to do. I must find a new leading man.'

Taking the flask as she set it down, he said, 'I'll give it to Tuttle.' He cleared his throat and murmured with a kind of shy bravado, 'I hope I am that leading man.'

It was her turn to be uncomfortable. She made light of his remark, hoping he would accept the hint.

'If life were a theatre, the Marches would be stars wherever they cared to perform.' When he looked discomfited and kept all his attention on her, she said brightly, 'It was dear of you to come and tell me how the poor Captain is coming on.'

He made no effort to deliver his message about Captain Hawtree.

When he seemed tongue-tied she began again. 'See how difficult it is to choose one new player? Tregaran has deserted me; so I have all these sketches, portraits, reviews to consider. All the tedious hours it takes!'

He was certainly behaving oddly and the idea made her more uneasy. He dropped the flask on the bare mahogany table. This made her jump.

'Sorry. Did I break it?' The little laudanum flask rolled toward him and he picked it up, giving her a flickering smile.

'My darling.' He played with the narrow flask, rolling it nervously back and forth between his fingers. 'My darling Elisa, I love you.'

She stiffened. This was not at all like his usual declarations. It sounded very much as if he meant it. She felt a deep affection for him but she had repeatedly implied that the difference in their ages and experience was insurmountable.

She had mentioned the barrier between them hundreds of times. Why had she accepted those ear-bobs? It must have seemed conclusive proof that she returned his love.

She saw now that he had never believed her protests. She was filled with shame at her own part in those expectations.

'Arthur, I beg your pardon. In some ways I do love you.'

'Elisa.'

She raised her hand, sorry she had made him unduly optimistic. 'You are a dear, kind person. You have never shown me the contempt so many men of your class show an actress.'

'Of course not. I made Jeremy see. You aren't in the least like other actresses. He even gave me his blessing after I explained that you loved me'.

'His blessing?' She became aware of a coldness creeping over her flesh.

'Why do you think Jeremy came to see you at the theatre, and defended you before the audience?' He sounded horribly reasonable. 'Why did he invite you to the affair at March House? He wanted to show you he had changed his mind. I told him this morning that you had loved me for this age. I pointed out to him that for my sake you even forgave him for his bad manners to you.'

'You told him that?'

'I confess, he was stunned. But the dear old boy gave me his blessing. Said he regretted he ever doubted your feelings, that he knew now you were sincere. Not one of those . . . others.'

'Oh, God!'

Arthur went on eagerly, 'I told him the straight of it. Said I wanted to make you Mrs Arthur March.'

It was a sickening blow to all her recent hopes.

But another person had been hurt by her incredible blindness, her selfishness. She took a deep breath before assuring him, 'I do care for you, Arthur. But not in the way you mean. I am so much older.'

'I have a birthday in a fortnight.'

'Even so, Arthur, eight long years lie between us. And I am so much older in experience. There have been other men. You know that. Arthur, I couldn't hold you more dear if you were my own young –'

'Don't say it. Not a brother.' To his embarrassment his voice cracked, making him more frantic. He got up, shaking with emotion. 'You did love me. You know you did. Someone else has come between us. When we were together that day at March House before Hawtree came in drunk, you loved me.' Another idea occurred to him then. His eyes widened with pain. 'You stopped loving me then, because I shot Hawtree.'

'No. Not at all.'

'It was that. You think I'm like that. A clumsy killer.'

'I don't. Arthur, listen to me.'

It was no use. He went rushing on. 'But I'm not like that. Elisa, you couldn't change so quickly. You still love me. You know you do.' He reached for her but she backed away.

'As a very dear brother.'

She put one hand out to him but he pulled his clenched fists away from her.

'It was because I shot him. You're too kind to admit it. I did it myself. I ruined three lives. His. And yours –' He swallowed hard. 'And mine.'

She was sorry for his misunderstanding but it would be more cruel to encourage him now. She said quietly, 'Captain Hawtree is fully as responsible as you. I might say the same of myself. Without meaning to, I encouraged emotions I could not return. I sincerely regret that. But not our friendship.'

'Don't!' he choked. 'You know I can't live without you.' Dropping the laudanum flask in his fob pocket to free his hands, he reached for her. Before she could draw back he caught her painfully around the waist and rained awkward kisses on her cheek, her chin and then her mouth. 'You love me. I'll make you love me.'

It was time to end these dramatics. She pulled herself out of his nervous clutches. 'Arthur, you have the whole world before you. You will laugh at that foolish remark in a month's time.'

106

He reached for her again but he must have read the pity in her face. This shook him more than her physical effort to repulse him.

'Much you know about it. They were right. You are icy-hearted. A tease. You led me to believe . . .'

She patted his sleeve, trying to soothe him. Her well-meant gesture was the last straw. Before she could stop him he ended the painful scene by jerking away and rushing across the room. He passed Tuttle in the doorway as she came in with the tea tray. Elisa started after Arthur, then gave up the effort to catch him.

Tuttle frowned. 'What's the lad been about? Wanting a night with you, I'll be bound.'

Elisa shook her head, saddened by many things. She had lost Arthur March's friendship and disillusioned him. Worse. She had never possessed his brother's affections except, with his reluctant approval, as a wife for the young Arthur. Jeremy March would certainly never take her word against his brother's, in any case.

Tuttle set the tray down on the table. Belatedly aroused by her action, Elisa said, 'Take care. Don't set it on the laudanum vial.'

Tuttle shifted the tray, then raised the pile of portraits and reviews.

'Whereabouts? No laudanum here.'

Not too interested, Elisa looked around. 'It probably fell on the floor. Mr March and I both handled it.'

Tuttle knelt, felt around and then stared at her with some suspicion.

'You sure you don't have it?'

'Certainly, I'm sure. What do you take me for? An addict?'

'Well, if you don't have it, and it's not here, then your late lamented Mr March must have gone off with it.'

Elisa said, 'Don't be ridiculous. What would Arthur March want with a half-filled vial of laudanum?'

'Took it absent-mindedly, I daresay.' Tuttle shrugged. 'How would I be knowing? In his state, anything's possible.'

It was annoying but if Arthur had taken it with him he would feel rather foolish when he recovered his normally happy spirits later in the day.

'Them things can be deadly,' Tuttle reminded her. 'I'm always telling you that.'

'Oh, hush up!' She wished Tuttle hadn't planted the ridiculous little idea in her mind. The boy was much too sensible to let one abortive love affair depress his spirits for very long.

CHAPTER NINE

Tuttle's warning stayed with Elisa. While dressing in the theatre that night she was still wondering if it would be a mistake to write a note of apology to Arthur March. Had she been a lady of the Regent's circle she could never send a written communication to anyone except her husband, but no actress was considered a 'lady'. She was deeply sorry for the impression she had given him and she still hadn't figured out how to return his grandmother's earrings without further humiliating him.

Her mood of uneasiness was aggravated by the feeling that her audience did not seem to be with her. It was a rare event when they did not laugh with her during the afterpiece. Here, customarily, the theatre audience was entertained, its spirits raised after the more sombre events of the plays or readings that preceded it.

In the ordinary course of events, after Elisa lost a leading player and was forced to change the night's program, her romantic readings would be greeted by much applause. Her lone appearances on-stage proved more popular than the ensemble plays. When these were followed by the lightly humorous afterpiece she often heard cheers and 'bravos' from her special followers.

But tonight was subtly different.

The applause at the final curtain sounded uninspired, respectable but not enthusiastic. It terrified her to think of the theatregoers out there in that bejewelled dark as her enemies. Their very presence and their warmth toward her relieved those fears that haunted her life.

Had she lost them? She knew many of them believed the lies spread about 'Circe, the Wicked Enchantress.' Her reputation had originally made her famous. Was it now about to destroy her?

She hurried to her dressing-room. The door slammed shut after her but luckily Tuttle got it open immediately. She was matter-of-fact and practical as always.

'I sent away some of your young sprigs. You look tired to me.'

While Elisa removed powder, rouge, and a little of the kohl mixture she used on her eyes, she asked, 'Was anything wrong tonight? Are they gossiping again?'

'Not that I've heard. It's just a mood. The fog tonight, most like. And then you . . . Here. The pink muslin. You should wear this deep pink more often. It brings out the color of your hair.'

'Like an ingenue.'

'Not this shade.'

Elisa crumpled and threw down the soft cloths she had been working with. 'You started to say something. Something about my performance. What was wrong?'

'Nothing. Like I said, you looked a bit sad. You'll have to practise that sparkle. It's worth hundreds of guineas, and well you know it.'

Propping her chin on her knuckles, Elisa stared at her reflection. 'This mirror needs silvering. It's getting old.'

Tuttle looked into the mirror over Elisa's head.

'That's the trouble with mirrors. The longer you look, the older they get.'

'Don't be impertinent.'

'Well, don't practise those la-di-da airs with me, my girl. I remember Elsie Catlow.'

Elisa carefully ignored this. She stood up and let herself be fastened into the slim muslin gown, hoping the brightness would bring out her own color. Curiously enough, it called attention to the pallor of her cheeks and a haunted look in her eyes. She reached for the rouge pot.

Tuttle watched her with rough concern.

110

'If you're fretting about that audience, you needn't. If you wasn't their better, they wouldn't be paying their shillings to see you. A deal of those shillings are hard come by.'

'I know. Tuttle, I half-hoped I would see Arthur March in the boxes, ready to forgive me. Or, at least, his brother. I should think His Lordship would thank me. He can't have been enthusiastic about that absurd marriage proposal.'

'Hard to say. There. You look mightily fetching. And you've a young army out in the alley waiting to escort you to the carriage. Hoping for a further invitation, I'll be bound.'

Elisa breathed deeply, managed her celebrated smile, and walked out to meet the admirers who had made Elisa Carlisle famous. Or infamous, she thought wryly.

They were there waiting – a few females, most of them her loyal 'claque' from the galleries and the rest were males, many elegant members of the aristocracy. The clamor of all their voices out of the chill night fog normally warmed her by their proof that her popularity had not faded, and by the sincerity of her friends in the galleries. Tonight she wondered if all their enthusiasm was mere curiosity about a notorious woman.

She spoke individually to those whose names she recalled. She made it a rule to associate names with faces, especially among her gallery claque to whom she owed so much. The sprigs of the aristocracy could be dealt with in her light, teasing way, promising much with her eyes and her smile, while her words gave away nothing.

But at the last minute she couldn't resist asking one young man, 'You are not with Mr Arthur March tonight? It is always so reassuring to look up at the Right-Front Stage Box and see you handsome gentlemen.'

The Honorable Harry Chalfont apologized. 'Expected him myself, matter of fact. Dashed odd business. Never arrived. Never knew him to miss a night when you were performing alone, Ma'am. Family business, I expect.'

'I expect. Then I will say good night, Sir.'

When she and Tuttle were alone in the carriage, Tuttle said, 'Pretty abrupt with those fancy gents, wasn't you?'

111

Elisa did not argue the matter. She felt discouraged and troubled without knowing precisely way. It was not the first time she had experienced a failure in the theatre, or even the first time she had refused a marriage proposal from a highly eligible young aristocrat.

The night was little better.

She remained awake for a long time, hearing the voices of the night watch frequently, and once the drunken young sons of her neighbor, an old general, as they were taken up by the night watch, (called the 'Charleys') for rowdy behavior. They would be home by morning, boasting of their adventure.

Shortly before dawn her entire household was aroused by rifle shots in the big square. Their target sounded dangerously close to Elisa's house. Then she heard loud voices within the house. She sat up, cold and uneasy, felt for her velvet wrapper and went out into the hall, belatedly aware of her long, tumbled hair and her state of dishevelment.

In the light of the lamp on the newel post she saw McFee and Tuttle arguing halfway down the pristine white staircase. The sturdy little man had pulled on breeches but his broad chest, matted with hair, was naked and the hairs on his head stood straight up like rusty spikes.

Elisa's mood hadn't improved during the night. She demanded, 'What the devil are you about? You know I sleep late after a performance.'

Tuttle shrugged. 'This one says the house was fired on by young ruffians.'

'Good God! It seems the French Revolution has finally reached these shores.' Elisa laughed without humor. 'If so, they are a trifle late, and certainly in the wrong house. I'm no aristocrat.'

'No, Ma'am,' McFee explained. 'Not a revolution exactly. Seems they must've read about you. There's a musket-ball landed right in the middle of your music room shutters.'

'A bit of horseplay, I trust.'

'I trust, Ma'am. But I best go out and make sure and certain. Tuttle here says I shouldn't. As if I was afeared of them pretty toffs.'

'They hold me to blame for Captain Hawtree's shooting.' Elisa started down the staircase. 'I am a poor actress if I can't reason with a pair of drunken young noblemen.'

They both got in her way, Tuttle insisting, 'Go to bed now, do, Miss. You need sleep. Nobody'd pay two farthings to see you right this minute, looking like you do.'

Elisa suspected there was some truth to this flat statement in spite of McFee's shocked and hasty denial. She went back up the stairs without troubling to find the musket-ball in the shutters downstairs. She stepped into the drawing room whose long windows opened on the square. After a quick exchange of whispers Tuttle and McFee followed her. She looked down onto the square. It appeared deserted in the pale dawn light.

'There is no one about now.' She smiled at their anxiety. 'Very well, I won't go out there. In any case, it would solve nothing. Good night, you two. I may as well take Tuttle's advice and sleep myself into beauty.'

McFee bent his small body almost double in a bow as she passed him. 'No need for sleep, Ma'am. You'll always be beautiful. And well you know it.'

'Liar!' she said fondly, resting a hand on his shoulder. Then she returned to her bedchamber, hoping sleep would follow.

But with sleep came dreams. She saw Lord Jeremy March watching her in that penetrating way he used to have before he gave consent to his brother's courtship. His eyes were alight, but not with affection. There was a barrier between them. Perhaps wrought-iron window bars, she told herself.

Which of them, she or Jeremy, stood outside those bars?

She sat straight up in bed. No delicate, wrought-iron bars separated them in that dream. She knew better but hadn't wanted to admit it. She was behind a locked door in Bedlam Asylum and for some strange, malignant reason of his own, Jeremy March was one of those visitors permitted to view the inmates, the way a theatregoer watches the comic antics on-stage. In her dream he had been peering at her from a safe distance and with that sombre smile.

. She shook herself, pounded her pillow into another shape, and lay down again. But a hazy sun drifted down around the city like a pretty gauze curtain, and she knew it was time to face the day. She must talk to Strawbridge before the night's performance, make a decision about a new leading man, and decide whether to accept a Paris offer for ten performances around Christmas. It would remove her from London, but there was still the entire autumn season to get through.

Later that morning she was discussing the week's menu with the new cook, a female this time, named Grandmaison, when she heard carriage wheels on the stones outside.

'Strawbridge must have abandoned that noble old mare of his,' she remarked to Tuttle who came to announce the arrival of a visitor. 'From the sound it is a landaulet at the very least.'

'Contrariwise,' Tuttle grumbled. 'It's a curricle.'

'What? Strawbridge tooling a dainty curricle? I must see this.'

As the two women started to the front of the house, Tuttle explained. 'It's not Strawbridge. Was you expecting Lady Hawtree?'

Elisa was ambivalent about her friend's arrival. She knew Gwenna Hawtree would want to know the full details of Arthur's proposal and her answer. On the other hand, she might have some information about Arthur's reaction and whether his brother was relieved at Arthur's escape or not.

Elisa said, 'I suppose I should have expected her.'

'She's all the plagues of Egypt, that female!' was Tuttle's firm opinion. 'Don't you believe anything she says.'

'Nonsense. She is enthusiastic about a liaison between Lord March and me. She can't be too great a plague.'

'I don't like the look of her, especially today,' Tuttle insisted.

Elisa shook her head at Tuttle's intransigence but Tuttle pursued the subject. 'Wait 'til you see the woman.'

This sounded mysterious and Elisa was intrigued, wondering what on earth Gwenna's condition might be to raise all Tuttle's hackles.

She saw quickly enough. Lady Hawtree had been shown into the Small drawing room opening off the elegant reception hall.

114

She was shrouded in black except for her white collar and her hat with a dyed green feather. Black was not Gwenna Hawtree's color, and this sight seemed overdone to Elisa who started back in surprise. She suddenly feared the worst about Gwenna's step-son.

'Not – oh, surely not the Captain!'

Lady Hawtree's forehead wrinkled in perplexity. 'My dear, what can you mean?' Belatedly, she appeared to understand. 'No, no. Ronald is doing well enough. He seems to have found comfort with a pretty young creature Sir Hugo hired to assist him. He must learn to do for himself as though he were a child.' She sighed. 'Poor boy.' She paused, looking down her nose at Elisa, as if she wanted to read her innermost thoughts.

Elisa was in no mood for her games. 'Lady Hawtree, you came here with some purpose. I know that look. Tuttle, would you ask Tabitha to bring tea? Or is it coffee?'

'Coffee, for my nerves, if you've no objection.' Her Ladyship sighed again.

Damn her! Elisa wanted to shake her until her prominent teeth rattled. She sat down beside Lady Gwenna who welcomed the arrival of the coffee tray. The two women turned their attention to the coffee heavily laced with milk. Sipping it and making faces, Her Ladyship studied her hostess over the rim of the cup.

'You are a truly remarkable actress, Elisa. I confess, I admire your—shall we say—your courage?'

'Why not say it, if you choose.' Elisa had no doubt that something exceedingly unpleasant was coming.

Lady Gwenna gave up the game and blurted out, 'I do believe you know nothing of this awful business. You must be the last innocent in London.'

Elisa announced, 'I am going to perform a great service for you, My Lady.'

Her Ladyship's eyes widened. 'How so?'

'I am going to let you tell me what calamity has occurred.'

Lady Gwenna set her cup down and moved closer to her hostess. It was as if she had been imbued with new blood, new excitement.

'My dear, he is dead.'

Not Jeremy March. Please God, no!

She moistened her lips. 'How did it happen? An accident?'

'Suicide. With laudanum, of all absurdities.'

'Jeremy took laudanum?'

Lady Gwenna stared at her, then suddenly gave a little trill of laughter which she stifled with her hand.

'I am sorry. It was unforgivable. But you misunderstood me. Young Arthur took laudanum.' She stopped; she studied Elisa's pale features. 'Elisa! Surely, you knew his mood when he left you. I am told he wrote his brother a note, something dreadful naming you, and—according to rumor—he then drank the laudanum you had given him . . . They say you taunted him with it, told him it would solve his problems.'

Elisa sat quite still. She was too shaken to feel anything except a creeping chill that left her numb.

For the first time Lady Hawtree was left with little to say. She almost seemed embarrassed. She reached out and touched Elisa's hand.

'My dear, these things happen.'

'Only to sensitive boys like Arthur March.'

Her Ladyship shrugged. 'One must accept such weaknesses in mankind. I once knew a lad—hardly more than a stableboy, mind—and he fell in love with me. It was absurd. He had merely taken me in his arms a few times as I dismounted. You know how easily these things come about. A touch. A pinch. A squeeze. One presses against all that aroused masculinity. Then the poor fool calls it love and deliberately takes a toss from a stallion he knows he can't handle. What nonsense!'

'Don't.'

'Not Arthur, of course. What a dear, naive boy he was! Think of it. Never to see that sweet face of his again . . . By the by, he will be put to rest in the churchyard near March Hall, Sir Hugo tells me. All the Marches are buried there. We shall be present at services, naturally. We ride over from Hawtree Place. Imagine. He'd barely reached his eighteenth birthday. Dear Arthur.'

Elisa said nothing. She was remembering the miniature laudanum vial. Tuttle warned her that it was dangerous. Why hadn't she run after him, made him understand the unsuitability of such a match? Why had she let him go?

She looked down at her fingertips. They were icy with the shock of her own guilt. By her manner, by some coolness or sharp dismissal, had she actually suggested that he destroy himself?

Perhaps he was right. The stories about her were right. To love her was to be accursed. She brought horror and death to those she cared for. Even Molly her mother. And the Duke of Pentland's son. Then Captain Hawtree. Now, Arthur March, another gentle innocent like her mother.

Dear God! How Jeremy March must hate her! And he was right to do so.

What would he do to her now to avenge his beloved brother's death?

She wished she could cry. Instead, she felt the world of darkness closing in upon her as it had destroyed Molly Catlow. There was no light left. Only this freezing dark.

Somehow, she must make Arthur March understand that she had not despised and tricked him. If she could only visit his place of burial, perhaps pray, hoping he would hear and understand . . . Maybe then her guilt would be wiped away, in part.

Strawbridge hurried to Portman Square in the afternoon to tell her what she already knew.

'No performances in the immediate future.' He added with a touch of grandiloquence, 'The winds of public opinion are against you.'

'I have no intention of appearing. Heaven knows whether I will ever be able to perform in London again.'

A trifle nervous, he assured her, 'I am persuaded you will win them over eventually. You never looked more beautiful.'

'That kind of talk is unnecessary. No one cares what I look like. They believe I gave that boy laudanum and taunted him into swallowing it. I am a murderess in their eyes.'

'Beg pardon, Miss Elisa, but they do care. Eventually, you are going to find your beauty brings them back. They will be

117

curious, for one thing. They will ask themselves, what does this woman have that she can drive men to self-destruction?'

'Please. That is disgusting.'

'But true; so let's have one of your famous smiles. The future isn't all black.'

She raised her head sharply. How could he know?

'I have no plans and no future, at the moment. Later, I may give thought to the Paris offer.'

He hesitated. He had his own finances to consider and Elisa Carlisle was his most profitable client. He cracked his knuckles nervously, remembered how much she disliked the habit and stopped, but he realized after a minute or two that her thoughts were elsewhere. He began again, hopefully.

'Have you given thought to performing in the provinces? In the west or the north? If you find that satisfying, there is always America.'

'America!' It was like the moon. An alien moon. 'We've only just finished our second war with the Yankees. Why would they want to see an English actress who was in disgrace in her own country?'

'Think about it. Meanwhile, leave London for a fortnight. Give yourself some country air. Walk along country lanes. Become – well, yourself, not that glittering public beauty, Elisa Carlisle.'

Become Elsie Catlow, she thought, and shuddered.

'I will consider it. Has the story spread over London?'

He admitted, 'Through the better classes, I believe. It may not be true, but I am informed that His Highness has asked for the details.'

She laughed shortly. 'Imagine having Prinny, with his past, call me "The Wicked Enchantress"!'

Feeling more and more awkward, Strawbridge soon made his departure, complete with a bow that would have done credit to McFee. As he was leaving, Tuttle almost fell into the room. Obviously, she had heard part of the conversation.

'What does he say? Thinks it's all going to draw in the crowds, I make no doubt.'

'He wants me to go to America. Or Liverpool. I'm not sure. Whichever is further from London.'

Tuttle was rocked by the consequences of Arthur March's suicide, but she braved it out.

'That's ridiculous. Your public loves you. They'd forgive you anything.'

'Even murder?'

'No such thing. He took the laudanum flask with him by accident. You weren't anywhere near the Marches.'

'Morally, they regard me as his murderess. I don't mind the opinion of others, but Arthur—I wish to God I could have made him understand.'

She walked up and down past the long windows, looking out, aware of the unusual attraction her house held for casual strollers. She turned away, angry for the first time. Her reaction burned out a little of the darkness that surrounded her.

'If I could only have attended his funeral —'

'Elsie Catlow!'

She shrugged. 'Very well. I am innocent but no one will believe me. Strawbridge is right on that score. He suggested I go into the country.'

Tuttle was astonished. 'Rusticate! Elisa Carlisle off wandering through strange copses and milking cows?'

Even Elisa forced a smile. 'Copses, yes. Cows, no. I'd like to leave flowers at Arthur's grave.'

'And his brother will promptly murder you.'

Elisa waved this aside. 'When His Lordship returns to London, of course. We must be quite certain that he has left the Midlands. Then we may go on to some quiet, lovely place where no one has ever heard of That Wicked *Circe*.' She made an effort to display at good spirits. 'Tuttle, you and I are going to disappear, and we are going to forget Elisa Carlisle for a few weeks.'

'Easily said. Let me tell you, Girl, no good will come of running away. You've got to brave it out.'

Elisa was too tired to argue. She ignored this.

119

'Don't let anyone pack for me. I shall pack for myself. And if you wish to escape with me, you had better do some packing yourself.'

'Just don't let His Lordship catch you, that's all. I've been hearing things from McFee. He's been gossiping with that Hawtree woman's coachman. They say Jeremy March is in what they call "a quiet rage" toward you. He believes what that wretched boy wrote him about you before he died.'

Elisa was firm on that subject, at least.

'I intend to avoid him at all costs, so we must be certain we don't go near the Gloucestershire countryside until His Lordship is back in London.'

Tuttle nodded. 'That I can safely promise.'

CHAPTER TEN

Less than a fortnight after the burial, Lord Jeremy March returned to London to take his seat in the House of Lords. Many of Elisa's acquaintances took it upon themselves to inform her, since, as they put it, 'You will not wish to be in his vicinity until the wound is healed.'

From the further descriptions she guessed how deeply his young brother's death had affected the peer. *Grim*, everyone said and stressed the word. Lady Hawtree wrote to her:

'He is handsome as ever, my dear Elisa, but a trifle pale, and so very grim.'

Elisa was not in London to profit by all the advice from well-meaning busybodies. She and Tuttle had taken the overcrowded, swaying Bristol Mail to Bath, and after a few depressing days in seclusion had gone north to a Gloucestershire village within half a day's ride from March Hall. They took two bedchambers and the private parlour at a coaching inn and were disturbed frequently by the racketing coaches that came and went at all hours.

The noise troubled Tuttle, but Elisa, with her craving for company, found the excitement of the comings and goings a little like the theatre and its audiences. She was grateful for the friendly attentions she received when she walked out occasionally, or drove around the countryside with Tuttle, having hired an ancient gig and a goodnatured mare. No one seemed to recognize her, a fact that made it easier for her to remain out of doors.

At night she was surprisingly relieved when awakened by noisy travellers, the screech of wheels and ageing coaches. All

121

this violent 'life' drove away her demons for the moment. She hadn't suffered one nightmare since her arrival. However, as Tuttle claimed, 'You've given them to me, Girl!'

It was at this inn that Elisa received her delayed London mail from MacFee as well as a letter from Brian Clifford. As usual, to prevent servants from talking he had seen to it that his daughter inscribed the address. Then he took care to have the local M.P. frank the letter.

Elisa smiled at his precautions, although Tuttle thought them very proper.

'You ought to be glad the fellow takes such care for your reputation. There's not many that would.'

'Thank you, Tuttle. You are such a comfort.'

Tuttle overlooked the sarcasm. 'If he is a man of sense, he'll tell you to stay away from the villages those Marches own. And that includes graveyards and vaults.'

'Do they own all of Gloucestershire? I think not. In any case, I want to spend time by the boy's grave.'

'By their vault. The tapster says the Marches have a vault in the village graveyard.'

'Very well. The vault. I won't be able to enter, but I am surely permitted a prayer for the boy's soul. Perhaps, somehow, he will know how deeply I regret what happened.' She looked at Tuttle while her fingers broke the seal of Brian Clifford's letter. She couldn't hide the emotion that crept into her voice.

'I miss Arthur March. He seems now like a lost young brother. I dream about him. I even know a little of how Lord March must feel.'

'He was a young fool,' Tuttle insisted. 'And he lied about you in the most cruel way there is. He lied so no one could ever know he lied. Except you.'

Elisa's fingers curled around the corner of the letter she unfolded. She confessed the thing that haunted her. 'Maybe it wasn't a lie. I must have given him a hope.' She ended suddenly, 'Never mind. It's too late now for everything, even regrets.' She bent her head to read Brian's letter.

122

It was a curious message that did not leave her the happier for having read it. Plainly, Brian had been exposed to the bitter hatred of those at March Hall, beginning with Lord Jeremy. For some reason it hurt even more to find that Susan Clifford also seemed to blame her for Arthur's death. Whether this was Brian's fault or the gossip around March Hall, it was hard for Elisa to guess from the letter.

A great deal too much of both, she suspected.

Brian said:

'Elisa my dear, the news was ghastly. A young man scarcely out of boyhood, to destroy all the hopes and plans of those who love him, merely on a whim, a ridiculous penchant for an older woman, no matter how lovely.

'It is your wretched profession, Elisa. We both know that. Since it has now destroyed another promising young life, surely you must see what a disaster it is.

'If you are concerned for your future, I swear to you there are respectable posts where your manners and charm would be appreciated. On Monday last I was a guest for tea at the estate of Lady Hobwith, near Exeter. She spoke of needing a companion, a post that would suit you admirably.'

'I can imagine,' Elisa murmured.

Tuttle peered over her shoulder, trying to decipher the rest of the letter. She had learned to read long ago and was well able to cue Elisa in her roles, but the doctor's scrawl was another matter.

Elisa said, 'It is nearly ended, and it doesn't improve.'

"'I fear that your notions of a suitable profession would not include a post as governess, but it is a highly respectable profession and would make you acceptable everywhere. I know how much you have grieved over what the theatre has done to your reputation.

"'My dear friend, you must be aware that I care for you. I have always done so. As my wife you would have a certain financial security and all my protection. And you would not have these dreadful qualms of conscience that must trouble your nights."'

Tuttle sniffed. 'He's got a notion you're guilty. He's worse than His Lordship. At least His Lordship has reasons –' Elisa looked

123

at her and Tuttle went on firmly, 'Well, he has. He doesn't know how it really was, or that the lad was lying, out of pride and anger and disappointment and such.'

'Do you think I should marry Dr Clifford?'

'No!'

It was a curious reaction but Elisa felt that Tuttle was the one person whom she could always count upon for the truth.

'Why?'

Tuttle picked a small, pink rose off the branch that climbed the wall beside the open window. She winced at the stab of a thorn and examined the ball of her thumb.

'Because it's my opinion that lad is mad to own the actress, not little Elsie Catlow that he knew a long time ago. He wasn't in love with you then, was he? No matter what he says, the thought's there. And remember, he's a doctor. Not a gentleman.'

'I am no lady. It wouldn't matter that the man I marry is no gentleman. I don't even know my father. I am not legitimate. A strolling player, he was. That's a deal worse than Brian Clifford.'

'He's not what you want,' Tuttle reminded her. 'That's the important thing.' She sucked her sore thumb and Elisa let the matter drop for the moment.

'At all events, he is kinder than Susan.' She showed the end of the letter to Tuttle. 'What do you make of that?'

Tuttle squinted and tilted her head in order to read the single line:

'*How could you? You never loved him.*' This was followed by the big, scrawled '*S*'.

'I should think she wrote this after Brian gave her the letter to have franked. I don't think he would approve quite such a direct accusation.' Elisa thought of the eager, bubbling, ambitious young Susan, her only god-daughter, and shook her head. 'Imagine how she would feel, a child like that, to whom Arthur must seem like a golden knight in a fairy tale. Glorious and gallant. Shining.'

Tuttle looked unconvinced. 'We talking about the same lad? Maybe little Miss Susan's eyes was on his inheritance, not his golden looks.'

'Tuttle, why are you always saying hateful things against anyone I happen to like? Were you never young and romantic? To Susan, he was all those things.'

Tuttle reconsidered. 'Well, he was a fine-looking one, that boy. For all the mischief he caused.' She rubbed her sore thumb on a handkerchief and glanced out of the window at the offending rose bush that climbed the old wall of the inn.

Determinedly, Elisa shook off the mood of defeat and self-recrimination that had darkened her world since Gwenna Hawtree brought the news to her. 'Hurry and change. Tomorrow is Sunday, and these country folk are pattern-cards of respectability. No immoral habits. They insist it is most improper – or is it immoral? – to travel on Sunday; so we are going today, in our elegant gig, with that dear Gillyflower.'

'Gillyflower!'

'The mare, Tuttle. The mare.'

Tuttle snorted at this familiarity with a borrowed horse but did as she was told. While she changed to her black and white striped cambric gown and her usual dark pelisse, Elisa picked a delicate little bouquet of the climbing roses beside the window. Arthur had always liked that particular shade of pink.

The two women found the young ostler and the tapster along with a stableboy, waiting eagerly to assist them when the rickety little black gig was brought out and Gillyflower accepted the light harness. The young men knocked each other about, trying to see which of them would assist Elisa, but the grizzled tapster had a weather eye out for Tuttle and made much of his chance to lift her up beside Elisa who took the reins. Holding the roses, Tuttle was elaborately unaware of the tapster's attentions, but took care to grin at him just as Gillyflower ambled off across the innyard.

'Now to Marchland,' she said a few minutes later, having memorized the directions from the tapster. 'Take the coach road until we find a little river winding away to the south, so he says. Follow the path beside this river until you come to a stone bridge.'

In the brisk morning air Elisa tooled the vehicle over the dusty road. She breathed deeply, her spirits brightening while she discovered the surprising benefits of the country-side.

'Pretty country,' Tuttle remarked, watching the healthy change in Elisa as the countryside seemed to ease the pressure of her thoughts. Since deep mourning would be resented by those close to the March family, the actress compromised with a violet-spotted silk gown, shawl and straw hat. They were flattering on her, bringing out her skin's porcelain delicacy and the lustrous bronze of her hair.

Elisa looked around at the pleasant, pastoral scene of wide fields, occasional marshy lowland, and frequent little copses of dark trees.

'I would prefer a bit of life in it, animal or human. We might be on the moon. I haven't seen anything move except those trees beyond the road.'

But Tuttle was already pointing out some very active animal life, a gaggle of gray geese hissing and quarreling on the bank of a stream that snaked its way through high, blowing grass. Gillyflower clip-clopped across the high road and onto the path beside the meandering stream. Here Tuttle pointed out a flotilla of ducks proceeding in the same direction and giving further fuel to her claim that Elisa was surrounded by 'life'.

'I do like this open feeling,' the actress confessed. 'No iron-barred doors clanging shut out here.' She took a long, deep breath again and nodded with satisfaction. 'An odd, sweet kind of odor. Not like London or the North Country, but very pleasant all the same.'

'Nature,' Tuttle explained. 'It only proves London isn't the whole world.'

'The London theatre is, for me. I played the provinces too long.'

Nevertheless, the two women were in excellent spirits by the time they reached the stone bridge emptying into the little village of Marchland. The village itself consisted of a single dusty street riven with cart tracks and bordered on both sides by low, stone houses cheek by jowl with half-timbered Tudor buildings. All of them were well kept, which said a great deal for Lord

Jeremy March's interest in the properties. Everything in any way concerned with His Lordship still fascinated Elisa.

Tuttle leaned out from the cramped space in the gig and asked if the road, gloriously named High Street, led on to the Marchland graveyard. The young rustic she called to had just come out of the local tavern but seemed more bucolic than 'bosky'.

'Aye, Mum.' His apple-red cheeks glowed with good health and he spoke of their destination with local pride. 'That fine stretch of green aside the church vestry. Canna miss it, Mum.' He pointed, then squinted at Elisa who had smiled her thanks. To Tuttle he confided as though Elisa had been deaf, 'Yon Lady does fair start the eyes outa me head.'

As Gillyflower resumed her stately pace, Tuttle remarked, 'That, my lass, was a compliment of no mean order.'

Elisa looked back at the youth and waved. He seemed to be dumbstruck. He kept staring. She felt the warmth of his admiration and hoped it was a good omen. She would pray near the March vault and perhaps Arthur might know. She had often prayed and even talked to her mother in her desolation after Molly Catlow's hideous death.

Some day, if God proved kinder than her experience with Him, Lord March might forgive her. But that was in the distant, veiled future.

The last building in the village was a two-storey, half-timbered house which appeared to be a combined inn and theatre. The theatre had obviously once been a stable but ineffectual efforts had been made to refurbish the exterior without removing the picturesque creeper that burned red upon the walls after the first autumn nights. A crudely painted board planted in the grass announced 'The Bristol Strolling Players in Sheridan's "*The Rivals*"' for the night of 20th May.

As it was now September, it seemed clear that no plays had been performed since, perhaps due to the condition of the building. Nevertheless, the sight of this makeshift theatre brought back memories of Elisa's early days with just such itinerant companies. She wondered, not for the first time, if she would ever regain her former hold over the audiences of London. Her whole life seemed to have collapsed with Arthur March's suicide and all the resentment she had carefully concealed, even from herself, came to the fore now.

It wasn't her fault that the boy had been so sensitive, imagining what did not exist at all.

Gillyflower ambled along for several miles while Elisa nursed her resentment.

'You're mightily quiet,' the observant Tuttle remarked at last when the square tower of Cotswold stone loomed up on the horizon around a turn in the tree-lined road.

Elisa avoided the truth. 'I've nothing to say.' It was enough that all her acquaintances and admirers thought her a heartless, wicked enchantress. Why should she add her only friend to that vast audience of enemies? Then she looked at Tuttle and saw that this woman with her worn, leathery face and knowing eyes understood all too well what her thoughts were. The important thing was that it didn't matter to Tuttle. She was either too foolish or too wise to care.

Almost at once they came upon the square tower that dominated the little country churchyard. The church itself was small and low, with peaked roofs. It looked more comfortable and certainly closer to its original purpose than some of the cathedrals where Elisa had worshipped.

Tuttle peered out at the far end of the graveyard. 'That must be the vault. Don't look too bad with the ivy and all. I hope there's no old ghosts and haunts about the place.'

Will there be any spirit, any touch of Arthur March in that depressing stone vault? Elisa wondered.

She closed the gate between the low stone walls of the church grounds and let Gillyflower wander around, grazing with the light gig behind her. Elisa and Tuttle seemed to be the only visitors to the churchyard at this hour of a warm Saturday afternoon. A huge workman bent over a bundle of broomstraws far across the graveyard, dusting off some of the tombstones that had long ago fallen flat on the sunken ground.

128

'Thank heaven, there doesn't seem to be anyone here from March Hall,' Elisa remarked as they strolled past the varied tombstones, some almost indecipherable due to the depradations of age and lichen. The grassy earth sank beneath the feet of the two intruders when they crossed each grave.

Tuttle said, 'I hope you don't make this a habit. They fair give me chills, all these sinking places and all.'

From the side they approached the vault with its deep-cut letters spelling March over the entrance and Elisa wondered aloud, 'Shall I put the roses inside the hasp of the lock?'

'Don't much matter. I think we've been found. That huge lad with the broomstraws over by the stone wall don't look like no vicar to me. Hunched over like that, he kind of makes me think of a "Natural" I once knew. No sense, you know.'

Elisa looked around. 'Oh, no! He will ask questions and then tell Lord March.'

Tuttle gave her a little push. 'Go on. Alone. If you'd like to spend a few minutes here in front of the old place, I'll go over and talk to the fellow. He looks harmless.'

Elisa could only nod. The imagination that gave her conquest of the stage was all too active now that she stood so close to the vault which held the remains of Arthur March, the boy who had loved her. She hugged her chilled arms and dropped the roses. Picking them up, she saw Tuttle making her way across the graves, many of the older ones half-covered by the overturned stones. She wished Tuttle hadn't left her, but she despised her own cowardice.

Pulling together the shreds of her courage, she stepped over to the March vault and held up the roses, to tuck them into the lock. At her first touch the heavy, iron-bound door screeched open an inch or two.

She jumped back, terrified by the echo of sounds that brought back terrible memories of metal shrieking down the halls of Bedlam Asylum. She studied the door and pushed it open. There were no windows, but there were lanterns. Probably the caretaker was responsible for those left on the coffin whose plaque announced: 'EARL OF MARCH, Born 1592, Died for King,

Religion and Throne in 1649.' Coffins were laid on shelves on either side of the vault, each carefully identified by a small wooden plaque. It seemed to her particularly horrifying that a vital youth Arthur's age should be lying here among ancestors dating from the sixteenth century. She made out his coffin at once by the remnants of flowers and plants that remained where they had fallen when the petals and leaves wilted. The stone floor was littered with them.

She had no intention of being locked in this place, which in some ways was worse than the cell in Bedlam. She found a heavy stone near the entrance and wedged it under the door that now stood half open.

She walked lightly into the vault, with some notion that she did not want to disturb all these dead Marches. Reaching up, she laid the roses on Arthur's coffin and whispered as the thoughts poured out, 'Please forgive me. I did love you in my way. You were very dear.'

Does he know? she asked herself. *And does God know how much I regret the mistakes, the false impression I gave that boy?*

Who could ever say?

She rearranged the roses, concentrating on her now silent plea to Arthur, trying hard not to think about her surroundings and the memories they evoked.

She found herself in a miasma of the old horror, remembering the time so many years ago when she brought one rose to her mother, in that other place, and the rose had smelled like these roses . . . dying.

A footstep grated on the stepping stones at the entrance to the vault. With her thoughts on the dead Marches she was chilled to the bone when the iron-bound door began to screech as it moved.

'No!' she screamed, hardly moving, paralyzed with fright. The roses dropped and scattered over the floor. 'Please don't touch the door.'

The sunlight slowly vanished as the door began to close. Meanwhile, the man who had stepped into this vault with her answered in an amused and contemptuous way that was certainly a part of the very real world.

'May one ask why not?'

She knew that voice before she turned and saw the tall, trim figure standing there with the closed door behind him.

'Sir,' she began. 'You see, I cannot bear this.'

'This?' Lord March repeated. She did not flatter herself that his was a welcoming smile. Obviously, he enjoyed her discomfort. Her terror.

'The confinement.' She sensed the fallen roses die under her shoe but did not look down. All she could think of was the open air, sunlight. Freedom from that place, from Bedlam.

He put one arm out and barred her way. She found herself helpless to move.

'Surely, you can stand this confinement for a few minutes. My brother must stand it for all eternity.'

For a dreadful few seconds she thought she would faint. Then, angered by her own weakness, she reached around his body to the heavy, rusted door latch but his free hand touched her face, cupping her chin in his palm.

She found herself forced to stare up into his eyes. His expression seemed to change, slowly, as if curiosity replaced that earlier contempt.

'I believe the girl is genuinely afraid. Arthur won't hurt you. He never hurt a living thing in his short life. And he loved you. To his sorrow.'

CHAPTER ELEVEN

She moistened her dry lips. 'It is this place.'

'Among the dead? They can't hurt you. Not as the living can hurt.'

'I mean, among the living. The living have been in such places.'

Her reply caught him unawares. His sensitive fingers caressed her cheek with an absent gesture. Apparently, her tears troubled him.

'My dear child, you and I are the only living creatures here.'

She tried again. She had never felt more helpless to explain. 'I knew someone once who was locked in a place like this.'

'Yes. I remember your earlier difficulties. This someone, he was locked in accidentally?'

'Deliberately. By law.'

'I see.' He still sounded thoughtful, as if debating whether to believe her. He asked her suddenly, 'Was the laudanum yours?'

'Laudanum?' Her mind was numb.

'That killed my brother.'

'It was mine. Arthur picked it up. He meant to give it to Tuttle. But he forgot.' She looked up. 'Please let me go. I must get out of here.'

'I do believe it is your conscience that is troubling you, not this old house of the dead.' He looked into her eyes with an almost tender amusement. She knew he was playing with her, teasing, making her suffer, but she clung to the small hope that he might be on the verge of forgiving her.

The ridiculous and humiliating tears were drying on her cheeks. She apologized. 'I never meant to be so cowardly. It was not today but long ago that troubled me. Things I can't forget.'

'Memories can be deadly weapons sometimes.'

As he stared at her, moved by one of those sudden, unexpected compulsions she remembered so well, he lowered his head and his lips covered hers. Their touch was whisper-soft at first, but then lingering, with a hard pressure, his mouth possessing hers so completely she couldn't breathe. Her struggles only inflamed whatever emotion had made him act in this violent way.

This is certainly not love, her disordered senses told her. It is hate.

But still, breathless and struggling, a part of her craved to be possessed by a man with any kind of genuine feeling for her. A man like Jeremy March. She knew why she had taken no lovers since her early meetings with Lord March. It had been some absurd effort to be true to her own passionate longings.

Outside in the blessed sunlight they could hear voices. Rescue. One, loud and angry, had to be Tuttle, but there were others, male voices. One of them sounded like Brian Clifford.

Thank God!

And yet, she still loved this hard bitter man who kissed her. She knew why he suffered and why his passion was cruel, not gentle. She could not blame him.

When Jeremy released her and she could take short, gasping breaths, she was sure she would spend her empty hours in the hope that she would feel again that hot, burning passion of his flesh on hers.

She understood that whatever motives had moved him to behave toward her in this manner, they could not be motives of pure hatred and contempt, nor even an understanding of her terror. He felt something for her and fought against it. The violence in his kiss was directed as much against his own desire as against her. Instinctively, she felt this.

No man had ever stirred her by his kisses, or his touch, as this man had, although with a rough kiss. She hungered for him to understand what had happened between her and his brother.

133

When she tried to call out to her 'rescuers' she found her voice gone. His kiss, she thought wryly.

He pulled the door open and ushered Elisa out into the pale sunlight which looked glorious to Elisa. While he explained that he had found their 'visitor' in the vault and the door had closed upon them, she blinked under the stares of Tuttle, Brian Clifford, his scowling daughter Susan, and a huge and hairy creature glaring at her. He must be the caretaker Tuttle had seen. Obviously, he too was embittered by Arthur's death.

It took an effort to hold her ground but she did so, trying to make clear what she was doing here in enemy territory.

'I trust Tuttle has explained. I thought we would be alone. We would never have intruded if we had known anyone from March Hall would be visiting today.'

Brian tried to cover her intrusion. 'Most natural, Elisa. I am persuaded His Lordship understands. You came here, like my Susan and me, to leave flowers for the poor boy.'

Jeremy March had been staring back at the open vault. Elisa ached to comfort him but suspected that, in spite of that violent kiss, anything she said to him about Arthur would only rekindle his bitterness toward her. If, indeed, the wound had begun to heal. After a minute or so he signalled the caretaker who shrugged loosely and loped away to close and lock the vault.

'Abel is, to all intents and purposes, a mute,' Brian explained, seeing Elisa's uneasiness concerning the heavy-browed caretaker. 'But quite harmless.'

To Elisa's enormous relief and surprise March then cut in warmly, 'Very true, Clifford. As to Miss Carlisle, she has also been leaving flowers. A gracious gesture. At all events, when I entered, the door slammed shut.' He considered Elisa while everyone waited in suspense. 'You came over from Hawtree Estates, no doubt. May I have a message sent to them that you are dining at March Hall?'

'I'm afraid I am not staying at –' she began.

134

'With suitable chaperones,' Jeremy March went on, further surprising them all. 'Dr Clifford. Miss Clifford too will join us, of course. Arthur would have it no other way. He was very fond of the Cliffords.'

Susan's gloomy silence ended at this bright prospect.

'If I am to be a housekeeper, I should know how the family itself goes on. Think of all I can learn.'

She seemed resigned to forgiving Elisa for the death of Arthur March, perhaps moved by the delightful prospect of dining with His Lordship.

Everyone laughed at her and the awkward moments were banished. Only Tuttle remained her watchful, suspicious self. When, despite Elisa's protests, Lord March went to see about the care of Gillyflower and the gig, Tuttle insisted in a low voice, 'It's a bad thing, this. He's not your sort, and well you know it. He's meant to be in London this month; so what is he doing here? Did he find out somehow that you were in the neighborhood? Is it a trick to trap you in some way? Mark me, there's havey-cavey business here.'

Susan put in quickly, 'Lord March came with us to leave flowers. Mrs Ponsonby and I come here all the time to leave flowers, and we nearly always see His Lordship. He's been excessively kind to me.'

Brian ignored this and kissed Elisa's hand. 'It will be His Lordship's pleasure to entertain you, I am sure. I have tried to explain your feelings and I'm persuaded he must have taken them to heart.'

'Yes, indeed,' Susan said when called away from her day-dreaming by her father.

'You are all kind. But you see, I am not dressed to dine with His Lordship. I don't think we should take his invitation too seriously. It was his gracious way of saying he holds no grievances against me. That is all.'

She could not forget the sombre glow in his eyes before he had kissed her in that surprising way, nor could she forget that he had done so in the very presence of his dead brother's coffin. He might have been moved by sudden memory of how his brother had loved her. Whatever it was, it had certainly been a fleeting emotion. He gave some indication of regretting it. He was very much his cool self now.

No matter, her other self told her: take what you can get, and hope to promote in him something of your own feelings.

She watched Lord March stride toward them against the rising afternoon wind that swept over the churchyard. He avoided the sunken graves without seeming to be conscious of it. She admired what she thought must be his sensitivity. She was collecting every possible indication of Jeremy March's kindness, his unexpected forgiveness. Maybe then her mind would assure her that his changed manner toward her was genuine.

He appeared to assume his invitation to Elisa had been accepted. He was in an excellent mood, so good it surprised Brian Clifford as well as Elisa. She could see Brian eyeing His Lordship in a curious way as they walked to the landaulet and the team that was being rubbed down by an old, bewhiskered coachman. The huge, frightening caretaker Elisa had noticed before stood leaning on a spade and staring at the big, bay horses. He reminded her of the warders of St Mary's of Bethlehem Asylum long ago.

Elisa and Susan Clifford were seated forward with Brian and Tuttle facing them. Lord March himself lightly took the coachman's box, motioning the old coachman to climb up beside him. It was with considerable relief that Elisa saw the last of the churchyard and the terrible darkness of that vault. She sat huddled in one corner, wishing she had worn a heavier wrap than her violet silk shawl.

She warned herself than Lord March had shown interest in her on several occasions – notably that unforgettable night when he visited her boudoir – only to turn from her, moved by gossip and foul lies. She must not let her own passion blind her to the aristocrat's true nature. He might desire her, but that was not the complete love she hungered for.

Torn one way and then the other, she saw her friends look at her curiously when she shivered. Brian asked if she was cold.

'We should arrive shortly. However, I must admit, March Hall is a stiff distance from almost every habitable place in this valley.'

'But there is always someone to keep you company on a stroll,' Susan put in thoughtfully.

Elisa remembered Susan's proud boast that Arthur March had walked with her on occasion. Elisa felt a kinship with her. She too knew how it felt to lose a dream.

Presently, as the coach rattled along the unpaved avenue between great horse chestnut and occasional oak trees, Susan sat up straight and pointed out of the open window on the left side of the carriage.

'Here it is. Isn't it splendid? Not in the least cold and gray, like other great houses.'

Elisa was curious about the home that had formed the totally different characters of Jeremy and Arthur March, but it was impossible to see the rambling house and its attached wings without falling over Susan; so she pretended a polite, moderate interest until the coach passed through the main gates of the high, forbidding coachhouse.

Having arrived within the walled grounds of March Hall, the coach halted before a modest series of steps that led up to double oaken doors hardly as impressive as the neat, freshly painted door of Elisa's own house in London. When the coach steps were let down Elisa found Lord March waiting with an arm held out to assist her. For a few seconds she was more interested in his gallantry than in the house, but when she was safely on the steps and he turned to help Susan she was able to study March Hall itself.

Her first conclusion was that happy accident permitted the long house with its many third-storey gables to glow like warm gold in the afternoon sunlight. Then she realized that the golden Cotswold limestone composition itself added to that illusion. She thought better and better of the Marches who had created this cheerful country seat.

While Brian escorted Susan and Tuttle up the steps, Elisa became aware that Lord March was watching her reaction with uncomfortably close attention.

'What do you think of it?'

What possible difference could it make to him? It had been in his family four hundred years.

'Very beautiful, Sir. It is a happy place. Much more cheerful than some other great houses.'

'Yes. I thought you would like it.'

Nevertheless, his smile was discomfiting. She tried to think of a word to describe that smile: it was cynical. He undoubtedly thought she was attracted by its monetary worth.

A round, bustling, smiling little woman met them as Susan's red-haired footman opened the door and bowed them in. To Elisa's amusement Susan ignored her footman like a great lady and then forgot her fine airs to hug the round little woman who treated her in a motherly way.

Susan called over her shoulder, 'Elisa, this is our dear Mrs Ponsonby, the housekeeper. She is teaching me all her secret arts.'

Little Mrs Ponsonby curtsied to Elisa, but just for an instant her bright blue eyes had closed as if caught unawares and striving to recover. Elisa felt sure her tight smile was forced. It was not surprising. Arthur March had probably been a favourite of hers.

Brian reminded his daughter, 'Susan, you are monopolizing Mrs Ponsonby. His Lordship is waiting to speak to her.'

'It's of no consequence,' Lord March assured them. 'Miss Clifford has completed the formalities. Yes, Miss Carlisle. This is our rod and our staff, so to speak. Mrs Ponsonby. She will see to your needs.'

'Thank you. We are most grateful. I had no notion of paying a visit. Tuttle and I are staying at a posting-house on the Gloucester High Road.' She knew she was talking too fast, but she felt the resentment of the servants surrounding her when they heard her name. Others had arrived, a pretty, foreign-looking blonde maid, and a grizzled old man who tugged at the housekeeper's skirts and inquired after 'the lady's portmanteaux and travelling cases'.

'There are none, thank you.'

He looked surprised, but caught Lord March's eyes and shrugged. A lady arriving without travelling cases was an oddity indeed.

Elisa caught glimpses of a large, sunlit room, probably the Great Hall, beyond the panelled entry. It looked far more welcoming than the human beings employed by the Marches.

None of these family retainers was happy to see Elisa. She could scarcely blame them. Still unsure of herself, she went on: 'I paid a visit of respect to Mr Arthur March. That is to say –' She felt the enmity around her and broke off awkwardly, wishing she had never accepted Jeremy March's invitation.

Brian started to say something in her defense but Lord March cut in with a voice like the edge of glass.

'We are fortunate in our guest. Anyone who was my brother's friend may count upon a welcome here; isn't that true, Mrs Ponsonby?'

Looking pale and nervous, Mrs Ponsonby bobbed a quick curtsy. 'As Your Lordship says. If Miss Carlisle will be pleased to follow me . . .'

In Elisa's view Lord March reverted to the smooth host much too quickly. 'Excellent. All seems to be clear. Now then, Clifford, come into the library with me. I want a report on the condition of those almshouses in Netherly. Are they as disgraceful as the villagers tell me?'

The two men went off together, Brian agreeing, 'Disgraceful is the word, Sir, since the last heavy rains. I fear three-quarters at least must be torn down and replaced. Quite uninhabitable, I give you my word.'

'I believe you. I was a fool to accept my estate manager's word. A lying rogue, if ever there was one. At all events, I have a proposition to make you. About replacing him with yourself. Come along. We'll discuss the matter.'

Mrs Ponsonby cleared her throat and Susan nudged Elisa.

'Shall we see you comfortable now, Elisa? Lord March is very punctual about dinner and it's near on three o'clock.'

Still uncertain and not quite sure why, Elisa went with Tuttle up the heavy, oak staircase after the little housekeeper and her acolyte, Susan. Elisa had caught glimpses of that glowing Great Hall to the right of the panelled entryway as they passed.

On the gallery above she saw the usual long, intimidating portrait line of family Marches. She studied them as she passed, noting any characteristics they had in common with Jeremy March.

The similarities were hard to find. None of the faces, even the recent eighteenth-century Marches, looked much like Jeremy March with his high-boned face and those strange eyes. The nose seemed to be legitimately arrived at, thin and high-bridged, and his ancestors had his mouth, wide, thin-lipped, with a humorous quirk at times, yet – in Lord March's case – undeniably voluptuous.

Several females, mother, grandmother and others, had bequeathed to Arthur March their look of gentle kindliness and pride. Many of them were blondes, like Arthur. She wondered if they had been happy as March wives.

Mrs Ponsonby unlocked a door on the west front of the building and Susan Clifford walked in as the elderly housekeeper stood aside. The girl looked around and turned back to Elisa and Tuttle.

'You see? I'm performing exactly as I should; aren't I, Ponsy?'

The little housekeeper pursed her lips. 'Very well, I'm sure, Miss Susan.' But when she saw that Elisa smiled over the little tableau, she went on less repressively, 'You learn promptly, Miss Susan.' She looked over her shoulder at Elisa. 'Will you come this way, Miss? I believe everything you need will be found here. If not, please to summon me by the bellpull beside the bed.'

The bed was broad and dark with a heavy, winter tester overhead and curtains of a surprisingly heavy emerald green velvet. Elisa wondered, if she would ever have shared that bed with him if things had been otherwise.

Susan hesitated when Mrs Ponsonby had gone. 'May I help you in any way, Elisa?'

'No, thank you, dear.'

'I'll come for you in a few minutes, then.' Susan smiled and then followed the housekeeper out, after carefully closing the door behind her.

Elisa shivered. She nodded to Tuttle who had already hastened to the door. She had to wrestle with the handle to get it open. Elisa found the palms of her hands sweating and started across the room to open the door herself.

'Hurry, Tuttle. Please, hurry!'

Having set the heavy oak-panelled door ajar, Tuttle eyed Elisa. She knew exactly why Elisa behaved in this ridiculous fashion but couldn't understand why the fear never left her after all these years. It was a weakness that the positive and assertive Tuttle despised.

'Best hurry,' she said. 'No point in putting His Lordship off now when he's ready to play the gentleman again.'

Silently, Elisa agreed. She went to the long, elegant credenza with its oak-framed mirror above and took her hat off. Her hair was somewhat dishevelled and she tried to arrange the Grecian coiffure neatly but could do very little until Tuttle produced a comb.

While Tuttle pushed the curls at the nape of her mistress's neck back into place in her usual, happy, slap-dash fashion, Elisa had an uneasy sense of being watched, as if unseen eyes stared at her. She raised her eyes from her own image to the portrait on the opposite wall reflected in the mirror.

Arthur March's eyes stared down at her, haunting her with the naive worship she remembered so well in their blue depths.

Was the presence of this portrait a deliberate reproach to her, a reminder of her 'crime'? But who had known she was going to be here, and in this bedchamber?

It was all nonsense. Lord March showed signs of forgiving her, at times, and the servants wouldn't dare to insinuate these needle-like darts against her. In this case, she was convinced that the fault was her own. She had become far too sensitive to every action, expecting each time that it was directed against her.

Tuttle said, 'They're waiting for you, Girl. Your audience. Go along.'

141

Elsie Catlow stood up. She forced herself to become Elisa Carlisle, the actress. It was her only salvation when all these doubts and fears engulfed her. She laughed, the calculated but warm little sound the critics called 'enchanting'.

'Wish me well, Tuttle. It is the opening curtain. Shall I dazzle them? Or be pelted by apples and oranges?'

'A little of both, very like,' Tuttle grunted.

CHAPTER TWELVE

At the head of the wide staircase with its warm, heavy, oaken glow she stopped as she would have done before making her stage entrance. But her pause was not long. She felt very strongly the sinister influence of all those Marches in the gallery looking down their noses at her back.

'Come,' she reminded herself. 'You have played to antagonistic audiences before. The Marches and their household staff cannot be worse than Peter Tregaran and his friends.'

Best not to think of the actor whose contemptuous dismissal of her overtures had been one of the worst blows to her self-esteem, bringing her back to the lonely rejection of her childhood.

Before she reached the bottom of the staircase Jeremy March rounded the newel post and stood there looking up at her. She tried to analyse his expression. Thoughtful, with a slight frown, but if he had been anyone else, she could have sworn there was desire in that look he gave her, studying her from her head to her slim, French-heeled shoes. It was almost as if he frowned at himself, at his own weakness. Perhaps that explained the violence of his kiss today.

She did not want to play the fool again, the insincere enchantress who had failed miserably with Tregaran; so she retained some of the gentle reserve that worked so well in the theatre.

'I hope I haven't delayed your customary dinner hour, Sir.'

'Not at all. It awaits the pleasure of the lovely *Circe*.'

She winced. 'Please.'

143

This time she could not pretend to misunderstand that smile. He said, 'I beg your pardon. But that is the name by which all of London knows you.' Seeing her eyes flash, he took the hand she tried to withdraw in hurt and indignation. He brought her fingers to his lips. It was easier to resist his touch, however much it excited her, than to resist his whimsical look which made him unexpectedly endearing. She hadn't thought him capable of this light, charming touch.

'Come now. Don't be cross. Let us be friends. He would expect it of us, you know.'

'He?'

'My brother. He always wanted us to be friends.'

'Yes, but –' Surely, Arthur would have been jealous if he suspected there was a grain of serious feeling between them. It was insensitive of Lord March and she became suspicious once more.

He went on making small talk. 'Ah! Here we have my new estate manager, Dr Clifford, and his delightful daughter.'

Elisa was still puzzled by His Lordship's manner toward her. He treated her as a particular guest of honor. She found herself seated at his right and consulted on every dish. There were so many of them and nearly all in French that she wondered, ever suspicious, if he intended to humiliate her.

If that was his hope, she would disappoint him. Her few suitors, and the many admirers with everything but marriage on their minds, had invited her to intimate suppers often enough where the menu was French. She was a quick study. Still, the only great house in which she ever sat down at dinner with aristocrats was the town house of the Hawtree family, and among the Hawtree guests, as she was perfectly aware, she had been a curiosity.

If that was Lord March's intention, she resolved to thwart his purpose. When he asked if she chose the *'turbot à l'Anglais'* she refused it politely, preferring the *'poularde à la Periguez'*. The footman-waiter standing behind her high-backed, brocade-cushioned chair, looked ahead stonily with his heaped silver tray held close to her ear. He seemed deaf, dumb and blind. She didn't know whether his impassive demeanor was aimed at her or if it was simply a part of his normal behavior.

When Lord March inquired after her taste in the *entremets*, of which there seemed a more than sufficient choice, she replied that she never ate the *gâteau Glacé au abricots*, preferring her *abricots* in *un petit soufflé*.

She saw Brian raise his head to give her a warning. Apparently, he was afraid she could not deal with His Lordship in French, but she went serenely on.

To all of this His Lordship seemed amused, even pleased. Had he really thought he could trap her into some gaucherie by ordering an elaborate meal to be served and then referring to it in French? If so, he would be disappointed.

When dinner was over and she reminded him that she and Tuttle must return to their inn before dark, he said brusquely, 'Rubbish. You will be properly escorted. Meanwhile, you might find some interest in a tour of this old building. It has quite a history.'

'Very much so, I am sure, Your Lordship. And you will prove that March Hall is in every respect superior to the Hawtree house.'

He flashed her a glance, as if suspecting a barb in that comment, but she merely smiled at him innocently.

Very much excited, Susan reminded her, 'Perhaps His Lordship will show you the secret stairs where his dead ancestors march up and down on rainy days. Mr Arthur showed me one day. He loved it. It was terribly mysterious and grim.'

There was a small silence at the mention of Arthur March's name, then Lord March protested teasingly, 'What of bright harvest nights with the moon at the full? And golden mornings when ghostly figures pass you soundlessly on the stairs?'

Susan gave out a little scream and covered her ears. The others laughed. Brian excused himself reluctantly, since it seemed clear that he would be an unwanted third.

Susan hurried off to join Mrs Ponsonby who was showing Tuttle the intricacies of the kitchen, stillroom and pantries. The housekeeper's manner had thawed considerably during her lectures to Tuttle on the proper feeding and care of 'persons with delicate appetites'. Elisa suspected that Tuttle had very early found that good woman's weakness for teaching and was now playing upon it.

Lord March laughed at the situation. 'We are alone, it appears. Shall it be the Ghostly Staircase first? Or the very impressive Great Drawing Room which is only used when we are entertaining royalty? Or the –'

'No, no, I beg you. Something simple, if you please.'

He took her arm. 'I do please. Very easily. I daresay you have seen enough of grandeur.'

'I?'

'In the theatre. You are forever playing empresses, princesses, all the crowned heads.'

'Paper crowns.'

He waved toward the sun-drenched room at the end of the hall. 'Come. The solar, as they called it when the house was built. It was my mother's favorite retreat.' He hesitated as they walked in under the lintel of the big room. 'It was also my brother's favorite as a child. So much light, I imagine. He was a creature of light.' He looked around. 'One could almost believe the boy was still here.' He cleared his throat and pointed toward the far west windows.

She had begun to resent the indelicacy of his reminder until he finished speaking. Then she realized that his true feelings had come to the fore. He said nothing for a minute but strolled across the room with her, toward the most astonishingly effective set of windows she had ever seen.

Whatever else he might think of her, she knew he was utterly sincere when he pointed with her own fingers in his: 'There. That is the place he loved above all else. He would sit curled up there beneath that glorious window and dream.'

'Dreams of his glorious future,' she murmured and avoided his eyes. She felt the painful moment. She was sure that was his intention.

He ignored the chance to twist a knife in the wound. 'He was very like our mother. An innocent. He needed so much

146

affection, care. Other than from his father and his brother, he would never receive it in this family. Ambition is our curse, you know. And the expectation that the boy should be exactly like us.' He laughed harshly. 'And the irony is, I despised my father.'

It was a strange thing to confess, considering his bitterness against her as the cause of Arthur's suicide. Was it possible he had blamed her so violently because he had found it too painful to blame himself and the others in his family?

In the center of the big room Elisa stopped to take a long, awed view of the 'March Window' that Arthur had loved.

The magnificent dais window with what appeared to be a thousand panes, was at least two storeys high. Every pane glowed in the light like topaz. At its foot a cushioned window-seat looked exactly like the place where a lonely boy would curl up and dream of all his future life. Including the woman he loved. She closed her eyes, finding the thought once more hard to dwell on.

Jeremy March never seemed willing to let her explain fully about her relationship with Arthur. Perhaps some guilt of his own, even an interest in her (though that sounded in her ears very like a monstrous conceit) might explain his deafness to her story. Why couldn't he see that Arthur's story of her cold-blooded dismissal of him had been the aberration of a furious, humiliated boy?

She tried once more as they looked around, sensing his presence everywhere in the room.

'Arthur was a boy, I know. He carried that laudanum away unconsciously, and then, in a child's angry way, he swallowed it to make everyone suffer. It was a momentary thing.'

'And his letter to me?' Before she could speak, he made one of his swift changes and said rapidly, 'He was always a dreamy child, and here in this room was his dream castle.'

She accepted the hint. 'I never knew his interests, his way of life. Did he hunt? Ride to hounds? Or attempt those curricle races the Prince's friends are so fond of?'

'No. He and Prinny never got on. He liked the farms and knew a surprising amount about them. He often walked with the farm girls and boys. Or the young folk of the village. I caught

147

him once explaining exactly where the best violets and the most edible cress could be found. And he was quite serious. I tried not to smile. He was right, of course, and I was wrong. There were very few flirtations, but, I daresay, some of those pretty girls may have gained another impression. Several claimed to be heartbroken when he spent so much time in London recently.'

Before she could bridle at this hint that his London sojourn was in pursuit of her, His Lordship's mood changed again. He smiled at a memory. It softened his hard, chiselled good looks. 'Those country walks were all very proper, I've no doubt.'

'Yes,' she said, remembering Arthur and his naive ways that made him so dear. 'I know.'

He gave her a sharp look. The tenderness was gone. 'I don't doubt it.'

Before she could find a polite, noncommittal answer he changed the subject. The new subject astonished her.

'Do you miss the theatre?'

She stared at him, wondering if there was a barb in this too. 'I have been away less than a month.'

'Very true. Nevertheless, I rather suspect there are those who would pay a handsome figure to see you perform again.'

The insult was coming. She could feel it.

'Possibly. But even I prefer not to flaunt my bad taste. You see, My Lord, I know why my audience would be coming to view me.' A sudden flash of pain affected her voice. She rushed on, to push the old terror behind her. 'Like one of the human animals caged at Bedlam . . . Are you familiar with St Mary's of Bethlehem, Sir?'

She had startled him. 'Not altogether. I know of it, naturally. You have visited the place?'

She bit off the words. 'Certainly not! An actress entirely concerned with her own pleasure? You are amusing yourself, I think.'

He was puzzled by her change of mood, but after studying the topaz glow of the great window he continued this curious conversation.

'Two days ago in the City your friend, Lady Hawtree, discussed with me the conditions for the elderly in the local almshouses of the shire. She seemed to feel that some amateur theatricals might induce the locals to join in the contribution. The Hawtrees and the March Estate will provide the greater portion, but we want the entire country to take a part in the rebuilding.'

'Admirable, My Lord. But I hardly think they would welcome a London actress, especially one who –' She said no more. He, of all people, must understand.

He pretended not to see her bitter confusion.

'Gwenna Hawtree shares my belief that a lady of your accomplishments would certainly attract them. I even agree to her further suggestion, though you may be shocked by it.'

'I can't imagine anyone daring to disagree with a suggestion to which you agree, Your Lordship.'

He managed to smile. 'However that may be, Gwenna Hawtree has stolen a story from one of Lord Byron's friends, a man named Poladori. They say Byron himself penned it, which seems much more likely. Whoever wrote it is unlikely to recognize it after Her Ladyship has completed her little touches. I refer, of course, to *The Vampyr.*'

What an extraordinary idea! Was it his way of calling her a vampyr? A creature who existed on the blood of her victims? If so, she was fully up to the challenge.

'A delightful notion, Sir. We have only to find some gentleman willing to impersonate the victim of this dreaded Vampyr.'

He was blandly confident. 'But Poladori's – or Byron's – Vampyr is male. You will play his lovely victim. I have no doubt the man will come forward willing to victimize you, for charity. In the county spirit, you might say.'

She shook her head at his incredible suggestion. Or was it Lady Hawtree's scheme? It seemed especially incredible that he should have fallen into Gwenna's usual trap. Surely, he knew Gwenna Hawtree loved manipulating people.

'You must be mad! The world would believe I made a mockery of the recent tragedies.'

'Not if you are the victim,' he reminded her. 'But you would have the satisfaction as well of performing in a noble cause. Is there no charity in your heart?'

The entire idea of flouting good taste in this way was odious. Still, he seemed to be very taken, almost obsessed by the necessity of persuading her, and she cared more for his opinion than that of the Regent's society.

Then, too, the days since she heard of Arthur March's suicide had been lonely and wasted, haunted by her own feelings of guilt. She longed to cast aside these feelings, to return to the only profession for which she had any gift. Perhaps in this way, sponsored by Lady Gwenna and Lord March, she might be accepted again on the stage. But she didn't want to give him the satisfaction of agreeing at once. Despite his arguments, he would be sure to think the worse of her for a swift capitulation.

She looked at the low western light through the hundreds of window panes and said, changing the subject, 'I'm afraid I must deny myself the pleasure of visiting the ghostly stairs. Tuttle and I will be in eternal disgrace if we arrive at the inn after dark.'

'You are afraid to meet our ghosts. Admit it.'

She smiled but refused to be joked into remaining.

He accepted this and ordered the closed carriage to be brought around. Tuttle was in excellent spirits when they located her in Mrs Ponsonby's cold-room.

'There'll be changes with that new cook of yours, Girl – I mean, Miss Carlisle. All her high-nosed airs won't cover bad sauces. I've learned a deal about that today, Ma'am.'

She addressed this to Mrs Ponsonby who warned her in reply, 'Mind now, Mrs Tuttle. No nonsense from them. They take their orders from you, seeing that you've no butler in your household.'

'I'll do that, Ma'am. And many thanks.'

Elisa and Susan embraced, with Susan informing her, 'Papa went off in a great huff. He says he has patients in the village, but I'll wager he's jealous because His Lordship pays you such attention.'

Elisa hoped Lord March didn't hear this. He would be sure to imagine she was 'getting above herself' by taking the gossip seriously.

But then, his entire conduct was mysterious. 'More mysterious than his absurd Haunted Staircase,' she told Tuttle later that night.

Tuttle was already suspicious about what seemed to be taking place between Elisa and Lord March, who escorted them all the way to the coaching inn. Elisa knew the older woman would be happy to believe Jeremy March was sincere. But, like Elisa, she kept wondering why he had made this spectacular change.

During the ride he was highly sociable, talking as though he expected Elisa to see more of March Hall, discussing local problems that could hardly interest anyone but a member of the March household. He capped his gallant behavior by lingering over Elisa's hand when they said good night. Bringing it to his lips he looked at her in what Tuttle claimed was a very 'speaking' way.

His final words to Elisa were encompassed in the plea, 'Do think over our plan for the almshouses, Miss Carlisle. I feel certain your generous heart will urge you to accept.'

Whatever her uneasy suspicions, she thought it best to answer him with an enigmatic smile and no more.

CHAPTER THIRTEEN

Gwenna Hawtree, totally innocent of previous experience in the art, had written a reading version of something she called *The Vampyr Of London*. She had no false modesty and promised Elisa at once, 'You will adore it. My dear, the original was too dreadful. I had no notion. But it is quite irresistible now. Come, do read it aloud and imagine yourself in my heroine's role.'

It was evidently meant to be read from some elevated floor in imitation of a stage, as if it were a simple reading of the sort conducted by writers for their own profit or, more often, for the charity of celebrated players fallen on hard times.

Elisa had no objection. Her most popular works were those she performed alone, as readings. She was amused at Her Ladyship's assumption of full credit for the story's authorship, but she had to admit that the 'play' was better than she had feared. So much had been changed, including character names, that neither John Poladori nor Lord Byron would have recognized the blood-curdling result.

The reading was to be performed in the great salon of the Hawtree country mansion, which loomed up in the gothic style of an old Scottish castle over the mist-shrouded hills from March Hall.

Sir Hugo Hawtree still avoided her, obviously holding her responsible for the loss of his son's arm and his military career, but he remained polite when they met – and his wife, of course, was in her glory.

'Magnificent,' she would say to Elisa, clapping her hands with enthusiasm as Elisa finished a monologue of rising terror. 'But my dear, forgive me. You do not quite suggest the ultimate in terror just yet. It needs work.'

'This is all very well, but am I to drain my own blood?' Elisa complained one evening at the end of a gruelling day during which she had read and re-read Gwenna Hawtree's florid lines, never entirely satisfying the author.

Nothing disturbed Lady Hawtree whose eyes still sparkled with excitement. 'Come, come, you must have faith. As for locating a "Lord Raven" – I do adore that name! – well, you must trust me. And our neighbors. What do you think of dear old Simon Diddlecome as Lord Raven? He breathes hard every time I mention the lack of a male lead.'

Elisa rolled her eyes heavenward. 'Squire Diddlecome would require more blood than I can provide, at his weight.'

'Well then, we might borrow a London actor for the single night of our play.' Lady Hawtree was intent upon her fingernails. 'Yes. Young Tregaran might just do. He has a certain following; so he cannot be too unattractive.'

She knew perfectly well how troublesome he had been to Elisa, who said sweetly, 'An excellent suggestion. Indeed, he is so popular you might not be forced to rely upon my name.'

'My dear Elisa . . .'

'The more I consider the idea, the better it seems. And it would free me to make an American tour which Strawbridge has in mind for me.'

'You are being deliberately obtuse. You must not, you *cannot* desert us now. March would never forgive me.'

'March?' Elisa was all attention, though she tried hard to show little of her real feelings.

'Naturally. It was all his idea. He wants to show you he holds no bitterness over that wretched boy's suicide. Anyone may guess that. But being a proud man, he choses this devious way to tell you.' Gwenna Hawtree tapped Elisa's shoulder with one slim finger slightly curled in her feline way. 'It is my opinion that his resentment against you was pure jealousy of his brother. But with his brother gone he is free to engage in –' she shrugged and grinned – 'whatever you and he may engage in.'

153

'If Your Ladyship were not who you are, I would say the suggestion is disgusting.'

Lady Hawtree sighed, unoffended. 'What a hypocrite you are, Elisa!'

It was hard to fool Gwenna Hawtree.

Even Tuttle was beginning to wonder if *The Vampyr Of London* would remain a performance with one player. Lady Hawtree had insisted that Elisa remain at the Hawtree house until the night when *The Vampyr* attracted the purses of the countryside. While she smoothed out the gown Elisa had carelessly hung on a peg in the big clothespress, Tuttle muttered, 'You needn't feel you're going to be left alone on stage – or whatever you call that platform they're laying in the room downstairs.'

'Whatever do you mean?'

Tuttle's laugh was a single bark. 'Her Fine Ladyship. She's practising up and down those big rooms, reading that other female's lines. The Lady Vampyr.'

After a surprised moment Elisa laughed too. 'Aha! So that explains her interest in theatricals.'

But it didn't explain Lady Hawtree's remark about Jeremy March. This ridiculous business had been inspired by him. It just happened to suit the plans of Gwenna Hawtree who thrived on intrigue.

As the night of the Charity Entertainment approached, Elisa found it difficult to contain her amusement at the efforts of the neighbourhood gentry to read 'Lord Raven's' role opposite her.

'It simply will not play. I may expect to have my blood drained by a war-axe,' she told Gwenna. The two had found themselves hysterical with laughter over the reading by Cedric, Marquess of Anglestoke. He was now galloping away on his huge black charger, in great satisfaction with himself after ranting through twenty pages of dialogue and offering to arm himself with the very war-axe his ancestor had bloodied at Hastings.

Gwenna controlled her giggles with an effort. She did not seem in the least disturbed about their failure to find a leading man.

'You are being very foolish. I give you the word of a Hawtree –' she giggled again – 'whatever that may be

154

worth – that you will have your Lord Raven before Friday next.'

She looked up then, beaming in her light, charming way and waved to her husband. 'Hugo, do come. We need a Lord Raven. You must read for us.'

Elisa stiffened with uneasiness. By this time she was well aware that his feelings toward her had not softened. From the large, overfurnished reception hall the stout little man nodded to them, a gesture that indicated good manners but nothing warmer. He pretended he had not heard his wife.

Lady Hawtree was not troubled. 'Dear Hugo,' she confided to Elisa. 'He spends all his waking hours with his dreadful stud-groom. As though his precious horses and his dogs were more important than his wife. At least, he is not the sort to dabble with bits-of-muslin.'

Unlike his wife who dabbled with admirers here and there, Elisa thought, but she laughed, used to this frankness. She did wish Sir Hugo would forgive her. She could not feel responsible for his son's drunken conduct, no matter how deeply she regretted the disaster. But the dreadful coincidence of his tragedy and that of Arthur March had fallen so close together they gave her dreams that left her freezing cold when she awoke in the night.

She had several times returned to London during the fortnight that Lady Hawtree was planning the Almshouse Performance, as she referred to it, but was always lured back, once by Lady Hawtree's supposed conversation with Lord March. According to Her Ladyship, Jeremy March talked of nothing but Elisa and was most anxious for her return. Even Sir Hugo pretended to welcome her, but she felt that the poor man had been over-persuaded and was only trying to oblige his wife.

Though Elisa still found something troubling about Lord March's interest in the ludicrous *Vampyr Of London*, she welcomed his frequent short visits to the Hawtree house when she was present. She tried to quell any hopes of his genuine feeling for her, but there was always the secret thought. On the other hand, Gwenna Hawtree's constant assurances that he loved her madly managed to annoy more than they encouraged her.

155

The countryside around the ugly gothic pile of chimneys and parapets that was the Hawtree house offered Elisa an escape of sorts. The busy valley on the Hawtree side of the hills was quite unlike the serene splendor of the hills she had observed from the topaz window of March Hall. Their beauty merely accentuated her fear of their awful loneliness.

One early autumn day, sick to death of the bloodthirsty play and Gwenna's absurd efforts to persuade her of Lord March's feelings, Elisa left the great house on her own, something she rarely did in London or in the country. But Tuttle had insisted on remaking Elisa's costumes, which fitted a trifle loosely on her, and the Hawtrees were entertaining one of the Prince Regent's cronies who did not feel it suitable to meet the notorious Elisa Carlisle socially.

Luckily, considering the actress's fear of finding herself alone, there were many villagers abroad; the Hawtree house stood prominently apart from the Tudor village that huddled below the Hawtree gates. Elisa was greeted with cool respect, which she returned in the gently gracious way she had reacted to those in the theatre who came to gape at The Wicked Enchantress.

She was curious to see the outside of the almshouses and also their elderly tenants, but she dared not go too close and dredge up memories. She thought the almshouses themselves would give her more incentive to play the wretched 'Auriane' opposite whichever of the county gentry read 'Lord Raven's' part.

The story was ridiculous. Incredible. Elisa wondered why it frightened her so much when she read her lines. She knew there were no 'vampyrs', whatever the public believed about Elisa Carlisle herself. If some rotund squire with a bulbous, drinker's nose and rosy cheeks should read 'Lord Raven', it would be more laughable than frightening.

She was so busy puzzling over what they would do if no 'Lord Raven' appeared tomorrow night that she reached the row of gray stone almshouses at the end of the lane without being aware of it.

The low-built dwellings with their small windows appeared to be very dark within. The thin morning sun barely reached through the thick mullioned panes and Elisa could well imagine the interior gloom.

Her mother's parents had died in such a place.

Instinctively, she shifted her closed parasol to her left hand and raised gloved fingers to her throat. Her pink pearls were safe. They had been her first personal investment. Her friend at Rundle's, the London jewellers, had reminded her, 'Quality like this is always of value, Madam. One never knows when a few hundred guineas might be useful.'

She had smiled, as though such a crass thought never occurred to her, but the pearls were only one of many such investments, including, she thought in a moment of regret, the jewels she had accepted from those who claimed to 'admire' her. Greed, some would call it, with Lord March among them, but they had never known real poverty.

In view of her thoughts it was a shock to see Jeremy March himself come out of a door in front of her, wearing a jerkin rather than a neat riding coat to match his riding breeches and boots. He had removed his cravat and the breeze of the morning ruffled the full, dusty sleeves of his shirt. He was discussing with Brian Clifford the problem of adding to this row of almshouses. He did not notice her at first.

At Brian's startled look he stopped in mid-sentence and turned to see Elisa. She wondered what he thought in that first glance. His frown was not promising. Then he gave her the puzzling smile that seemed to tell her: *I know you. I have found you out.*

He hadn't, of course. He had no notion of the real Elisa Carlisle. How could he? Lord Jeremy March had never heard of Elsie Catlow.

'Miss Carlisle, a happy meeting,' he greeted her, coming forward to take her hand. Then he saw how dusty his own hand was and excused himself. 'You must do the honors, Clifford. You, at least, look the gentleman.'

Brian took her hand in his and looked into her eyes warmly. 'I think you will find your cause a worthy one, Elisa. I only wish a more worthy vehicle might have been chosen.'

157

'Rubbish!' His Lordship argued. 'Nothing could be more appropriate. The wringing of a few farthings from some of these squires is like tapping drops of blood from them.'

Brian laughed politely but Elisa remained quiet, still close to her memories. Evidently, her silence surprised and perplexed His Lordship.

'I imagine almshouses are not in Miss Carlisle's theatre of experience,' he remarked pleasantly enough, but the intimation that she knew nothing of real life was all too clear.

Indignant at this injustice, Brian started to correct His Lordship, but Elisa was angry enough to stop him.

'Perhaps I am more at home in my London house. Poverty and age are so depressing.' She added savagely, 'Mama always said so.'

Brian gasped but Lord March agreed at once, as if happy to see Elisa Carlisle in her true selfish colors.

'That is well, because I have always rather fancied myself hovering over a frail and delicate "Auriane". It would hardly be the same at all if she were spotted with mud and showered with the dust of common folk.'

It would be difficult to say which of them, Elisa or Brian, was more caught by surprise but Elisa recovered first.

'How delightful, My Lord! You are to play that bloodthirsty beast, Lord Raven. I do hope you will be as successful in your reading as Squire Diddlecomb was.'

His Lordship further confounded Brian Clifford by the grave answer that did not quite extinguish the mischievous light in his eyes.

'I promise to do my best, though I can see the competition of Squire Diddlecomb is severe. I will trust you to give me every assistance, Miss Carlisle.'

'Your obedient servant as always, Sir.' She curtsied low.

Before she could withdraw from the forceful grip of his fingers he took her by the wrist and pulled her across the ground to the open door of the almshouse. She went, protesting all the way. An aged, gray face stared from the doorway but gave no indication that the man (or was it female?) noticed Elisa. He reached out a clawed hand and mumbled something as Lord March passed.

His Lordship's voice, sardonic, teasing and sometimes insulting when he spoke to Elisa, was surprisingly warm as he gave the man reassurance: 'Your new blanket will arrive within the hour, Neddy. That will make you snug.'

Then he turned his attention to Elisa. 'Eleven people in one room. Three families. You see the good you will be accomplishing with the *Vampyr*?'

'Yes, yes. Please, let me go.'

She tried to wrench her hand away from him. No doubt he thought she had no feelings, that she was cold to these gray, defeated faces and what they told her of their life. Quite the reverse was true. Her dreams were too often crowded with such phantoms. She knew a great deal more about them than did Jeremy March.

It was Brian who said firmly, 'Sir, you are hurting Miss Carlisle.'

She gave him a grateful look, aware at the same time that several of the room's wretched inhabitants were looking anxiously from her to Lord March, afraid a quarrel might put His Lordship in a bad mood with them. The scene and his own actions had clearly embarrassed March who released her at once with a brusque, 'Sorry!'

Then he went on inquiring as to the problems of the men and women who crowded around him now. There were half a dozen cots and trundle beds in the room, besides the table and a big, worn dish rack on the wall. Instead of dishes, however, the shelves were loaded down with the lifetime possessions of the tenants, bundles containing clothing and various little treasures.

Elisa was ashamed of her cowardice, especially as she could not help hearing the complaints of the others who had been sitting on stools around the old, scarred deal table. Their wants were curious; yet they were also heartbreaking to her. They evoked thoughts almost too painful to bear.

A witch-like female, with an exceedingly sharp nose and no teeth, mumbled, 'A cloth for the table, Sir. That'll make it all tidy-like. Last one went and wore out.'

159

A younger woman with hands red and swollen by chilblains and cold water, asked for 'More spoons, if it please Your Ludship. They's some as steals 'em.'

A child peeped out from behind the woman's skirts which had been turned several times, the way Molly Catlow used to turn and resew clothing for herself and the child Elsie. This child, a plain girl about seven, with speaking eyes, pointed to Elisa.

'Y'er a fair one. So fair.'

With a lump in her throat Elisa thanked her and tried to give her a smile. The girl was so fascinated by Elisa's jonquil silk and lace parasol that she lost interest in 'the fair one'. While March and Brian Clifford watched, the child reach out stealthily to touch the parasol. She passed gentle, grubby fingers over the lace. Her mother warned her in a low voice, 'Maggie, yer hands ain't washed,' but the girl was too enthralled to notice.

'Does it open up?'

'Very easily. Come and see.' Elisa led her out of doors into the blessed air and pushed open the parasol. Maggie shivered with pleasure.

'It be like a coteen you was to live under. A sunny coteen.'

'Very like.' Elisa struggled to keep her thoughts from wandering back and back. She liked the child. She pitied the mother and all the others. But she wanted to drive away these haunting memories, not drag them out to relive again. She looked to Brian for help. Brian would understand.

'I want her to have the parasol. Then I want to go. Will you walk back with me?'

'Certainly. Here, little girl. The pretty lady gives you the parasol. All for you.'

This produced confusion on all sides. Elisa knew it was a poor substitute for personal interest, or gifts of food or clothing, but she started to walk rapidly past the length of the almshouses toward the distant Hawtree house. She was aware that her quick departure had made a bad impression on everyone, especially Jeremy March, but she could not help it.

Brian hurried after her.

She said quickly, 'Come with me. I'll give you a purse for them, but I couldn't stay there. It is like reliving those years.'

'You contribute to them by the reading. You are doing enough.'

'I must give them something. For my cowardice. I'm running away from my past.' She hesitated. 'Lord March said something to you. What was it?'

'Nothing.' He was far too quick with his denial.

'Tell me.'

He blurted out, 'March doesn't understand. I think you should tell him.'

'Doesn't understand what? That I don't like poverty and wretchedness?'

'That you lived through this long ago. That it affects you. You are obsessed by those painful memories.'

It was maddening to have her own words and, worse, her own thoughts, hurled back at her. She stopped in the road, shaking with anger. 'Are you telling me I am a candidate for Bedlam?'

'Good God, no, Elisa! I merely wanted to explain why he said that to you just now. He didn't know the truth.'

She glanced over her shoulder. Lord March was still taking note of the needs and desires of the tenants at the various doorways. 'What did he say?'

Brian was uncomfortable. 'Some nonsense in bad taste. About that play the two of you are performing with Lady Hawtree.'

'What nonsense?'

'Something about your blood being very cold to drink but he would do his best. He was trying to be amusing. You know how sardonic he can be at times.'

She had been excited and thrilled when she first learned that Lord March would play Lord Raven. Now, she thought: 'By heaven! we will see whose blood is cold, my fine vampyr!'

CHAPTER FOURTEEN

All those guests who had paid even a farthing over twenty guineas to the Almshouse Project were permitted to visit the 'actresses' backstage. This produced a traffic problem in the music room (females) and Sir Hugo's bookroom (males) where the players waited on either side of the Grand Salon for their entrance.

Eventually, it was agreed that no one should stay more than five minutes. It was also agreed by all who saw them that Gwenna Hawtree and Elisa Carlisle presented a breathtaking contrast.

Gwenna, her long body gowned in black with an assortment of gold jewelry, was the evil vampyr, consort of the demonic King Vampyr, Lord Raven. Elisa, all in white silk-gauze over an underdress of silk, wore her diamond parure, a set of jewels that had been carefully chosen over the years, modest by comparison with some of the ladies in the Prince Regent's set, and some in the audience, but exquisite in their cut. She wore her lustrous hair unconfined and took care to accentuate this delicate look by wearing light paint and powder.

With genuine feeling Brian Clifford informed the ladies that the profits would be far more handsome than they had expected.

'You underestimated your neighbors' generosity,' he told Lady Hawtree but she laughed at his naiveté.

'Not in the least, my dear boy. You underestimate their curiosity to see the infamous Miss Carlisle –' as Elisa frowned she summed up – 'and the absurd Lady Hawtree. They fully expect me to make a cake of myself before them all.' She winked at Brian who was not unmoved by all this attention. 'How disappointed they will be if I fail them!'

A bit flustered, he contradicted her politely. 'I am certain that Your Ladyship could never do that.'

Both Lady Hawtree and Elisa laughed, just as his daughter Susan arrived to warn him that Lord March wanted to see him about some estate business.

Lady Hawtree cried, 'What? At a time like this? Ridiculous! I devoutly hope and trust he is at least dressed to go on-stage!

Susan's eyes sparkled. 'Indeed yes, My Lady. He is Lord Raven, right enough. Some of those silly females keep saying they adore him in that dreadful part. The Marchioness is in the bookroom with some other ladies. She says he looks like a handsome Lucifer.'

Lady Hawtree, who was pleased with herself over the settings, asked, 'Have you seen our stage? Did you find the lights too dim? Clever of me to have the lamps placed behind those great lengths of blue gauze for the first act; don't you think? I borrowed every painting in the shire that could masquerade as a Grecian scene. You know: temple ruins; moonlight on the vine-dark sea.'

When Brian and Susan had gone Tuttle grumbled, 'The lass is right, you know. There's summat about that gentleman. I don't trust his likes. He watches you when you've no notion of it.'

'What could be more natural?' Gwenna Hawtree put in. She missed nothing. 'He loves you.'

But Tuttle was unflatteringly doubtful. 'Excusing the liberty, Ma'am, oh, he wants Elsie – Miss Carlisle. But there's more to it. A deal more. It's like a cat watching a – a bird.'

'What a very odd notion!' Lady Hawtree observed. 'And not entirely flattering to you, my dear. I should prefer to be the cat, myself.'

Somewhat belatedly, Elisa recovered from the chilling idea Tuttle had put forth.

'I agree with Her Ladyship.'

The sharp ringing of a silver dinner bell brought them all to attention.

'Curtain,' Lady Hawtree called. 'Our butler seems determined that we are all deaf. Where are those two silly parlor maids? They must follow me on-stage. And then you, Elisa. Ready?'

163

Amused by all this authority from a woman who had never set foot on a stage, Elisa nodded. She watched Gwenna Hawtree stride across the music room, neatly avoiding the harp in its protective cover, and step out into the narrow passage that separated the music room from the Salon and the improvised stage. Her two trembling maids followed her. One of them stumbled over her black robes but recovered before she entered the scene.

Leaving Tuttle behind her, Elisa moved out into the dark passage which was kept without illumination to protect the obscure lighting of the 'Stage'. The door closed behind her and she swung around nervously. Just as she was about to push the door ajar, Tuttle opened it from the inside and whispered hoarsely, 'All's well. Best luck, Girl.'

'Dear Tuttle, thank you.'

The darkness was not so oppressive with good, dependable Tuttle sharing it. Elisa straightened for her entrance, realizing that she had never been more nervous. The reason was not hard to guess. All that had been said about Jeremy March preyed upon her fears and, worse, upon her emotions.

She wanted him physically, his touch, his presence near her, and at the same time she was afraid of his motives. She knew that his feelings for her were ambivalent, but were they sinister? She could only hope Tuttle's suspicions were false.

She heard her cue and stepped gracefully onto the stage, looking about her as if in fear of her surroundings. She played an innocent young English traveler who has been deserted by her Greek guide and finds herself lost on some obscure Greek isle. Her fate was already foreseen by the 'wicked' Gwenna Hawtree and her minions who informed the audience that they would tell their master, Lord Raven. He was always looking for fresh blood, preferably virgin.

Elisa had been afraid of audience reaction over casting the notorious Elisa Carlisle as a virgin, but the set and particularly the lighting had been so well planned that the crowded salon didn't have time to do more than murmur for a few seconds before Elisa wandered, wraith-like and terrified, onto the scene.

Her usual command of the audience did not fail her now. Among those bejewelled creatures in the darkness and the gossiping whispers about her there were murmurs of admiration that reached her across the covered footlight lamps. They renewed her faith in her own small but special talent.

'Auriane' searched for the guide who had deserted her in this godforsaken spot. One of the parlor maids fluttered around upstage behind her, adding a bit of atmosphere. When the girl exited Elisa sensed the tension in herself as she spoke the lines which cued the first entrance of 'Lord Raven'.

From the stir and buzz of excitement in the audience she knew Lord Jeremy March had emerged onto the scene, moving through the deep blue light behind her. She felt a twinge of genuine terror. What did he look like? Some monstrous black apparition, hovering over her as those great wings had beaten relentlessly over her when she was a child, bringing ill-fortune and death?

Her fingers curled into her palms. The sharp little pain strengthened her. She was stronger than her mother. She would not let herself be cowed by whatever shocks Jeremy March had planned for her. She turned slowly on cue, beginning to recite her lines, during which she would ask if this stranger could show her the correct path to the village below.

The sight of him startled her in spite of all her preconceived ideas. Neither Susan Clifford's comments nor the obvious excitement of those who had seen His Lordship in the male dressing-room quite prepared her. She was shaken by his actual presence. He stood on a makeshift rock some yards behind her, his tall figure shrouded in a black cloak very like the wings she had dreamed of when she was a child. The blue light made him look as pale as the Undead when surrounded by so much darkness. His hair, his cloak, even his cravat accentuated his evil persona. But that was all mere theatre.

What shocked and fascinated her most was his easy command of the stage, the way as he moved forward his eyes caught the faint, muffled glow of the footlight lamps and burned like pinpoints of fire as they gazed down at her.

165

It seemed to her that at this minute he took his amateur acting role too seriously. It was obvious that the audience believed he was Lucifer. There were moments when Elisa almost shared that belief.

He spoke his lines to her in his low, well-modulated voice that had just a faint throb of something else: the promise of passion. Still, he was all politeness to the young stranger who had lost her guide, introduced himself as Lord Raven and offered to escort her back to the villa of her English friends.

They played out the scene and the audience relaxed, but out of the corner of her eye Elisa noticed the women leaning forward in chairs, sofas and fauteuils. They did not want to miss a single nuance of these doings between their own Lord March and the notorious Carlisle woman. From their tense positions and almost suspended breath it was clear that they expected scandalous events to come.

When the mysterious Lord Raven bent over her hand and his lips brushed her fingertips in a highly erotic way, Elisa heard a single sigh that rose from more than one female in the audience. She could not blame them. She found her own senses aroused. Worst of all, he must have guessed as much; for his gaze was fixed upon her breasts with their thin veiling of silk and gauze which did not conceal her rapid pulse-beat.

From this first familiarity he led her toward what was presumably the downward path to civilization across the stage. He had chosen to believe the role required him to run his hand between the gauze and the silk of her costume and clasp her tightly under her warm breasts. There was a well-defined moan of pleasure – and envy? – from some women in the audience.

His whisper to her was meant to convey some sinister spell. What he actually said was: 'Your flesh is softer than ever. It recalls a certain delightful encounter. I behaved stupidly that night.'

She smiled up into his eyes in her role as 'Auriane', showing her teeth, while she whispered sharply, 'Your insult was unforgivable.'

'Not entirely, I hope.'

166

How smug he was! As they made their exit off-stage she could only rely upon the ancient complaint, 'Let me go. You are behaving like a brute.'

'If I must.' But his eyes were amused. He did not take her seriously. He released her and her flesh felt uncomfortably cold after the heat of his embrace. Damn him!

The end of the first act brought enthusiastic and prolonged applause. Backstage in the music room Gwenna Hawtree pronounced the evening a huge success.

'My dear,' she confided to Elisa who was busy changing with Tuttle's help, 'I truly believe the man would have attacked you on-stage but for the audience.'

Elisa hoped to silence all this speculation.

'He was inspired by the applause and all those gushing women in the audience.'

'I shouldn't be at all sure of that.' Gwenna stopped match-making long enough to scold her abigail for scratching her check while rearranging Her Ladyship's coiffure. 'Especially,' she added in her tantalizing way, 'since his hints about a prospective Lady March.'

'What!'

Elisa was not the only one who reacted violently. Tuttle muttered, 'God save us!'

'He is thinking of you, my dear.'

But Elisa recovered enough to dismiss the preposterous notion that Lord March's intentions toward her were legitimate. She was the woman he blamed for his brother's suicide. And there were other insurmountable barriers. A man of Jeremy March's family and lineage would never soil his name by joining it to that Wicked Enchantress, that 'Circe' who turned men into swine.

'Lady Hawtree's humor takes an odd turn at times. May we change the subject?'

Gwenna laughed and shrugged. 'By all means.'

The second act included some gory but amusing by-play between Lady Hawtree and her 'victim', a local Greek merchant, played by Squire Diddlecomb under the handicap of extreme stage fright. The squire read aloud his entire role, including

167

the stage directions originally dictated by Lady Hawtree to her bookish abigail. This was not easy during a scene in which Lady Hawtree led the fat squire off-stage to drink his blood. The audience tittered and then guffawed, and the squire beamed with pride. He had provided entertainment despite his artistic limitations.

While Elisa played a scene with Gwenna Hawtree and then with the squire who ogled her neck hungrily – he had been turned into a vampyr by Her Ladyship – Elisa tried to prepare her nerves for the King Vampyr's appearance and the seduction to follow. She was determined not to give him any indication of his effect upon her.

All in vain. The nervous tension beginning to sweep through the audience was contagious. When Lord Raven appeared on-stage to rescue her from the squire's attentions Elisa too expected the worst, whatever that might be. But he played lightly, charmingly, with scarcely a hint of what Gwenna Hawtree had referred to in the dialogue as 'his fell design'. He flirted with Elisa, presenting himself as her rescuer, and gradually, as the scene progressed, becoming the smooth but powerful aggressor.

The audience rustled excitedly, hoping that the worst would be enacted in front of them. Gossip had already reached them about the peer's strange interest in the woman responsible for his young brother's suicide.

Elisa had been lulled into false security by his easy manner early in the scene. She knew that it would end with herself in Lord Raven's arms, with his head bent over her throat as Lady Hawtree's best emerald drapes slowly closed. She was prepared to writhe out of his clasp – and if he caused trouble, she would raise her voice, making his efforts absurd.

Having thought over Gwenna's suspicions, she decided the whole affair was Jeremy March's deliberate scheme to sleep with her, and then turn from her. Perhaps that was meant to be part of his revenge for Arthur's death. He had known Gwenna Hawtree would tell her those preposterous suspicions of hers. He must think Elisa was so ambitious she would be easy to seduce. She

168

had never objected to his unexpected kisses. If this was indeed his plan, it was despicable.

But all her excellent preparations for defense had not allowed for his performance. He approached the climax of the scene with the same ease that marked the rest of his acting in Lady Hawtree's little melodrama. He wove his sensuous spell over the helpless 'Auriane', as required, drawing her to him while she played her part. He bent his head to her lips and she steeled herself to feel nothing, but he was using Lord Raven to help Lord March's conquest. He lowered his head further, his mouth lingering on her throat.

There were no words of guidance in the manuscript to indicate the power of his lovemaking. She found it impossible to resist, despite the script's instructions to fight him off. She was sure his lips burned the flesh of her throat and breast, but he was surprisingly strong and she found herself clinging to him, sharing the sensual excitement of his mouth and hands, and his body.

She almost forgot where she was and what she must do. She was expected to cry for help as the curtains closed. She remembered barely in time.

When they were beyond the Argus-eyes of the audience, she tried to slip out of his arms. Her effort produced nothing but the tightening of the vice that held her hard against his groin and thigh.

She twisted her head to avoid his lips, but she fancied that his kiss pierced her flesh like a vampyr's bite.

Desperate to avoid her own weakness, she whispered, 'The scene is over. Finished.'

'No.' He silenced her protests, his mouth covering hers with a passion he evidently could not control. She was frightened by her own mixed response.

The voices of those backstage separated them at last. Luckily, Elisa thought, everyone considered the predicament of the two leading characters amusing. Lady Hawtree warned them with bubbles of amusement in her voice. 'You must save some of that passion for the final act, else our friends out there will feel cheated.'

Elisa did not look at Lord March. She was still a trifle dazed by the extent of her own feelings, an emotion she once reserved only for the stage. It was strange and terrifying to be so enthralled by another human being.

She could scarcely imagine how they would get through the last two acts with the passionate confrontation between Auriane and Lord Raven, and the vanquishing of the vampyr, but when the curtains parted for the third act Elisa was surprised to find that Jeremy March behaved with the most maddening indifference. A young Greek fisherman (played by the Honorable Barnabus Rudd, aged sixteen, with boyish devotion to the famed actress) rescued Auriane before the monstrous vampyr could reduce her to one of his bloodsucking followers.

By the end of the act Elisa began to wonder if she had imagined March's earlier passion. Was it her own desire that had disturbed her so much? Still puzzled, she passed indifferently before March on her way to the music room, ignoring his smile and his wave of the hand as she passed him. In the hall, illuminated by the light from the music room, she was stopped abruptly by a sight she had dreaded.

Captain Ronald Hawtree barred her way. She was shocked by the change in the dashing young officer who had spent so much time pursuing her not so long ago. Unwillingly, she had glanced first at the empty sleeve. But the change went further. His highly correct evening attire did not suit him nearly as well as the scarlet tunic of former days. And the arrogant confidence was gone. His full face had thinned noticeably. His heavy lips turned down at the corners. He looked less hard than cynical.

'Ma'am? You're looking your usual enchanting self.'

She could not miss the resentment in his voice and manner. 'Thank you, Captain. I am happy to see you.' She had never felt so ill-at-ease. 'I trust the theatricals will be a success. The cause is well worth it.'

'How can it fail, Ma'am? With my father's wife so busy at the helm.'

She gave him her hand with some hope of making peace between them. He did not seem to see it and she went on to the

170

music room. She turned as she passed the big, covered harp, and glanced back. It was disturbing to see that he was now in close conversation with Jeremy March. Both men looked her way and then continued their conversation.

She took a deep breath, crossed the room and motioned to Tuttle who brought her final costume. This was a curious, shroud-like drapery of black over the white gown of her first scenes. She would make the transformation from darkness to light, black to white, in the final moments of Gwenna Hawtree's play.

Everyone else was so busy discussing mistakes in the previous acts, or the lively conduct of the audience, that, fortunately, no one mentioned Captain Hawtree to her. It was an enormous relief. She was afraid Gwenna Hawtree might say something cutting and contemptuous about her step-son, as she always did.

The unexpected sight of Captain Hawtree had further unnerved Elisa and she went through her later scenes in a mechanical fashion, occasionally forgetting lines and dropping cues. The audience seemed unaware of her condition but it was noticed by some backstage and, of course, Tuttle knew at once.

'You afraid of that man?' She demanded audibly enough to be heard by the marchioness who had decided at last to visit the ladies in their 'tiring room'.

'Not in the least.' Elisa pulled Tuttle over to the long windows overlooking the Italian Garden and a tiny, decorative lake that shimmered in the moonlight. Elisa avoided the view. It reminded her too vividly of Lord Raven's entrance tonight. She still remembered the terrifying effect it had on her when she turned suddenly to find his eyes upon her with that mesmerizing power.

'Tuttle, the young Captain is here. He hates me. I'm sure of it.'

Tuttle said, 'I seen him. His kind has to blame somebody and you make it easy.' She looked hard at Elisa. 'Elsie, was it you that give him the gun he was going to use on the March lad? Did you tell him things he believed that wasn't true, like you being his mistress and his alone?'

171

Elisa thought back. 'No. I never tell anyone, in so many words.'

'Well, it aint your fault he mistook you.'

Was it though, in truth? Had she given Hawtree, and especially Arthur March, some such idea because she liked them, needed their devotion, and because of the gifts? Was it in payment for the diamond trinkets with which they showered her? Undoubtedly, they understood that the jewels were the price of her favors.

She was not happy when she returned to the stage for her final scene in which she would stand up to Lord Raven, defy him with crucifix and holy wafers and see him slink away into the darkness. The hall was empty. Captain Hawtree must have gone back to his chair. Since both Gwenna and the Rudd boy played their parts very professionally, Elisa began to relax.

Then came the climax in which she would drive back the forces of darkness and stand triumphant as the velvet portieres used as theatre curtains came together. Lord Raven entered, looking much like Jeremy March entering his box at the theatre. More at ease now, Elisa spoke her lines, aware of an intense relief that his playing on her emotions was about to end.

He stalked her slowly, according to his stage directions, and across the room she removed the rosary and crucifix Lady Hawtree had borrowed from the Catholic marchioness. As she started to extend them before her, her attention was caught by a movement at the side door which opened from the hall and the music room beyond. Captain Ronald Hawtree stood in the doorway, unseen by the audience, his body – especially the empty sleeve – outlined by the light in the distant music room.

It was all wrong. He mustn't be there. Outlined as he was in that strange way, he appeared to be a phantom. His presence destroyed her concentration. She raised the crucifix with a slender hand that shook noticeably. All her lines had been expunged from her mind.

Still, Lord Raven came on. His eyes held her, willing her to remain motionless. She fought with the reminder that if he had been any other man she might believe in his love. But his brother's death had not been forgiven as she hoped. It was too

172

great a tragedy to go unpunished. Jeremy March could not have changed this rapidly. He was goading her, as he had done in the vault. He wanted her to believe in the honesty of his intentions. And then what? The presence of Captain Hawtree and his close conversation with Lord March had warned her.

March's fingers touched hers. The rosary dropped into his palm. This was not a part of the action and she knew it. He reached for her. She tried to move, to retreat, but her body would not respond. She could not run in the other direction. She would come face to face with the armless man. Her head ached too much to let her think properly.

With an enormous effort she swung around to avoid March, crashed against a long Chippendale table behind her, and became aware of a humming in her head that made her think she was in a meadow on a warm summer day.

Aware of impending collapse, she tried to fall with all her well-trained grace.

She remembered nothing more.

CHAPTER FIFTEEN

The ridiculous collapse, the first that had ever happened to Elisa on-stage, ended on the long sofa by the hearth in Sir Hugo's study, where she was taken to recover. She opened her eyes to find at least a dozen people, mostly women, crowded around her, staring, curious. She was sure only Tuttle really cared.

Elisa was well aware that her problem had been emotional. She was eternally terrified of hearing those terrible words that condemned her mother: 'She belongs in Bedlam.' She murmured a more prosaic explanation, blaming a physical injury.

'My side. When I turned I must have bruised my ribs.' She grimaced. 'Here.' She tried to sit up but was surprised to find that her entire body ached as if it really had been injured.

'Best leave the lass to sleep it off. She's been wretchedly frightened,' Tuttle said, but nobody paid much attention to her.

'Small wonder. His Lordship put a scare in me as well,' Susan Clifford remarked as her father touched Elisa's side through her silk stage garments in a professional way.

'Does it hurt here? Or here?' Brian's manner was sympathetic as always and when Elisa looked up into his kindly eyes she was ashamed for deceiving him.

'It only aches. I don't believe anything was broken. I shouldn't have turned so suddenly. It was because – because –'

'Because I had asked the lady to marry me,' a well-known voice cut in from somewhere behind the eager, interested women. Heads screwed around as if at a mechanic's touch. Elisa's eyes opened as wide as anyone else's. There could be no mistaking Lord Jeremy March's sardonic tones. During the time they all stared, he made his way between Lady Hawtree and a shocked and resentful Brian Clifford, who told him severely, 'At a moment like this, your humor is out of place, Sir.'

Lord March did not take offense.

'But I am quite in earnest. I will admit my ardor took even me by surprise, and I fear I was too precipitate in announcing it to Miss Carlisle.'

Elisa's heart was beating fast and she covered her throat with one hand so that no one would notice the betrayal of her rapid pulse. How they would laugh at her behind her back for taking him seriously, no matter what his protests might be!

'Precipitate and absurd, My Lord, as you are entirely aware.' He still looked like a romantic Lord Raven. She thought he was handsome enough to spin his web once more. This time she would be on her guard.

Everyone was looking from Lord March to Elisa and back again. It was now His Lordship's turn to toss the ball. He seemed unaffected by his audience.

'Not absurd to anyone who saw you tonight, Miss Carlisle. And I am quite in earnest, with all these charming ladies for witness. Not to mention my friend Clifford here.'

Brian was not mollified. He cushioned Elisa's neck with his arm so she could sit up. He ignored Lord March's remark. The proposal had been conducted in blatant bad taste but, like many aristocrats, perhaps His Lordship felt above such prosaic things as good manners.

'Do go away,' was all the answer he received from Elisa. Sitting up now she was able to see men gathered in the doorway, curious to discover her condition. The two men she saw at once were plump Sir Hugo Hawtree frowning, and beside him, Captain Hawtree, with the empty sleeve that haunted Elisa. He was studying Lord March in a reflective way. Probably questioning his sincerity, if not his sanity. Elisa could scarcely blame him.

Tuttle bustled around elbowing ladies out of the way with considerably more authority than that permitted to the Hawtree servants.

'The girl is tired after all that performing falderal. She needs rest. Go about your business, Ladies.' She added her last jab for Lord March. 'And you too, my lad. We've had enough of your jesting for this night.'

'Aye. As you say, Mam.'

Lord March pretended to be cowed by her but he reached for Elisa who shrank away. She didn't want a repeat of his tantalizing jests. He was all innocence, except his eyes which did not hide a glint of mischief.

'I'll just carry Miss Carlisle to her chamber, where she may rest until we can work out the time and place where the bans will be posted.'

Brian thrust him aside. 'I'll take the lady. We are old and very close friends.'

Lord March yielded gracefully but kept watching Elisa's face. Was it her imagination or did he look less amused now? Perhaps he expected her to take seriously his preposterous proposal. Until very recently she would have given her soul to hear that, but suspicion gripped her, especially after his cruel attempt to embarrass and humiliate her with Captain Hawtree tonight.

Still, she wanted him. She had never known any feeling as strong in her as this passion for Jeremy March. But could he forget Arthur's death, bury it under his desire to have her? She could not believe in such a miracle.

Brian picked her up. He followed Lady Hawtree, who took a lamp from her abigail and lighted the way into the hall and up the heavy staircase. Tuttle trailed behind, admonishing everyone. 'Go about telling your audience Miss Carlisle's all right and tight again. She was just set afright by His Lordship.' She gave Lord March a parting shot. 'You was too fearsome by far, Sir. Mustn't take your part so serious-like.'

Lord March bowed. 'You are quite right, Mam. I must remember, next time I tread the boards.'

Some of the women laughed but Elisa, in Brian's arms, distinctly heard him say at the foot of the stairs, 'All the same, Ladies, my offer was perfectly genuine. I intend to make Miss Carlisle Lady March.'

176

Giggles and gasps followed this disclosure. Only Sir Hugo demanded,'You cannot mean it, March? Not with that female's past. Good Lord, man. You'll be cut by every acquaintance.' There was a little silence. Elisa held her breath. Then Lord March said, 'Yes. I suppose we shall be. That would seem to be inevitable.' These words sounded a bit grim. Almost flatly so. A challenge.

Or a promise?

Dr Clifford left Elisa on an Elizabethan bed under its heavy tester and velvet curtains that Elisa herself pushed open. No one made an effort to undress her. Brian suggested to Tuttle, 'Let her rest. Don't permit His Lordship, with his bad taste and ridiculous jokes, to see her until she is stronger. I'll ride over tomorrow.'

By the time Elisa tried to thank him he was gone. She found herself alone with Tuttle who had run everyone but Lady Hawtree out of the bed chamber. Gwenna too left after a last reassurance: 'My dear, he means it. I could swear he intends to marry you.'

'That's as may be. He lied about the cause of my absurd faint. He had not asked me to marry him. That was a later idea of his. He knew it would disconcert me.'

'Disconcert? To receive a genuine offer from the most eligible man of your acquaintance?'

'Am I to be flattered by his public proposal? It was almost insulting.'

'Let me tell you, Elisa, you will never achieve anything better. A peer of the realm. A war hero. And to think, I promoted the marriage. What triumph! Marrying him would set all those tales about you at an end. Sleep well and dream of playing your greatest role. Lady Elisa March. You will be enormously rich, my dear. Beyond your wildest dreams.'

She left then, careful to leave the door ajar after a knowing glance at Elisa who sat up, pushing against Tuttle's hand.

'This is all pointless. I am perfectly well. We've finished the reading. They say it has done well for their charity. So – it is time we return to London. Strawbridge must find a theatre that will accept me without too many oranges thrown at me.'

177

'If you will talk rubbish, Girl, at least wait 'til you've had some sleep. You best change to your bedclothes. What say?'

Elisa ached too much to argue the matter. But one vision still haunted her. 'You did see Captain Hawtree. I know he curses me. I felt it when I was on-stage.' She raised up again with an effort, leaning back on her elbows. 'Tuttle, dear, would you look out into the hall and see if he is hovering somewhere about?'

Muttering, Tuttle obeyed her, crossing the room, peering up and down the hall and shaking her head. She came back to announce, 'He's not about. You really think that silly fellow could put the evil eye on you?'

The absurdity of the idea should have struck Elisa, but she couldn't forget what she herself had read into the young Captain's blank stare. It was so different from the lively, arrogant self-confidence she remembered in Captain Hawtree's expression before his accident.

Nevertheless, she didn't want Tuttle to guess how shattered her nerves had become of late. She was anxious that no one, including Tuttle, should know how desperately she hoped that Jeremy March was sincere in his proposal, preposterous though the whole idea might be.

Elisa was surprised to find herself dropping off to sleep before changing to her night things.

When she awakened shortly after dawn her fantastic hopes of the previous night had dissolved. She realized how absurd was his disclosure and yet, how typical of Lord March's humor. No doubt this was just another form of his revenge against her for her past.

With this in mind, she washed and dressed and was ready to travel when Tuttle pushed the door open, knocked on the panel and brought in fresh warm water. Even knowing Elisa, she was surprised to find her thoroughly ready for the long journey back to London.

'Do we walk?' Tuttle asked flatly.

'I hope not. I intend to speak to a stableboy. Or the second coachman, if I don't run upon Lady Hawtree in the meanwhile.'

A minute's reflection decided Tuttle. 'It's as well. There's nothing for us here.'

Half an hour later, thanks to the insistence of Sir Hugo Hawtree, Elisa and Tuttle were on their way to London in one of the Hawtree closed carriages, behind two of Sir Hugo's matched pairs. The women had come upon him on the path to the stables and the meeting was not a pleasant one, in spite of Elisa's efforts. She knew he despised her. This knowledge only made his perfect manners harder to endure. They were so different from the easy, joking, flirtatious manner of the stout man she had known before the accident.

He was startled to see the women. He had obviously been out riding and was returning to the house, tired, breathless, and dusty. But he managed to ask pleasantly enough, 'Do you care to ride, Ladies? I'll speak to Rees. He knows our mounts very well and can help you.'

Elisa had explained that they must return to London at once. 'Some pressing business.'

He had leaped upon this excuse with embarrassing haste and led both women to the stables. After that, it was only a matter of minutes before the women were on their way. They were escorted by a trusted coachman, and even a footman-outrider armed with a pistol against highwaymen.

They remained two nights at local inns where the coachman saw to the needs of the ladies. He demanded each time they receive the best bedchamber with its adjoining private parlour, and argued when Elisa insisted on paying the reckoning.

The usually suspicious Tuttle was impressed.

'That Sir Hugo, I think he's forgot all his crotchets. He has a fondness for you again. Like he used to.'

'To the contrary. He is desperately anxious to be quit of us.'

By the time they reached the outskirts of London it seemed clear that Elisa was right. The last hours of the ride threatened to become a race with any vehicle they encountered. When the two Hawtree servants had set the women down on their doorstep in Portman Square, they scarcely stayed long enough to accept

179

Elisa's thanks or the money she pressed into their palms in gratitude for their efforts.

McFee, his small body puffed up with importance, met Elisa with a catalogue of problems which he poured out from the moment she entered the immaculate white reception hall and all the way up the stairs to the sitting-room that adjoined her bedroom.

'The new cook's been nipping at the port.'

'All cooks nip at the port, when they don't nip at the Madeira or some other potion. I believe it's in their agreement when they are hired.'

'And that actor that caused you all the trouble, he was here.'

This startled her. 'Not Tregaran!'

'Aye. The very same. Sat in that striped satin chair in the Small salon and said he'd come to make amends for his behavior.'

'What? I can't believe it. He is much too proud.'

'He's much too anxious to be seen in your acting company,' Tuttle put in.

Still and all, it was good news of a sort. 'I must confess, he was a good actor, even if his feelings for me are less than cordial.'

'They aren't all like young Master Tregaran, with their nasty little reasons. Others is different. His Ludship, he was right pleasant, you might say.'

She sat up straight. 'Lord March? Here?'

'Sure and certain, Ma'am. You missed him by half the day, at that Hawtree place. He comes riding up to London this morning and wanting to see you, Ma'am. Where was you, he wants to know. Says he stopped by the Hawtree female and she sends him here. Mighty fast travelling, I'd say.'

'I can't imagine what sent His Lordship to see me.' She closed her mind to the obvious hope.

'As you say, Ma'am. There's a few other matters but Tuttle and me, between us, we can settle them.'

180

He was leaving when he added, 'This Ludship, he says he'll be back.'

She tried not to sound too excited. 'Really?' She made a pretense of calm. 'We must be certain the best Madeira is available.'

Ignoring His Lordship's presence in London, Elisa sent off a message to Enos Strawbridge, asking the theatrical manager to find her bookings where her recent bad reputation would have no effect on the box office. She added that Peter Tregaran had returned to the fold.

'Could even bring in more folk to gawk at him and the Enchantress,' Tuttle reminded her hopefully. 'You two were mighty popular together.'

'Don't,' Elisa walked away, tired after the journey, uncertain about her future, and made more nervous by the possibility of Lord March's return.

Late in the afternoon she heard the elegant old fox-head door knocker rap several times and hurried down the stairs, relieved that at least her manager had not failed her.

She was so pleased by his loyalty that she called out, 'Strawbridge, how good of you to come at once! We must discuss all our new plans...'

Her voice trailed off in confusion. Lord March looked up at her as she stopped, dumbfounded, on the staircase. His smile, she thought, was not so much warm as amused. He offered his hat and a six-caped greatcoat to the efficient Tabitha who had trained under Tuttle.

Adopting what she assumed was his own mood, Elisa walked down the rest of the stairs with much more dignity. She extended her hand and welcomed him with gracious formality, as though she had forgotten his extraordinary behavior during the performance of *The Vampyr*.

'Good evening, My Lord. This is an unexpected –'

'Pleasure?' he asked, with an eyebrow raised in mockery.

'Honor, I was about to say. You must be carrying a message from the Cliffords. Or perhaps Lady Hawtree?'

'May I not carry a message of my own, Miss Carlisle?'

181

·While she fumbled for a suitable reply, he moved her gently aside with one hand and made a sweeping gesture toward the staircase.

'I am perfectly prepared to settle the necessary matters here in the hall, but I should imagine any discussions about the special license, our place of residence, et cetera, might be conducted in more privacy. Let us say – that romantic boudoir of tender memory.'

It was too much. She backed away. Her knees were trembling. 'Please don't go on and on with this game, My Lord. If you wish to make me suffer, you have succeeded.' She reached for the door latch. 'Your brother would show mercy.'

For the first time she had caught him unawares. She was sure she gave him something he had not thought about before. His gaze softened while he studied her face. But something happened then, an all too familiar hardness, and she wondered if she had lost him forever.

He laughed. It was a light, easy laugh, but it hurt. 'Arthur's little gift becomes you, *Circe.*'

Guiltily, she touched her ears with fingers that shook. She was wearing a pair of diamond ear-bobs. She had purchased them in London after her first triumph at the Adelphi Theatre. The knowledge that Jeremy March had been wrong in his suspicion gave her a wonderful sense of triumph.

'I am afraid Arthur would not recognize these, Your Lordship. Are you acquainted with Rundle's, the jewellers?'

She had confused him and was delighted. He gave her a wry little look. 'I know them. Perhaps too well.' He felt even less sure of himself when she took off one of the jewels and forced it into his palm.

'You will see a very small pearl at the upper point of the diamond cut. It is not a March heirloom.'

He examined the diamond, seeing at once that the stone was not flawless, nor was it as large as the heirloom she had received from Arthur March.

'I returned the March heirloom after you so kindly mentioned it to me,' she reminded him, pouring on the coals of fire.

182

'I see. It must have slipped my mind.'

A precious heirloom had slipped his mind.

Anger, pride and a sickening disappointment were all carefully concealed by her polite farewell.

'And now, Your Lordship, I believe we have no more business with each other. I will bid you a very good day.'

It was astonishing but this little error on his part had affected him curiously. She suspected he wasn't used to finding himself wrong.

He juggled the earring in his hand absently. He had already forgotten it.

'I have been unpardonably rude to you.'

She found the word too soft for the offense but she smiled and nodded. 'Rude? Yes.'

He was recovering, however. 'So let me put the matter to you, now that you have had time to think. I assume a special license would be preferable. Anything more elaborate –' He cleared his throat and started again. 'Because of my brother.'

She fumbled for a chair, finding nothing but the wall behind her. 'You are being absurd. You don't love me.'

He did not argue the point as she hoped he would. He stopped her retreat by stretching one hand out toward the wall, so close his knuckles caressed her hair as his arm imprisoned her.

'I have never known precisely what love is. Perhaps you are the one to teach me.' He looked down into her eyes.

She read some emotion there, probably more passion than love. Whatever it was, the knowledge that it existed was exciting to her.

Was he tempting her only to hurt her again? But she could not bear to lose the passion that his eyes promised.

She managed to moisten her lips long enough to whisper, 'Let me teach you. I love you enough for both of us.'

She believed it. It must be so. She wanted so desperately to have it so.

CHAPTER SIXTEEN

The carriage of Lord and Lady March pulled up before the Cotswold gold front of March Hall on a matching golden day in October. They were met by the Cliffords, little Mrs Ponsonby, and assorted unknown but welcoming servants – everyone, in fact, except Tuttle and Elisa's own household.

At this moment Elisa Carlisle March said to her husband, 'I never knew I could be so happy.' She did know that she had said this once, somewhere on-stage, before a glittering jewelled audience, her voice throbbing with tenderness. But today she meant it and found there was no new way to express her joy, except to kiss the hand he offered to help her down the coach steps.

'It is a comfortable old place,' he agreed absently. He was studying her as she descended.

During three days of travel since their quiet marriage ceremony performed by the vicar of a church near Oxford, he had often watched her. She assumed that, like a newly hired parlour maid, she was still on her preferment. She must pass certain tests before he accepted her affections as genuine.

As for his love, she found it fully equal to her own, though he preferred to call it passion. His assaults upon her body were sometimes unexpected but never unwelcome. He knew exactly how to arouse her, which was not surprising when she remembered what Arthur had said about him, that he had his 'lady-birds' but never took love seriously. He remembered his father too well, according to Arthur.

184

Sir Jeremiah March, his father, who was not a peer despite his ancestral glories, had been a crony of the Regent in earlier days when the first gentleman of Europe was only the Prince of Wales. As a result of his association with acknowledged mistresses, he had given his wife much grief and humiliation. Elisa suspected that Lord Jeremy March inherited his father's passion and for some inexplicable reason he had chosen to expend it upon Elisa. She welcomed this exquisitely sensuous invasion of her body with the same degree of passion. Her erotic charm had been tender in dealing with Arthur, practised in her dealings with Captain Hawtree, capricious with others. Before she met Jeremy March all her knowledge of male weaknesses had been carefully cultivated. If she still did not understand why he had chosen to marry her, of all women, she was so desperate for his love that she simply told herself if she lived entirely for him, some day he would know what love is.

Hardest of all was the temporary loss of Tuttle. Jeremy wanted to bring Elisa at once to March Hall. She agreed. He explained that he wished her to rely upon him and not to upset March Hall's staff so soon by new authority from her own servants. 'Therefore, it would be best for the first few weeks if Tuttle remained behind, in charge of your London house.'

This seemed reasonable, painful though it was to accept, and a little frightening, too. No one knew her so well as Tuttle. Still, Elisa understood that Tuttle did not trust Lord March. Perhaps His Lordship sensed this.

Having seen to it that Tuttle and McFee witnessed the wedding itself, Elisa agreed to the rest, despite Tuttle's gruff, private warnings. Elisa would have agreed to anything if it made Jeremy discover he loved her. She wanted him to understand that she offered him this genuine emotion. No matter how much they 'made love', she was afraid he had not yet come to believe she gave him more than a sexual pleasure.

Nevertheless, the few days of their marriage had been the happiest of her life. She was no longer alone in the world, cut off from blood ties, from her mother long dead and her father, that unknown actor, who would never have acknowledged her.

185

Now, she belonged to someone and the world was bright, warm, comforting.

Moving gracefully up the long, shallow steps of the old house that welcomed her in the sunlight, Elisa did not reveal any of her uncertainties, or even her hopes, as she greeted Brian and a suddenly grown up Susan who seemed to ape the little housekeeper's self-satisfied and possessive manner. She was learning fast, Elisa thought. But she was very glad to see the girl, a familiar, friendly face among a dozen men and women who (Elisa was sure) knew her identity and resented her. There had been no mistress of March Hall in many years. She would have to use every grain of the charm that had been celebrated in the theatre.

Brian understood her feelings and tried to hide his own, but she knew he disapproved of what he saw as a fantastic misalliance.

While her husband spoke to the various servants individually, she murmured to Brian, only half-teasing, 'I know. You are shocked.'

'I am,' he confessed and then added surprisingly, 'You deserve better, Elisa.'

She laughed. 'But does Elsie Catlow?'

She read the deep sincerity in his eyes and looked away as he told her what he had always insisted, 'You know I have always preferred the honesty of Elsie Catlow. I am sorry you are ashamed of her. I never was.'

'My dear,' she said in tones worthy of Gwenna Hawtree, 'I despise Elsie Catlow. I have spent my life running away from that wretched little creature who was put upon by the entire world.'

'Then I am sorry for you.' He stepped aside, making way for Jeremy March.

His Lordship took Elisa's arm, drew her close to his body in one of the spontaneous gestures that gave her hope. It was not calculated but instinctive, and it seemed to prove to her that he genuinely cared for her in a way almost divorced from the sexual.

'Do you remember the first time you walked up those steps?' he asked.

'Very well. Though I scarcely thought I would return in quite this way.'

'Are you certain?' There was an edge to his voice now, one of the few times since their marriage three days before. She did not know how to convince him that her love for him had never been concerned with the material things he could offer her. It had been the same two nights ago when he insisted on adorning her satin and lace night robe with a necklace of dazzling rectangular-cut rubies, then fastening the long, drop, ruby earrings onto her ears. He had lifted her up in an impressively easy way and tossed her onto the bed.

He made love to her while the jewels pressed icily against her bare flesh. It was only afterward, when he slept and she stealthily removed the jewels, that she wondered if, once again, he was paying for the use of her body.

In any case, she seldom wore rubies. They were not flattering to her. Even more important, Captain Hawtree had once given her a ruby ring in an antique gold setting, and now, whenever she saw it, she was reminded of the blood he had shed in his quarrel over her.

She decided to return the ruby set to Jeremy the following morning, but when she packed to leave the inn she took up the heavy, blood-red jewels and ran them through her fingers, while the insidious thoughts nagged at her:

What if you are abandoned by him? What if, through some trick of fate, you find yourself as helpless as Molly Catlow was? These could pay for your freedom. Even if the world decides you are 'mad', as they said of your mother, this might be the only bribe left to you. Who knows?

She had thrust the velvet case down deep in her bandbox, beneath another of her husband's gifts, the set of lace lingerie made by the nuns of a Belgian convent. She drew her hand out of the bandbox, with the prickly sense of being watched. She turned her head and saw Jeremy looking at her with the little smile that she was afraid to read.

Today, the doors of her new home opened for Lord and Lady March and she answered her husband's jibe with glittering sweetness: 'I am quite certain, My Lord. It was not I who made the first advances that day.'

She had annoyed, or perhaps embarrassed him. He actually seemed to redden a little, probably because he remembered how he had kissed her while they stood in the very shadow of Arthur March's tomb. He was ashamed of that, as well he might be.

Stebbings, the March butler, saved the moment by his stiffly correct greeting. 'Welcome to March Hall, Your Ladyship.'

To Lord March he merely inclined his head, saying, 'Sir, it is good to have you back. Your Lordship was missed.'

As always, Elisa noted, her husband was interested in his properties and the lives he guarded.

'More trouble in the cottages? How are the new drains? You have found a lodging for Granny Skeen? And someone to look after her?'

Stebbings bowed. 'I believe Dr Clifford is attending to the matter of the Skeen woman. The drains are coming on. The cottages, as I am informed, will be fully repaired before Christmas.'

'Excellent. I see I must absent myself more often.' He looked around and motioned to Mrs Ponsonby who had come in behind them. 'Did I give you enough time to arrange the master apartments?'

'Yes, indeed, Your Lordship. Eight days. Quite ample.' The little woman bobbed two rapid curtsys. 'And Miss Clifford has been of great assistance to me. We hope – indeed, we trust – that Her Ladyship and you will find the apartments satisfactory.' She hadn't once looked at Elisa.

But Elisa was concerned about another piece of information she has just learned. Mrs Ponsonby's remarks betrayed the fact that on the day after the performance of the *The Vampyr* Jeremy March had known Elisa would marry him.

His certainty about her response troubled her. One might almost think their entire relationship, from the time he stopped publicly snubbing her, had been a carefully worked out plan.

With what purpose?

She reminded herself that all this did not matter. She had married him with the hope of making him share the love she felt for him. It would take time. Crossing him, as she had done a minute ago, was a foolish way to achieve that.

They followed Mrs Ponsonby and the proud, smiling Susan up the main staircase with its warm, brown-gold balustrade and treads. Jeremy reminded Elisa, 'This is all yours now, my love. If you see anything you disapprove of – any furnishings, colors, or conduct by these good people – you must make your objections known.'

She said truthfully, 'Oh, I leave all those things to Tuttle.'

She sensed at once that this was a mistake. The backs of both the housekeeper and Susan stiffened perceptibly. Watching them, Elisa saw the side glance they exchanged.

Jeremy dismissed the matter with ease.

'Meanwhile, you will find our Mrs Ponsonby more than adequate. As for Susan –' Elisa envied the warmth of the smile he gave to Susan as she looked around in her pert way 'You have heard Ponsonby on the subject of Miss Clifford. As an old friend of yours, Susan would know precisely the qualities of an abigail that would suit you.'

Susan beamed under this flattery, but the red-haired young footman, Belliver, passed them in the gallery, bowing to the Marches, then gave Susan a furtive grin. She ignored him after a flirtatious look at Jeremy.

Jeremy murmured, 'Ah, to be sixteen again!'

Not I, Elisa thought. He caught her swift shake of the head, so quick it was like a nervous twitch.

'An unhappy childhood, my love?'

Every time he called her 'my love' the sound grated on her ears. It was facile, insincere. And yet, there were other moments, perhaps moments in which he didn't quite understand his own feelings, when she was certain he loved her. She told herself that she must forget everything else.

'The usual childhood of a struggling player. Not quite like theirs.' She indicated the long series of age-darkened portraits that lined the gallery wall.

He raised his head, glancing at his ancestors as if he had never seen them before.

'No. Their problems were of a different nature. Chiefly political. Lost their heads over one female or another. If it wasn't Mary Stuart, it was Mary Tudor. If not Mary Tudor, it was the redoubtable Elisabeth Tudor. I believe one of my noble forebears was imprisoned for following Monmouth, but he was an aberration. Didn't like females.'

Mrs Ponsonby ushered Lord and Lady March up three floors to the private apartments which faced the rear of the building and a green rolling hill. Halfway up the hill the green of the grass dissolved in a copse of trees dense enough to appear dark and gloomy on a sunless day.

With considerable pride Mrs Ponsonby pointed out the suite of rooms.

'Here in the center is the master chamber. On the right, with two exposures, east and south, is Her Ladyship's boudoir. On the left is His Lordship's dressing-room.'

It was all breathtaking, not for its splendor – it was far less rich than her own London suite – but for its warm feeling that generations had been born and died here in view of those dark woods on the hillside.

As a child who belonged nowhere and was wanted by no one, Elisa was more than ever impressed by these signs of family continuity. To 'belong' seemed the most important ambition that had ever consumed her. For the benefit of her sophisticated husband and these servants who would despise too much naive enthusiasm, she tried to restrain herself, but it was impossible in this case to present the blasé acceptance practised by his titled friends.

'How beautiful it is! This room, the furnishings, the feeling it gives one of – of . . .'

She saw that she had puzzled her husband. 'The furnishing are far from new,' he admitted as he ruefully surveyed the big oak bed with its short posts and no tester. He seemed determined to find fault. 'That clothes-press must be centuries old. I sincerely hope you've aired it for ghosts.'

'Naturally, My Lord. Most of Her Ladyship's boxes and cases have been opened. The contents are in place.' Mrs Ponsonby looked at Elisa. 'The valises and bandboxes Your Ladyship brought . . . Do you have a preference for one of the girls here to act as your maid?'

Elisa said pleasantly, 'Until Tuttle comes I will need someone. As you say, Miss Clifford will know the sort of girl I need.' She caught Brian's grateful smile.

The girl assured Elisa in her most grown-up voice. 'I'd be most happy to do so, Ma'am.' She was pleased by Elisa's assumption of her new, if temporary, position.

'Thank you, Miss Clifford. I know I can count upon you.'

Shortly afterward, as if by magic, the servants drifted away. Jeremy March kissed Elisa's cheek, apologizing, 'I'm off to examine Clifford's work with the terrace houses. I hope you like the arrangements. If not, blame Ponsonby. If you do approve, you may thank me in your inimitable way, my love.'

She pretended to be pleased, but she would have felt a deal better if she could have spent her first few hours in March Hall with her husband.

During the first hour after the departure of the two men, the servants came and went, bringing pewter jugs of water, towels, her remaining baggage, and then silence fell over the entire house. This lengthened minute by minute as sun set, piercing all the westerly views with a crimson light.

Elisa found it impossible to remain in her own boudoir, even with the door left carefully ajar. She had hoped against hope that this warm, golden house would free her of all the dreads and fantasies that haunted her in London. With this resolution she started out to explore the major rooms and corridors. She hoped that familiarity would make the house seem more like her own home.

She was not encouraged by the enclosed sensation she received from the upper floor containing the master bedchamber. One after another, the doors quietly closed behind her as she moved from room to room. It was necessary to retrace her steps and place some obstacle, usually a rug, in each doorway. She knew these obstacles would be removed as soon as she left the area, but for the moment she felt safer.

On the ground floor she spent time in the solar, that great, lovely hall with its many panes of glass that formed a window two storeys high and filtered in a golden light. She loved the room but couldn't help remembering that it had been Arthur March's favorite hiding-place from the world.

She was not imaginative enough to see Arthur's ghost on that window-seat, but his warm, young, ingenuous personality seemed to wrap itself around her as she stood there, enjoying the big room.

Hearing footsteps outside the solar, she confessed to herself a certain relief. She thanked heaven that the servants hadn't deserted en masse. She was uncomfortable enough while her husband and her best friends, the Cliffords, were off – God knew where! At least, with the servants present, she would not be alone. But this was the first sign of them that she had heard in the last half-hour.

She called out, 'Who is it? Has Lord March returned?'

The footsteps ceased. Because she was growing more and more anxious for human company she returned to the big double doors which remained open as she had left them. There was no sign of the servant whose footsteps she had heard. Evidently, whoever it was had already gone. But were they the steps of a man?

A man wearing boots. Yes. That was it.

The hall was sombre, after the brightness of the solar. Elisa fought her own cowardly instincts and called again, so loudly she head a note of fear, 'I am Lady March. Speak to me at once.'

She stood there uncertain, half-inclined to believe she had imagined the sounds, out of hunger for company. On her left was the long, tapestry-covered wall of a formal salon. The panelled doors were further down the hall.

On her right she made out a long, narrow tapestry depicting a medieval knight holding a chalice, perhaps the Holy Grail. One curious detail attracted her attention. The tapestry trembled a little, as though there were a faint passage of air behind it.

She remembered suddenly that in giving her a tour of the lower floors several weeks ago Jeremy March had mentioned a so-called 'secret' passage. She had no intention of trapping

192

herself inside such a dark and dusty passage, but it seemed likely that the footsteps she heard had been heading toward this passage, or was it a staircase? Logically enough, they would have been silenced once the servant stepped into the passage.

However sinister such a place might sound, the entire family, and particularly Arthur, had used it, according to Lord March. She touched the edge of the tapestry, looked behind it, and made out, as she had expected, a narrow door, old and metal-bound. The iron latch was blackened with age. She pressed down on the latch and opened the door quite easily. No creaking noises; no deadly 'Count Montoni' popped out at her, as in the popular Gothic romance, *Mysteries Of Udolpho*.

A stone staircase, dimly but adequately lighted around the first turn, seemed harmless enough.

A second later she had a shock that made her cry out. A hand tapped her shoulder. She swung around and saw the young red-haired footman named Belliver. He was embarrassed but ever-obliging.

'Beg pardon, My Lady. Might I light your way up? We call this the Secret Staircase. It's quite safe. Keeps right on up to the roof. Most interesting, Ma'am, though a bit coolish when the sun goes down. Servants use it mostly, them and Master Ronald Hawtree when him and Master Arthur was boys. Games they played on the roof, so long as Master Arthur's mother wasn't about to forbid it.'

'Why don't they remove the tapestry, instead of going through that absurd charade?'

'Well, Ma'am, it wouldn't be a secret staircase then, would it?'

She had to admit it was true, ridiculous as it might be.

'I take it that one of the servants was on the so-called Secret Staircase about five minutes ago.'

He looked at her, expressionless, but his voice was very positive.

'Impossible, Your Ladyship.'

'Why, for heaven's sake?'

'Because there are no servants in the house, Ma'am. I only came back for a minute because I thought I saw someone on the roof. If it was Master Ronald Hawtree, it would've been my place to fetch up some whisky and make him comfortable.'

She was more annoyed than puzzled. 'May I ask why the staff chose this particular time to desert the house?'

He shrugged apologetically. 'There was a slight—altercation in the stables. Then old Neame, the coachman, was stricken. A seizure, so Mrs Ponsonby says.'

This banished her small problems. 'May I help? Which is the shortest way to the stables?'

'No, Ma'am. Please. All's well. I think they'd rather manage things without –'

'Without my interference?' She tried not to let herself be hurt.

'I mean to say, without hindrance from those outside.'

'I am not outside the family. That shall be mended. However . . .' She realized her husband would undoubtedly be on the side of the servants. Her attention reverted to his earlier remark. 'The person you saw on the roof, he must have been the man I heard in the hall.'

'Very likely, Ma'am.'

'What on earth did Captain Hawtree and Arthur do on the rooftop?'

Belliver appeared surprised at her question. 'Him and Master Arthur, they had games they played. Who could walk closest to the edge, like. And how close could they catch a ball. Things like that.'

'I certainly didn't see him go up there.'

'No, My Lady. And he hasn't paid his respect to you or His Lordship yet. But then, he goes his own way these days, does the Captain.'

'I'm afraid he always did,' she murmured, wondering desperately if it might not be better to find herself alone than to face an embittered Captain Hawtree.

Belliver pulled the tapestry aside again. The door was still ajar as she had left it. He went up the stairs, turned and passed the little hanging lamp that lighted the way. The stairs were almost free of dust. This 'secret staircase' was as well-travelled as the Bristol High Road.

194

She watched the lengthening of Belliver's shadow against the wall. In a short time, scarcely more than a couple of minutes, he returned to the lower floor.

'He's gone now, My Lady. Must've went out by the main staircase.'

She was relieved.

She turned away, wondering what to do, how to occupy herself until her husband, or the Cliffords, or all of them, came back. She had always worked, since they took her mother away long ago, and now it was strange, uncomfortable, to find herself with nothing useful to do.

Her behavior the last half-hour had been ridiculous. It was another sign that her nerves and her imagination were travelling the road her mother had travelled.

She was so terrified of finding herself alone and imagining things again that she barely restrained herself from going down to join the household in the stables, or wherever the devil they were!

Pride held her back.

And there was something else. She didn't want her husband to hear her scolding his servants for deserting her in this bad hour. He must not guess the secrets that were revealed by this fear of finding herself alone.

As luck would have it, he witnessed her at her worst.

CHAPTER SEVENTEEN

The household staff drifted back only minutes before Jeremy March and the Cliffords returned. The fact, coincidental or not, had its effect upon Elisa's nerves and, ultimately, her temper. She was in the midst of making her feelings clear when her husband appeared to witness quite a different Elisa from the compliant woman he had married.

She had waylaid Mrs Ponsonby and the butler, Stebbings, as they came in to the main hall through a passage from the housekeeper's private parlour and the servants' quarters. They found her alone in the hall.

Mrs Ponsonby seemed insolent, treating her with none of the respect and deference she showed His Lordship, and Stebbings was worse, bowing slightly from considerably above the waist, and giving her a nasty smirk as he left Mrs Ponsonby to put the new 'mistress' in her place. Obviously, to these important March Hall appendages, she was still the wanton actress, not the Lady of the House.

Mrs Ponsonby's round eyes opened wider in assumed surprise and disapproval. Elisa's presence in the hall outside the main salon was not the expected state of affairs.

'May I assist you, Madam? Your apartments are at the top of the staircase above the gallery, and to the right.'

'I chose to be here,' she snapped icily. 'Since I could not arouse anyone when I summoned you, or the rest of the staff.'

'There were difficulties in the stables, Madam. The first coachman, old Neame, was stricken. We thought, perhaps, it might be an apoplexy. Happily, it was not.'

'Are you a physician?' Elisa asked, not allowing herself to be placed in the wrong by this ploy.

'Certainly not, Your Ladyship. I am the housekeeper for Lord March.'

That is surely meant for me, Elisa thought, and her temper was not improved. 'Then I see no reason why the entire household was permitted to slacken its duties and run away to watch fisticuffs among the stableboys.'

Apparently, the woman wasn't aware that Elisa had heard about the original trouble. She bit her pudgy lower lip and explained. 'There were difficulties, My Lady. It was thought that I might settle the matter between them.'

'I can't conceive of a butler asking the housekeeper to settle a dispute between stableboys. Just what purpose did Stebbings himself serve?'

Mrs Ponsonby stood on ceremony. 'That is not for me to say, Miss – that is, Your Ladyship.'

Several faces in the post-sunset dusk behind her looked uneasily at each other.

'Henceforth,' Elisa said firmly, 'when the doings of stableboys call you from your duties, please see that a sufficient staff remains in the house. At least so they may announce visitors like Captain Hawtree.'

There was a moment's pause, pregnant with angry emotions. Suddenly, to Elisa's consternation, the woman's eyes welled up with tears, accompanied by the wretched, nervous plea, 'I beg Your Ladyship's pardon. Your Ladyship is quite right. The second kitchen maid is not the most competent in the world, but the two parlour maids and two footmen seemed enough to . . . Not that I would contradict Your Ladyship. No, indeed.' The warmth, the caring, had come into Mrs Ponsonby's voice as she looked at someone behind Elisa.

Of course it had been a lie about the five servants available in the house half an hour ago. It did not take more than a second or two for Elisa to guess who stood behind her and had heard that last theatrical plea complete with tears. But she was so unnerved by having been completely cut off from humanity in a strange

197

place full of closed doors that she refused to continue the sweet, compliant game she had been playing to win her husband's love.

She said, 'I want it strictly understood that there are servants on call in the house at all times when I am present.'

Mrs Ponsonby gave Lord March a simpering smile as she curtsied deeply to Elisa.

'At all times, Ma'am. Just as they were today.'

Liar, Elisa thought. No servant had been in the house until Belliver appeared. The cluster of servants behind the housekeeper now proved that.

Before Elisa could answer the lie – making it sound like a petty dispute between two children: 'I did!' 'You didn't!' – Lord March said easily, 'We know you will always see to it, Ponsy. Thank you. Now, we musn't take any more of your valuable time. Go along. All is well. Lady March is sorry for having misjudged you, but you must remember she doesn't know you as I do.'

Mrs Ponsonby's tight little smile, directed at Lord March with calf-like devotion, seemed an added insult to Elisa who considered that, in spite of her husband's words, all was 'far from well'. She was convinced the whole scene had been staged to place her in the wrong before her husband. She had no notion why this should be done to her and she was furious at having been maneuvered into the wrong when she was right.

Jeremy took her arm rather more firmly than was necessary. 'Come along, my love. We are late for dinner already. We don't want the cook put out also.'

'I did not put anyone out. And may I inform you that Captain Hawtree was wandering over the rooftops? He left without greeting anyone.'

'He is often here. He and Arthur and I made up our differences after the shooting. But of course, you know that. You saw him at our little venture into melodrama at his father's house.'

As though she had forgotten!

The two of them moved along the hall with graceful propriety to the main staircase. They looked like a long-married pair of aristocrats, exchanging cool nothings.

When they were alone his comment was tipped with ice. 'My house is not a stage where you may play off your temperament against servants who have looked after March Hall since before Arthur and I were born.'

She wanted to flare up, to remind him that he had made her his wife and this was also her household staff, but his reprimand explained the real cause of the staff's animosity. They had loved Arthur, and they regarded Elisa Carlisle as his murderess. Unlike Jeremy March, they had no reason to believe her protests of innocence. There were many moments when she wondered if her husband actually did believe her.

The anger and indignation drained from her. As they went up the stairs she murmured softly, 'I'm sorry. Of course, they resent me. If I could only make them understand that I was fond of Arthur! On that last visit, I tried to make him see the impossibility – the difference in our ages, our positions –'

'And yet,' he pointed out, 'you and I find ourselves here.'

'But this is not the same thing at all. Our ages and our positions are quite different, and then –'

'Yes,' he agreed, his voice curiously rough, perhaps with emotions he did not often reveal. 'We are quite unlike you and Arthur.' His sudden laugh and change of mood startled her. 'Which reminds me. We cannot have you appear in the March dining hall without the March pearls. So come along.'

Evidently, he was 'forgiving her' for his servants' insolence and incompetence. It was kind of him and she appreciated his generosity. It must prove that he loved her, at least a little.

She tried to make her protest as warm and endearing as possible.

'Why not save the March pearls for your heirs?'

'Because I assume they will be your heirs as well. What ideas are you getting in that lovely head of yours?'

'Nevertheless, I wish you would keep them for –'

'I want you to wear them. I'm sure you will do so, to oblige me.'

She felt scolded in a polite, patronizing way. As usual in his presence, she abandoned any idea of revolt or argument.

199

'I will, if it means so much to you.'

'I rather thought you might.'

Her reaction was oversensitive but she couldn't prevent the disappointment at his tone, his cool confidence that held a tinge of sarcasm. She said nothing when he made small talk for the next few minutes. They arrived in the master suite and she started past the big bed to the door of her boudoir, still without saying anything.

In the standing oval mirror of the boudoir she saw her husband's reflection in the bedchamber. He was staring after her, frowning. Whatever was going on in his mind, he still had doubts, one way or another. At least, he had not been totally convinced that she was the greedy harpy of his imaginings.

A plain, gawky girl about Susan's age had been sent to act as Elisa's abigail. In great excitement she blurted out that she was called Dilly Skeen. She seemed unlikely as a ladies' maid. She was totally lacking in grace and immediately overset Elisa's miniature snuffbox of rice powder. The delicate gold-hinged little Limoges box had been one of Elisa's early gifts, which she regarded as a sign that she was no longer a poverty-stricken, despised urchin. The girl was still apologizing and wringing her hands helplessly while Elisa cleared away the powder as best she could with a towel snatched up from the elegant, marble-topped commode. Most of the powder had seeped into the heavy carpet.

'Never mind.' Elisa waved away the girl's endless chattering apologies which made her more and more nervous. The girl would have done better to help clear away the debris, including the broken pieces of the precious box. 'If you will be so good as to order up a hip-bath for me . . .'

'Ay, Mum. Order a hip-bath.' Dilly Skeen swung around, anxiously eyeing every wall, every corner, but failing to locate anything that looked like a bell-pull. She gave up the search finally and started out the hall door, with the apparent intention of fetching the hip-bath herself.

'There are two, Dilly. One is beside the door.'

200

Dilly fumbled apologies again while she tugged at the petit-point bell-pull. Then she returned, grinning with pleasure at her success.

'Is there summat else you'd like o'me, Mum?'

The girl would have been useful in pouring heated water from pots and jars onto Elisa's shoulders. But it was equally obvious Dilly Skeen knew nothing of such niceties. Susan Clifford was supposed to have sent her up. Was Susan a part of this domestic plot against the new Lady March?

The thought of treachery from the Cliffords hurt, but Elisa told herself it shouldn't surprise her. She had considered herself a cynic for years.

'Dilly, Miss Clifford told you about your duties here, didn't she?'

Dilly flashed her amiable grin again. 'Oh, no, Mum. Miss Susan, she's off looking out after me Granny. Granny Skeen.'

'Then how did you happen to be chosen?'

Dilly scratched her head; her hair badly needed washing. 'Reckon it was Mr Stebbings. Him and old Ponsy – I mean to say Mrs Ponsonby. They had their heads together and, next thing, they was sending me up to you, Mum.'

This knowledge considerably softened Elisa's feelings toward the girl. Another thought occurred to her. She remembered the housekeeper's remark about an incompetent kitchenmaid. 'Were you formerly in the kitchen, Dilly?'

Dilly was nothing if not enthusiastic. 'Aye, Mum. That I was. But Cook, she said I made her that jumpy she near stewed her own thumb, and old Ponsy, she said we'd be thrown on the parish, me and Granny Skeen, if you didn't take to me.' Her dull blue eyes fired up with a desperation Elisa remembered all too well from her own childhood. 'If you please, Mum, I'd be ever so obliged if you'd take me on to train up, like.'

Elisa sighed. The girl was a disaster. Even now she was handling the other articles on the commode, including combs, brushes and a lip rouge, with fingers whose nails seemed never to have been clean. This, compounded with her awkwardness,

201

meant that her training would have to begin with the bare essentials.

On the other hand, Elisa had no doubt the housekeeper would see to it that, if she sent the girl back to the kitchen, Jeremy March would be told of his wife's 'cruelty', her arrogant behavior toward a helpless girl who was trying to fit into her new role.

Well, old Ponsy, she thought, looking up at Dilly Skeen's hopeful, pleading eyes, you have outsmarted yourself. I'll make an abigail of this girl if it kills me.

She said, 'Dilly, you must tell me honestly. Would you like to remain as my abigail, my personal maid, until Tuttle comes? Tuttle has been with me all my professional life, you know.'

Dilly clapped her hands, dropping the silver-backed mirror. Elisa caught it by a long-armed reach and got to her feet in front of the oval mirror.

Dilly was exclaiming, 'I'd be that happy, you've no notion! Me, Dilly Skeen, an abigail! Granny Skeen's sure to say I'm making fun.'

'There won't be much fun, I'm afraid. At certain times you will be exceedingly busy.' The girl looked back at her, all eagerness. Elisa added encouragingly, 'But on other occasions your time may be free. However, there are several habits you must cultivate.'

'Aye, Mum. You've only to say. Brush your pretty hair? Get your gown out of the press? Fetch your jewels?'

'No, Dilly. Just take the pewter bowl and the water in that jug, and the perfumed soap, and wash — your hands. Then use this brush on your nails.'

It was this curious scene into which Jeremy March intruded after a light knock on the door that stood ajar as Elisa had left it. He scarcely noticed Dilly Skeen as he came up behind Elisa, his gaze fixed intently on her reflection in the big oval mirror.

She was puzzled by his intensity, but pleased, too, every time he showed any real emotion toward her, whether it was in her favor or not. Her greatest fear was his typically amused, mocking attitude. His hands wandered over her shoulders, warmly sliding the soft, silken material of her gown off her shoulders until the pale flesh was bare down to the swell of her breasts.

'Shall we just see how they are going to look on you?' he asked; and then, before she could react, he dropped a heavy, opalescent, five-strand necklace of pearls over her throat. The necklace was heavy. The pearls had a yellow sheen considered superior by many, but unflattering on Elisa. In her eyes they seemed to drag her down. They had none of the delicate lightness of her own pearl necklace.

'What do you think?' Jeremy asked, leaning over her with his chin on the crown of her head.

She tried to speak but had no notion of what to say. Luckily, Dilly Skeen said it for her.

'Oh, Mum, it's that grand, Queen Charlotte herself would be wishing she was you!'

'Very likely,' Jeremy agreed, his eyes on Elisa's face, this time her true face, rather than the reflection which showed left to be right, and vice versa. 'Well, my love?'

She pulled her thoughts together. 'It's worthy of all the Lady Marches, My Lord.'

He assured her, 'You will grace the jewels as they grace you.' All the same, to her sharp view, he looked a shade disappointed.

Good heavens! He must have wanted her to refuse the jewels. These little games of his were beginning to annoy her. She became the gracious actress, thanking her admirers for their applause.

'You are too generous, My Lord. Isn't he, Dilly?'

For the first time he looked at his wife's new maid and stared in surprise. 'Dilly Skeen! What the devil are you doing up here?' He glanced at the pewter bowl beside the girl and laughed shortly. He turned to Elisa for an explanation.

She was matter-of-fact about it. 'Certainly. Mrs Ponsonby and Stebbings thought I might train her. She is Granny Skeen's granddaughter.'

'Yes. I know. But what are they thinking of, sending up a girl –' He broke off, obviously to spare the girl's feelings.

Elisa cut into the awkward moment of silence. 'She is perfectly willing, and a willing girl is worth a great deal. Dilly, would you mind going down to Mrs Ponsonby and telling her Lady March would like a hip-bath carried up to her?'

The girl started off with a clumsy, loping stride. She was slightly crippled. One of her heavy shoes turned inward. This problem only made Elisa's decision more firm. She would make a successful maid, an abigail, of the girl and confound the household.

Elisa called, 'Don't run, Dilly. Just tell the housekeeper I said you are to be treated with the respect due to my abigail. Tell her Lady March said so.'

'Aye, M'lady. I will so. She'll be that surprised!' The girl loped out into the hall, giggling.

'That was very good of you,' Jeremy told Elisa.

'Surprisingly so?'

'I didn't say that. But you do puzzle me.'

She smiled up at him, a bit archly, she thought, but he didn't seem to mind. His head was very close to hers and she felt, even before his movement, that he was about to kiss her. She remained carefully still, wondering at his changeful moods, but no less fascinated by them.

When his lips touched her it was on the slender porcelain column of her neck, just beneath her ear, and she shivered with the pleasure of it. His hands drew her head back against him, moving then to her bosom where he had pulled away her gown and sleeves to display the heavy necklace. Below the pearls he uncovered her breasts, manipulating the flesh of the delicate globes to the darker nipples that hardened with excitement under his skilled fingers.

While she was a willing prisoner to his touch, his lips closed over hers. He held her prisoner with his mouth until she began to struggle unwillingly, desperate to take a breath.

He released her, and then stood there laughing as he watched her awkward attempt to cover her breasts. The silk neckline of the gown had torn.

All the same, even while she struggled to regain her composure, she was glad to see that his color had heightened and he, too, was aroused by their brief, passionate contact. She could only smile and shrug helplessly. It was all he needed. He reached for her.

A scratching on the hall door was followed by Dilly Skeen who tripped on the rug and stumbled into the room.

Jeremy's greeting stopped her in mid-stride.

'Damn!'

She looked anxiously from Lord March to his lady.

'They said they would, Mum. Right soon. The Hip-bath –'

'Later!' Jeremy snapped.

Dilly wasn't taking *his* word. After all, Lady March was the fairy godmother who had transformed her into an abigail. 'Mum?'

Elisa glanced at Jeremy, warned by the look in his eyes. 'Yes, Dilly. Later.'

When Dilly bowed herself out Elisa started after her, trying not to make her pleas sound so desperate: 'Don't close the door. Please, don't close . . .' But the door had already slammed. The old, smothering sensation enveloped her and she began to shake.

She was not immediately aware of Jeremy's hand on her arm until she felt herself being drawn to him. He lifted her into his arms, obviously not aware of her panic. She set her teeth hard in her lower lip to keep from crying out, but he saw her face and his own excitement faded.

For an endless few seconds, while she tried to control her inward terrors, he studied her closely. His first anger, and perhaps humiliation, turned to puzzlement. She, for her part, made the greatest effort of her life, to conquer her hideous smothering sensation. She tried to speak but made no sound.

With surprising tenderness he kissed her mouth lightly, a mere brushing of the lips, and then raised his head and studied her, thoughtfully.

'Do I repulse you?'

She managed to whisper hoarsely, 'No. Never.'

'But you are frightened.'

'Not of you.'

'Nor of our sexual — pleasure. What, then?'

'Nothing. She – Dilly – slammed the door. It startled me.'

She had not really answered his troubled questions but she roused herself, wriggling in his arms until her face was close to his. She freed one arm, caught his shoulder to give her leverage, and crushed his mouth with hers, forcing his lips apart, almost shocking him by the heat and passion she poured into that kiss.

While he responded with all the enthusiasm she could have desired, he carried her across the boudoir, kicked the bedchamber door open wider and didn't stop until he set her down on the high master bed. Then he stood back, hands on hips, and looked down at her. She was delighted to find him breathless as she had been a few minutes ago. She sat up, leaning back provocatively with her weight on her arms and wrists behind her, enticing him in her torn gown, with much of her bosom displayed, and moist lips parted.

She laughed as he stared at her. Soon, very soon, she told herself, his desire for her must turn to genuine feeling.

He reached for her, dragged her across the bed to his body and she clung to him, loving his closeness, the feeling that was a part of him, belonged to him.

They made love with a nervous urgency. They joined quickly, violently – a lightning stroke, she thought. It seemed to her that he buried a part of himself within her body which she locked around him. He drove and twisted, sealing his possession of her, she told herself. She wanted to hold him within her forever. It would mean — what? That, as long as they remained sexually bound, they belonged to each other?

She entangled her fingers in his crisp, black hair, hearing herself whispering desperately, urgently, 'Love me, my darling – please – please love me . . .'

She had broken the spell. He let her go, drawing back from her far enough so that he could study her. Worst of all, he laughed. Not in a jeering, nasty way, but humorously, as if she amused and puzzled him.

He ran one finger over the curve of her breast, a feather touch over the nipple, and down over her stomach, reaching its true destination amid the golden hairs between her thighs.

'My dear Elisa, what do you call this if it isn't lovemaking?'

Her body responded with delight, but her mind was closed to any sensation beyond disappointment. He had not understood her in the least.

Unbidden, a memory came to her from long ago of some boy who had sworn he loved her 'more than life'. And he had cried in his despair, 'You ask for love. Always, you ask. *But do you give your love?*'

The foolish boy. She had given him her body. Wasn't that love?

Dimly, she began to understand that foolish boy.

CHAPTER EIGHTEEN

On her first night as 'Lady' of March Hall, Elisa had no further complaints about loneliness. The evening went rapidly, full of the delight of her husband's company. He insisted on personally introducing her to every corner of the Hall.

Mrs Ponsonby offered to act as Her Ladyship's guide when Brian Clifford arrived to discuss the needed expenditures from the Charity Performance, but to Elisa's profound relief Jeremy dismissed all business for the evening.

Elisa knew what all his friends thought of Lord March's marriage to the notorious Elisa Carlisle. Very few cards had been left at March Hall by those who might, in other circumstances, have come to congratulate him. He was being ostracized, but he didn't seem to care. It was very odd, but his attitude was warmly flattering to her.

As she had suspected on her first visit, the house possessed a welcoming quality. She began to develop new respect for the Marches who had built, furnished and lived in the house. Remembering the Hawtree house with its crowded, over-decorated look, its elaborate gothic additions to the exterior, and the attempts to display all their wealth ostentatiously, she was even more impressed by what her husband stood for.

'Curious,' she remarked when they passed through the Ladies withdrawing parlour. 'The furnishings are worn, the portières a trifle faded' – they were golden brown and added cheerfulness to the room with its heavy casement windows – 'but I already feel a fondness for it. Comfortable in every way.'

He examined the backing of the portières, admitting wryly, 'We have not always been able to afford what is new or fashionable.'

'I am glad.'

She had pleased him. She was prepared to love every stick of furniture, every family portrait, even every drafty chamber, though there weren't many, until they came to the so-called Secret Staircase, that favorite of Arthur March, concealed behind the Grail tapestry. She wanted to omit this aspect of the 'tour'. No secret passages. No ghostly oubliettes. Her imagination was too vivid, but Jeremy taunted her laugiaingly.

'We will omit Arthur's favorite secret staircase. Belliver tells me you are afraid of it.'

'Belliver is mistaken. Unless, of course, there is some danger from ancient family ghosts.'

Jeremy pointed out that the Secret Staircase was the most direct way to reach the roof of the Hall. She thought that was ridiculous when the roofs were all steeply pitched, but he assured her that there was an area behind the crenelated section on the southwest front.

'The view would impress you. That area of the roof is often used by the laundresses for drying bed linens. It used to be a point of challenge between us – Ronald and Arthur, in particular. But if you are afraid . . .?'

It was all nonsense. As to the view, what could they see at this hour of the night? One would think he deliberately wanted to frighten her. Nevertheless, she insisted, 'Well then, at night I won't be able to see any apparitions.'

He said, 'Good. No cowards in this family.'

Elisa wanted to please him. She took the shawl one of the parlour maids brought to her and then pinched up an inch or two of her satin and lace skirts between her gloved fingers, to keep the hems from sweeping the dust. She followed her husband behind the tapestry. The stairs were not dusty and the walls seemed to be cleaned fairly often. She hoped for the best.

The first lamp in its little niche was protected by glass but the light flickered; so there must be a draft from somewhere. She was relieved. This meant that they were not closed in tightly. Somewhere, a door might be open.

Jeremy reached back for her hand as the staircase spiralled narrowly as it neared the gallery floor.

'Take care. The steps taper off to nothing at these turns.'

It was fortunate she had taken the hand he offered. A minute later, as they passed the narrow door that presumably opened into the gallery, her pale brocade shoe grated on something that caused her to turn her ankle. She was not hurt but she hated appearing clumsy before him. She knew quite well that her looks and grace were all she had to attract him and any fall from perfection might lose him.

'Sorry,' he said and then became interested in what had caused her accident. He stooped and picked up the object she had stepped on. 'A button. From a cuff, I should think.' He weighed it in his palm. 'Of course. I remember now. Arthur had a hacking-jacket he often wore in the country.'

She looked at the little silver button. It was still untarnished. There was something engraved on its surface, a griffon, evidently the symbol of the March family. It shone brightly, even in the flickering lamplight. Arthur had lost it very recently, else why would it be so shiny?

It took all her will to keep from looking behind her, into the shadowy staircase below.

Was Arthur everywhere in this house? Or did those who loved him merely want her to keep him constantly in mind as some kind of penance?

Her heart almost stopped beating when she asked herself silently, Is my husband a part of this conspiracy? He certainly appeared very active in promoting it.

Anything was better than this suspicion.

Don't let him be a part of it, she prayed . . . *Anything else I can accept. But not that . . .*

He said energetically, 'Come along. We've another floor and then the attics before we come out upon the view.' He stopped after another few minutes and studied her under the light of the lamp swinging from a hook in the wall. 'Am I going too fast? Are you all right?'

'Certainly, I am,' she snapped. 'I am able to climb stairs, you know. It's my skirts.' They tangled around her legs as she mounted the steps. Such an idiotic idea, anyway, in her evening clothes! Her long white gloves were already soiled.

'Sorry. I only thought — you do look pale.'

'I assure you, I am not.'

He reached down, slipped an arm around her waist and they took the last steps together. They passed the attic door which was smaller than the others. A man would have to stoop a little to enter that corridor.

Jeremy explained, 'The servants' quarters are along the length of the house, both east and westerly view. We Marches pride ourselves that they are the best quarters of their kind in the country. Dormer windows and slanting roofs, of course. But adequate furnishings, and air. There is a fireplace in one of the north parlours where they may get coal for their warming pans before bed.'

She found it surprising that he cared, or even that servants had warming pans. What a difference such comforts would have made to Molly Catlow and her infant daughter! Before she could remark on the family's kindness they reached the heavy oaken door opening onto the roof, and while she waited on the small landing he put his shoulder to the door and pushed it open.

Cool night air met them, but in spite of her thin evening dress Elisa welcomed the scent of the woods from the east slope behind the kitchen gardens, mingled with autumn earth in every direction, and smoke from the many chimneys of March Hall. Her lace sleeves and shawl did not keep out the cold; she hugged her arms while Jeremy leaned far over the low crenellations that decorated this part of the roof, pointing out various natural protuberances in the land-scape.

'That uneven row of hills to the west, silhouetted by the moon – it separates our valley from the Hawtrees on the far side. Can you see it?'

She peered into the distant skyline where, in spite of a quarter-moon behind her in the east, it was hard to make out the humped line of hills against the night-blue sky in the west. She searched in vain among all that darkness for any sign of human habitation. Even a lantern light from a shepherd's hut would have been welcome. She pretended to joke about what seemed to her an appalling lack.

'Are there no human beings within the neighborhood?'

'None whatever,' he agreed cheerfully. 'If you mean permanent habitation. Naturally, the sheep and goats and other livestock are grazed on some of those fields, among the copses of trees and the willows by the streams. We have a number of tenants who do very well.' He looked over at her. 'You must be chilled. Come here. We mustn't have you freezing. You'll be getting a bad impression of your new home.'

She moved across pebbles, blown dirt and leaves, plus considerable soot, to join him, becoming conscious, at the same time, of something that moved just at the corner of her vision. She turned her head and saw a black figure standing in the shadow where the steep slant of the main roof began. She wanted to cry out but found her throat dry.

She stopped in her tracks. How long had the thing – fantasy or man – been standing there watching her and Jeremy, listening to them?

Surprised by her behavior, for she stood with one gloved hand closed around her throat, Jeremy turned and saw the thing.

'Good God! What –?' Then, to Elisa's anger and relief, he started toward the shadowy watcher with one hand extended. 'Damme, man, do you live on this rooftop? We took you for a ghost. Did you ride over? My wife says we missed you this afternoon. Let's go below and warm ourselves with a glass or two of Madeira.'

'Any French brandy, my dear fellow?' the phantom asked, coming out into the moonlight. 'It was a deucedly cold ride. I'm still having trouble training Rigel to my somewhat eccentric new riding habits.'

Captain Ronald Hawtree, who had tried to shoot the March brothers, appeared to make himself free with their house and Jeremy welcomed him as he had at the Hawtree theatricals. Strange were the ways of men who had seen service, Elisa thought. She hesitated a few seconds but the Captain's bitterness seemed to have vanished. With his good arm he took the hand she offered, bringing almost to his lips the little circle of bared flesh just beyond the glove fastening.

'My sincerest good wishes, Lady March,' he said smoothly, but when he raised his head she was reminded of a pattern doll she had once seen, a doll with two colored eyes made of glass that had absolutely no expression. Ronald Hawtree's eyes did not flicker in the slightest as they stared at her. She was sure he had deliberately staged these rooftop scenes, hoping to frighten or at least disconcert her. And Jeremy seemed willing to help him. Had they plotted it together?

'Thank you, Captain. It was very good of you to call, even so unceremoniously.' She looked at her husband. He seemed to accept all this strange and somewhat sinister behavior without surprise.

Very possibly, he wasn't surprised.

'Well, Captain, it's clear you haven't forgotten those rough games you used to play with Arthur up here on the roof.' Jeremy shook hands with him, ignoring the awkwardness of the left hand. He went on conversationally, 'Have you seen Prinny lately? Does he have any late report on His Majesty's health? I've no doubt he is counting the hours until he can wear the crown in his own right.'

The Captain showed little of the lively conceit of his earlier days. Elisa found this more sad than the terrible empty sleeve that was pinned up. He seemed to have lost all the youthful exuberance that made Elisa think of a cock in a hen yard.

She went before the two men, down the steps, still secretly angered by the way the Captain had terrified her. How dared he sneak up the stairs before them and then say nothing when he stood in the darkness watching them? He had listened to them as well. It was despicable.

213

Giving his conduct more and more consideration, she suspected that someone else, not Jeremy, had told him she and Jeremy were going up to the roof. He must have hurried up another staircase and joined the Secret Stairs from the attic rooms, or even the family floor where the master bedchamber was situated. To Elisa's way of thinking, he knew too much about the house.

Meanwhile, he had several messages to deliver from his family. 'My father's wife –' he corrected himself punctiliously – 'that is to say, Lady Gwenna offers you her congratulations and assures you and Lady March that she will soon be calling upon you.'

He made it clear without saying so that he had never accepted Gwenna as his stepmother, and Jeremy seemed to understand. Elisa admitted to herself that the young Captain's feelings were understandable. He had some reason to mistrust his stepmother. Gwenna certainly regarded her husband's son as an obstacle to her inheritance.

Elisa could not blame him but, all the same, he troubled her. Considering the March household as well as Captain Hawtree, she was surrounded by enemies.

She was relieved when they all left the rooftop and Captain Hawtree started home.

Before Jeremy visited Neame, the old first coachman, to see to his comfort, he suggested that Elisa might care meanwhile to discuss the week's menu with the cook.

'That will be your affair now, my love.'

She agreed because he suggested it, but she wondered if the cook, like Mrs Ponsonby, would resent her interference.

Her scene with the cook, a powerful woman with a hard-scrubbed complexion and knuckles as red as her unruly hair, took her mind off the problem of Captain Hawtree. In almost every way the cook was the antithesis of stout, sweet-faced little Mrs Ponsonby.

She nodded to Elisa and barked at her, 'Save your pretty clothes, Ma'am. You're mightily near my stillroom.' She was carrying a haunch of mutton over one shoulder of her stained, homespun pinafore.

'I beg pardon.' Elisa jumped and moved away from the doorway, toward the very modern Rumford enclosed stove. On the other side of the big kitchen was the huge, open hearth, stained black with age, its fire burned out now. To Elisa, even across the room, it smelled of good, broiled meats, roasts – the odors that had fascinated her as a child, representing unattainable delicacies.

The cook returned from the stillroom without the mutton. Seeing Elisa still there, staring across the room at the open hearth, she grinned.

'Aye. The old ways taste better. But this is quicker. Easier, modern. And the Good Lord knows we've got to be modern, come what may.'

Elisa smiled. She had learned long ago not to shake hands with servants, but this woman's manner was so like Tuttle's that she offered her hand.

'You are a knowing woman. What is your name? I am Lady March.'

'Hannah Fincastle. Can't be taking that hand, Ma'am. I make it a rule. Never touch all that pretty animal skin.'

Elisa looked at the stained white glove and began to peel it off. 'I'd forgotten.'

'You wanted to see me, Ma'am?'

'Yes. About the week's menus.'

Hannah Fincastle looked her over. 'Old Ponsy know about this?'

Elisa raised her head. Her authority must be asserted sometime. 'Your concern is with me, Hannah.'

'Ha! You say. Must be nice, new-wed to His Ludship.' But the woman did not say it unpleasantly. She accepted Elisa's authority, for the moment.

The two women discussed the week's menus, getting on with the same rough amiability that Tuttle practiced with Elisa. It was not until they had completed the subject to their satisfaction that Mrs Ponsonby appeared. She gave Elisa her sweet, pursed smile, adding that, 'Your Ladyship must be tired after your busy day. I will direct myself to Fincastle's plans for the meals. There will likely be guests.' After a tiny pause she added, 'Paying their respects to the new Lady March.'

'How kind of them!' Elisa murmured. 'Hannah reminded me of the likelihood, and we have allowed for that. I believe the menus are set. Good night, Mrs Ponsonby. And I believe I may thank you for my temporary abigail – the girl, Dilly Skeen.'

She left the kitchen, and two surprised women. She heard the cook repeat, 'Holy Saints! Not our Dilly Skeen?' and Mrs Ponsonby's regretful, 'I fear so.'

Elisa went up, smiling, to her bedchamber and was still remarkably cheerful when Jeremy came to bed. Her mood obviously pleased him, and when she went into his waiting arms he seemed to her a trifle different – more tender, less violent, perhaps closer to that ideal she so desperately needed: a man – no, a *person* who loved her.

Because of her years in the theatre, she was not used to rising at dawn, which she soon found to be Jeremy's habit. He kissed her on the nose, pinched her chin, and told her he saw no reason why she should be up so early. Then, on most days, he left her to her own devices.

While she lay there luxuriating in the richness of the linens and the warmth where her husband had lain, she thought about the future, the long, golden years with the only man she had ever loved.

But even while she planned these years, she did not really believe them. He would find her out, discover Elsie Catlow, who had lived anywhere that there was space for a child of three or four, or seven or eight. Alleys, deep cellars that dripped with Thames water. Darkness. Sometimes – the worst times – a door was inadvertently locked on her and Molly.

Molly had sometimes appeared the younger of the two. She cried so much and clung to Elsie, murmuring brokenly, 'My big girl will save us. My Elsie is going to be pretty enough to feed us and keep us in fresh sheets every night

216

. . . You won't never leave your Mama, will you, Elsie-lamb? Swear!'

'Never, Mama. I'll see to you. I'll get all the pretty sparkles and sell 'em and you'll never get hungry again.'

But of course that was before they came and took Mama away and the last thing Mama cried, holding out her frail hands to Elsie from behind the bars, was: 'Don't leave me . . . Don't leave me alone . . .'

But of course they did – except for the visitors who were allowed to watch the antics of the 'creatures' in Bedlam. But Molly was dead now. Alone in the dark forever.

Elisa sat straight up in bed.

'Who is it? What do you want?'

The answer came noisily. Dilly Skeen stumbled into the room carrying a jug of chocolate and a pot of tea among other breakables. Luckily, she did not go down and the broken cup and saucer on the floor were empty, though they looked to Elisa very like valuable china.

'There's water for washing over on the chest, M'lady.'

'Thank you, Dilly. And leave the broken china. I'll pick it up. What kind of day is it?'

'Awfully fine, M'lady. There's still roses nigh the walls of the gatehouse, and some bird racketing away in the ivy by the gatehouse door. In front, yon know.'

Flowers. Her mother's unknown grave haunted her. But there was another grave and she felt some responsibility for Arthur's grave, as well.

'Dilly, would you fetch down my green –' She caught herself. 'Let me see your hands.'

The girl thrust them out proudly, fingers spread.

'Oh, aye, Ma'am. All clean, like.'

All but her nails. The dirt had accumulated beneath those brittle nails as usual.

Elisa signed. 'Never mind.' She looked more carefully at the girl's face. Dilly's round left cheek was badly puffed out. Small wonder that her clumsiness was more pronounced. Elisa's pleasant, impersonal tone warmed in sympathy.

217

'Dilly, are you suffering with a toothache?'

Dilly grinned valiantly. 'It'll be fine as silk, Ma'am. Cook says she'll put a hot baked onion on it when I come back.'

'I'm so sorry – I mean, about the pain. Why don't you send up one of the parlour maids later to remove the tray. You should go and lie down until the heat of the onion does its work.'

'No, Ma'am. If it's all the same to you, Cook says I can drink anything you leave on your tray. She sent up your choice, them being from your own sort.'

Elisa studied the tray. 'Tuttle must have packed them. Which do you prefer, Dilly? Tea or chocolate?'

Dilly's eyes were wide. 'Oh, the chocolate, pleasin' Your Ladyship. All foamy and sweet.'

'Good. Then the chocolate is yours.'

'Thank'ee.' Dilly turned away in a hurry and hit the open door which rattled back against Jeremy's mahogany tall boy. She grinned at Elisa and went out, luckily leaving the door ajar.

Dressing alone, Elisa was reminded of her earliest days in the company of travelling players when her entire appearance, and perhaps the winning of her audience, depended on her own miniscule talents. She had learned quickly, copying from other actresses all that seemed to be successful, and remembering not to get either bosky-drunk or boisterous when celebrating a local (and infrequent) triumph at York or Lincoln, or even as far west as Bristol.

She had learned to use male admirers and to give as little as possible in return. She saw what happened to the actresses who let themselves fall in love or who enjoyed sex so much they cheapened their bargaining price. She planned all her movements, even her emotions.

Now, at last, she knew what some of those early female friends of hers had tried to tell her.

'You'll fall in love one day, mark me, Elisa. And if he don't match your feelings, or if he toys with you, making you believe what isn't true for him, you'll know what it's like for them toffs that loves you.'

218

'I do know,' she whispered that morning at March Hall as she fastened and buttoned herself into the grass-green redingote over her matching green and ecru gown. Where had they gone, all the actresses who had shared her youth in the theatre? They had used themselves up too fast, given too much, and taken gifts of the moment – food and wine, not gems that would keep them during the long years after their beauty and charm faded.

Carefully setting the modish straw hat on the high-piled Grecian coiffure that she had arranged herself, Elisa thought of the heavy heirloom necklace that Jeremy had given her to wear. It would be impossible to sell it, since she understood very well that it was only hers on loan, as the present Lady March. But she liked to plan ahead, to be safe, and she had received no salary from her theatre work this month. The logical move was to sell her own pearl necklace and lock the money away for the future, should she ever need it.

She sat down at the little desk of a magnificent polished golden wood unknown to her, and wrote a note:

'Dear Tuttle, do send McFee to me. I have an errand for you. I wish you to get the best price possible for the pearl necklace with the diamond clasp that I am sending to you. You know what to do with the proceeds . . . My dearest affection to you and the others.'

She re-read the brief scrawl, then signed, 'Elisa Carlisle,' adding 'Lady March'.

When she was leaving the house a few minutes later she met Stebbings on the staircase and almost gave him the sealed note to deliver, but discretion got the better of that impetuous idea. She knew she could not trust him. He would tell Ponsonby. She was not afraid Jeremy would find out. She intended to tell him herself. The necklace was her own property.

Then she remembered. According to law, all her own precious jewels and property, even her London house, now belonged to her husband.

No matter. It was not Jeremy she was afraid of, but the gossip that would spread through the household if it was thought that she had been forced to sell her own jewels.

219

In front of the Hall Brian Clifford solved her problem. He had estate errands in town and was bringing Susan's two bandboxes, a portmanteau and several boxes out to the old March landaulet where Susan sat in queenly splendor.

She waved to Elisa and leaned out to boast proudly, 'Aren't we splendid? Since Father must go to London, he is taking me with him for a week before I go into Ponsy's hands and earn my five guineas per annum as her assistant.'

She looked enchanting in her yellow gown and pelisse, with a bright straw hat perched on the back of her head.

'Think how quiet and peaceful it will be at the Hall without my chatterbox!' Brian said. He squeezed his daughter's small hand in its jonquil yellow glove.

He went back to the gatehouse for the next load and Elisa followed him.

'Brian, will you favor me by staying at my London house?' He hesitated, pride holding him back. She added quickly, 'I need someone to deliver a packet to Tuttle. Someone I can trust. It will take a few minutes for me to fetch it down. Can you wait?'

'Of course.'

Luckily, the footman, Belliver, passed them at that minute and Susan was so interested in him she paid little attention to the doings of her elders. Brian put in the last of the luggage and went back up to Elisa's boudoir while she wrapped the necklace case in a lawn neckerchief.

As he put it into his own valise, still without asking questions, she embraced him impulsively.

'Dear Brian. Dear friend.'

It disappointed her that he should be so serious. He removed her arms with a kind of reluctant finality. His eyes seemed to look into her mind, even her soul. It was a disturbing sensation.

'Elsie –'

'Elisa.'

'Elsie Catlow,' he repeated, still holding her off. 'You are a beautiful, capricious, totally insincere — actress.'

She found this ridiculous. What else had she ever been?

'Do you think I want to be Elsie Catlow? I hate being Elsie.'

220

She felt her lips go dry. 'I despise her, Brian. You must know that.'

His hands shook her shoulders. He was in a curious state, not his calm, rational self, at all.

'I do know it. But you see, I love that Elsie, that dear and suffering girl. She was honest. Sincere. Every year you grow further away from her.' He looked at her a long moment, awkward for both of them. Then he moved toward her, staring at her mouth. She let him kiss her. He was her trusted friend. It was the least she could offer him. She felt his lips, the earnest pressure . . .

When he backed away she murmured again, 'I do care for you, Brian. You are my closest friend.'

He swallowed and said coldly, 'I will carry out Your Ladyship's commission.'

It was not a happy parting. She went out with him again in order to say goodbye to Susan once more, and when the coachman got up on his box and Brian was beside his daughter, Elisa reached out and held his hand, caressing it with the fingers of her left hand.

'Thank you again, my friend.'

He nodded but let Susan speak for him as the coachman gave the signal and the team started off at a spanking pace. Susan shrieked and held onto her hat. It was her goodbye wave that Elisa saw at the last.

She went slowly around the gatehouse to the front where Dilly Skeen said the roses were still blooming. She had that other tomb to decorate, since she couldn't pay her tribute to Molly Catlow's grave.

This time, however, she wouldn't go inside and let herself be caught as she had been by Lord March's arrival.

On the other hand – and she began to feel cheerful again – perhaps she wouldn't be married to him now if she hadn't been trapped inside that tomb with him.

CHAPTER NINETEEN

It was a long walk and unusually quiet. She had not met a single creature, man or animal. She might almost have been walking on some obscure planet at the end of the universe. But she reached the graveyard at last. It was a welcome sight, even the fallen tombstones and sunken grass. Her delicate, light-soled shoes were not the most comfortable for a country walk.

There was no likelihood of Elisa being closed into the March vault. The new lock on the door was so heavy she thought ironically: does it keep the living out, or the dead within?

She arranged the full, blowsy, sweet-scented roses in the lock and made a prayer to the eager young Arthur March she remembered. Then she turned from the vault, only to collide with 'Abel', the hulking mute. She gave him a nervous smile, thinking that he couldn't be too much of a brute, if Jeremy was his friend. She hoped to win him as she had hostile audiences.

He looked down at her from his great height. It was difficult to tell what feelings she had aroused in those muddy yellow eyes.

She managed a civilized introduction, holding out her hand. 'How do you do? I am Lady March. Do you have the care of this graveyard?'

He nodded. His fierce look, she saw now, was the natural result of his facial construction. His heavy brow over-shadowed his eyes, and she suspected his frown indicated his difficulty in understanding, perhaps even in seeing her.

She said, 'Do you work for the Marches?'

Abel grunted. She thought she made out an agreement. He pointed one finger over her head toward the vault door.

'The Marches?' she asked.

He nodded, then abruptly shook his head. He made noises in his throat. She stared at him, looked at the vault and then at the flowers she had left by the lock. Arthur's flowers.

'Arthur March?'

He seemed genuinely happy that she understood. What was he trying to tell her about the dead youth?

'You were Arthur's friend? Arthur came here?' It seemed an odd place for a young man Arthur's age. She was about to leave the matter and start back to March Hall when he grunted again and pointed to the roses with the same forefinger. While she puzzled this out he raised another finger and brought the two fingers together. He then pointed to his mouth with both fingers. An odd business altogether.

She understood vaguely. 'Arthur talking to someone?'

He shrugged his heavy shoulders. It did not seem likely that she had guessed rightly and her imagination went no further.

When she left him he called in that rasping grunt, 'Ah!' and again, 'Ah!'

Whatever the word he wanted to get out, it was unintelligible. But he had tried. He caught her by the shoulder and then made a flat, cutting motion. She shook her head.

Finally giving up, he shuffled out of the way and she started along the path. He remained there looking after her. She stopped abruptly, went back and held out her hand. He rubbed a big paw on his stained and patched jerkin, then stuck it out. Her hand was lost in his.

She stood motionless for a few seconds, aware of an overwhelming gratitude. This strange, frightening man knew nothing about her, had no reason to be kind to her; yet he offered his friendship. It was a gratifying experience, especially after Brian Clifford's severe judgement of her.

She said finally, 'Thank you, my friend. And we *are* friends, aren't we?'

He made a noise in his throat and scowled, but he did not fool her this time. She said, 'Good day,' smiled again, and went on her way around the grave-stones.

The long, lonely walk back to March Hall was not easy and she was relieved when, sometime before noon, she heard a wagon harness rattling along the road toward her. The wheels rolled into and out of every rut and hole. She was surprised to see Jeremy holding the reins loosely and dressed like any country yeoman, in a homespun shirt, an old jerkin, breeches and boots that had seen a long life.

'Good Lord, is it you?' he called out to her. 'Here, my love, give me your hands.'

She hesitated, wondering if the mare would stop, but she needn't have been concerned. Apparently, the good creature was used to her master's moods. She drew up just beyond Elisa who raised her arms to her husband. Seconds afterward she was seated beside him on the old board seat. He put his free arm around her like any farmer with his lass. She leaned toward him and kissed his cheek. His face was very close to hers when he looked at her, tilting his head back to see her better.

'You are looking like a girl who isn't used to a country walk.'

'Nor am I. But I'm glad I went. I have a new friend.'

He seemed genuinely surprised. 'One of the tenants?'

'The mute who sees after the graveyard.'

She could feel the muscles in his arm tighten as he held her.

'You went to the vault?'

'Dilly Skeen said there were still roses growing around the gatehouse.'

'That was good of you. Incidentally, Dilly Skeen is my reason for this ride. She has a toothache.'

'Yes. I know. The cook promised to apply a hot onion, I believe.'

'She will do better with professional help. There is a good man in the village. He sells drugs for various aches and pains. The tooth may have to be drawn and since Clifford has gone, Sam Yarrow may just do. I'm sorry Clifford left before he could see to poor Dilly.' He gave her a side-glance. 'You get on very well with Clifford.'

224

'Sometimes.' She was remembering his stern attitude today, his effort to make her into what she wasn't, a noble, selfless lady bountiful.

'Why did you never marry him? I'm sure he loves you.'

She hoped he was jealous but she doubted it.

'Most importantly, because I never could love so pure and noble a man.' He laughed and she added, 'Also because, in his eyes, I have become a selfish, manipulative, scarlet woman.'

This time he looked directly at her. 'And are you?'

She didn't snap out the indignant answer that first occurred to her. She said after a little silence, 'My new mute friend accepts me for what I am.'

He must have recognized that this was meant for him as well as Brian Clifford. He remarked thoughtfully, 'It is a wise human being who understands what he is. I'm not sure I know what I am.'

She said, 'You are kind and thoughtful and, best of all, helpful –'

'Ah.'

'To your social and economic inferiors.'

He opened his mouth to say something automatic like, 'Thank you.' But he closed his mouth immediately after. It took him a minute or so to recover from the barb she had concealed in all those compliments.

'And to the rest of mankind?' he asked finally.

'But only you can answer that.'

'Ironic. And all this time I thought you were the one with the –'

'Problem?' She let a note of irony creep in.

'Sorry. That was clumsy.' But he didn't deny it.

The thought made her a little sick. She said nothing more as they jogged along toward the village.

They found Samuel Yarrow tending his garden behind a narrow, terraced house in the village. He proved to be a cherubic little man, more concerned about his rows of carrots and turnips than with the usual obsequious manner of the villagers toward Lord March. During the first few minutes of introductions he almost offended Elisa by his casual indifference to her. She immediately assumed he resented her and perhaps knew her reputation.

'Aye. It's Her Ladyship, is it? . . . Now, then, Sir, what's the difficulty?'

Jeremy told him about Dilly Skeen. He heard it all, nodding sagely, and after a last, regretful look at his garden where he had been caressing the feathery carrot-tops, he led the way into his tiny house. So far as Elisa could see, he ate, slept and read his collection of books in his two rooms, surrounded by mortars, pestles, green bottles, yellow and amber bottles, even some that glowed like rich wine. Somewhat to Elisa's surprise he took down a box of white powder, poured a small amount onto a square of paper and, folding the paper in upon itself, he slipped it into his waistcoat.

Jeremy looked at Elisa and grimaced when little Mister Yarrow next hefted a double-pronged metal instrument that looked like steel shears.

'It sometimes comes to this,' he told the Marches cheerfully. 'But the Skeens are tough wenches. If I can save the tooth, I'd rather. Old Granny Skeen still has most of hers. Comes of the hard bread she used to bake. Mighty good chewing, as I well recall.'

'By the by, don't worry about dinner,' Jeremy told him. 'Mrs Ponsonby will see that you dine at her table. We'll send you back in one of the carriages.'

'So I figured, seeing Ponsy and I are such old friends.'

The little man's stout hips took up space on the wagon, but Jeremy drew Elisa closer and she was happy with the arrangement.

Oddly enough, just when Elisa no longer desperately hoped to find some form of civilization on the road, Jeremy and Sam Yarrow saw a dozen acquaintances, passing on foot, or working in the fields, or driving their flocks. There was much joking back and forth, a great many calls and greetings.

A few passersby, strangers to Elisa, politely raised two fingers to a forelock in acknowledgement of her. She returned these gestures, inclining her head and smiling. But she was not foolish

226

enough to think the friendly acknowledgements had anything to do with her as an individual. She was Lord March's bride. This was her sole qualification. She had yet to earn their respect as an individual.

They passed the graveyard caretaker, and Elisa was especially pleased when the mute made big strides out to the wagon and held up a gigantic hand. Jeremy offered his own hand but Abel grunted and shook his head. Hardly daring to hope she had been singled out for this favor, Elisa extended her hand and Abel took it in his, squeezing hard. Then he nodded to the two men and shuffled back into the graveyard.

Elisa turned and waved to him as they rode on. She was well aware that Jeremy and Sam Yarrow looked at her with new respect. It delighted her.

Sam Yarrow pushed his wide-brimmed hat back on his thick, white hair.

'I never saw that before. Most females are afraid of poor old Abel.'

'My wife is exceptional,' Jeremy boasted.

It was the first really sincere and heartfelt compliment she could recall from her husband; she told herself that if this glorious state continued she might yet win what she craved most of all: Jeremy March's love.

They reached the Hall a little after midday, shortly before dinner time. Elisa volunteered to find Dilly Skeen when Mrs Ponsonby proved more interested in Mister Yarrow than in the whereabouts of the new abigail. She assumed that Hannah Fincastle, the cook, would know, since Dilly had last been seen returning to the kitchen quarters with Elisa's tray.

The cook agreed that Yarrow was needed.

'I've had them toothaches in my time. Nasty business. Dilly Skeen is a bit clumsy now and again. That's the bad leg. Born with it. But she was nigh onto crying when she fetched down your tray. I doubt the onion helped over-much. I felt right bad for the lass.'

'Where did she go?'

Hannah shrugged. 'Hard to say. I'd my ragout of lamb to attend to, and my fricassee of chicken and asparaus. And the rest. So I sent her on her way. Told her to ask old Granny who always had a notion or two. Old Granny Skeen still has a deal of good sense. Most likely, you'll find her there.'

It seemed reasonable. Elisa went back to Mrs Ponsonby and Sam Yarrow. Unfortunately, she interrupted a personal moment. The housekeeper resented her enough in the present circumstances. The feud would grow worse if Elisa interrupted what appeared to be the progress of a romance.

Elisa passed them by in silence, hoping to find Jeremy, but Stebbings informed her loftily that he had gone to oversee the drainage repairs at the almshouses.

'And Granny Skeen? Where will I find her?'

Stebbings' eyebrows went up. 'Your Ladyship wishes to carry food to old Granny? I believe that would prove unnecessary. Baskets of food and ale were delivered to her and to her neighbors yesterday.'

It would take somewhat longer to win over the pompous fellow. Elisa dismissed him with as much cool confidence as she could muster.

'This is quite a different matter. Mr Yarrow is here to treat Dilly Skeen's tooth.'

Stebbings was unimpressed. 'Mrs Ponsonby sent for the girl. It is within walking distance. If the girl is in enough pain, she will come at once.'

Elisa was determined to do someone some good. She would give Dilly a ride back to the Hall. She went to the stables, wondering if there, too, she would be rejected. The old coachman, Neame, was still in bed in his room over the stables, recovering from his heart seizure, but Belliver, the young red-haired footman, was there, harnessing a neat gray mare to a curricle.

Seeing Elisa, he assured her with naive anxiety, 'His Lordship said please exercise the mare. He had no time and Mr Clifford is gone. I could take Your Ladyship for a little drive.'

'Exactly what I was about to suggest. Can you take me to Granny Skeen? I've no notion where to find her.'

He was flattered. 'An honor, Ma'am. Granny is just across the river. Staying with one of the shepherds and his family.'

He helped her up over the fragile, high wheel of the curricle and minutes later they were driving over the little limestone bridge toward the shepherd's cottage.

The shepherd's wife had been out on the bank of the meandering stream, washing clothes. Now she was spreading long, hip-length, homespun shirts, belonging to her husband and sons, over bushes above the water. The woman whom Belliver pointed out as Granny Skeen was wrapped in a fleecy cloak and hood and huddled in the sunlight on the step of a cottage. The building itself appeared to have started life as a one-room coteen but now, with additions on both sides, it could accommodate an entire family.

The old woman looked ancient enough to be Dilly's great-grandmother. Her skin was the color of parchment and her hands curled like claws upon themselves. But when she looked up at the visitors in the fine curricle she grinned and revealed a number of excellent teeth. Sam Yarrow was right. She or her diet had taken good care of those teeth.

Belliver brought Elisa to the old woman, while the shepherd's wife looked up from the grassy bank, rolling down her sleeves and getting ready to join the newcomers. It must be annoying, Elisa thought, to have to stop work and pay your respects to someone you probably didn't even respect.

Elisa called, 'Please don't let me interrupt you. I'm Lady March. I would like to speak to Granny Skeen.'

The woman nodded, dipped a very slight curtsy, and returned to her work, looking back over her shoulder several times.

Belliver cautioned Elisa, ''Fraid you'll have to speak up, Ma'am. Granny doesn't hear too well.'

Elisa raised her voice. 'May I speak to your granddaughter, or has she left already?'

'Left?' the old woman repeated in the peculiar, high-pitched voice of the aged deaf. 'Dilly's no been here. Dilly's up at t'Hall.'

I've certainly made myself a figure of fun, Elisa thought. But she tried once more.

'Your granddaughter was suffering with a toothache. I'm told she came here.'

Granny squinted at the distant shepherd's wife in perplexity. The woman took a few steps toward them. 'Your La'ship looking for Dilly? She'll be up at t'Hall. She's a room there. Hasn't been here all the day.'

Probably Stebbings or the housekeeper thought it was amusing to send Elisa here, interrupting the woman at her work and making a cake of herself. Elisa thanked the two women and Belliver lifted her neatly into the curricle.

'Awful strange, Ma'am,' he remarked as they rode back over the bridge and soon came within sight of the golden Cotswold facade that always impressed Elisa.

'Not strange at all. Just a bit of sly fun on the part of that wretched housekeeper and her minions.'

Belliver was shocked. 'Surely not, Your Ladyship. They wouldn't dare.'

'Oh, wouldn't they! Do you know where Dilly's room is?'

'Well now, not to visit, like, Ma'am,' he said stiffly. 'Dilly Skeen not being in my –'

'Class?'

'Just so, Ma'am. We all have our place, and Dilly isn't my class, just like I'm not equal to Miss Clifford, in a manner of speaking.'

If they all felt this way, it certainly explained the prejudice against herself. She had been born into a social state lower than Dilly's and now she called herself Lady March, the wife of a peer of the realm. How they must despise and resent her.

No one was about when Elisa entered the Hall, leaving Belliver on his way to the stables. From the staircase Elisa could hear Sam Yarrow and Mrs Ponsonby in the south corridor, now discussing the dinner he would share with her in a very few minutes. She went on up to the top floor, repeating Belliver's instructions: 'Second door on the east, one of those overlooking the kitchen gardens.'

At such moments she understood why the servants preferred to use Arthur's 'Secret Staircase'. It was considerably more direct. The top floor hall proved to be narrower and darker than the others in March Hall, even at this hour, early in the afternoon.

She tried the second door, but it was locked. She called Dilly's name and rattled the latch. When she heard Stebbings marching along the hall she was actually glad to see him. He looked surprised to find her in this area.

'Dilly Skeen, Madam? I understood she had gone to old Granny Skeen.'

'It seems not. Would you please unlock the door? She may be in pain.'

Making no effort to conceal his impatience, the butler produced a bundle of keys, trying two of them before he pushed the door open.

'As one might expect. The girl was never reliable. Resting at this hour! She will certainly be needed when Your Ladyship dresses for dinner.'

As lightly as possible Elisa crossed the little room under the slanting roof. The girl was still asleep. The sound of the door opening had not disturbed her. She was curled up in a child-like bundle, with her tousled head burrowed into the straw mattress.

Elisa reached out to touch the girl's hand, but hesitated. It seemed better to let her wake up naturally. A sudden awakening now might start the pain again. Stebbings approached the narrow bed with its pile of excellent quality bedding folded against the footboard. She signalled to him, whispering 'Sh!'

After looking down at Dilly for a few seconds he was about to turn away indifferently but, to her annoyance, he stopped, frowned and picked up Dilly's bare hand by the wrist.

'The girl is never clean. You see?'

There was a ring of dirt around the girl's wrist, just above where she had obediently washed her hand. At least, he hadn't awakened the girl.

'The toothache?' Elisa brought him back to business.

He was still frowning. With unexpected gentleness he offered Dilly's hand to Elisa.

'If you please, Your Ladyship.'

Puzzled by his behaviour, she took Dilly's hand in her palm. She was alarmed by the chill of the fingers, and something more, a peculiar moistness that sickened her.

'What is it? What happened?'

'Undeniably dead. I should say she took a drug for the toothache. Something deadly.'

'I don't believe it! I saw only her a few hours ago. She wouldn't do such a stupid thing.' But of course, she might. It could happen to anyone.

Elisa caressed the pathetic hand absently. She began to shiver. When she roused herself to the present she saw Stebbings staring at her thoughtfully.

CHAPTER TWENTY

Dilly Skeen had been a friendly, ingenuous girl – perhaps foolish, and undoubtedly not very quick-witted – a girl who happened to die at her own hands, so to speak. But her eagerness and willingness had been poignant and attractive to Elisa.

'Stupid up here,' the cook said, tapping her head. 'Like as not, the girl took a few drops of summat, then forgot and took a few more. Happens common enough.'

'What does "summat" mean?' Elisa asked, to receive shrugs. 'Such accidents,' the cook said, 'were common.'

'It's a great pity. A dreadful business,' Miss Ponsonby said. Elisa was just thinking with surprise that the woman could actually show compassion when Ponsonby added, 'Imagine that girl doing such a thing under His Lordship's own roof! Dreadful!'

Elisa resented everyone's attitude. She had never known the girl well. But a human being had died. Someone should at least try to discover how it happened.

She was gratified and relieved that Jeremy cared enough to ask questions. He investigated Dilly's room, as well as the room that Dilly had shared with her 'Granny' before the drains were repaired. The answer was always the same.

After Dilly had been taken to the shepherd's cottage to be shrouded, Elisa went with Jeremy to point out all the details of her discovery, or, more properly, the discovery by the butler.

'When they keep saying "summat" or "somewhat", are they talking about a particular drug?' she asked Jeremy.

He shook his head. 'They use old remedies – powdered tree bark, the leaves off bushes, a hundred things – for

233

headaches, earaches, toothaches. Laudanum is fairly common, however.'

Laudanum again.

The small pinches of fear that had troubled her from the first crystalized now. 'Is laudanum so easily obtained?'

He looked at her, puzzled by the tension in her voice. 'Certainly. Anyone may buy it. It has a dozen good uses.'

'In liquid, for instance?'

'Yes, one way. Certainly, you are acquainted with laudanum to calm the nerves, to put you to sleep. After a performance, perhaps?'

The sarcasm was unmistakable. She knew he was thinking of the laudanum that had killed Arthur. Laudanum Arthur had taken from her.

'Tuttle says I use it too many times.' She tried to excuse herself. 'There is a tension I often feel after a performance, as you say.'

'Yes. I can understand that.'

He had been studying the bed and now the little stool beside it where were gathered Dilly Skeen's treasures: a pattern of wood anemones pressed between pieces of broken glass; a broken saucer of genuine porcelain that had been mended with lumpy glue (it held a half-eaten currant muffin); a bit of hemp with a loop in it, probably once used as a lead for a small pet animal.

Elisa turned away, aware of an overwhelming ache in her breast. She stared out of the narrow dormer window, seeing nothing but the top of the wooded hill and the pale eastern sky at mid-afternoon.

Jeremy had been speaking. When he got no reply he watched her, puzzled.

'Did you know Dilly that well?'

She thought, am I that selfish? Does everyone's misfortune bring back memories? She said aloud, 'No. It was just that she reminded me of a woman I once knew. She used to save pressed flowers and broken crockery.'

'I see.' He fingered Dilly's treasures a bit helplessly. 'I'm sorry. I didn't know.' He replaced the glass shards. Then he reached for her hand. 'This isn't anyone's fault, though I do think Yarrow might have gone to her instead of waiting for her in the solar. It is a cruel thing, but life is cruel.'

She left the room with him. Her head seemed to be buzzing with weird ideas, suspicions only half-clear to her. They were noisy as bees, and they formed one hideous pattern whose centerpiece was *laudanum*.

But the girl took the drug on occasion, as everyone informed Elisa. It happened when Dilly had an operation on her splay foot, and it was said that she gave it to her dying father when he was in pain. The drug was commonplace, though expensive. All the same, Elisa had her troubled thoughts.

Dilly Skeen's burial, supervised by Abel, the mute, under the instruction of the local vicar's curate, was treated with a casualness that shocked Elisa. Granny Skeen appeared to have accepted her granddaughter's death with very little emotion, but she developed a painful habit of speaking about Dilly as if the girl were just across the river at March Hall.

Elisa caught faint flickers of surprise in Jeremy's eyes when she made it clear she would attend the burial with him. Elisa was also interested in the others who were present, notably the shepherd's wife and one son, an adenoidal boy who earned Elisa's sympathy by his genuine grief at the passing of a friend. Sam Yarrow arrived and was welcomed by everyone, though Elisa's greeting was not effusive. She felt that he had some responsibility for Dilly's death. He might at least have broken out of the housekeeper's clutches long enough to minister to the girl. Had he done so, he might have awakened her and saved her life.

A day later Elisa tried unsuccessfully to discuss the subject of laudanum with Jeremy. She suspected the drug brought back to him all too vividly the pain of his brother's death. He dismissed the subject for 'another time'.

Then, Captain Hawtree rode by on a lively stallion, demonstrating his remarkable, one-handed horsemanship. The Captain carried a message from his father and stepmother, that Lord March was needed to mediate the division of the profits from the charity performance.

Elisa's thoughts about the drug were chaotic by this time. Except for sadly regretting Dilly Skeen's appalling mistake, her mind seemed to whirl around an experience of her own.

The poisoned champagne . . . Perhaps enough to kill.

Then, Arthur March's death. Laudanum again. Elisa's thoughts raced on.

And now another innocent, Dilly Skeen. The only thing to be said in this case was that Dilly, like Arthur, had administered it to herself. Dilly, however, was an involuntary suicide.

When had she taken the drug? Probably while waiting in her little bedchamber for Sam Yarrow. She must have suffered the gnawing, nerve-racking pain and poured a few drops of the liquid drug.

Elisa didn't really expect to solve this gruesome puzzle, but the original thought nagged at her. Both of the other laudanum poisonings were connected with Elisa Carlisle.

She wondered if one of those clever little Bow Street Runners from London, so useful when hired to pursue a criminal, could serve her now. But it would take time to hire one and Jeremy would probably be outraged at this invasion of March Hall's sacred portals.

What if I tried to think like a Bow Street Runner? she asked herself. Suddenly, she decided to act upon her idea.

She found Hannah Fincastle in one corner of the kitchen-garden. The herbs formed a rectangular patch of greenery brightened by an occasional mauve blossom. A tiny stream headed down from the wooded hill above and ran along one length of the garden. It was here that Hannah waved a handful of tiny circular leaves with lengthy, fragile stems.

'Cress. My favorite kind, Ma'am. This perfect sort is hard to grow in our particular soil. Feel the softness. You might rub it on your cheek.' She took out one leaf, smaller in size than a shilling piece, and rubbed it over the back of her freckled hand.

Elisa enjoyed watercress but her mind was on other, more urgent matters.

'Tell me, Mrs Fincastle, what did Dilly Skeen eat or drink the day she died?'

Hannah's gaze sharpened, but she asked no question.

'Had porridge at dawn. Couldn't eat it. Complained about her tooth, poor thing. I promised to give her a roasted onion after she finished serving you. To press against her tooth, you know. She was excited about serving Your Ladyship. She sometimes drank whatever was left on the tea tray.' She stopped and considered the cress in her fist. 'But Your Ladyship drank the tea, if that's what you're meaning. Still, she could've put the drops in what was left.'

'And the chocolate pot?'

Mrs Fincastle's chin went up. 'I'd clean forgot, Your Ladyship being the only one that drinks it. Old Busy-Ponsy come to me about that chocolate pot. It was missing.'

'The pot? Or the chocolate itself?'

The cook was puzzled. 'The pot, Ma'am. It never come back. Me, I was busy with the mutton and I didn't notice. But Dilly should've come back with the two empty pots. Both tea and chocolate. Poor lass. She was on the clumsy side, as you may have seen, and it was like her to break it and hide the pieces.'

'Yes. I know. She saved them.'

Hannah leaned toward her, confiding, 'China and crockery disappear now and again. Odd bits, you know. And that chocolate pot had violets on it. Real pretty. She might've broke it on purpose, as you could say. So she could keep it.'

'But she would have returned it, perhaps broken, as you say. Then she would ask for the pieces.'

Hannah shrugged. 'Well, her being dead, poor creature, made that impossible.'

The two women walked together into the stillroom. They were both silent and Elisa wondered if the cook shared her confused suspicions. Apparently not. When they reached the kitchen Hannah excused herself politely.

'I'll be seeing to the turbot and the cauliflowers. Got a celery *espanole* I'm going to try tonight. Hope His Lordship has a taste for oddments.'

'One more question.' Elisa remembered this as she was leaving the kitchen. 'Apparently, when Dilly Skeen returned to the kitchen with the tray, you didn't notice that the chocolate pot was missing.'

Hannah was already issuing orders to a kitchen girl of about twelve and she resented the implication that she had been at fault.

'Your Ladyship, I was mighty busy at that hour.'

'I understand. I'm sorry.'

Elisa went out through the service passage and into the main hall. She hesitated by the Grail tapestry, knowing this was by far the most direct way to reach the servants' floor. Disgusted by her own cowardice, she passed the concealed door and went on to the main staircase.

The house was its usual quiet self at this hour. She deliberately put extra weight on each foot as she went up to Dilly Skeen's room. The sound of her own footsteps was not particularly reassuring. They produced an unsettling echo.

Playing Lady of the Manor without any real 'stage business' did not make her happy. She wanted to help Jeremy with the poor on the estate. No one was better motivated. She understood the people of the almshouses a great deal better than she understood the aristocrats to whom Gwenna Hawtree was forever introducing her.

The old doubts appeared as she made this decision. Sooner or later, Jeremy would know about Elsie Catlow. If he had despised the actress Elisa Carlisle and had obviously fallen in love with her after great reluctance, he would feel even more contempt for the real Elsie, a bastard child whose mother ended her life in a Bedlam cell.

I must enjoy whatever emotions he offers me, while they exist. Even now, he prefers to be gone from me for most of the day and evening, Elisa told herself.

Why not? What had she to offer? She took great care with her appearance. She let him know her sensuous desires. But he knew little of her desperate fears.

Elisa Carlise was a hollow woman. Elsie Catlow was real. When would Jeremy discover this? Sometimes she was sure he knew it already.

She thought of the hollow Elisa when she entered Dilly Skeen's room on the attic floor, because Dilly was so very real. Nothing in the least like the actress, Elisa. Dilly had no pretenses.

The room had been given a slap-dash cleaning and dusting. The broken dishes and the pressed violets that had been Dilly's treasures were piled in a heap on the center of the bed.

Elisa looked them over, examining the dish, wondering if Dilly had sneaked Elisa's tray down to the kitchen area and then returned to her room, put drops of laudanum into the chocolate pot and poured a drink, hoping the drug of the rapidly cooling chocolate would soothe her pain.

Where was the chocolate pot now?

She looked around the room, seeing only the few personal items that had belonged to Dilly Skeen. Several garments were still hanging on pegs across the room. Beneath them a pair of patterns had been carelessly thrown. Bits of mud and decayed leaves still clung to them. There was nothing of death about this room. Dilly had expected to live many, many years.

Elisa examined the bed and Dilly's treasures. The three-legged stool on which they had formerly been displayed was over in a corner. It occurred to Elisa that something might have fallen off the stool when it was near the bed. There was hardly room on the stool's surface to hold all Dilly's little treasures.

She felt around the edge of the bed and then knelt to look beneath it. Obviously, the cleaning broomstraws had not reached beneath the bed. Dust and bits of fluff made her sneeze, but she paid little attention to this when she saw the violet-sprigged chocolate pot sitting in shadowy splendor far under the bed.

Ignoring what this crawling around might do to the creamy silk folds of her gown, she reached for the chocolate pot.

The handle was cracked, whether deliberately or accidentally no one would ever know. But it seemed likely that Dilly had placed it here intending to add it to her little collection.

Elisa removed the top. Some chocolate remained in the bottom. She sniffed it but she had no way of knowing whether the drug had been in the chocolate. She poured a few drops onto her finger and tasted it. She couldn't come to any conclusion.

Perhaps the cook or Mrs Ponsonby could tell. With the chocolate pot in her hand she looked around the room once again before leaving.

She had a sudden, vivid memory of Dilly Skeen carrying the tray, almost dropping it, telling her: 'The tea and the chocolate come with your cases and valises, Ma'am.' And Elisa had said, 'My people must have packed it for me.' Perhaps not those exact words, but something very like them.

She had been incredibly blind!

With her hand on the door latch she suddenly felt the full horror of an idea that had been playing about in her brain and never fully admitted. What if Dilly Skeen had never taken laudanum for her toothache? It was all so obvious. Dilly had merely drunk Elisa's chocolate.

She catalogued the laudanum attacks in her mind: the champagne; the chocolate; the laudanum death of Arthur was the only event that proceeded logically from her legitimate possession of the drug.

Who was responsible for those other 'gifts'? What enemy *hated* her? Who would profit by her death? It was ironic that she would have said a month ago, 'Only Arthur's brother hates me so much.'

Her will left specific jewels and a handsome annuity to Tuttle, with another account set up for Brian to pay for the care of patients at St Mary's of Bethlehem Asylum. Brian himself would receive a tidy sum, with smaller sums to McFee and Strawbridge. Now, of course, by law her husband would be her heir. She must make certain that Tuttle and the others were provided for.

Holding the chocolate pot carefully in one hand, she closed the door and started toward the front staircase. Stebbings was just going down. He had reached a landing and looked back, perhaps hearing her footsteps. She retreated. In her present condition, stiff with the horror of her thoughts, she didn't want to be seen yet by the butler who had already demonstrated his dislike and contempt. Doubtless, her present condition would delight him. He would immediately go to Mrs Ponsonby so they could enjoy it together.

She hurried along the hall, found a door ajar and opened it. Luckily, it was another staircase. She had already started down when she realized this was the 'Secret Staircase' so beloved of Arthur March. Her mood was such that she stopped and listened, praying that her imagination would not begin to work now, as it so often did during her waking nightmares.

At first, the narrow staircase seemed far less sinister by daylight. Being an inside staircase, it still required the lamps she had noticed the night she followed Jeremy to the roof. The oil must be replaced daily because most of the lamps were flickering or glowing today. She had to take care, since the treads themselves were short, and the heels of her shoes were curved and narrow. She held the chocolate pot in her right hand with great care, pressing her left hand occasionally against the whitewashed wall to keep her balance.

She had gone half the way to the floor on which the bedchambers were situated when she became aware that the echo of footsteps she heard was not her own. She stopped, listening. She was sure she heard her own heart beating. Nothing else.

She went on, listening with each step. She stopped suddenly. This time she heard the sound somewhere above her. A heavier step, probably a man's boot. It could be anyone, a servant, or even a friend of the family, like Captain Hawtree. But in her present, terrified state, haunted by the knowledge that the chocolate served to her may have been drugged, her imagination took possession of her.

This was Arthur March's favorite haunt. Arthur had cursed her with his dying breath.

She took the next few steps to the door of the family floor and tried the latch.

Locked.

She turned back, heard nothing, and shook her head in disgust at her own susceptibility.

She had taken several more steps, heading downward toward the gallery floor, when the 'echoes' began again. Furious at her imagination, she hurried downward, swung around a turn where the steps narrowed to nothing on the turn, and put out her free hand to brace herself.

Too late. She felt for the vanished step and plunged down a dozen steps to the landing in front of the gallery door. She knocked her head against the door latch, the buzzing noise increased, and she was aware of a deep, breath-cutting pain in her right arm.

None of these facts seemed to matter before she lost consciousness. She was aware only of a keen annoyance that she had broken the little chocolate pot.

CHAPTER TWENTY-ONE

Except on the stage, she had always disliked being stared at while her eyes were closed. She hated knowing that she was completely at the mercy of someone else at such a moment. Yet, here she was, lying in the big bed she shared with Jeremy, and a face seemed to be very close above hers. She opened her eyes abruptly.

Gwenna Hawtree's long, amusing features, framed by their wig of bright red hair, hovered above Elisa's face. She greeted Elisa's recovery with satisfaction.

'Ah! Back to this mundane world, my dear. You relieve us all. Especially your household.'

Elisa found it difficult to talk for a minute and asked hoarsely, 'The household cares? Your Ladyship's humor is always appreciated.'

Gwenna seemed surprised. Perhaps she didn't know the situation, after all.

'Whatever do you mean? Little Mrs Ponsonby has been running about looking pale and sending off messengers in all directions to find March. And there is that pretty fellow, Belliver, who found you and stands around wringing his hands, saying he must have pushed the door open upon you, and –'

Elisa tried to sit up, groaned and muttered, 'My head! No. My arm.'

'Both, I regret to say. The entire house was in an uproar when I arrived. I came over to pay my call – to show you all the courtesies; I am nothing if not correct in my manners, you know.'

Elisa grinned at that. 'But of course. You are the soul of propriety. Never mind. Belliver found me. Was he on the staircase behind me?'

'No, no. You have it all wrong-side to. Belliver was about to enter the staircase from the gallery floor. He pushed the door open against what he thought for an instant was your dead body.'

'He was not on the staircase?'

'Not a bit of it. But can you imagine the scandal if Lord March's bride had been found dead in her own home, with the wedding a mere week or so behind them? A quarrel. A quick blow. A toss down the stairs . . .'

'Please, Your Ladyship.'

'But in your case a mere broken chocolate pot and a broken shoe heel.'

Elisa said quickly, 'What happened to the chocolate pot?'

'Heavens! Thrown away, of course. Quite worthless now.'

Elisa tried to sit up. 'I'd like to see it, all the same. Can someone bring the pieces to me?'

Lady Hawtree was puzzled. 'Impossible. That sort of thing has gone out with the rubbish. They would never find it by this time.' She held up the right shoe that Elisa was wearing when she tumbled down the stairs. The curving heel had been wrenched off in Elisa's fall. 'You should concern yourself with this.'

'I remember.' Elisa glanced at her left arm which had taken the brunt of her fall when her right foot tripped. The arm seemed to be loosely encased in a silk shawl whose ends were looped around her neck. 'Is it broken? It hurts.'

Lady Gwenna shrugged. 'Unlikely. I believe you were a bit pulled about. But just before you opened your eyes you clenched your fist.' She looked around the big, comfortable bedchamber, obviously no longer interested in her friend's accident. 'I begin to wonder. Can this dreary place make up to you for all you have surrendered? I'm sure I should prefer the theatre.'

'I was pretending in the theatre. Trying to play various roles that would make me forget Elsie Catlow.'

'Who?'

Too late, Elisa fancied she could see Lady Gwenna's ears prick up.

'A girl I once knew. In my years with those travelling players. I'd almost forgotten.'

Her Ladyship grinned, a peculiar smile, as though she grinned at herself. 'Do not fancy you are the only woman with disreputable antecedents. My dear, why do you think I took you up in the first place? Because I despise my father's class. I can match your Elsie person and riposte, as the duellists says, with my sainted father. You see, we both have our buried scandals.'

The unexpected bitterness vanished. She became the incurable gossip again. 'Tell me, how is it with you and March? Is he still the lover he seemed to be that night of the *Vampyr* reading?'

'You see "how it is with me".'

'Don't evade. Is he the lover he seems to be?'

'In every way.' The effort to be cautious with Gwenna Hawtree was beginning to tell on Elisa's nerves and her battered body. She resettled herself and made the mistake of trying to touch the swelling on her left temple. Someone had placed a pad of cotton cloth against it and unguents wafted their way to her nostrils. She cried out at the pain of her touch and Lady Gwenna took the hint. She reached for the ribbons of the deep-crowned silk bonnet that she had dropped on the small leather-topped table near the bed.

'I have stayed too long, my dear. Another time. Tell that glorious husband of yours he must take better care of you. Happy brides are not usually left to their own devices in deserted houses.'

She adjusted her bonnet, touched the fingers of Elisa's injured arm sympathetically and looked as if she would leave, but seemed to make an abrupt decision.

'Elisa?'

Her tone surprised Elisa who could not recall a time in their acquaintance when Lady Gwenna's manner had seemed to be so serious, even doubtful. Her Ladyship was never in doubt about anything.

'Your Ladyship?'

Gwenna walked back a step or two toward the bed. 'Has it ever occurred to you that March's swift about-face with you was odd?'

Elisa surprised her by a quick assent. 'Often. A month ago, or a little more, he despised me. He believed I was responsible for Mr Arthur March's suicide.' She suspected Gwenna was about her usual tricks, hoping to disturb her. It was particularly cruel at such a time, but that had never stopped Lady Hawtree before.

'Then why did you marry him?'

Since Gwenna was largely responsible for bringing them together and had incessantly urged Elisa to seduce him, it seemed a brazen question. Elisa answered in the same mood.

'Because you made it so easy for me.'

Gwenna remained in that uncharacteristic mood, thoughtful, even doubtful, as she tied the ribbons of her new poke bonnet.

'Hoist by my own petard. To confess the truth, Elisa, I was warned not to discuss this with you. It could be perceived as bad taste.'

'Who warned you?'

'My wretched Hugo. He sees little that goes on and understands less, but he has been putting some very odd notions in my head.' Having fastened the green bow in a very stylish way, she patted Elisa's good hand. 'Good luck, my dear. Take care, won't you?'

Surprisingly unsubtle for a woman with Gwenna Hawtree's gift for troublemaking.

Lady Hawtree's departure left Elisa angry and resentful. How dare she try to stir up Elisa's suspicions of the man she loved?

Surely, her Jeremy wasn't capable of plotting such a devious and labyrinthine revenge as to marry her out of hatred! True, he had never been as direct and uncomplicated as his young brother, and he certainly had hated her until very recently, but now he was rapidly coming to love her. If he still hated her and sought some long revenge, he would have to be an astonishingly good actor to fool her so completely.

Wouldn't he?

The household had been hovering around the hall door waiting for Lady Hawtree's departure. They poured in as soon as she left. Mrs Ponsonby hurried across the room, with Stebbings and Belliver striding after her, trying not to overtake the little woman. Several housemaids clustered around the open door, gawking in at Elisa's battered and wrapped figure on the bed.

Elisa now trusted no one, for a great many imagined reasons. In spite of her fears she closed her eyes and pretended to be asleep. The housekeeper fussed around the bed, smoothing the elaborately worked coverlet, trying to tuck the sheet up around Elisa's arms. She looked over her shoulder at Stebbings.

'I thought you heard her speaking to Lady Hawtree.'

'So I did. It may be the head injury. Consciousness comes and goes.'

Young Belliver murmured, 'Poor lady, she's that beautiful, you wouldn't credit it! Looks like a wall-painting, so she does.'

Elisa wanted to smile but was curious to hear what the others had to say. She remained immobile.

It was just as well that she didn't let Belliver's praise go to her head. Stebbings apparently stood there staring at her before he dismissed Belliver's opinion.

'Common, boy. A commonplace prettiness. You see it quite often in the cheaper theatres. Not Shakespearean, you understand. They call this one *Circe,* after the creature who seduced men and turned them into swine.'

Belliver rolled his eyes. 'Lord-a-day!' But he added more warmly, 'All the same, she's a mighty pretty Sursy – or what you said.'

Elisa opened her eyes very slowly, giving young Belliver the full effect of her long lashes and what had been called the 'dazzling' effect of her celebrated eyes. He caught his breath and was still under her spell when she murmured sensuously, 'Thank you, Belliver.'

She had won him over, but what amused her even more was the reaction of the butler who realized she had heard his sour comments about her. She looked up at him, all provocative innocence, and was sure he had flushed with embarrassment.

Good. He deserved it. But for him, she might have descended by the front staircase.

This hardly seemed fair. He hadn't driven her to take Arthur's Secret Staircase. How did he know she wished to avoid him? Still, she was meanly pleased.

Mrs Ponsonby, who hadn't insulted her aloud in the last few minutes, was overdoing her solicitude. She fussed too much and looked anxious. Perhaps she was afraid of Lord March's reaction. Looking squarely at the matter, Elisa had to admit it was Jeremy and not Mrs Ponsonby who had invited her to try Arthur's staircase in the first place.

A sinister thought: was it Jeremy who had first mentioned that the staircase was Arthur's favorite? Was it Jeremy who planted the deadly notion that Arthur might be following her down those stairs today? She couldn't quite remember. Her own imagined terrors had done the worst damage.

Anyway, the suspicion of Jeremy was ridiculous. Mrs Ponsonby's chubby little face with those daring, anxious eyes, appeared much more guilty.

'Were you about to say something, Mrs Ponsonby?'

The housekeeper almost stammered. 'Will you be w-wanting something, Ma'am? Are you hurting anywhere?' Elisa smiled, which seemed to increase the housekeeper's anxiety. 'I mean to say, may we bring you something to make Your Ladyship more comfortable?'

Elisa's voice sharpened. 'Something like laudanum?'

All three of her visitors looked at each other; Stebbings expressed the general feeling, whatever that might be, of guilt, shock, or simply surprise.

After that awkward and shared hesitation Mrs Ponsonby said, 'If Your Ladyship has any laudanum, I'd be pleased to put a few drops in water; but you see, there's none in the house now. Not since Dilly Skeen.'

This was news. Not that Elisa believed it.

'Isn't that a trifle after the fact?'

'Quite right, Ma'am. But it was His Lordship's order. He said it was criminal stuff and two people had died because they found

248

it to hand, as you might say. He was speaking of Mr Arthur, I collect.'

'Yes. So I understand. Never mind. I don't wish any drugs.'

Stebbings cleared his throat. 'Mrs Ponsonby has sent for Sam Yarrow to attend Your Ladyship. He's a good hand when Dr Clifford isn't about.'

She said tartly, 'I trust he can be more useful to me than he was to poor Dilly Skeen.'

They all understood this as a rebuke to the staff and were relieved when she reverted to facts they could answer efficiently.

'Was it you who discovered me, Belliver? It was very obliging of you.'

'Quite by accident, M'lady.' Nevertheless, he was flattered. 'I was meaning to get up to the room I share with Biggs. He's the second footman, as you may know, Ma'am. And there you was, all of a heap. I was that scared! Thought you might be dead, like Dilly Skeen.'

'That will do, Belliver,' Stebbings said repressively. 'Your babble prevents Her Ladyship from resting. If you wish anything, Ma'am, you've only to ring.'

He made gestures ordering Belliver out of the room, but he had infringed on Mrs Ponsonby's prerogatives. She started forward, smoothed Elisa's bedcovers and reminded her with some emphasis, 'I'll be pleased to oblige in any way possible, Ma'am. Me and mine, that is.' She gave the butler a scowl. 'And I'll be sure and certain to send up Sam Yarrow.'

Stebbings capped her offer with a checkmate.

'I shall direct His Lordship to you the minute he arrives, Your Ladyship.'

Mrs Ponsonby sniffed. 'Hump. His Lordship won't need directions from Mr Stebbings, Ma'am. He'll come direct of his own accord.'

With this *coup de grace* she curtsied to Elisa and left the room, shooing the gaping servants away from the doorway as she swooped out into the hall. Stebbings followed at a dignified pace, letting Belliver go before him to herald the way.

249

Elisa scarcely waited until they were out of the bedchamber before she burst out laughing. She thought she had discovered at last how to handle the two dragons, Stebbings and Ponsonby. She would merely play one off against the other.

She was sorry when they had gone. Too many thoughts came rushing in. Was it possible that one of these people had put the drops in the chocolate? If not, had the chocolate been poisoned before it left her London house? The idea of Tuttle's or McFee's guilt was even less credible.

Another strand in the deadly braid: there was the gift containing laudanum that arrived in the London house.

She closed her eyes to Lady Hawtree's insinuations and turned to other thoughts, such as Gwenna's coincidental visit, and with this she remembered the hatred of two men in the Hawtree family. Sir Hugo, who had been so proud of his son's brilliant military career, and Captain Ronald Hawtree, who – she was convinced of it – still hated her. A much more likely pair of possibilities than Jeremy or Tuttle, or McFee.

Curious, though. The first laudanum attack had come when Arthur was very much alive and in pursuit of her. The drug might have been sent by someone who didn't intend to kill her, but merely to warn her, remind her of what might happen if she went further in the relationship.

Who was likely to warn her away from Arthur in those days? The answer was obvious. Only one man made his feelings evident.

Back to Jeremy again.

Infuriated by her own ridiculous suspicions, she clenched her fists, which brought back the ache of bruised muscles and flesh. No matter. She had to be ready for any further assaults, and especially for her own fears which brought about tumbles down narrow staircases. That, at least, she couldn't blame on anyone else. She had imagined she heard the sound of a man's footsteps behind her. All gentlemen wore boots of one sort or another during daylight. It might even have been a servant who left the staircase when he reached the floor above.

Female servants wore heavy shoes. Mrs Ponsonby's feet were sturdily clad, to carry that plump figure of hers, no doubt. There were a dozen reasons for someone to have been above her on the staircase. Her imagination had always been dangerously active. Originally, it was useful in escaping the death-in-life she feared when her mother was locked away. Later, it created Elisa Carlisle. An imagination could be very useful, within limits.

She knew she could not lie here in bed all day, like the weak and helpless victim of a danger that might come from any direction. She tried to push herself up by one elbow, but even this effort made her grit her teeth. She eased herself back among the bedclothes, closed her eyes and sighed with relief.

Despite her firm resolve to stay alert, she dozed off and only awoke when she felt the pressure near her as someone sat down on the side of the bed. She stiffened to awareness of danger. Just as she opened her eyes, her husband leaned over her and kissed the bandage on her forehead. He seemed to be sincere She hoped she read deep concern in his eyes.

'You are looking pale, my love. How do you feel?'

She forced a bright, confident smile. 'As well as I deserve for having been so clumsy. I missed a step on that narrow twisting staircase.'

'You are anything but clumsy. However, Stebbings believes there was no serious harm done.' His fingertips touched her arm in its improvised sling. It was a sensitive touch and she was almost grateful for the accident that produced this change in his manner toward her. He had not often been either sensitive or tender to her.

But he was still dissatisfied. He studied her, frowning. 'You are very tense. Are you sure you feel more fit?'

'Certainly. See?' She held up her good hand, clenched into a fist. 'Strong as a –' She couldn't think of a comparison and then added triumphantly, 'Strong as our mute friend Abel.'

That made him smile but his eyes still searched her face in a troubled way.

'That may be, but you certainly don't look it.' He pinched her chin between thumb and forefinger. 'I know precisely what you need.' He reached over her shoulder and beyond the bed to the nearest bell-pull.

In a matter of minutes the hall door opened and a parlour maid, whose name Elisa didn't know, looked in and curtsied.

Jeremy said, 'Ask Stebbings for the brandy.'

'It isn't necessary,' Elisa protested. 'Truly, it isn't.'

He was smiling but firm. 'And I say it is.'

When the brandy arrived it was on a tray in the butler's hands.

'Our best, I trust,' Jeremy said.

'Naturally, Your Lordship.' Stebbings poured brandy into one of the glasses and was about to pour a generous amount into the other.

Jeremy took the first glass, waving away the other.

'None for me. I've work to do this afternoon.'

Elisa felt a sudden prickling chill. 'I don't think I should. I haven't eaten.' She tried to joke. 'I might become bosky.'

'Nonsense. Just the thing you need, to bring back that lovely color to your cheeks. Isn't it so, Stebbings?'

'Quite so, My Lord.'

Jeremy raised the glass to her lips. She started to object, realized it would only arouse suspicion, and said with nervous brightness, 'Do let me. I'll show you I am very much myself.'

She took the glass from him with her good hand and raised it high with a toast: 'To March Hall, and everyone's good health.'

'Easy, sweetheart,' Jeremy warned her. He had never called her that before.

She began to lower the glass, twisted her wrist carefully, cried out, and the glass fell from her fingers, over the side of the bed and onto the floor, its contents spilling over the rug.

She groaned histrionically.

'I told you I was clumsy. I do hope it didn't break.'

Jeremy looked over the edge of the bed. 'Seems to be in several pieces, but it's hardly irreplaceable.'

'Broken? I'm so sorry.' She saw the butler biting his lip as he assessed the damage, and added, 'I really don't want any spirits in any case.'

'If the lady won't drink, she won't.' Jeremy picked up the shards of glass and dropped them on Stebbings' tray.

Elisa found her forehead damp with perspiration around the improvised bandages. She didn't know whether she had been very clever or insanely suspicious. Her action put her forceably in mind of many odd things Molly Catlow had done, before the strange men came and took her away.

It was with enormous relief that she felt Jeremy's arm around her. He sat on the edge of the bed and drew her to him. She saw Stebbings' eyes on her as she raised her face and Jeremy's warm lips were gentle but insistent upon her mouth.

Doubtless, like most of them at March Hall, Stebbings thought his master was caressing the female who 'killed' Master Arthur.

CHAPTER TWENTY-TWO

She had a nervous sense of triumph for several hours after the episode of the spilled brandy. If the butler, working for some enemy of hers, had actually put something in the brandy, he would realize by now that she wasn't a complete fool.

As for Jeremy, she was less sure. She caught him watching her at odd times, and knew her behaviour had puzzled him, made him a trifle suspicious – of what? That she was not quite herself? One thought made her shiver. Someone might find out about her mother and suspect Elisa, too, was showing signs of madness.

In spite of her fears that someone in the household was dangerous to her, she knew she must walk a very thin line to avoid the appearance of 'odd' behavior. Nothing in her life had ever been as dreadful as her fear of Bedlam, not even the probability that an attempt was afoot to poison her.

She had never wanted to be left completely alone; yet, after her recent experiences, she felt unsafe in the company of any single person, without reinforcements from others. Always excepting her husband. Of course.

She came down to dinner when the loneliness of the bedchamber proved too much for her. With her sore arm and aching head suitably wrapped, the one in the shawl sling and the other concealed by a romantic silk bandage, she was hailed as a heroine by Jeremy. Strangely enough, Mrs Ponsonby and Belliver also conveyed their respect to her, the housekeeper remarking on 'Her Ladyship's bravery'.

During the meal Elisa informed Jeremy that she intended to make his estate problems less onerous by taking some from his

254

hands, especially the problems of the poor. To her surprise, she saw that she had puzzled him, nor was she certain that he had been pleased.

'Unless you feel I do not know the situations well enough,' she added with whimsical assurance. 'I promise you to be on my very best behavior. No London airs, no Bond Street elegance.'

He laughed. 'I'm sure of that. It's simply that I was given the impression you were not sympathetic to the poor. Well, that was a mistake, obviously. You are happy, then?'

'Happy?' Sensitive to these undercurrents, she asked, 'Should I not be? Unless these impression-gatherers of yours think I should smile when I tumble downstairs.'

'Far from it.' He promised, as one does to a child, 'When your battle scars are healed, we will see if you are still of the same mind.'

She said coolly, 'I shall be.'

It was disappointing. She had hoped for more enthusiasm from him.

It was frightening, too.

At first, she tried to eat only the foods she saw her husband take from the plates on the trays offered him, but she didn't want to make her movements obvious to the staff, one of whom might be watching for the result.

In the evening Lady Hawtree sent over a servant to discover Elisa's condition. She enclosed a sealed message to both Elisa and Jeremy. When Elisa waved it away impatiently Jeremy cut the seal with his forefinger and read it.

He got up, walked the length of the table, and showed her the paper. She read:

'My dear Elisa and Lord March, I do trust your poor bones are mending.'

Embarrassed, she looked up. 'She hopes you have consoled and cosseted me.'

He leaned nearer. 'May I cosset you, my love?'

'Absolutely. At once.'

He studied her. 'How are you feeling now? Did the champagne soothe the aches and pains?'

She had a sudden fear that he might think she was too fragile or clumsy, even too old to enjoy his vigorous life. She wiggled the fingers of her left hand, waving them before him.

'Quite, quite normal. You see?'

He took her fingers and kissed the knuckles, gazing at her over her hand. It was thrilling to read the warmth and caring in those eyes that had once frightened her by their glittering hatred. 'I see very clearly. It occurs to me that you winced just then.'

It was a new experience to be cared for, fussed over by a man who now genuinely seemed to love her. Except for Brian, who was almost a brother, she couldn't remember another man who cared about her in this way. Always, before, the motive had been sexual in the most selfish way, the desire to join that select little party of Regency bucks 'who had been favored by *Circe*'.

But was Jeremy actually different from those others?

She found herself praying that this was so.

He asked, 'Are you certain you feel more yourself? That bump on your temple was no love tap.'

On the other hand, she became uneasy again at the depth of his concern, as if he thought she might not be herself. If this was only his concern for her physical wellbeing, she would be delighted. But if he had begun to suspect her mental condition – dear God, no!

She assured him brightly, 'You mustn't think I spend all my days tumbling about so clumsily. Truly, I am in excellent spirits. To prove it, lend me your glass.'

Still troubled, he reached for her champagne glass. She stopped him.

'No. You will ruin my romantic gesture.'

He was puzzled but he did as she asked. There were still dregs in his glass. She touched her lips to the rim of the glass and drank the dregs.

'You see, my darling?' she asked. 'I want my lips to touch only what you have touched.'

She thought this sounded romantic. In a play it would have been a sensuous moment. Unfortunately, the theatrical idea occurred to him at the same time.

He reached for the glass in her hand. She was so surprised she let her fingers weaken in his and surrendered the glass.

'My love, that was spoken very like a line from one of your plays.'

She flushed angrily; her feelings were hurt.

'You forget, My Lord. I am an actress and sometimes I behave like one. It is not a profession you favor, as I know all too well.'

'But I prefer that you remain yourself. You have been changing out of all recognition lately and I love you for it.' He leaned over her. She raised her chin proudly but he ignored this sign of pique. He startled her by touching her soft, sensuous mouth with his lips and then lingering over his kiss.

Surrendering to his touch, she made a determined effort to banish all her fears, including the suspicions that had threatened to consume her life. Dilly Skeen had administered the laudanum herself. It was a part of the pattern when anyone suffered pain. Only Elisa's overactive imagination had produced these fears based upon several coincidences, any one of which could be explained away, and upon Lady Hawtree's tiresome efforts to arouse her suspicions.

Besides, Elisa had a passionate desire to believe it was all coincidence!

After dinner, with Jeremy's firm, gentle help, Elisa walked around the grounds until the blue haze of dusk had darkened to reveal the first starlight. Jeremy found it admirable that she insisted on walking up the grassy slope with him toward the dark woods that crowned the hill.

'Afraid?' he teased her as they entered the little copse and she clung to him, aware of the awful, closed-in feeling that such places inspired in her.

'Not afraid of these trees,' she tried to explain while guarding the true reasons, the memory of how Molly Catlow had ended and how – perhaps – her daughter would end. 'It is the sense of being imprisoned by walls. And the silence.'

He was surprisingly gentle with her and she permitted herself to hope that, whatever happened, he would not let her die as her mother had died.

'Stop here, my love. Now, take a step. On these dry leaves. Do you hear that crackle? Listen again. That little bubbling sound? The stream that runs below us, beside the herb garden.'

She felt the contagion of his effort to raise her spirits. She added, 'And the wind rustling the leaves overhead. I hear that.'

'Then you aren't alone, even when no one is with you here in this little copse.' He looked into her face as it was partially illuminated by the first starlight. 'You see? You look better already. How is your arm?'

'A little stiff, but nothing broken.'

He put out a hand and closed it on the fingers she moved experimentally.

'Let the muscles heal. Don't overdo. And your forehead?'

'I don't feel a thing. I believe the swelling is gone.'

'Good.' They started back down the hill on the dirt path. Without looking at her, but tucking her good arm in his, he said unexpectedly, 'It would be a loss to all of us if anything happened to that brow of yours.'

'What? Nonsense.' She was pleased but curiously embarrassed, as though she had never heard such a compliment before. Perhaps, she thought, this was the first time he had been sincere.

He still looked straight ahead, almost as if he wanted to avoid her eyes.

'Not nonsense at all. When I used to sit in that theatre box and watch you, despising you – as I told myself – because you used Arthur for your own purposes, I thought I had never seen so fair a brow.' He laughed suddenly at his own susceptibility. 'You never knew I could wax poetic, did you?'

Her voice was soft and so low he turned his head slightly to hear it. 'I knew.'

He said nothing after his half-confession. Perhaps he had never understood this about himself before. It seemed probable that he, like Elisa, had belatedly discovered these real motives and feelings. It was a great step forward in their relationship, the greatest since he had astonished and delighted her by his proposal.

Warm and close, they returned to the Hall.

They retired early. Jeremy was firm about it. 'You need your rest after that fall.' Seeing her quick, anxious look, he added with his little smile, 'I intend to be there, to see that you follow my orders.'

Ultimately, in spite of her bruises, the night proved to be the most perfect in their marriage. Elisa felt that they gave of themselves, feeling for the first time that they could be utterly sincere. She found him lighthearted, playful, trying not to hurt her, then, with her encouragement, warmly passionate, exciting her with his body, the touch and exploration of his skillful fingers.

Her own reaction was spontaneous and natural. She forgot that only a few hours ago she had tumbled down the stairs. She knew only that she would remember tonight all the rest of her life.

Though he had been carried away that night by fresh emotions Elisa discovered only two days later that he had not forgotten her injuries, after all. She was just returning to the Hall in the pony cart, after leaving food and bed supplies for the indigent elderly of the terrace lodgings, when she saw the March family closed carriage, big and lumbering, pull up before the front steps.

Puzzled as to which of Jeremy's distant relatives would be arriving unannounced in the carriage with its polished armorial bearings, Elisa pulled up short and was lifted out of the pony cart by the young footman named Griggs. She hurried along to the visitors'coach as the steps were let down. It was a delight to see Brian climb out and then Susan, her golden curls arranged in a very sophisticated fashion.

Upon closer examination she looked older in many ways than Elisa remembered, and there was an excitement about her that was obviously the result of her anxiety to be back at the job she really cared for, that of apprentice housekeeper.

'Thanks to His Lordship, we are home again. Time to begin my new post. I love visiting London, but I shouldn't like to live there. Though the most famous thing did happen.

259

Mr Strawbridge called on papa at our hotel and sent you a message.'

'A message? "Stay away from London," I've no doubt.'

'No, no,' Brian put in. 'He arranged for us to have a box to see Peter Tregaran. A small theatre, very obscure. A nice little talent there, though not well attended that night. But we were invited backstage to meet him and my Susan took a great fancy to the lad.'

'Papa, really!' Susan said in her most adult voice.

'Well, I can only thank providence Susan was so busy being fitted for her respectable housekeeper's wardrobe that she hadn't time to press me about seeing this Tregaran again.'

Susan rolled her eyes. 'Nothing of the sort, Papa.'

Brian shook his head. 'Was I ever so young and so fickle?'

His daughter objected to this with such vehemence it surprised both Elisa and her father.

Elisa embraced her. 'You are looking very much the thing. The color in your cheeks, those bright eyes. How glad all the handsome young men in the neighborhood will be to see you!'

Susan looked blank for a moment. 'Oh – of course.' Then she confided to Elisa, 'I would love to see you and Tregaran play together in one of your great romances. You would be sublime. Tregaran thinks so, too. I know he is sorry about the difficulty between you. He lays it to temperament, you know. An actor's nerves are so easily shattered.'

Elisa laughed at this and turned to Brian. He had been ordering the boxes and valises down. The old coachman saw to the matter and waved Brian away as if he were intruding.

'Never mind, Brian,' Elisa advised him. 'We have so much to say. Do come along.'

'Very well, Your Ladyship.' Very correctly, Brian bent over her hand and would have touched it with his lips but she drew her hand back, hugging him instead.

'Come now. No formality. Our friendship goes back too far. How proud you must be of Susan! She looks so much the lady of fashion.'

Brian pressed Elisa to him with a quick, almost secretive movement, then released her, still holding her hand. He looked fondly at his daughter who was chattering away to both Belliver and Griggs, the two footmen, while she glanced around at the facade of the noble old house.

'She loves March Hall.' He added thoughtfully, 'Or, at all events, some portions of the Hall.'

Elisa assured him, 'So long as her heart seems divided, you may breathe easily.'

As they entered the Hall together, hearing the light, high-pitched flirtation of Susan behind them, Brian explained that His Lordship had wanted them to return as soon as possible.

'It was all His Lordship's notion. He told us about your fall and said he wanted to be certain you had sustained no ill-effects. Not that we weren't coming anyway.'

She was so touched by the gesture of the man she loved that she surprised even her old friend. He studied her with interest but she wasn't entirely sure he had been pleased by what he suspected.

'You really do love him, don't you?'

'More than my life,' she said and heard herself as she had seldom listened when she was Elisa Carlisle, the actress. Jeremy had taught her to listen. She shook her head. 'I'm sorry. That was a theatrical line. Let it read *almost as much as* my life.'

He smiled, but not too happily. 'I trust he feels the same way.'

'I'm certain he does.' *I pray he does.* 'He is off in Marchland on estate business.'

'And how are you feeling?' He sounded very professional.

'Splendid. Just a bit of a bruise on my forehead. I was unconscious for an hour, I believe. But I have been growing better every hour since. My arm is practically perfect.'

He touched the bruise on her temple, then stopped to greet Mrs Ponsonby who had curtsied to Elisa and now was pleased when Brian took her hand. But her real interest was his daughter. Susan threw her arms around her in an impulsive way and, abandoning the two footmen, went off arm in arm with her 'to talk secrets', as she confided to her father. 'About the dreadful housekeeping in London.'

This worried Elisa. 'Heavens! I do hope she isn't talking about Tuttle. I really should see her soon. I owe her so much.'

'She owes you so much,' Brian corrected her stiffly. 'She had no hesitation in letting us know her deep animosity toward His Lordship. As a matter of fact, she regards him as the author of all your troubles. She even accuses him of causing your accident.'

'What?' She was badly shaken.

Susan hurried past them into the solar, followed by Mrs Ponsonby, trotting along, trying to keep pace with her. Susan flung herself onto the window seat beneath the high golden window panes.

'Oh, Ponsy, you've changed the cushion covers. You promised you wouldn't.'

While she agonized over this, Brian murmured to Elisa, 'The household seems determined that everything should remain as young Arthur left it.'

'They act as though they had enshrined everything he touched.' Then she added guiltily, 'I didn't know it had been changed. I complained yesterday about the dust and it was attended to at once. Obviously, my mistake.'

'Surely, as mistress of March Hall you have the right to change cushions or make any other alterations you wish.' He raised his voice. 'Susan, you are not the lady of this house. You mustn't presume to criticise.'

Susan rolled her eyes in the manner of all youth being unfairly scolded. 'I might have known. Ponsy, one day I shall insist that my word is law.' Seeing that Brian was about to chide her again, Susan added directly to Mrs Ponsonby, 'I mean, when I am a real, true housekeeper.'

'That you shall, Miss Susan, and nobody better suited,' her chubby champion promised.

This talk of housekeeping jobs troubled Elisa, bringing back memories of Tuttle's accusation. It made things doubly difficult just when she needed Tuttle after the tragedy of Dilly Skeen's death. She hesitated until they were beyond the hearing of the servants, then told Brian about the girl's death.

At first, he couldn't place Dilly Skeen, but he knew Granny Skeen well and, remembering the connection, was very sorry on the old woman's account.

'But I'm afraid it isn't too surprising. The girl – if she is the one I am thinking of – seems to have been almost simple-minded. A natural. Like poor Abel in the graveyard.'

She smiled at the thought of that odd friendship she had made. 'I do believe that winning Abel's good will was my greatest triumph since I came.'

She became aware of his gaze, earnest and troubled. 'Winning March was not your great triumph?'

She felt trapped by the question and resented it.

'I hope our marriage was a mutual triumph. I love my husband and I have every reason to believe he loves me.'

'I'm glad.'

She thought his comment was genuine, but when he made an explanation she wished he had simply left the matter with his first brief remark.

'I suppose it was that woman who made me think about the matter.'

'Woman? What woman?'

'I mean Tuttle, of course. I believe her to be obsessed by the idea that you are some kind of jewel she found and polished. I've always felt that she was a menace to you.' Seeing her bristle beside him, he pursued the matter doggedly. 'You permit her the most personal actions. She might conceivably rob you of all you have earned.'

'That is the most unworthy thing you ever said, Brian. I have entrusted her with very delicate matters and she has never betrayed me.' She was reminded of one especially delicate matter. 'Incidentally, did you give her the packet?'

He flushed at the implication that he might not have done so. 'Certainly. She sent you some sort of communication from Rundles, the London jewelers. It is in my valise.' Since he had raised his voice, both Susan and Mrs Ponsonby looked around, curious about what began to sound like a quarrel.

Brian was always sensitive to his position. Elisa suspected he would rather die than behave crudely or with anything approaching bad manners. Quite unlike Jeremy's disregard, she decided. She felt an inner glow at the thought of her recent relationship with her husband.

Brian cleared his throat. 'Mrs Ponsonby, would you please ask Griggs to bring my small valise to me here in the solar?'

The little housekeeper bustled off, just as voices in the hall told Elisa that Jeremy had returned and was talking to his valet, Philbey.

'They've arrived, have they? Excellent. I left Sam Yarrow with Granny Skeen, but I haven't too much confidence in that lad since he failed poor Dilly. I hope he has seen Her Ladyship.'

Elisa went to the doorway to meet him. She was thrilled by the brightening of his features when he saw her, his warm smile which was unfamiliar enough to make her especially delighted since their new understanding. He slipped an arm around her waist, brought her close and kissed her, while Brian watched without expression.

Still holding her, Jeremy put out his free hand to Brian. 'Good to see you back, Clifford.' He waved to Susan who got up from the window seat, thrilled by his notice. 'And our lovely golden lass.'

Susan beamed. 'It was ever so kind of Your Lordship, to bring us home again.'

'His Lordship did not bring us home to oblige you, Susan,' her father reminded her. It seemed to Elisa that Brian's annoyance with the Tuttle matter had given him a sharper tone than he habitually used toward his much loved child.

But it was clear that Jeremy wanted everyone else to share his own mood. He assured Susan, 'Your dutiful father is only half correct. We needed your bright presence here.' He squeezed Elisa's waist. 'Didn't we, darling?'

Elisa said, 'Absolutely. Susan, you must finish showing me all the wonders of your March Hall.' Seeing Susan's tension over her father's criticism, she said quickly, 'If you are to be Mrs Ponsonby's successor, March Hall is truly yours.'

Susan raised her tawny eyebrows and looked at Jeremy, who said, 'Absolutely.' She grinned. She started to burst out excitedly but was silenced by the confusion behind Jeremy and Elisa in the doorway.

Mrs Ponsonby was fussing with young Griggs about some baggage.

'I said I will take it now. Give it to me, boy!'

'Beg pardon, Ma'am. But I was told to deliver it into Dr Clifford's – '

'At once!'

'But Ma'am –'

Jeremy turned to ask 'What the devil?' just as the housekeeper jerked the valise out of the footman's hands. The leather straps of the aged little case pulled away under this tugging and the contents spilled out over the floor.

Accompanied by the buzz of low-voiced altercation between the two combatants, everyone else set about picking up Brian's possessions, to his profound embarrassment.

He pleaded, 'No, no, Your Lordship – Elisa – let me. I can – if you please . . .'

But since the clean shirt, a book on 'Medical Matters', a nicely laundered cravat, a loosely sealed paper, and less mentionable items had spilled over Jeremy's boots, it was he who rescued most of them. He had been surprised by the accident and especially the conduct of his servants, but he was in an excellent mood when he presented most of the interesting assortment to Brian who crammed them all into the battered valise with its broken, hanging straps.

Elisa remembered afterward that her husband was still amused at the accident when the letter floated out of Brian's collection of belongings. Its seal had cracked and it lay half-opened as Jeremy retrieved it. Unavoidably, he read the signature.

'Well, Clifford, I see you deal with Rundle's Jewelers. The best. A good, trustworthy company.' He noticed the curious stillness that suddenly engulfed both the doctor and

Elisa. Puzzled, he glanced at the superscription, adding, 'Sorry. I see it belongs to my wife. Darling, have I ruined a – surprise?' The last word came automatically. His thoughts were fixed upon something else, the operative words in the letter from the celebrated jewelers.

He scanned the letter very briefly, then offered it to her. She looked it over silently:

'Undoubtedly an heirloom belonging to Your Ladyship's fore-bears. Be assured the pearls will fetch Your Ladyship a handsome price. This shall be applied to Your Ladyship's banking and bond accounts as your agent requests.'

The thought struck Elisa that Jeremy must resent the selling of her old jewels and the investing of the funds for herself without consulting him. No respectable and proper ladies would dream of such underhanded conduct. Their husbands handled all such matters.

But respectable ladies did not have her fears and her past.

Susan was the first to try and restore some kind of normality to the scene.

'Papa, we haven't unpacked yet and those shirts and cravats will have to be laundered again. Ponsy, is the laundress in the Hall today?'

'On the roof, hanging sheets, Miss Susan. If Her Ladyship will excuse me, I'll be about the work now.' Not unexpectedly, the little woman was anxious to remove herself from what appeared to be an embarrassing scene.

Elisa said abruptly, 'Yes. Please go. All of you.'

She knew her husband was deeply angered by the discovery that she was selling her own jewelry and investing it. She supposed it must be family pride. Whatever his reason for this chilling change of mood, she did not want anyone else to witness whatever followed between them.

CHAPTER TWENTY-THREE

He did not directly accuse her of anything – of greed in collecting her own private income or of failing to tell him about this private fund in her name that, by her marriage and by law, should now belong entirely to her husband.

Unless it was her lack of trust in his generosity which produced so profound a reaction, she wasn't sure why he should have reverted suddenly to that handsome, cold aristocrat, his feelings carefully hidden.

All those early days rushed by in her memory. She sensed a return of his contempt for her, probably due to her passionate craving to collect material gain in negotiable form. He would never understand what it was to be really poor, not like those country people he took such good care of, but city denizens in the stews of London. If she described what had happened to Molly and Elsie Catlow his revulsion would only grow.

It looked as though he would continue to study her in silence. What did he expect of her? Sobs and crawling, humble pleas for forgiveness because she had sold a pearl necklace that she herself had purchased from her own theatre earnings?

Unable to stand the silence, she said quietly, 'I have not thanked you for bringing the Cliffords back home.'

'Home?'

Her frigid manner matched his. By drawing on her skill as Elisa Carlisle she could pretend to banish all those hideous feelings of insecurity in the world of this aristocrat.

'I trust I may refer to the March estate as the home of your estate manager and his daughter.'

He had the grace to look slightly discomfited.

'Of course, it is their home, though Arthur and I always felt that they were capable of something better. That child should be in an academy, being turned out as a lady.'

'What? And ruin her conquest of all the footmen in Gloucestershire?' His expression softened slightly but she apologized. 'Actually, I agree with you. But she has always been a trifle spoiled. It wouldn't do to force her.'

'No. Perhaps not.' He wasn't thinking of the subject that occupied them. He was watching her, studying her again, waiting for something, perhaps an explanation.

She started to leave the room, but stopped as she passed him. She said briefly, 'By the by, you are doubtless waiting for an explanation of this letter from Rundle's.'

'A matter of curiosity, yes.'

Her chin went up again as it often did when she had been challenged. 'I was once very poor. I never forgot it. Let me assure you, My Lord, that nothing you may mention is worse than poverty.'

He glanced at the letter. 'I am sure you believe that. Are all women so indifferent to honor?'

She knew that to a man this would be the worst insult. Did he actually feel so passionately about the fact that she had concealed money from him, money that English law gave to him the moment they were married?

'Honor?' she echoed. 'What an enchanting word! So much prettier than starvation, or an agonizing death!'

She left him then, knowing she had shaken him by her vehemence. Undoubtedly she had puzzled him as well.

She went up to her boudoir-sitting room, closed the door into the bedchamber she shared with Jeremy, and stood for a long time staring down at the gatehouse and the road beyond. What had happened to the beautiful marriage that seemed so perfect an hour ago?

Not quite perfect, she reminded herself. There was the subject of the laudanum that seemed to hang over her life recently like a deadly miasma. That mystery remained unsolved. Brian's arrival would certainly be helpful. He was a good listener and level-headed. Having been in her London house for several days, he might even have a few ideas on the matter.

So long as he did not mention Tuttle in that connection.

A few minutes' thought gave her a possible answer to his dislike of Tuttle. The woman had been her closest companion and confidante during most of Elisa's life, a position that Tuttle occasionally shared with Brian. Elisa had suffered from jealousy herself, especially of other performers, and recognized it in both Brian and Tuttle.

She was still wondering how much she dared tell Brian about the laudanum – she didn't want him suspecting Jeremy! – when her attention was caught again by the activity below her window as a landaulet, smartly tooled by the Hawtree coachman with two footmen, came rolling under the archway of the gatehouse and onto the pebbled drive.

She asked Belliver to send her the second parlor maid, Mary Rose, to help her change her dress the better to challenge the overpowering Lady Hawtree.

She wore white as usual and, because she wanted her husband to know she did not sell all her jewelry, she wore the charming little emerald set given to her long ago by . . . She tried to place the admirer precisely in her memory. He was young, fickle, lighthearted, and she was sure she loved him. He boasted to his friends about his conquest of 'that enchanting new actress', but before he lost interest in her he did teach her a few airs and graces, manners important to know when she found herself in the company of people like the Hawtrees.

She looked at the emerald ear-bobs in her palm and weighed them thoughtfully with an ironic thought: Perhaps it was you who gave me the beginnings of my reputation, but it seems you paid for it. You hurt me once. Now, I can't even remember your name. That is true vengeance, my friend. That and these little emeralds which lasted a deal longer than my memory of you.

The parlor maid was delighted to become Elisa's 'abigail', even temporarily, but she made the mistake of chattering about Elisa's jewels. This painfully reminded Elisa of the quarrel with Jeremy.

'Oh, Your La'ship, if I was Your La'ship, I'd put on them diamonds, too. Makes the green sparkle right nice.'

'One set is quite enough,' Elisa said repressively, but she gave Mary Rose a smile as she left the room. She was thinking that once she herself would have said that.

She made an entrance into the big, sunlit solar that would have done credit to Elisa Carlisle at Drury Lane. Her special look was in place, that sensuous smile which promised endless mystery and romance. She was determined to show a little courage after her earlier cowardice in the face of her husband's mood.

Her effort had its effect on Sir Hugo. Even Captain Hawtree stared at her wide-eyed.

Gwenna touched her hand as Elisa passed and murmured, 'Splendid. You are looking marvelous, as you should.' This would have been kind if it hadn't made Elisa wonder why she should be congratulated for looking well. As if she hadn't been expected to look healthy!

But there ahead of her was Jeremy, obviously impressed, his eyes with that well-remembered light in them; yet his manner was cool. Following the two Hawtree men in bringing her hand near their lips, he said pleasantly, 'Good. Feeling better, I trust, my love?'

If there was one habit she wanted to break him of, it was that cutting and sardonic 'my love'!

She was equally polite, equally casual.

'Very much myself, I assure you. How good to see you, Sir Hugo! And Captain Hawtree. Did you know? My dear Lady Hawtree was the very first person to see me after my absurd fall. Except for the servants, of course.'

Gwenna laughed. 'I should certainly not make an exception of those precious servants. Let me tell you, my dear March, I do believe your wife survived despite your servants.'

This was startling enough to make them all stare at her, including Elisa. Jeremy's polite smile froze in place.

'May one ask why?'

'Really, Gwenna,' her husband began. His son had raised his head and was studying Elisa. For the first time since his accident

Elisa felt that he looked at her with interest – almost, but not quite, with sympathy.

Gwenna shrugged.

'But what else is one to think when my poor friend is beset by accidents even on her own staircase?'

This was unfair in one respect, because she knew her fall had been an accident, unless someone deliberately followed her down the stairs to frighten her, pretending to be a ghostly Arthur March. But she reverted to her earlier suspicions. Dilly Skeen may not have deliberately taken laudanum for her toothache. Suppose the poisonous sleeping draught had been in powder form, meant for Elisa, and placed in the chocolate that Tuttle packed in Elisa's wedding luggage.

Ridiculous!

For what reason? How would it profit Tuttle if Elisa died? Still, a good deal of Elisa's money went through Tuttle's hands. Tuttle would do very well financially if Elisa died before she could make her estate over to its new legal owner, her husband. Tuttle knew where so much money was invested and, above all, she was the only person who knew exactly where most of Elisa's jewelry was to be found.

Jeremy took this hint about her fall seriously. Reaching out, he drew Elisa closer with his fingers around her wrist.

'Is there more to this fall of yours then you have told me? Don't be afraid. If you have reason to believe any of the servants is responsible, I must know.'

Since her possible danger was drawing sympathy from men who had been angry and resentful toward her, she was almost sorry to relieve all the tension in the room by her denial. 'It was exactly as I have said.'

She was about to mention Dilly Skeen's death but Jeremy answered her first statement by saying, 'Thank heaven for that. Hawtree, your son and I have evolved a new scheme for the almshouses. Ronald believes, as my estate manager does, that the drain problem may be solved quite easily if we make use of the old irrigation channel. If the ladies will excuse us, I'd like to take you over to the gatehouse. Clifford has returned from London and can be very helpful in handling our problem, when he isn't attending to his sick duties.'

'Please oblige us by leaving, gentlemen.' Lady Hawtree waved them away and gestured for Elisa to join her in Arthur March's window seat under the golden light of the great windows.

This was not as satisfactory an arrangement as Elisa hoped for. A few minutes ago it had looked as though Jeremy was concerned enough about her safety to forget his curious pique over the sale of her pearls, but he took the first excuse to leave her. And worse. He left her to the tender mercies of still another person she was learning to mistrust.

'Now, my dear,' Gwenna said with the all-too-familiar excitement in her eyes, 'you and I must solve this business because – mark me – there are some havey-cavey doings going on around us.'

Elisa was all innocence. 'What can you mean, Lady Gwenna?'

'Secrets. This tiresome habit you have of preventing anyone from assisting you.' She obviously sensed a stiffening in Elisa's manner but went stabbing on, it seemed to Elisa, like a needle through heavy tapestry. 'You are ashamed of your past. As I should be, in your place. An actress, with doubtful antecedants and the usual past. But my dear, it is a mere commonplace.'

With all her worst fears of Gwenna Hawtree coming to the fore, Elisa tried to retain a few shreds of angry dignity.

'But you are not in my place. And if I may say so, there are undoubtedly moments in your life which Your Ladyship would not care to expose before the gaping world.'

Gwenna Hawtree batted her sparse eyelashes but laughed, too, as she astonished Elisa by her frankness.

'You are right. My childhood with a drunken, besotted peer of the land, my honored father. Or another tender memory, certain moments of which, the less said the better, when one or two of his friends, equally besotted, tried to mistake me for one of his lights-of-love . . . And I should not like our beloved Prinny's world to know I acquired Hugo through the oldest and most absurd of tricks. I confessed I was in the family way. How His Highness would laugh!'

This was such a well-worn trick that Elisa despised it, though it amused her. The rest of Gwenna's story seemed to her very nearly as scandalous as her own background.

'Obviously, you were not pregnant.'

'Detestable word. Remember, my dear, when in Prinny's society one does not use such words. The Prince believes in practising whatever vileness appeals to one, but it must always be done circumspectly, under a different name. Now then. I shall play the Bow Street Runner for you and solve your mystery.'

'Your spy system would do credit to a Bow Street Runner, My Lady.'

Her Ladyship motioned toward the bell-pull. 'Would you be good enough to ring for one of Stebbings' handsome young footmen? I have a raving thirst. Too much cheap rum this morning when I was questioning your champion, Abel.'

Too shaken to do more than obey, Elisa waited until Lady Gwenna was sipping sherry and nibbling at a biscuit before she demanded, 'What were you doing in the Marchland graveyard? And why did you question Abel? In point of fact, *how* did you question him?'

'Rum has a surprising effect on servants when one confides in them. Or seems to. I visited the vault of my sainted mother-in-law early this afternoon. Odious creature. But one does one's duty. And Abel came to me, all eloquence, with his gestures and signs and grunts. He often confides in me. Astonishing how much I learn from the lower orders about the higher. I am very democratic. Who knows better than you, my dear?'

'Who indeed?' Elisa echoed. 'What secrets did he confide?'

'That is the intriguing part. He wished to communicate with you here at the Hall and has twice been turned away this morning. I persuaded that tiresome little curate at Marchland to fetch me some rum. Nearly half a jug, and I fed it to Abel. I call him my Monstre Sacré. Dear, grotesque lad that he is, but so helpful. At all events, he tells me they refuse him admission to see you.'

Looking like a colorful parrot, she cocked her head on one side and stared at Elisa. She repeated, 'He is refused admission to see the mistress of the house. Why? Doesn't that intrigue you?'

To Elisa this was a distinct anticlimax.

Gwenna said, pursuing the matter, 'After all this laudanum nonsense that seems to surround you? Your maid died of it. Now, you tumble down the stairs.'

'I assure you, laudanum had nothing whatever to do with it. We are confusing an accident with – with – '

'Murder. I do not hesitate to admit the word.'

Elisa remembered the chocolate pot that had been broken in her fall, but this did not point to anyone in particular. She asked abruptly, 'Why should anyone murder me?' Before Gwenna could answer she added, 'And what could Abel possibly know of any doings at March Hall?'

'I regret to say that even I, with my cheap rum, could not elicit the answer to that, though I may have my suspicions.' Gwenna frowned and touched the fresher cushions around her, seeming to caress them. 'I see you have changed the decor since young Arthur's day. But no matter. Poor foolish boy! You must remember that your arrival here was a direct blow to all those who loved him. One would think it was done to punish you, have you near at hand for the fatal blow, as it were.'

'Gwenna, your imagination is incredible!' Elisa was so impatient at this preposterous – or perhaps not so preposterous – notion that she forgot the respect she had always shown 'Her Ladyship'.

Gwenna waved away her complaint. 'I remember how popular the boy was here with servants, with the local females, squires' daughters, serving maids. It was always the same. Not that he behaved in any but the most correct way, from all I gather, but they must have dreamed of becoming his wife and inheriting March Hall before he went up to London and fell head over heels in love with you. Everyone assumed, of course, that your Jeremy would leave no legitimate heirs. I adore this sort of situation.'

'I can well imagine.'

'Because, my dear, if I were to solve your little problem, think what delicious self-satisfaction I should know. And how very much you would owe to me for, who knows, perhaps saving your life.'

Elisa wondered if this entire conversation had been conducted merely to disturb her. It hadn't succeeded, since she doubted most of what Gwenna Hawtree had told her, except the confession about Gwenna's childhood and the sickening events in her father's house. That had the ring of truth.

Just possibly, Gwenna was sincere in her protest that she and Elisa had pasts in common. She had gone out of her way to give Elisa a weapon of gossip which could be used to shame her own family.

There were many facets to Gwenna Hawtree.

Still, Elisa dismissed all nonsense about Abel. There were a thousand reasons why he might have come to March Hall this morning and 'asked' to see Lady March. She said so aloud.

Gwenna made her disappointment amply clear.

'Is it possible I must send the poor fellow on his way without even seeing you? I should think mere curiosity would induce you to question him.'

Elisa sat up straight. 'My dear Gwenna, you must be quite mad. Abel is here?'

'He walked here, poor fellow. I knew my noble husband would not take him up beside the footmen.' She turned and looked out of the great window. 'I can just see him. He is under the arch of the gatehouse, studying the flowers March Hall produces with such ease. I wish I knew your secret. Of the roses, that is.'

Elisa was anxious to find an excuse that would take her away from this room with its haunting memories of Arthur March. She stood up and started across the room. Gwenna followed her.

'You do mean to see him, then? Excellent. I shall be your witness.'

Elisa shivered. 'If someone means to destroy me, Your Ladyship may receive your wish and become my rescuer.'

Gwenna promised, 'I shall stand by you through laudanum, opium, and whatever other little pleasures your admirers conjure up for you.'

From the steps that led down to the drive Elisa could see the great, hulking graveyard attendant under the far side of the archway. She went to meet him with her trained step that was rapid

275

but carefully attuned to the ripple of the slim skirts she habitually wore. Abel had seen a bush, still heavy with yellow roses despite the lateness of the season, and was bent over it, examining stems, thorns and petals, probably with an eye to planting one like it in the graveyard.

He looked up when their shadows lengthened across the drive. He was surprisingly nervous for such a powerful man, but he gave the two women a smile, wide enough to exhibit the toothless areas of his mouth. He nodded eagerly to Lady Hawtree and gave Elisa an awkward sketch of a bow.

Elisa was reasonably sure that Gwenna had exaggerated, since she couldn't think of anything Abel might know that would shed light on her problems. But the poor fellow was so anxious, she tried to ease the moment as much as possible.

'Abel, Lady Hawtree tells me you wish to speak to me.'

He looked over his shoulder at the ancient gatehouse door with its new brass fittings polished by one of Mrs Ponsonby's girls under Susan Clifford's directions. Abel shrugged, indicating the door. For a moment Elisa was puzzled but Gwenna understood at once.

'No, Abel. The gentlemen have gone to the almshouses. No one will hear you. Tell Lady March your secret. I will translate.' The word 'translate' was beyond him but Gwenna went on in her confident way. 'You indicated to me that you know something important to Her Ladyship.'

'First,' Elisa cut in, 'tell me who forbade you to see me. Was it Mrs Ponsonby, the housekeeper?'

He nodded, then perversely shook his head. She pursued the matter. 'And someone else? Stebbings, the butler?' He looked at Gwenna, hesitated, then nodded.

Gwenna said again, 'Something important to Her Ladyship?'

His rugged features were still strained. It was curious and satisfying to Elisa that he no longer looked as ugly as she had thought him on her first meeting. He grunted and pointed to the Hall. Then he raised his huge hand and levelled off twice with his hand flat.

276

'Height,' Elisa exclaimed. 'Two people.'

He seemed delighted by her reading of his gestures. He grinned and pointed again to the Hall. Gwenna Hawtree burst out triumphantly, 'I knew it. Something about the two Marches. But note, Elisa. It is March's brother Arthur.'

Elisa did not know how she came to that conclusion but Abel shook his head. His deep-set eyes glittered and he grunted with an effort, 'Aa!Aad!'

Gwenna cried suddenly, in triumph, 'Bad!'

To Elisa's surprise he nodded and kept repeating the sounds. 'Not Lady March, surely,' Gwenna went on.

He further confounded them by nodding and then shaking his head. 'Of one thing we can be certain,' Gwenna said. 'It is about you. Something "bad" concerns you.'

Abel nodded vigorously. He was still making wild gestures when the door of the gatehouse opened behind him and Jeremy stepped out, speaking over his shoulder to his guests, his estate manager and the housekeeper.

Abel heard his voice and the slight commotion behind Jeremy as the others came out. Abruptly, Abel closed his mouth and sidled away from the men. Since Elisa had very little confidence in anything he might say, she wasn't particularly disturbed; but Gwenna Hawtree, whose dream of playing the Bow Street Runner with its resultant furore had passed her by, went after the mute, still insisting, 'Abel, we are your friends. You may confide in us. Abel!'

But Abel was already loping off down the drive, looking back over his shoulder. He stumbled, tripped, caught himself and continued homeward, leaving a confused Elisa and an infuriated Gwenna who turned back and studied with narrowed eyes Jeremy, Sir Hugo, Captain Hawtree and the Cliffords. Her mood did not change when stout little Mrs Ponsonby came out to speak with Susan.

Sir Hugo found Abel's presence highly irregular.

'Isn't that the brute who tends the graves?'

Jeremy remarked casually, 'Abel often comes around for a basket of food. I hope he wasn't frightened off.'

277

'Susan will have a basket sent to him,' Brian promised as the girl headed toward the kitchen quarters and her work with the housekeeper.

Jeremy and the Hawtrees escorted the two women back to the Hall. It was not a comfortable group. Gwenna was still muttering to Elisa about the chance that was missed, but Elisa had less faith in the mute's 'important evidence'. She suspected his tale was concocted in order to obtain extra food, just as Jeremy had implied.

Her own interest was concentrated on Jeremy's casual, supercilious mood which still seemed inexplicable. Their relationship seemed to have reverted to its state on those terrible occasions before their wedding when she felt that he despised her.

She couldn't endure much more of this uncertainty. Would it never end? When would he trust her? And if her forgave her for this, the sale of her own jewels without his permission, what would prevent his turning away from her the next time she made a personal decision?

Perhaps, if she left him temporarily, he might miss her enough to break this pattern of mental torture he was putting her through.

But the gamble was great. If she broke with him, he would very probably learn to live without her. He had lived without her for half a lifetime.

She was in an agony of indecision. She was sure of only one fact: if he continued this game, she might be driven to her mother's dreadful end.

CHAPTER TWENTY-FOUR

Since the Hawtrees were dressed for an afternoon call, the postponed dinner would be informal, though Elisa was always surprised by the richness and elegance of what the Regent's circle considered 'informal' attire.

Before the two women joined the gentlemen for the absurdly formal stroll into the dining salon, Lady Hawtree promised Elisa, 'I shall pursue Abel on this. You may count upon me.'

It was not a priority in Elisa's mind. 'I daresay you will learn something scandalous.'

But her mind was asking her sadly, is it over, this up-and-down relationship with Jeremy? Can I go on, never knowing the next time he will mistrust me and grow cold over some fancied wrong?

'Of course. Nothing else is so entertaining. My beloved Papa taught me that,' Gwenna said, brightly sardonic.

Elisa opened the case which contained the March heirloom pearls, those heavy, uncomfortable jewels that Jeremy had been so proud of. She fastened the necklace while watching Gwenna in the mirror. 'The Earl, your father, was very important in your life?'

'Despised him. And his wretched death.'

'How did the Earl die?'

'Blew his head off in my dressing-room with one of my duelling pistols. Manton's best. I am considered an excellent shot.'

Elisa shuddered. 'Why did he choose to destroy himself in your room?'

To her surprise Her Ladyship turned away from the looking-glass, avoiding Elisa's eyes. Elisa thought her voice was almost too devoid of feeling, as if she strained to make it so.

'He wanted the last remnants of my inheritance from Grandpapa. My jewels. I refused him. I exchanged blood for rubies, one might say.' She turned back with a light laugh. 'They were excellent stones. Now, my dear, shall we join the gentlemen?'

Somewhat shaken, Elisa agreed. While walking down the great staircase with her, Elisa said, 'I see that there are several ways in which one can meet tragedy: with fear of the world, as I did; with revenge against the world; or with understanding.'

Gwenna said brightly, 'I never was a forgiving soul. Nor am I a coward. I'm sorry to say that leaves but one reaction. Enough of serious talk. Men always seem so distressed by it.'

Elisa remembered very little of that dinner. Her thoughts were occupied with Gwenna Hawtree's grisly confession and the malaise brought on by Jeremy's indifference. She was seated at the lower end of the table, in the chair customarily occupied by the hostess, as far as possible from Jeremy, with Sir Hugo on her right and Captain Hawtree on her left. The Cliffords had been invited to dinner and sat opposite each other at the center of the long table.

It was impossible not to notice Captain Hawtree's difficulty with the meats and fish and she longed to help him, but the moment she so much as looked at his plate he glared at her. Fortunately, someone had spoken to Belliver, who served the captain chiefly bite-sized morsels.

Almost as bad, Sir Hugo made light conversation with her but managed to distract her attention by staring at his son every time the Captain took a bite.

Elisa had hoped that the pleasant chatter over an informal meal would help to restore at least a semblance of friendship between Ronald Hawtree and herself when they went in to dinner together. They made a good start. He placed her hand on his good arm and said, 'Damme, for some reason I have a roaring appetite after all that talk of drains and irrigation works!'

When she laughed and said she certainly hoped so, he had grinned in the old way. But his difficulties at the table temporarily changed all that. It was Brian Clifford who took her arm as they all left the table. Sir Hugo had decided to play the gallant with pretty Susan, who adored sitting at the great table with all the attendant formality.

As they were crossing the reception hall toward the comfortable Small salon, Sir Hugo saw Elisa's necklace of pearls and remarked to Jeremy, almost in tones of accusation, 'Ah, March, you have brought out the great March pearls, I see. Mighty handsome. I always said so. How well I remember them around the throat of your sainted mother!'

Elisa touched the big yellow pearls, feeling their coldness. At the same time Jeremy moved forward, leaving an alert Gwenna Hawtree. He studied the necklace. His tense expression astonished Elisa. He seemed to be shocked. She could not imagine why until he said in an odd, uncertain voice totally unlike him, 'I had thought they were – lost.'

This was absurd to Elisa. Surely, he remembered giving them to her!

For the rest of the evening he seemed curiously abstracted, often not hearing a remark by the Hawtrees. Even more strange, his manner toward Elisa changed. He was once again kind, attentive, as if he hoped to make up to her for his previous indifference.

It was Gwenna who pointed unerringly to the pearls, the culprit in all this, as she and Elisa embraced and said good night.

'My dear,' she murmured in Elisa's ears, 'His moods are deplorable. Those wretched pearls. He appeared surprised to see them. Did he think you had lost them? Or had he forbidden you to wear them?' She brushed Elisa's knuckles with her gloves. 'I advise you to stop pandering to his moods. It is most unwise in a wife. Gives these dear creatures notions about their superiority.'

Elisa found Jeremy's new mood as mysterious as his old one, but Gwenna's advice was salutary. Jeremy had put her through so much anguish and suspicion before and after their wedding that she was beginning to wonder if it was wise to love him so much.

She was thinking of this as Ronald Hawtree kissed her hand before joining his father and stepmother in the carriage.

It took an instant for the importance of his words and manner to penetrate when he looked into her eyes and said, 'I wish you well, Lady March. I do quite sincerely.'

When she understood that he was offering his friendship again, she smiled, greatly relieved. One less enemy, she thought, but she also remembered with tenderness her old, half-humorous affection for him. Her smile made him add in a whisper, 'Lady March, you will always be the Divine Enchantress to me.'

She touched his fingers gently. 'Thank you, my dear friend. Thank you especially for your friendship.'

Standing in the drive watching their carriage depart, she felt Jeremy move closer until his arm was around her waist and they stood together.

Yet, she felt further away from him than ever. He was kind and loving now. But hours ago, since he knew she had sold her necklace, he had been sardonic and suspicious, like the Lord March she remembered months ago.

Probably he had resented her secrecy. But if a man of his background ever learned about her mother and Bedlam, he would see Molly Catlow's fate in everything Elisa did or said. She dared not tell him.

Her relations with the man she loved were terrifyingly insecure. She was deeply depressed.

Brian and his daughter had gone off to the gatehouse, leaving her alone with Jeremy. For the first time she wished they had remained. Her thoughtful gaze travelled up the golden Cotswold stone front of the Hall to the roof over the south wing of the building. She had been frightened that first night when Jeremy insisted on forcing her to climb 'Arthur's Secret Staircase'. When they reached the roof she had been terrified by Ronald Hawtree standing behind them, looking ghostly and silvered in the rising moonlight.

Was there a deliberate plan in it all, an effort to make her suffer for Arthur's death? Was this the real reason why Jeremy had made the fantastic proposal of marriage in the first place? So he could bring her here to the tender mercies of servants who had adored Arthur? All of it done to make her aware of what his young brother had meant to the people of this valley. But none of this explained his conduct about the sale of her own pearls and then, tonight, his abrupt reversal. Surely, he hadn't thought her capable of selling his family's heirlooms, and in secret?

If he thought that, he thought she was still the cheap *Circe* he had hated months ago.

Of course, he believed that!

She was suddenly sure of it.

She said aloud, 'You believed me capable of selling this heirloom necklace for my own profit, didn't you? Stealing it, in fact. Did it ever occur to you that I might have pearls of my own and wish to sell them?'

She felt the slow withdrawal of his arm from around her waist. His eyes were undeniably troubled as they looked down into hers. His voice was almost humble, or as humble as Jeremy March could ever be, she thought.

'I know better now.' As he tried to take her hand, she tried to free her fingers, then let them remain, cool and dead, in his hand. He began, 'My love, I wish I could make you understand.'

'Please, Your Lordship, do not call me "my love". I have always felt its insincerity, though I tried not to admit it, even to myself.' She thought that would annoy or even anger him, and was infuriated when he responded gently.

'I beg your pardon. There is an explanation. I should have confessed the truth before this. I have been incredibly stupid. Insensitive. But that is going to be mended. Come, sweetheart.' He tilted her chin up with his free hand and added whimsically, 'Am I permitted to call you that?'

Twenty-four hours ago she would have died to hear him talk to her like this, she told herself silently. Aloud, she said, 'There is another thing you may do to oblige me, if you will.'

'Tell me.'

She removed her hand from his clasp and pointed up to the roof which was barely visible under the quarter moon.

'Take me up there. By the inside staircase.'

He could hardly believe he had heard her correctly. 'Arthur's stairs? They nearly broke that lovely neck of yours.'

But she remained adamant. In the end, as she knew he would, he agreed to take her, probably thinking it was a romantic whim to test his love. They walked back into the Hall, presenting the servants with an appearance of perfect harmony.

'I want to make a confession, sweetheart,' he said once, but she ignored this. She was now reasonably sure of what that confession would be.

The staircase behind the tapestry on the ground floor was nearly as ill-lighted as it had been that first night. Philbey, Jeremy's very correct little valet, was passing them as Jeremy held the tapestry aside. He gave his master a disapproving look and shook his head as he glanced at Jeremy's hair which the night wind had left in disorder. Lumley was so disturbed Jeremy grinned and explained.

'We are playing a little game, my dear fellow. You need not wait up for me.'

Further shocked by this *lèse majesté*, the valet bowed and went on his way. Elisa started up the stairs, wrapping her silk shawl more closely around her. She had not looked back during the exchange between the two men. She was sure Jeremy felt that a few soothing words would absolve him of all guilt. It hurt with a sharp, physical pain to know that this man she had so passionately loved could still produce violent feelings in her.

He came up the stairs behind her two at a time. He reached for her hand. When she resisted he took it anyway, holding it securely as he passed her and went up, keeping two steps above her.

'No tumbles this time.'

She told herself that at this moment he might actually love her and mean it. But his capacity to believe the worst of her, even after their recent life together, was too much to bear. It had pointed out to her a truth she hadn't wished to face: when he loudly announced their betrothal, when he pursued her to London to marry her, and even in those glorious first days of their marriage, he had been acting out some subtle, long-planned and terrible revenge.

He had brought her here knowing how his staff would hate her. He had even left her at their mercy when someone tried to kill her.

Surely, there had never been a real love here. At best, it was a sexual passion which would die as such fervour always died.

Now and again, she heard the creaking noises, sounds of an old house settling. Sounds also that suggested the presence of Arthur March's ghost. Jeremy and his servants had worked hard upon her imagination. How sweet their revenge must have been!

But no more.

They reached the door to the roof and Jeremy pushed it open. The night was much colder up here than it had been on the driveway. Jeremy looked down at her before permitting her to step out onto the roof. How concerned he looked, his dangerously fascinating eyes carefully warm, even anxious! She told herself he was a better actor than she had ever been.

'It is too cold for you up here. The wind has an icy bite.'

She ignored this and tried to move past him. He stepped aside, still watching her closely. The wind whipped across her face. He brushed back the tendrils of her hair with a gentle, loving gesture. How hard he was trying to renew the old spell of his! She would not be fooled again.

Weak. Like Molly Catlow. Elsie, too, had been used.

I *am* Molly Catlow, she thought and shut her eyes in horror. She heard his voice with its deep pretense of caring.

'What is it, sweetheart? Tell me. Let me help you.'

She borrowed strength by remembering her anger.

'You had Ronald Hawtree up here to frighten me that night, didn't you? *Didn't you?*'

She had shocked him again, unless this was a part of his pretense.

'Good God, Elisa! How would I know he was here? Why would I want to –?' He broke off, remembering something. It was some truth that gave the lie to his denial. His face looked pale in the faint evening light. He put out his two hands, grasping her arms. The pressure was painful but she did not immediately feel it.

'I don't know why Hawtree frightened you up here. He and Arthur loved their dangerous games on the roof. I admit I was a little amused by your fright. I was stupid. I thought Hawtree deserved a little revenge after you jilted him as you did the others. But –'

'I never promised any man my love. Except you.'

He moistened his lips and began again. 'I thought it would pay you back for those poor fools you pretended to love. I thought I could pretend.' He shook her slightly in his desperation to make her understand. 'But I began to discover qualities about you. Qualities I had never before found in a woman. I fell in love with you. Then, I was jolted again when I believed you had sold the March pearls in secret, to gain money for some purpose of your own.' He looked into her eyes. 'But sweetheart, I love you now, this minute. Can't you feel the difference?'

She forced herself to smile. Her features felt icy. 'You made love to me to further your revenge. You became betrothed to me and let me marry you, still hating me. My Lord, you belong on the stage at Drury Lane.'

He was holding her so tightly she winced.

'I never hated you for long. I wanted to, but I couldn't. Every time I began to see you as you are, something came between us. I was even jealous of my own brother. Jealous of Hawtree and those others. When Arthur told me you loved him, I forced myself to do the decent thing and encourage your marriage to him. Afterward, I hated you for what I thought of in my conceit as a web you spun around those fools, including myself. But I never stopped wanting you. Don't you know that?'

He pulled her to him roughly, ignoring the night and the wind and her own fragile body in his hands. He crushed her mouth with his, forcing her lips apart, possessing her by sheer and desperate force until she began to struggle, making helpless sounds in her throat.

She had known he wanted her. But that had nothing to do with love.

'When you brought me to this house, did you know they would hate me enough to wish me dead? To humiliate and then frighten, and finally poison me?'

He started at her, unbelieving.

'You can't mean that.'

She asked in her glittering voice, 'Did you think of killing me up here that night when Captain Hawtree frightened me? You may kill me now, so easily. I led you up here to show you how easily. Someone wants me dead. That I know. And then Arthur and Hawtree and da Spada and those others will all be avenged.'

She knew she had hurt him as deeply as he had ever wounded her.

After a terrible minute he asked, 'You really think I could do that?'

'Could you?'

His hands fell away from her. Her entire body felt cold now, even where his hands had seemed to scorch her flesh.

She turned and moved to the open doorway, the wind whipping her skirts hard against her slender body. He remained there, watching her. She felt his gaze upon her back. She had no idea what emotion was revealed in that gaze.

Though she still loved him and was sure she would always feel this desperate longing to have his love despite his deception, she had suspected from the beginning that this relationship must end as soon as he discovered her real past and her relationship to Molly Catlow.

Like any gentleman with that long gallery of noble ancestors, he would abandon her in haste when he learned that her mother had died a suicide in Bedlam.

She was doing the right thing now, turning from him while she had the strength to do so. Maybe then he would never know the worst about her.

She left the Secret Staircase at the first door and took the main staircase to her boudoir-sitting room. Moving mechanically, without volition, she bolted the door that opened into the bedchamber she had shared with Jeremy in her happiest hours. Then she began to dress for travel, tearing off the white silk

287

and lace gown where the buttons down her back proved recalcitrant.

She had scarcely picked out a travel gown and redingote when Jeremy tried the latch on the bolted door and then called to her.

'Elisa, let me talk to you.'

She wondered how to give herself time.

'In the morning, if you wish.'

There was a hesitation, then his voice again. 'In the morning, then, darling.'

She ignored the endearment. Talk was easy. No one knew this better than an actress.

She completed her change, not staying to pack so much as a bandbox. She tied the violet ribbons of her smallest, out-of-fashion bonnet and, taking up her reticule, listened at the corridor door until convinced by the silence that it was safe to leave.

She got as far as the reception hall before being discovered. The music room door opened almost in her face and Belliver came out. It would be hard to say which was the more startled. Belliver looked as if he had seen a ghost. Probably people didn't wander these halls at midnight as a usual thing.

He stammered, 'M-my duty, Ma'am. Mister Stebbings says: "Lock and bolt all doors on this floor."'

She put a finger to her lips. He looked around uneasily, afraid of being witnessed in something furtive. To her relief he then nodded and surprised her by hurrying to the front doors and unbolting both of them for her. Whatever his thoughts on her secretive, midnight departure, he made no difficulties.

She had forgotten how cold it was tonight. No matter. She started to run toward the gatehouse, ignoring such irrelevancies as the sharp pebbles underfoot and the fog rolling in over the hills that hid the Hawtrees' absurd gothic castle from view.

She looked back when she reached the gatehouse door under the archway, but Belliver had gone inside the Hall. She wondered what he thought. He had been her friend. Perhaps he believed his employer was a Bluebeard and his unfortunate bride fleeing from him in storybook fashion.

288

She scratched on the door in the polite, accepted way, then realized Brian could not hear. He would be upstairs, probably in bed. She hammered on the door with her bare hands and after a long minute or two sucked her bruised knuckles. She heard the bolt of the door being shot back and almost fell into Brian's arms before the door was entirely open.

'I must get back home. To London. Some way. Quickly. Before he discovers I'm gone.'

Brian held her close but made the usual, sensible objections. 'It can't be that bad. He is a good fellow. I'm sure he didn't mean to . . . What did he do?'

Thank heaven, Brian hadn't gone to bed yet! It wouldn't take him so long to get ready.

'It's all a fraud. He never loved me when he married me. I was a weak, gullible fool like –' She could only explain in vague terms. He probably wouldn't understand that she had been rejected like her mother, that all Jeremy's lovemaking and trust, their beautiful moments shared, were a lie.

'Nonsense!' Brian told her bracingly. 'You aren't in the least like your mother, if that is what you are afraid of. She died because she was not strong enough to face life. Life didn't reject her. She rejected life.'

After all her torn and anguished thoughts, it was intolerable to hear him insult her mother. She twisted in his arms, slapping him as hard as she could across the cheek and jaw.

'That is a lie. She was taken away because of me, because she couldn't find a job to feed me. It was my fault she died.'

He had flinched when she gave him the stinging slap but he kept looking at her with that sad, understanding look she hated. Pity. That was what she hated most. Only the weak deserved pity. It was all they had in life. He shook his head obstinately.

'You should let March explain. Settle matters with him. Perhaps it is only a misunderstanding.'

He hadn't wanted her to marry Lord March. It was maddening to have him fail her now. She struggled to free herself.

'Then I will go alone.'

Susan came clattering down the stairs in her shoes usually worn on muddy days. She had heard most of their conversation.

'Papa, Mrs Ponsonby told me the truth after poor Elisa fell downstairs. Lord March expected Elisa to be treated badly. It was horrid. But we thought he had changed. Ponsy says he has been much nicer to her until a day or so ago.'

'I don't believe it. No gentleman would –' Brian broke off. Susan's confession had sickened Elisa. It decided Brian.

'Very well. We must get Elisa out of her. Susie, you will have to explain to His Lordship what we have done.'

'Shouldn't I go with you?' Much as Susan loved March Hall and had a proprietary feeling for it, it looked like the excitement and drama of Elisa's problem were beginning to attract her. 'It would be more proper. And I'd give anything to see Mr Tregaran play opposite her. He wants to, desperately. He told me so.'

Brian appeared to have decided on Elisa's behalf. While Susan got Elisa a small glass of Madeira, promising, 'It will warm you for the journey,' Brian wrote a stiff but respectful note to Lord March, gave it to Susan to deliver, and was soon ready to accompany Elisa.

'It would be wise to take the little closed carriage used by the servants on occasion. It will arouse less attention. I will have the two-horse team and the buggy returned to His Lordship and we may make the rest of the trip by the Mail Coach. Not very comfortable, you know.'

'It won't be the first time.'

She hugged Susan, thanked the girl again, and watched with envy while Susan and her father embraced. Elisa had never known her own father, an itinerant actor, Molly said, and she often thought how different life might have been for her mother if that easy, irresponsible lover had only married her.

So much for love.

Elisa was already determined to resume her career, win over her audience again, and let men love her if they liked. As for her own softer passions, she would never again yield to them. She had been right about mankind in the first place.

Brian chided her in a gentle way as the little black carriage and casual, opinionated team took them out under the archway of the gatehouse and away from March Hall.

'You musn't keep looking back like that or I'll begin to think you regret leaving.'

'Certainly not.'

But still she looked, remembering painfully the hours during the few weeks here when she had been happier than at any time in all her twenty-six years.

CHAPTER TWENTY-FIVE

Two nights with scarcely any sleep had left Elisa thinking of nothing but her big, comfortable bed and the lonely security of her house in Portman Square. Her first reaction on meeting Tuttle and McFee was to embrace each of them.

They were both their gruff selves but showed their affection for her in their odd ways, McFee by bringing in gifts of flowers and even trinkets from her admirers, Tuttle by clearing her throat and admitting roughly, 'Missed you, girl. And the theatre's dead since you went off with that Lord. All your London lads missed you, come to that. I opine you'll be wanting to get back on-stage soon as ever you can.'

A little flicker of happiness lighted Elisa's thoughts. 'Then you think they will accept me?'

'Ask Strawbridge. Gad's life! The fellow makes this his second household. He's signed that Tregaran actor; so you're barely in time. He wants you together again.'

Brian, as usual, showed his dislike and mistrust of Tuttle in a polite way. He invariably addressed Elisa, suggesting she rest at once. 'Meanwhile, I must return to March Hall. I owe him some kind of explanation.'

'No. Please stay. Do rest a day or so. Here.'

He shook his head. He looked around, saw that they were alone and warned her sternly, 'In heaven's name, don't be so trusting with those servants of yours!'

'Tuttle is more than a servant. You know that. We've travelled a long way together since I hired her. She used to know Mama long ago.'

'That's as may be. But we can make hasty judgements. I believe I may have made one about March. I think he really cares for you . . . Now, forgive me. I must be on my way.'

She held out both hands, took his and briefly caressed them. 'Thank you, dear Brian. When I am back on the stage you must promise to come and see me. If I succeed, we will celebrate.' She managed a tired smile. 'If I don't, we will commiserate.'

He squeezed her hands affectionately, assuring her, 'You won't fail. They are waiting for you, your audience. They love you.'

She watched him summon the horse and cabby across the square and ride off to put himself on the waybill of the Gloucestershire coach.

'I'm glad to see the back of that lad,' Tuttle muttered behind her. 'Mark me, I've never trusted him and his spoiled brat of a daughter. Telling me all that was wrong with my housekeeping. Making sly remarks about all the food. Dishes not clean. Cook not to be trusted. And what-all.'

Susan's anxiety to be a good housekeeper had given her the neophyte's usual habit of finding fault with everyone else.

Elisa was almost relieved at these complaints, though she said, 'Tuttle, in heaven's name, don't you start!'

Tuttle ordered the hip-bath carried up to Elisa's bedchamber, where it was set before the fire in the adjoining boudoir and Elisa was able to rest her tired, aching body while Tabitha and another maid poured pails of hot water over her back.

It was the new maid who assured Elisa, 'Folk will be that glad to see you back, Mum, you've no notion. That Bessie Maulders, she got hissed t'other night. Mister Tregaran, he got right put about over it. Said he'd be damned if he'd come pleading for you to play again. But ever-body knew it was in his thoughts.'

Elisa was aroused to a little of her former confidence by this news.

'Have they really discussed my coming back? Don't they know I am married?'

'Aye, Mum. But Mister Strawbridge, he signed Mister Tregaran to a paper and what he says is what Mister Tregaran has to do. He said you'll be back more famous than ever, and here you are.'

It was comforting. She still had the love of her audience out there in the darkness beyond the footlight candles. She went to bed, warmed by Tuttle's gruff voice.

'Sleep well, lass. Tomorrow will look a deal brighter.'

The deep, exhausted sleep came first. It was not until late in the night that the oldest dream began, the dream that she thought she had buried when success came to her as Elisa Carlisle.

. . . *She was the child Elsie Catlow again, and it was night. She slept curled up in a ball and with reasonable comfort in this position, warmed by a form of self-heat. An occasional stray cat, and once a lost dog, joined her in this lodging-house near the river. She and her mother lived in the small room that was transformed from a kind of root cellar to living quarters. It still held the odd, musty smell of unwashed vegetables, but its single cot, a table with three drawers, and a little shaving mirror left by the previous inhabitant, had served Molly and Elsie as a reasonable lodging.*

At first, Molly's careful mending and embroidery earned them enough to pay the rent, but then, after an experience in the streets that she would not discuss with Elsie, she became uncommunicative, like a somnambulist. Kind young Dr Clifford, who lived two streets away with his tiny, motherless daughter, explained when called to attend Molly, that she had 'lost the will to live'.

It explained nothing to Elsie who had a passionate will to live. Dr Clifford told her gently, 'It is up here. In the head. We do not understand these things, but they exist. We must be very kind to such people, but we should also urge them to rouse themselves. They must be active, set their minds on outward things. Other people. Do you understand me?'

Elsie understood very little. Besides, it was some 'outward experience', perhaps with a strange man, that had brought on her mother's condition. It became impossible to make her mother 'rouse herself'. Molly sat hour after hour, sometimes weeping, sometimes just staring. Elsie stole food from a lodger who drank and left his door unbolted. She ran errands, carrying packets

294

from the greengrocer's and others to neighbourhood women of the streets.

In the end the men took Molly away one afternoon while her daughter was out in the street running an errand.

It was Dr Clifford who found out where they had confined Molly. He took Elsie several times to see her mother at St Mary's of Bethlehem Asylum. Each time he tried to persuade the warders that he could care for the woman if they would assign her to him.

The matter would be discussed, he was told.

Elsie was convinced for a time that this place was a hospice, a place for the sick. But it was very strange, the way she imagined an ancient fortress to be, and it smelled of age and secrets. Then, after her first visit, she heard things, dreadful little cries. Helpless people, tortured, she thought. But Dr Clifford explained that they were tortured by their own thoughts. He did not like it when some of the 'patients' were beaten or hung in shackles.

That was wicked, he said.

But she knew then that though Dr Clifford was tall and fine looking, he was helpless against those who had power and money.

Then, there was the last visit. On a previous occasion Molly had seemed to recognize her daughter, though she would not speak. Sometimes a warder or a turnkey would let Elsie in to the cell and she would go to her mother who hugged her very hard. That was all. But it was enough. She might be getting better. This was a place where sick people were taken. Surely . . .

The last visit was different. While Dr Clifford talked to the officials, Elsie was taken through aged corridors past barred doors, to her mother's cell.

Separated from her mother by the door with its barred aperture, Elsie was lifted up to the bars by a goodnatured turnkey.

But she couldn't see her mother, only pieces of material tied to one of the bars.

'Where is she?'

Impatiently, the turnkey set her down. Elsie heard metallic noises. The key was turned in the lock. The big, muscular turnkey had a hard time opening the door. There was an obstacle. The turnkey cursed, scaring Elsie who peeked in under his arm.

The obstacle proved to be a life-sized rag doll, hanging from one bar. It looked like Molly, but for the bloated, unrecognizable face. The noose had been made from many strips of cloth – Molly's old, stained petticoat. How patiently she must have torn it into strips, sometimes with her teeth, perhaps with her small fingers.

Elsie began to shiver. They had taken her mother away, she thought, and left that rag doll in her place. The turnkey muttered 'God! God!' He looked very pale. He pushed Elsie away so hard she fell against the next cell door. Close above her head someone laughed, a curious, tuneless laugh, and fingers squeezed out between the bars, groping to her.

A voice, neither male nor female, pleaded, 'Let me see you. Let me see –'

The horror was real. The thing had once been human.

Elsie began to run, stumbling, picking herself up, running. Corridors. Steps. Strange, sinister, ancient walls. Then a street she did not recognize. Amid the distant noises of the world's biggest city she kept calling for her mother. Where had they taken her?

After nightfall she came to the little room she had shared with her mother, curled up in a ball, and slept. In the morning, when she woke up, Molly might be here in this room, the natural place to come after she ran away from that dreadful prison.

Poor Brian! It was always his duty to bring her pain. He found her almost a day later. By that time she had accepted the reality of what she saw at Bedlam.

What she did not know was that she would still be living this anguish when she was twenty-six years old.

In the deep night she reached out to touch the hanging doll that everyone insisted was Molly Catlow.

She awoke.

She sat up and stared into the dark of her elegant bedchamber in Portman Square. There was nothing to fear. She was alone.

The thought did not comfort her.

She threw a peignoir around her chilled shoulders and went into the boudoir. By good luck there were still burning embers in the gate. She stirred them up and sat down in front of the fire. After a while the chill went away. She closed her eyes to memories of Molly Catlow. She refused to think of Jeremy, who was still her husband. She would think of the theatre, of her future, the only place where she was genuinely loved.

'They won't pack me off to Bedlam. By God, they won't!'

Twelve hours later there were distractions to raise her spirits. She felt that the answer to everything lay in her career, since she had never really possessed Jeremy's love. Enos Strawbridge brought a certain happiness to her with his enthusiastic offer.

He kissed her hand, embraced her, and assured her with sweeping gestures, 'London awaits you, dear Enchantress. It does more: it salutes you.'

'You forget the scandal. I thought I was a wicked *Circe*, turning men into swine. I was a danger to the Regent's entire male circle.'

Strawbridge, who had suggested sending her off to the wilds of America only a few months ago, now took the reverse line.

'You couldn't have returned at a better time. Four nights ago we performed your triumph, *Our Lady Of Victory*. Tregaran had a passion to repeat his Bonaparte role. Alas, dear Enchantress, there was no one but Bessie Maulders to play the Empress Josephine. Tregaran insisted he would train her to the role. Disaster! Howling disaster. They hissed her off the stage. The lads who cleaned up afterward tell me they picked up enough rotting apples – and quite a few oranges – to feed a starving army.'

'I trust they haven't saved some for me.'

Strawbridge raised both arms eloquently. 'Ah, but that is the best of it. Can you guess what they cried out from every quarter – the pit, the galleries, the boxes? "Give us back our Lady of Victory." "Give us our *Circe*." "We demand Carlisle!" Yes. Their very words.'

'Tregaran must have loved that.'

Strawbridge shrugged. 'No more than Bonaparte, I daresay, when his armies cried, "Bring back our Lady of Victory!"'

It was a pity Strawbridge had signed Tregaran for the season, without knowing for a certainty that he meant to conduct himself properly. But then, Elisa warmed as always to the thought of the love that poured across the footlights to her from out of that great jewelled darkness.

Sensing her indecision, Strawbridge reminded her, 'I ordered Tregaran to make me a solemn promise. He must behave like a mature and seasoned performer or it's out for him, no matter how popular he may become. And he's that, you know.'

'Well then, we seem to have the matter settled.' She tried to cultivate the old excitement, the old ambition, but she kept seeing Jeremy's face in those last moments between them on the rooftop of March Hall. How tender he had been, how desperate that look in his eyes!

Perhaps he did love Elisa Carlisle a little. He would never be able to love Elsie Catlow.

By the time Strawbridge left Portman Square fifteen minutes later, she began to concentrate on her theatrical future. It would be good to start again with *Our Lady Of Victory*. There were advantages for her in that particular role. After her many years before audiences she knew the qualities, the traits and assets that proved most successful with them.

Even her costumes were circumscribed by their popularity with her admirers. The role of the charmingly fickle Josephine seemed easy for Elisa. It was the role she had played through most of her life.

It was burned in her heart that love had destroyed her mother, and the only time Elisa herself was foolish enough to fall in love she had been deeply hurt, her life threatened.

She told herself Strawbridge is clever. I must play Josephine while my age still permits the illusion.

Peter Tregaran came to visit Elisa two mornings later. She was uncomfortable about how Tregaran would react to her after their last encounter when he stormed off the stage.

Upon meeting her he put her in mind of the young General Bonaparte making a tactical recovery from a military miscalculation. He bowed awkwardly, with stiff reluctance, accepted the hand she extended, and returned it to her. Though he was on his dignity, he was young enough for his haughty attitude to seem merely petulant. She, for her part, reacted with her celebrated warm smile – almost, but not quite, promising whatever it was he might seek.

'My dear Tregaran,' she began, gesturing him to the tufted gold sofa in the Small salon, 'how good it is to see you again, and to tell you how very much your fame has preceded you about the country. Even down in Gloucestershire we heard of your triumphs.'

Relieved and a bit smug, he settled back on the sofa. She seated herself in the armchair beside the sofa, still giving him the full effect of her admiring gaze.

'There was an unfortunate audience that last performance of *Our Lady*,' he explained hurriedly. 'I'm afraid the reports . . .'

'Oh, but Strawbridge assures me you yourself had a complete triumph. I can only envy you. To play the greatest genius of our time – though he was an enemy – well, that is an honor in itself. And to arouse such comments! Strawbridge says there was nothing but praise for you.'

He bent toward her eagerly, his dark face alight. 'You feel his genius, too? I mean Bonaparte's. Yes. I feel that when I play him. I sometimes think – I daresay you will laugh – but I do believe something of his personality comes over me when I play that role.'

You may well say that, she thought, but went on smiling. 'I am firmly of that opinion myself. I felt it the night we played *Our Lady* together. A happy teaming, I always thought, in spite of our little temperamental differences.'

It began to appear that she had gone too far and persuaded Tregaran that he himself was the genius he portrayed. The old arrogance returned, spiced with self-satisfaction. His meagre body, especially his chest, seemed to expand as he sat there on the sofa, expounding his ideas.

'I have broached to Strawbridge the happy notion of Bonaparte returning to Josephine on her deathbed. Perhaps stage center, in the lamplight beside her bed. A vision of what she has lost. A touching moment.'

And ruin my death scene? Not likely!

Aloud, she assured him, 'I shall certainly bring the idea to Strawbridge.'

And if he agrees, he may look for another star!

But she went on nodding and smiling while her thoughts wandered. She marvelled that she had once enjoyed this real life playacting. Now, all unbidden, came quick, flashing memories of genuine happiness: with Jeremy, walking through the herb garden, arm in arm; with Jeremy, as she melted into his lean, muscular body in that great ancestral bed; with Jeremy, laughing and teasing and sometimes flirting.

Only on her part, she reminded herself, had it been spontaneous. How well he had chosen his revenge, playacting with her, treating her as she had treated those men who thought they were conquering the celebrated Elisa Carlisle!

Something of her sad thoughts must have showed in her eyes. Tregaran stopped speaking in mid-sentence. Surprised by the unexpected silence, she looked at him. He was staring at the doorway where the double doors stood open to the reception hall. She turned her head, gasped, and flushed with nervous excitement.

She thought she had never seen any sight so welcome. Or so troubling.

Her husband stood there, looking dusty but magnificent, in a caped riding coat, his beaver hat in one hand and his riding crop in the other. He must have come all the way to London on horseback. He was smiling. Not perhaps, a cheerful smile, but one that appeared to promise much.

'I beg your pardon. I asked your man not to announce me. I was afraid you wouldn't see me . . . But I am interrupting you.' He stepped into the room. She noted that his topboots were mudstained, unusual for Jeremy March. 'I am March,' he said to the actor. 'And you, sir, are Peter Tregaran. I saw you as the Corsican. Excellent work. I knew the Emperor slightly and the resemblance is striking.'

'Thank you, My Lord.' Tregaran glanced from March to Elisa. 'I believe our business is at an end for the moment, Miss – that

300

is, Lady March.' He hesitated. 'Shall I tell Bessie Maulders that you are replacing her?'

It was an embarrassing moment. They hadn't discussed the Maulders problem, and, furthermore, she was afraid to find herself alone with Jeremy. She knew her weakness too well. 'Do you think she will play Marie-Louise? She would do excellently.'

Tregaran stopped. 'If she had another scene or two. Something to indicate the Emperor's affection for her. Then, losing the Josephine part would not be such a blow.'

The idea was to prevent more trouble with the audience, not to bring about another disaster. But Elisa promised, 'It shall certainly be discussed. Good day, Mr Tregaran.'

The young man looked so smug she knew he had not changed in the least. After an imperious nod of the head to her, he was on his way out. He went in the wake of a confused McFee, who gave Lord March a look and then questioned Elisa with raised eyebrows. She nodded. He stalked out, motioning Tregaran to follow him.

As the front door slammed behind Tregaran, Jeremy set his hat down and reached Elisa in two strides. She put her hands out to stop him.

'No. Someone can hear us.'

'What if they can? Darling, it is quite legitimate. We are man and wife. Had you forgotten?' It was said on a wistful note, as if he tried very hard to give it a light sound but was unsure of himself.

She shook her head, afraid he might win her love whenever he chose to exercise his charm over her. 'We were never man and wife, My Lord. You wanted revenge and I was the object of your hatred. The truth is, I was never your kind.'

He made a gesture of denial. He seemed so tense she could almost believe he was afraid he would fail with her. It was not at all like Jeremy March.

'Arthur told me you had offered him the laudanum, taunting him to take it if he chose. That you would not marry.

301

But he wasn't himself, I know that now. When I knew you better, I understood. You couldn't have done such a thing.'

'Thank you. You will recall I told you that.'

'Darling,' he went on, 'I started for London the minute I received Clifford's note. To make you understand. Come home with me. I'll prove my love. I swear to you, you will never have cause to doubt me again.'

'Please don't lie. It will happen the next time I sell a necklace that was my property.'

He flinched at that. 'You won't need to sell your jewels.' He brushed her protesting hands aside. Though he took her to him gently, his hands around her arms, her body close, with all its familiar excitement, he hesitated before kissing her. For the first time in their relationship she thought he was not certain of her response.

She managed a shadow of the smile she had used on Tregaran. 'My Lord, your revenge is complete. Even your brother would be satisfied. What more can you possibly want of me?'

He stared at her, shaking his head, but wordless.

She tried to free herself. Belatedly, his fingers slipped away from her flesh, a slow and reluctant movement. He asked at last, 'Have you never been wrong? Never made a mistake?'

'Certainly. But I was never quite so cruel.'

'Never?'

Surely not! There were men who had given her gifts, built her comfortable little financial nest that would save her from ending like her mother. But she had given them – what? A few hours of false passion. The same gift Jeremy had given her. And how valuable was that?

She looked up into his eyes, haunted by what might have been.

'If only you had loved me, just a little.'

Gradually, she realized that he was no longer touching her. He backed away. She imagined she saw on his face a return of the old, arrogant mask that had once fascinated her by its diamond-hard perfection.

'I see.' He turned away.

She tried to speak, failed, then got out the words finally.

'I wish you well, My Lord. Goodbye.'

CHAPTER TWENTY-SIX

Rehearsals began at once, for which Elisa was profoundly grateful. She was even relieved to find that plump, blonde Bessie Maulders bore her a deep grudge. This and Tregaran's scene-stealing tricks occupied her thoughts during most of her waking hours.

In the dead of night her bad dreams had returned, a circumstance Tuttle took as a personal affront.

'How is it you never had dreams when you was in that man's house? Him that you couldn't even share a bed with. A wicked business, that.'

During rehearsals she received a letter of warning from Brian:

'My dear Elisa, this is painful but I feel you should be prepared. A professional colleague of mine at St Mary's of B. informs me that your husband has been in London making inquiries about Molly.

'Lord March seemed most curious. 'Interested' is the word my friend used. I understand Lord March was excessively generous at the end of his several visits, but one would expect that of March. How it will affect your relationship I cannot hazard a guess, but I know how you fear the revelations about your mother and I felt it my duty to warn you.

'I wondered where His Lordship was put onto the subject but, according to my friend, March had heard someone mention Bedlam several times. I believe you may have done so inadvertently when you were distressed, and, of course, he must be aware of the provisions for Bedlam's inmates in your will. This seems the most likely source.

'*Naturally, I assure you I have never discussed it.*'

Elisa was surprised by her own relief when she read the letter. Her greatest fear, that Jeremy would discover the truth, had come to pass.

There was no possibility now of second thoughts, of moments when she would daydream about a reunion, telling herself his scheme of revenge didn't matter because he had learned to love her. Any lingering passion Jeremy might have for her would die the minute he entered Bedlam to investigate the fate of her mother and herself.

Then, a day later, when she looked up at the stage-right box during rehearsal she saw Lord March seated there, half-obscured by the faded curtain, and perhaps by his own deliberate intent. He did not stop at her dressing-room before or after the rehearsal. Probably because he knew now that her deception had been as great as his.

Strange that she had never before balanced the two, one against the other.

Meanwhile, she must go on with her life, ask of herself what she asked of Jeremy March: sincerity toward others.

When Tuttle arrived with Elisa's freshly pressed and refurbished costumes, she was astonished to find Strawbridge and her mistress discussing with an angry Tregaran the extra scene created by the Cornishman in which Bessie Maulders would shine. Disapproving strongly, Tuttle heard Elisa yield at last, but not before she had reminded Tregaran in her coolly gracious way that it would not matter in the end; 'her audience' would know what to think.

Once more, Tregaran went about threatening dire things, including an effort to show her up before her precious audience. It did not help matters when Strawbridge forced him to apologize to Elisa. This humiliation took place before the crew. It was regrettable to Elisa but Tuttle considered it a splendid thing.

'And no more than he deserves, the rogue!' Tuttle ended, 'What's he after now?'

'He wants to include a Napoleonic vision in my death scene.'

'I don't like it.'

'Never mind, Tuttle,' she said afterward when they were alone. 'It may be better this way. I have always been concerned with myself. I must change if I am to expect changes toward me.'

'Bosh! You just hope to win back His Lordship. Well, girl, you're giving away your professional advantages for nothing.'

Elisa did not agree. She felt a glow of pride in performing an unselfish act, and she hoped it would begin to change her self-involved thinking. For a few minutes that day she had examined more than her flawless skin. She had looked deeply into the flawed woman behind that facade.

In spite of Tuttle's sharp and observant objections Elisa thought the new rehearsals went reasonably well. Bessie Maulders stopped licking her sticky fingers long enough to make a plump, kittenish Marie-Louise. She still could not hold an entire scene, but this inadequacy was covered by the fiery theatrical quality of Peter Tregaran. His scene-stealing tricks served this scene well.

She looked up at the stage-right box during the last act rehearsal but the box seemed to be empty. Tregaran noticed her inattention and remarked loudly on it.

'The show is here, *Circe*. Not up there.'

She colored at the rebuke which was justified. She even let pass his offensive nickname for her. But when she finished the scene, got up from her deathbed, and walked rapidly off-stage, she noticed that Tregaran's sensual eyes took in the full sight of her body in its thin silk night-rail and flesh-colored tights. In earlier days the obvious working of his full lips, and the way he wet them unconsciously, would have amused her.

Tuttle met her in the wings with a warm shawl and a glum announcement. 'You ready for company?' She tilted her head roughly, to indicate the Carlisle dressing-room. 'Waiting yonder.'

Trembling with anxiety, Elisa ran toward the dressing-room. She forgot to remind herself that by now Lord March knew she came of disreputable stock. In his mind there must always be a taint that made her impossible as a wife. The door, which had been left open as always, revealed the tall man who turned, smiled at her and held out his hands.

'My dear Elisa, I am happy to see you looking so well. We are absolutely determined to be present for your triumph, Susan and I.'

She swallowed her disappointment. 'Dear Brian, thank you.' She looked over his broad shoulder. 'And Susan. You look prettier than ever.'

After a moment of silence, for she was absorbing the sight of the actress, Susan burst out, 'Do you think I may see Tregaran for a minute? He said I was to be admitted any time I called upon him backstage.'

'By all means. And you are looking splendid. So grown-up. How can he refuse to see such a beauty? He will be exceedingly flattered.'

Susan was too excited to do more than accept Elisa's embrace and wriggle out of it before she sped off to Peter Tregaran's dressing-room where the actor held court. She had slammed the corridor door behind her and Brian, remembering Elisa's peculiar terrors, obligingly pulled the door open.

'She is at the age where glamorous actors are her entire world.'

'Perhaps I had better warn her about Bessie Maulders.' But on second thoughts Elisa decided young Susan could manage the buxom Bessie without help. She and Brian could both hear the noisy chatter of Tregaran's admirers leaving his dressing-room.

Brian reacted nervously. 'I trust she isn't there alone. It would be extremely improper.'

They both heard laughter and several unintelligible comments. Among them they made out the shrill tones of Bessie Maulder's laugh.

Elisa reassured Brian. 'There are several in the room, including Maulders. Male and female. They will play lackeys and *vivandières* and soldiers in some of the scenes. They are unpaid. Did you know that?'

But he was not interested in the inner workings of the theatre. 'Elisa, how much trust do you place in Lady Hawtree?'

It was an unexpected subject. 'I am afraid Lady Hawtree is an incurable gossip. Nothing pleases her more than to spread poison.'

307

'Poison!'

'Gossip. Mental poison.'

He admitted that might be very true. 'She has even been frightening poor old Abel. I had to speak to her about it. I saw her trying to entice him into her carriage two days ago.' He seemed to feel that this required some explanation. 'I believe she wanted to hire him for some work about her gardens. At all events, I assume so. But he was terrified. Big Abel, terrified.'

'Abel? How very odd! Gwenna always thought Abel had some secret knowledge. He once got out the word 'bad'. About me, strangely enough.'

'My dear Elisa, you mustn't mind the opinion of your inferiors.'

She brushed this aside. 'He may know something bad that concerns me. Quite a different matter . . . Dear Brian, give me a few minutes. Tuttle will have me presentable for the street and I want you and Susan to stay with me as long as my — as Lord March will permit you. I know he may need you, but I need you as well.'

'A pleasure, as always, Elisa. I want to help you in any way possible – and, of course, nothing would make Susan happier.' He looked down the narrow hall to the source of considerable merriment and giggles. Tregaran's dressing-room. 'They seem to be in great spirits.'

He retired to the corridor, carefully leaving the door open. A minute later he brought his daughter out of the actor's dressing-room. She was pink with excitement.

'They are all excessively kind. And flattering, too.'

Hearing this, Elisa smiled and went with Tuttle to change behind the screen. She told herself she was relieved that her husband no longer seemed interested in troubling Elsie Catlow. She hadn't seen him again in the theatre box, though Bessie Maulders demanded the next day, during final rehearsals, 'Who's the nob that hides away in the boxes, spying on us?'

With her heart beating fast Elisa said nothing. It was Tregaran who dismissed the matter. 'Some nabob from India whose son is in the "ghost" scene. He may put money into Scunthorpe's career.'

So much for hopes and fears.

How appropriate, she thought on the night the play was to open. *Our Lady Of Victory* was to be played the very evening when the weather was frightful. Rain had fallen all day and a persistent wind rattled through the old theatre building. Just as the patrons were arriving late that afternoon for the six o'clock curtain a wet fog crept in off the Thames. Still, according to Strawbridge, the box office had never been busier.

'A genuine triumph,' the manager promised Elisa. 'And your name is on everyone's lips. It's so obvious, even that conceited pup, Tregaran, has heard the comments. He has his young spies gathering the gossip in the audience. Much good it may do him. Luckily, he is taking it well. Confessed to me that you would be unforgettable tonight. Which I don't doubt for a minute.'

There was something not quite natural about this reaction from Peter Tregaran, of all people. Was Tregaran planning an outrage on-stage, as publicly as possible?

'Did you see Lord March in one of the boxes?'

Strawbridge was uncomfortable. 'Not yet. But I daresay he will be late, like all these aristocrats.'

By the time of the first curtain Elisa was trembling within, though her long discipline in the theatre kept her from showing it.

'They're waiting for you, girl,' Tuttle assured her. 'Them that truly adores you. You go out and give them what they've come for, Elisa Carlisle.'

Elisa's smile flickered and faded. 'How long do you think all those loving creatures would adore Elsie Catlow?'

'You'll be asking God's truth? I don't think they would care.'

Laughing silently at what she considered Tuttle's naiveté, Elisa moved in her accustomed way to the wings where she would make her entrance well into the first act.

Her entrance would be meticulously staged, through the dialogue of other characters. Every mention of Josephine was guaranteed to arouse passionate anticipation in the audience. It

309

was also one of the careful methods by which she had built up her reputation as London's most popular actress. She knew the necessity of an arrival on-stage that was later than the arrival (accompanied by mindless chatter) of the occupants in the boxes that hovered over the stage.

She saw Brian Clifford in the opposite wing, separated from her by the stage. She was grateful for the warmth of his affection as he and Susan signalled their good wishes to her.

Suddenly Tuttle tapped her shoulder. It was an extraordinary action, destroying her concentration at the moment she most needed it. She shrugged off Tuttle's touch.

Tuttle muttered in her ear, 'He says he must see you between the acts.'

'Impossible.'

'He says it's vital. And you're not to speak to anyone else or have them in your dressing-room. No one.'

'Good God! Who is it? The Prince Regent himself?'

'It's him. His Lordship.'

'He must be mad. He knows better.' Her head whirled with questions. But she couldn't let this affect her now. She would make her all-important first entrance in less than two minutes and she couldn't afford to worry about his reactions to the Bedlam visit.

'Tell him, at the final curtain.'

Across the stage in the opposite wings Peter Tregaran came past Susan Clifford to make his entrance. He stopped, ran his forefinger along Susan's chin under the ribbons of her girlish pink bonnet, and grinned at her. She winked at him. Luckily, her father didn't see it. Nor did the ever possessive Bessie Maulders.

Tregaran made some remark, apparently in a low voice, for Brian looked around, frowning, and Tregaran broke off. A moment later he made his entrance on-stage, to some vigorous applause and a few shouts from the pit. There was general applause throughout the theatre, a little more than Elisa remembered from his last appearance with her. She tried to analyze the sounds, wondering if she could concentrate on them and not on the message from Jeremy.

Not for years had she permitted herself to be away from the stage for more than a few days, a fortnight at the most, and this contributed now to a strong irritation of the nerves; but even at this stage she could not miss the tension, the excitement, and the whispering in the audience just seconds before her cue was spoken by Tregaran as the youthful General Bonaparte.

Taking inventory, she made certain her 'charming' smile was in place, promising so much, that her eyes sparkled in the old, familiar way, and her Empire gown of shimmering white silk, bedecked with tiny paste diamonds and pearls, clung to her slender, fragile-looking body.

She could never afterward remember whether she spoke her opening lines as she made her own entrance, the feathered ivory fan in her fingers swaying gently. She was very much aware of the sounds like thunderous ocean waves pouring across the footlight lamps. For an instant she wondered if the storm outside had crept within these ancient walls.

It was Tregaran's reaction that made her aware of the individual voices shouting from the pit, the galleries, and even the boxes, as he approached her for the introduction of the two characters.

'Your admirers are out in force,' he murmured, lowering his head to kiss her hand.

Absurdly enough, she thought, he is being sarcastic. They are all his friends. He knows that.

She heard the individual voices now, calling – many of them shouting – her name, '*Circe,*' which made her shiver; but she forced her smile and played out the scene lightly, easily, transforming herself into the woman she had been before Jeremy March came into her life.

It was late in the first act when she was finally able to glance at the stage-right box. Her heart seemed to give a painful lurch. He was there, a stunning vision to her, all stark black and white, sitting forward, looking down into her eyes. Surely, love and pride were in that look . . .

Elisa had perfected her stage personality to such a point that she was a mechanism, acting without being aware of the effort.

311

She relied upon the tricks of charm and capturing an audience with personality. But the waves of affection from the audience, waves she felt distinctly, were warming, humanizing. By the end of the first act she was deep into her character, transformed inside as she had been on the surface.

Most remarkable was the behavior of Tregaran and Bessie Maulders. Tregaran in particular seemed almost excessively anxious to display Elisa at her best. There were none of his stage tricks that she had steeled herself to resist. He actually gave her some moments he had previously fought for, with every weapon of the born scene-stealer. She found all this strange, out of character. Tregaran's exceptional behavior troubled her as much as his open enmity might have done.

When she came off-stage after the second act Tuttle met Elisa in her usual disgruntled fashion. 'There's that female waiting to get into your dressing-room and gabble away. Claims she must see you.'

'Who?' she wondered aloud, her voice distant. 'I can't see anyone. You know that.'

It was bad enough to have her concentration ruined by the Regent's drunken friends before the performance. In her mind she was still Josephine de Beauharnais Bonaparte, Empress of France, and soon to be dethroned. She wanted no interruptions.

'That Lady Hawtree, she seemed mighty excited.'

'If I can't see Jeremy, I certainly won't see Gwenna Hawtree.'

She hurried to her dressing-room, aware that Gwenna Hawtree stood at the end of the passage, tapping impatiently on the seamed wall beside her with a white-gloved hand. Seeing Elisa, she started forward, waving at her wildly, but Tuttle got between them and Elisa slipped into her dressing-room, and slammed the door for the first time in Tuttle's memory.

When Tuttle joined her Elisa stopped stripping off the sensuous gown long enough to ask, 'Is she gone?'

Tuttle stuck her head out and studied the dark passage. Sounds of an animated conversation came from Tregaran's dressing-room, punctuated by female giggles and male guffaws. But in the passage there was no sign of Gwenna Hawtree.

312

'Probably in Bonaparte's room,' she decided. 'Causing more trouble than Josephine ever did.'

Elisa laughed abruptly. 'I don't doubt it . . . Tuttle, please. Leave the door open.'

Tuttle started to say something but changed her mind, left the door ajar, and crossed the room to help Elisa change into the elaborate Coronation gown for act three.

'Aint you wearing your real jewels?' Tuttle wanted to know.

'No. He – they will think I am flaunting my past.'

Tuttle's disapproving face hovered behind Elisa's shoulder in the looking-glass. As Elisa set the diadem with its great, false jewels on her hair, Tuttle's head shook very slowly. No question about it. The costume crown looked clumsy, overbalanced on the head beneath it.

'Bring the set I bought after the Drury Lane opening.'

Tuttle took out the key she wore around her neck. The key was still warm from its place between her sagging breasts. She unlocked the drawer Elisa had ordered to be made into the wooden stand that supported the looking-glass. The difference between this set and the paste jewels was phenomenal. Elisa set the little tiara in her hair, removed the necklace and earrings and substituted the genuine diamonds. Instead of a vulgar blaze, her figure now seemed to give off an aura of light.

The sounds from Tregaran's dressing-room became more audible, a burst of laughter, then low voices, and more laughter. Tregaran's friends who were to act as the spear-carriers had poured in to admire their Napoleonic leader, no doubt.

Tuttle groaned. 'I don't like it.'

Elisa's own nerves were on a knife-edge. She needed encouragement, not support for her own uneasiness.

'Nonsense. They laugh because he is their bear-leader. It is the price they pay for his patronage.'

With all her celebrated ease of movement Elisa made her way to the wings for the two scenes of the final act. She revealed none of her inner doubts and only Tuttle guessed they existed.

Throughout the Coronation scene and its climax, in which Josephine as Empress is put aside because she cannot give her

313

husband an heir to the throne, Elisa was at her best. Tregaran once more gave her the scene without a struggle or a trick. She felt the excitement in the audience, the passionate sympathy with her, which told her of their love even before the wave upon wave of applause began at the end of the scene.

Elisa glanced up at Jeremy's box in time to see Gwenna Hawtree appear behind him. Jeremy arose politely but gestured her to silence. What on earth could Gwenna have to say to him?

A more important question remained. What could Jeremy possibly say to Elisa that was so pressing? Pity? Yes. That might be the answer. He would be likely to sympathize over her childhood and Molly's fate. But she would not permit herself to hope he still wanted Elsie Catlow, with her tainted blood, as his wife.

Meanwhile, she had too much to think about on-stage. The timing of the final minutes was extremely important.

At last it was here. One final scene. Josephine's death. There were less than five minutes between scenes, just long enough for Elisa to remove her jewels in the wings and throw a robe over her gown, aided by Tuttle, before she rushed on-stage to her bed.

The set was a short one, arranged before a painted backdrop that concealed the elaborate previous scene and also represented the back wall of Josephine's bedchamber at Malmaison. The bowl of Parma violets was at hand, a prop to be used in her last moments as the curtains slowly closed upon the view of the violets, symbol of the Napoleonic cause, dropping petal by petal from her pale, dying fingers.

Her goodbye to her lady-in-waiting was an easy, if affecting, little scene which she had often rehearsed and played, but she was nervous about the moments afterward since they had only rehearsed once with Tregaran. She was to whisper his name and then the lamp, casting a dim light over stage center, would reveal Tregaran as Napoleon holding out his arms to her, fading at last as a deathbed vision.

She had never before felt her character so deeply. Trembling, she tried to keep Josephine under her emotional control.

All had gone well but still, in her highly nervous state, she wondered if something strange and unrehearsed was in the air tonight. It wasn't until her lamplight dimmed, turned down secretly with her own fingers, that she became aware of the first divergence from the script. The light that cast an eery glow over the scene was an ominous and sinister green, rather than the usual dimmed warm glow from the oil lamps.

It took some seconds for the muffled light to illuminate the man in stage center. Elisa turned her head slowly, as required by her role. She was to stretch her arm toward the vision, vainly groping for her lost love. In the flickering green light she saw – not the Napoleon she expected, but a slender, yellow-haired boy who must be *Arthur March*, staring at her with sorrow and reproach in his eyes.

A faint buzzing swept over the audience.

Elisa dropped her arm, backing away as if she might dissolve into the wall at one side of her bed. Her heart hammered in her breast. She made a gutteral sound that even she did not understand.

Another low series of murmurs in the audience . . . From somewhere on the darkened stage behind her the audience made out another figure. She tried to rise. She put her weight on one wrist and hand as she looked around past the low, wooden-back frame of her bed.

Who was that, faintly green-hued, in the gray shadows beyond the light?

A young man in uniform, the white bandoliers standing out against the dark, scarlet jacket. One arm of that jacket hung empty. Captain Ronald Hawtree?

The buzzing in her head told her:

I am going mad. They will cart me off to Bedlam. Like Mother . . . Dear God! Like Mother!

The room was full of motionless figures. In a far corner of the stage she saw someone else vaguely familiar. She had almost forgotten him. Wasn't that the chubby-cheeked, drunken boy, the Duke of Pentland's son, who threw himself off the Channel packet because he fancied he loved her?

315

There were others. Even in her distraught state she made out the faces of men she had refused, after leading them to believe they were favored. These phantoms began to move toward her with infinite cunning and stealth. It was like a hideous game, to catch them moving. When she stared at 'Captain Hawtree' he remained a statue; yet 'Arthur March' was closer. In mingled terror and fury she watched Arthur. Another phantom was close, very close. She could just catch his movement out of the corner of her eye.

She shrank further away until there was no longer any escape. She was trapped like Molly Catlow in that tiny cell. The stage reverberated with the metallic screech of a clanging cell door.

The walls were closing in upon her.

Huddled against the wall like Molly when they came to take her away, Elsie Catlow began to scream. There was no stopping the ghastly sound. It went on and on and on.

The curtains closed upon an audience in convulsions of excitement.

CHAPTER TWENTY-SEVEN

Even before she opened her eyes she sensed that it was Jeremy whose arm cradled her head and whose anxious face she would see first. He shouldn't be here. Didn't he realize? He had no place here on the stage. But was there more than pity in his eyes? She sensed the tenderness in his warm embrace. She wanted desperately to believe she was still safe in his arms, in their bed in March Hall, and that everything happening afterward was no more than a cruel nightmare.

The whirling, hideous world righted itself again, though the noise beyond the curtain sounded as if the building might be tumbling down. The audience? Were they hostile or friendly after her ghastly and unprofessional behavior?

Jeremy kissed her forehead that was still moist and cold with fear. Then he kissed her lips. The two facts which guided her life had come together. Jeremy loved her. And this was not St Mary's of Bethlehem Asylum. It was the final set used in *Our Lady Of Victory*, and Jeremy had seated himself on the edge of Josephine's deathbed, his body, in severely correct evening attire, close beside her. How had he come from the boxes to the stage so fast?

The lamplights were turned up. She looked around, seeing the youths who had frightened her. They were Tregaran's friends, dressed and even made up to resemble lovers in her past. What a credulous fool she had been!

As for the youths themselves, they looked aghast at what they had done to her. Thank God the heavy folds of the curtain separated her from the audience!

'You are safe now, sweetheart.'

Jeremy crushed her fingers in his until she winced, but it was a small price to pay to hear this proud man call her 'sweetheart' before so many gawking witnesses.

Beyond the curtain the audience roared on, calling her name. Jeremy kissed her cheek and gave her fresh courage.

'Take your bows, Enchantress. You've earned all their praise.'

He would have given her support when she got to her feet, but she moved forward, ignoring all the other helpful hands. The audience might be hostile. She couldn't blame them. But she must face them.

As she stood in the stage center before Strawbridge gave the order for the opening of the curtains, she realized that no matter what Peter Tregaran had done in contributing to that on-stage horror, he would be expected to share the final curtain calls.

Tregaran's young friends, giving each other scared looks, retreated to the wings with Jeremy. Elisa threw off the night robe and in her Coronation gown held her hand out to her leading man. He had been across the stage watching the hullabaloo with a scowl while his booted feet shifted nervously. He came forward to her beckoning hand and immediately became the gallant and generous leading man. Still badly shaken, Elisa turned up a smile as radiant as a porcelain lamp whose light was meant to dazzle the beholder.

When the two, Elisa and Tregaran, were seen by the audience the noise increased. Many in the pit stood on chairs cheering, '*Circe!*' '*Circe!*'

The galleries shrieked the word in an ecstasy of support and love. Most of them knew her past. They were aware of the gossip and most recognized the cruelty of the trick played upon her. They still gave her their support.

There was no escaping the odious '*Circe!*'; so she took it finally as a compliment. Aided by years of practice, she controlled the trembling in her limbs and sank in her celebrated curtsy. Not to be outdone, Tregaran bowed to her. She curtsied to him and, since the shouting still went on, he waved her forward to the footlight lamps and stepped back. Elisa was bombarded with violets, not the Parma variety in this case, but the deep-woods, English sweet violets that gave her the message of returning love from these people in the jewelled darkness whom she had wooed all her life.

At long last it was over. The heavy curtains again separated her from the crowded theatre auditorium and she made her way back to Josephine's bed, with Jeremy's help and that of the young man who had played 'Arthur March' in their charade. He seemed eager to make amends for the actions that had earlier sent her into such hysteria. Tregaran too looked uneasy.

She ignored the little group. 'Where are the Cliffords and Lady Hawtree?'

'I asked them to meet us at your house in Portman Square. Your friends are very concerned about you.'

'Could you send the others away?'

'They are going.' He added coldly, 'All but the Little Corporal.'

One by one the others began a shuffling, uncertain retreat, along with the property men who had been dismissed by Strawbridge. The blond 'Arthur' was stopped by Jeremy who called to him, 'You there with the yellow hair, who gave you that suit? I know those cuffs. The suit was made for my brother.'

The youth stammered, 'It w-was to be a jest, Sir. Scurvy thing to do, Ma'am. Someone suggested it to Peter. One of his admirers, it was. That's where we got your brother's suit and some of the details, Sir.'

The blond youth slunk away then, leaving only an anxious, watchful Strawbridge and Tregaran. The actor's dark face looked belligerent, although he shifted from one foot to the other. He kept glancing toward the dressing-rooms and the passage to the street, but Strawbridge stood in his way.

Jeremy raised his voice. It had that chilling note Elisa remembered from her early relationship with him.

'Strawbridge, have this creature's story of tonight's events delivered to Her Ladyship's house within the hour. I want names.'

Tregaran glanced at Strawbridge. It was clear that his chief concern was whether this fiasco would injure his career.

Strawbridge took his arm. 'You best do it, lad. Now! That is to say, if you ever want to set foot on a London stage again.'

While Strawbridge ushered Tregaran off to his dressing-room, the actor was still complaining. 'It wasn't my notion. Damme! I've nothing to hide. Fetch me a pen and an ink standish. I'll set down the truth. With pleasure.'

Elisa looked around the deserted stage. Only one lamp burned low. The place smelled of weathered old wood and of a heavily perfumed powder used by the actors and often found on their clothing. It probably came from the costumes lying where Tregaran's young friends had dropped them after the shock of her collapse.

Jeremy was watching her face with a deep concern she had never noticed before in his eyes. It might have been there but she had never permitted herself to believe it was genuine.

He said, 'You shall have the truth at home, darling, where you can be comfortable. It isn't very pleasant, but at least it will be ended tonight.' She got to her feet with his help. She headed for her own dressing-room with Jeremy beside her. He urged her, 'Don't change your costume. I'll just throw this cloak around you. You are still trembling.'

This was not the eloquent, cutting and cruel aristocrat she had first known. This was the compassionate and caring man who spent so much time trying to alleviate the conditions of the less fortunate. As for herself, she had never been so cosseted in her life and she loved his gentle care of her. But she knew the blow had only been delayed.

In her present exhaustion, brought on by the ghastly fears of that last stage scene, she wasn't sure she ever wanted to know the real menace that had nearly destroyed her.

They were home before she was ready for the encounters that must come. Tuttle met them at the door. Her rough-skinned face looked as if it had been cut out of stone. She ignored His Lordship's friendly, 'Good evening, Tuttle.'

'You best have a hip-bath brought, Ma'am. You look like you've seen a ghost.'

'I have, Tuttle. Believe me.'

Jeremy said, 'Send brandy to my wife's boudoir and then ask Lady Hawtree and her guest to come up.'

'And Mr Clifford, Sir?'

'Send the Cliffords a trifle later. As soon as Strawbridge delivers a letter, see that it is brought up at once.'

'I understand, Sir.'

Walking into Elisa's boudoir together, she and Jeremy shared a vivid memory of their first passionate embrace and their first kisses.

'How angry you were that night!' she reminded him.

'I was impossible, if that's any comfort to you.' He settled her on the tufted satin chaise longue, carefully removed her while silk Coronation shoes used in the play and raised her feet to rest on the chaise. Meanwhile, he told her, 'I had some notion of proving to Arthur that you would love any March, that it was the name you wanted, not the man. Well, I managed to coil myself in your lovely net. I found that my feelings for you were much stronger than I had supposed. After that, I had myself to fight as well as Arthur's very understandable passion for you. I thought I was being noble when I gave my approval to Arthur's betrothal ideas. But I may tell you, sweetheart, I envied Arthur from the bottom of my heart.'

'And then you thought I had played him false.'

'I thought I would lead you on, make you understand what it was to love and be rejected. Vain hope! I still wanted you so much I told myself I was marrying you only to make you what my own mother had been. A victim. Hoist by my own petard, my darling.'

'Were you, love?' She caressed his cheek with her chill, trembling fingers and he turned his head slightly, kissing the tips of her fingers, trying to warm them.

Examining her fingers, he murmured, 'I resent only one thing, Elisa. When you knew I genuinely loved you, you should have had a little faith in me and told me about your mother's mistreatment all those years ago. Don't you know that during those same years I have worked to better the conditions of people like Molly Catlow?'

Though she loved him, she shook her head. 'You would never have looked twice at Elsie Catlow.'

'I married Elsie Catlow.'

The brandy came, borne by McFee, who easily accepted His Lordship as the new master of the Portman Square house. Jeremy drank his brandy rapidly. Elisa looked at hers a long moment, seeing warmth in it, and drank it down almost as fast as her husband had.

It gave her the courage she needed. 'Let's hear the truth. How did you discover it?'

'It is entirely Gwenna Hawtree's doing. She came to me with her story about Abel. It seemed unlikely to me. A few garbled words. But I had only to confront one of the parties involved, and—Shall we hear Gwenna?'

Elisa closed her eyes momentarily, hoping to gain strength for the confessions she dreaded. Someone she cared about, someone she trusted, would be unmasked.

'I am ready. Send for her, McFee.'

Jeremy seated himself on the edge of the chaise, still holding one of Elisa's hands.

When McFee was gone Elisa asked suddenly, on a secret note of hope, 'Was it Captain Hawtree who was back of this? I could understand that.'

'No, darling. Hawtree probably hated you during those first weeks after his injury, and during the play, for example. But that night on the rooftop at March Hall when he frightened you, he had no way of knowing you would come up there. He went to the rooftop, as he told me, to re-live those happy days when he and Arthur and their friends used to play their daredevil games and discuss their great dreams. Hawtree wanted glory and Arthur wanted happiness. Whatever that may mean to each of us.'

'Then who was it? Or were there more?'

Gwenna Hawtree came sweeping into the room and leaned over to touch Elisa's cheek with her own.

'You're certainly looking your years, my dear,' she announced in her frank way. 'But be cheerful. You've poor Abel to thank for straightening out your affairs. I translated a few of those grunts

322

and mutterings. Patience is the way of it. After that, it was only necessary to locate one of the two parties he overheard in the graveyard discussing their little schemes against you. They had come to leave posies for young Arthur.' She looked over her shoulder. 'And here is one of our gossipy little conspirators. Do come in and tell us why you should not be sent to Newgate for your part in these crimes.'

To Elisa's stupefaction, Mrs Ponsonby bustled in, dipping curtsies as fast as her pudgy little figure could manage. She was white with fear. Her eyes avoided Elisa. She addressed only Jeremy.

'Your Lordship, if old Abel tells the truth, and if you may understand his babbling, he'll admit I counselled against violence and I thought I was heeded. I understood that Dilly Skeen took the chocolate and dosed it with laudanum to relieve her toothache. The other things—well, you might say they were only in fun. We had a few laughs in the quarters, thinking of her that killed our Mister Arthur being feared of closed doors and being left alone in the house. And such like. It was a game. Sometimes the staff made little noises for the fun of it. Clomping down the stairs, making believe we – they, that is – were poor Mr Arthur's ghost. Him that she gave the laudanum to so cruel, like. It's what you thought, too, Sir. Only a joke. For Mister Arthur's sake.'

She took two steps toward Jeremy who warned her off with such disgust as Elisa hoped never to see on his face.

Mrs Ponsonby tried again. 'You, Sir. We thought you'd approve. Wasn't it why you brought the creature there – the lady, that is to say? To have her see what she'd done to your charge, your very own brother?'

'Oh, God!' Jeremy looked heavenward. Elisa sensed that he felt a little of Mrs Ponsonby's guilt had fallen upon his shoulders.

Elisa said stiffly, 'Abel tried to tell us there was something bad against me. Then the rest of you came out of the gatehouse and he ran away. He was afraid of you.'

The little woman cried in panic, 'Not me alone, Miss. For my part, there was to be no wickedness. I warned against it.'

From the doorway they heard a young, vibrant voice call to Mrs Ponsonby. 'Dear Ponsy, they've nothing against you. Everyone knows old Abel is a liar and a madman. He would make up anything to even the score. We sent him away from the house any number of times.'

Startled by the strength in that voice, Elisa stared at the doorway. Susan Clifford stood there, watching the housekeeper who avoided her eyes.

Brian had one arm around his daughter's shoulders and he said now, sternly, 'A half-witted natural is certainly no fit witness against respectable females like Mrs Ponsonby and my innocent child. Is that what you are about?'

Susan.

Elisa shivered. After a painful moment of silence, she murmured, 'There is no reason. It must be something Mrs Ponsonby did that perhaps persuaded her.'

The housekeeper pleated the edge of her frilled cuff nervously.

'If it please Your Lordship, whatever else I may be guilty of, it was the child's idea. She wanted to be Mister Arthur's wife. I thought it a splendid idea. But after walking out with her a few times and kissing her once there under the shadow of the gatehouse, he went away and fell under the spell of the actress.'

'He loved me. I know he did. I could tell.'

Mrs Ponsonby rushed on. 'Then poor little Susan thought of His Lordship. He was excessively kind to her, treated her almost like a daughter. Teased her a bit. And she thought if she stayed about March Hall, pretending to be learning my post, she might win him. We talked about it on occasion in the churchyard, before and after poor Mister Arthur was buried there. When we brought flowers to his tomb, and so on – we went regular, like. I daresay that creature, Abel, heard us. Then Your Lordship brought home the actress. This was my Susan's enemy doing her a bad turn again. There was no escaping that woman. I thought it cruel wicked to bring that evil woman into Mister Arthur's house. Poor Miss Susan talked quite wild, like. But to kill Dilly Skeen – that, no, never!'

Brian shouted, 'How dare you, you harridan! You put ideas into my child's head. My poor Susan wouldn't think of all those cruel things herself. The laudanum and the rest. My Susan isn't capable of such monstrous acts.'

To Elisa's astonishment Gwenna Hawtree interrupted with one of her cutting laughs. 'You all give the girl too much credit. She could not possibly have committed those acts. It would have taken a brilliant mind, a genius, to make herself responsible for such things. Certainly, that stupid child is incapable. Someone told her what to do, every step of the way.'

Stung by this, Susan broke away from her father. 'How dare you say such a thing, you horse-faced old witch! I don't need other brilliant minds to plan my future and to destroy someone who has spent her life ruining men.'

Looking pale and harried, Brian seized her, trying to silence her. 'They are goading you, don't you see? Be quiet!'

But she twisted away from him again. 'What a fool you were, Papa! Letting her cuzen you all those years with her insane fears. She's every bit as mad as her mother was before her! If you had locked her up in Bedlam, you'd have your hands on all those jewels she took from Mister Arthur and the Captain and those others. And you could have used it to help people, not to horde like her because she feared to die a pauper in Bedlam where she belongs.'

Elisa covered her eyes. Jeremy pulled her to him.

'My darling, it is this child who is mad. Not you.'

Tuttle elbowed Brian and the girl aside and stalked across the room to Jeremy. 'Your letter from Mr Strawbridge, Sir.'

Brian managed to quiet his daughter. His desperate anger found Elisa his easiest target.

'For many months, Elsie, I have thought you were bent upon your mother's path. Now, I can no longer doubt. You've arranged this lie to destroy a child you sense as a rival.'

Elisa was so surprised at this that she raised her head and looked into Susan's pale, staring eyes, seeing the bitter hatred there. She could no longer doubt.

Jeremy broke the seal and silently read the note written by Peter Tregaran. He recognized Brian's desperation and asked in a quiet voice, 'What do you think of the attack made on my wife on-stage tonight? Certainly, of all people, you must have recognized that someone very close to Elisa betrayed certain facts which were used against her in the cruellest way tonight.'

'Now, there is your enemy,' Brian insisted. 'The man who betrayed Elsie to that actor is responsible for tonight and all the other attacks on Elsie.'

'Then you will be interested in this letter from Peter Tregaran who admits to creating the scene.' Jeremy opened the letter with one hand; the other had closed around Elisa's fingers again.

'Your Lordship asks the truth about tonight's jest. The facts about Carlisle were brought to me by a friend of hers who knew her past. Even the clothing once worn by Arthur March was contributed to my friend Scunthorpe for his part.

'When she first came to me I thought she was one of my admirers. She was pretty. I listened to her. She returned with March's clothing and gave us all the details.

'Marcus Scunthorpe and three others heard her, as well as myself. She said her father thought she was having gowns fitted. That's how she got away to visit me.

'The blame is Susan Clifford's. Not mine. Ask any of the others who heard her. I opine now that she wanted to destroy Carlisle. Or maybe drive her mad. We only thought to embarrass Carlisle. Nothing more.

'That is God's truth.

Peter Tregaran'

Susan cried, 'It's a lie. Papa, don't believe them. He is lying to save himself.'

'And his four friends who witnessed your little game?' Jeremy asked gently. 'What of Arthur's clothing?'

No one said anything. Elisa's heart went out to Brian who reached for his daughter, trying to shield her from their stares as she began to sob. He stroked the girl's yellow curls. She calmed a little but realised at last in what danger she stood. Her broken voice was passionately sincere. Elisa had no doubt she believed everything she said.

'I didn't mean poor Dilly Skeen to die, Papa. She never hurt me. But Elisa! She took you from me. It was always Elisa-this and Elisa-that. As if you loved her more than me. And then Arthur. I'm glad I sent her that champagne. She deserved to suffer. Only she didn't. Then, when I'd set my thoughts on His Lordship, she stole him away, too. I'm just as pretty as she is. But she became the lady of March Hall. And that should have been me. Don't you see? She deserved to die.'

'Or be shut up in Bedlam?' Jeremy asked.

'Yes. Yes. Like her mother.'

Brian groaned.

Mrs Ponsonby explained loyally, 'She had this passion to be mistress of March Hall. And a pretty one she would have made, if I do say so. She has so many talents. Poor lamb.'

'Poor tigress!' Lady Hawtree put in, to which Elisa heard Tuttle muttering, 'Amen to that!'

Curious, she thought, how Tuttle had never quite trusted Susan.

Susan began to sob again against her father's waistcoat. Brian raised his ashen face.

'My Lord, couldn't I take her away? Out of the country? America. The Antipodes. I beg you.'

Jeremy looked into Elisa's eyes, read the question there, and relented in part.

'Clifford, we will talk about it tomorrow. I expect you to keep your daughter in charge meanwhile. If not, I will then inform the magistrates.' He turned again to Elisa. 'Sweetheart, you and I have a lifetime together to plan.'

The others took the hint and left the room, Lady Hawtree congratulating herself on having solved the whole affair, Mrs Ponsonby still assuring everyone who would listen, 'It was none of my doing. I but gave a little well-meant help to Miss Susan. A few tricks here and there. Naught but a game, when all's said.'

Tuttle was last, telling Jeremy she would be on the watch in case 'that yellow-haired hussy escapes in the night.'

Elisa watched them go. Then she looked up at her husband. 'Promise me to be generous with Susan.'

He stiffened a little. 'Susan Clifford may be mad. She has killed an innocent girl. She nearly destroyed you. God knows what else she is capable of. However, I have an idea that may help matters.'

She sat straight up in horror. 'Not a place like Bedlam.'

Gently, he drew her back to him. 'I have a friend in the north. Edinburgh. He has spent half a lifetime rehabilitating such cases. It will not be a place like Bedlam. I know what Bedlam means to you.'

My darling, she promised him silently, I will hold you to this. I will not let you send Susan Clifford to Bedlam. Somehow, we must find a way . . .

Perhaps he guessed her thoughts, but in any event he kissed her again.

She considered this his pledge to her, and to Molly Catlow, who could now sleep in peace.